ALL IN

Tyler Woodbridge

Acknowledgements

A grateful and eternal thank-you to my beta readers, Patrons, sponsors, and writer circle – this book would not have seen the light of day without you. You're amazing.

Rachel Bowdler | Elizabeth Ridge | Kayla Nickley

David Ansel Benson | Tess Jones | Jordan Kirian | Hien Nguyen

Meredith Violet Wells | Laura Woodbridge | The Klitzka Family

And a special thank-you to **Cult Talk Network (CTN)** for promotional consideration!

Dedication

Julia Claire, my sweet daughter.

Never be afraid to ask for help.

Follow your dreams.

I love you.

About "All In"

"All In" is a Thriller novel and a work of fiction. These characters aren't real people. Most creative works and real people referenced are done so out of a place of love and tribute.

This novel is a love letter to Ohio and the zany adventures I enjoyed as a young adult in and around Columbus. Care has been taken to accurately represent locations in and around Columbus.

Drake's Landing, Nawakwa, Perkins Township, Slade City, and Winterview State Park are fictional locations crafted to enhance the spirit of mystery and adventure in the foothills of Appalachia.

Please remember to practice gun safety. When operating motor vehicles, maintain safe speed and wear appropriate protection, including seat belts and/or helmets. Buzzed driving is drunk driving, and drunk driving is not cash money.

This work of fiction contains references to armed insurrection, organized crime, domestic violence, recreational drug usage, doing the Horizontal Bop, and Canadians. This is a story primarily about adult Ohioan criminals, and they cuss like adult Ohioan criminals. If the "fuck" word offends you, fair warning, you should probably turn back now.

Copyright

PROLOGUE

Bright lights flashed with the rhythm of the pulse-pounding beat. The bass rattled the club-goers' bones and urged their bodies to throb and press with the music. People reached out just to feel: on the wall, on one another, to feel alive. The broad splashes of glow-in-the-dark paint on the walls, neon green and yellow and pink, set the backdrop for a celebration of being.

Behind a rack of keyboards and computers, Captain Galactico stretched his arms wide as the beat quickened and the noise rose to a crescendo. Reminiscent of WWE's Ultimate Warrior, long blue and gold streamers dangled from Galactico's arm scarves. His tan, hairy chest contrasted the bright refraction of his silver shining cape. A bright geometric space-age mask coated in Chromalusion color-changing paint completed his ensemble.

Trinity Stone shuffled around alongside the stage. She whirled her dark brown hair around in circles and rocked her body up and down to the building beat. Trinity looked up at Captain Galactico. He pointed to her, and she saw a grin peek beneath his mask. She smiled beneath her own black and green mask, a relic from the pandemic, now repurposed for higher fashion. She pointed to the sky as she moved her body. A crowd rushed forward and mobbed the stage.

The beat dropped.

Captain Galactico used a makeshift flamethrower to cast fire upon a rack of small candles in front of his instrument rig. The reactions of the crowd were mixed. Some yelled excited swears in the face of the blaze. Others came over once the flame disappeared and all that was lit were the candles. They bent and danced over the stage and huffed the smoke deeply.

As Captain Galactico hammered out crunching dubstep riffs and an array of lasers spun all around him, Trinity came face to face with a dark-skinned woman of approximately her same size and build, her hair streaked with pink and blue and yellow. She slung her arms around Trinity and danced close, the two women's legs and hips tangling together to the music.

"You're cute..." the new girl whispered in Trinity's ear. Trinity smiled and tucked her hair behind her ear as they danced.

"Thank you... what's your name?" Trinity asked as the other woman ground against her, cheek-to-cheek.

"It doesn't matter what my name is," she said with a wry grin. "But you can call me Zoey."

"My name's Trinity. Are you having fun?" Trinity put her hands to Zoey's waist.

"I'd have more fun if you would follow me," Zoey whispered in Trinity's ear.

Trinity's blush could be seen even in the dim light of the club. Zoey's hand linked up with Trinity's, and she led her away from the throbbing and smoky dance floor as they pushed through a wall of sweaty, pulsing bodies.

The two women left the club and ran around the side, to the back. It was dark in the nightclub district, and late – most people out and about were revelers and thrill-seekers. Zoey and Trinity found themselves in a dim parking lot, no other soul around, shrouded by the shadow of a looming poplar tree at the end of the lot. Trinity jumped at the sight of something in the shadows but relaxed when it came to light; a discarded light blue face mask fluttered past on the breeze. Conscious of her own mask, Trinity pulled it to dangle off her left ear, exposing her wry, curious smile.

Zoey pushed Trinity against the brick wall of the club in the shade of the poplar. Trinity was acutely aware of the grit of the wall, the scent of the recently-applied graffiti paint around her. Trinity's breath increased as Zoey ripped an arm of her white tank top down and then pinned her waist to the brick with her other hand. She pressed herself against Trinity and whispered into her ear, "Do you know why I'm here?"

Trinity leaned forwards, tilting her head backward and opening her mouth ever so slightly. Zoey put a finger to Trinity's lips.

"Shhh..." Zoey said. Zoey put her whole palm against Trinity's mouth and produced a switchblade from her waistband. She held the edge of the blade against Trinity's ribs. It took a minute for her to register what was going on. Trinity shivered and shook, and her bloodshot eyes widened as she realized the imminence of danger.

"I'm here for you, but not in the way you want it..." Zoey said with a laugh. Trinity tried to scream through Zoey's fingers. Zoey pulled Trinity's face forward and then slammed it back against the brick.

"I swear to God if you scream, I'm going to gut you like a fish," Zoey said. "I'm here for the candles. Where do you get them?"

As soon as Zoey moved her hand so Trinity could answer, Trinity screamed. Zoey put her hand back up and moved the knife up to her throat. Zoey looked around quickly, and seeing that the coast was clear, she turned her attention back to Trinity.

"Another stunt like that will cost you your life. Let's try this again. If you don't answer, or if I don't like your answer, you're dead. Understand?"

Trinity nodded as much as she could in her compromised position. She fought back tears, her vision obstructed as they welled up.

"The candles, Trinity. Tell me who makes your candles and where I can get them."

Zoey removed her hand. Trinity gasped for air.

"Cowtown Candles. Columbus, Ohio... that's all I know... that's all I know," Trinity stammered among deep breaths.

Zoey lowered her knife back down to Trinity's ribs. Zoey nodded as she let the words simmer in her head.

"Columbus, Ohio... Cowtown Candles. Retail store or what?"

"I don't know. Please, please don't kill me, Zoey. I'm not a bad person. I don't deserve to die."

"Shut up!" Zoey barked. This had the opposite intended effect, as Trinity broke down even further and slumped against the wall. Zoey rolled her eyes and knelt alongside her.

"Listen... What you've shared has been a big help. I'm going to need a little more. Just give me one name. One name of someone that can lead us to the mother lode. And we will leave you alone. I promise."

Trinity put her head in her arms and muttered something. Zoey grabbed a handful of dark hair and yanked back hard, pressing her face against Trinity's once more.

"One more time, Trinity. *With feeling.*"

"...Manny. Manny Rezendes. That's Cap's connection. I don't know if it ends there or not."

"Manny Rezendes. Perfect. Hispanic guy?"

"Mixed, I think... please don't hurt him."

"I make no promises." Zoey stood up and put her knife away as she looked around one more time. "You're too cute to kill anyway. Now go. Go back to the club and have fun. Hold yourself high, act like nothing happened."

Trinity staggered to her feet and nodded. Zoey stepped in front of her as she went to walk away and pressed an index finger against Trinity's collar.

"No funny business, Trinity. I have people in that club that will be watching you. You know nothing."

Trinity nodded and walked quickly away, back into the club. Zoey retreated into the shadows.

Inside the dance club, as Trinity did her best to move and sway and grind to her friend Captain Galactico's punishing dubstep the rest of the night, she couldn't affix herself to the music and lose herself in the atmosphere the way she used to. Every time she turned, she would make eye contact with a different person who was staring at her. All white guys, all shifty, all unblinking. A muscular man in a soccer jersey, a taller one with a mustache, a shorter one with a side shave and blow over.

All watching. All waiting.

CHAPTER ONE

"Burn 'em and turn 'em, brother!"

Trevor MacKenzie's tilted voice cut through the tension in the room with grating confidence. He leered over the table, eyes unfocused and piercing green beneath the brim of his black Ottawa Senators snapback hat, sweat leaking out from beneath his blonde, shaggy locks, a half-smoked menthol dangling out of the corner of his mouth. The ashes crumbled onto the table, yet he sat still and glared at the cards and immense chip stack before him.

"Stack city bitch, stack stack city bitch," Trevor chanted as a muscular and broad-shouldered man flipped the three flop cards onto the felt green table.

The competitors all shared furtive glances at one another as the cards were revealed. Naev Broadnax, AKA "Anvil," was the dealer. The stocky James Glencroft, or "Jimmy" as his friends called him, sat on the small blind, still in the game and struggling to keep chips. Jimmy kept running his fingers through his thinning light brown hair. Brody Marlowe, the group's newest competitor, was in a similar short-stacked position at the big blind. Manuel Rezendes, a tall tan fellow with shaggy black hair, had a decent amount of chips. Trevor MacKenzie swayed to and fro, grinning maniacally.

The flop cards were a jack of hearts, a ten of spades, and a ten of hearts. Jimmy knocked on the table, signifying a check. Brody followed suit almost immediately, as did Manuel.

"Well boys, I'm gonna have to raise the stakes a little..." said Trevor as he pushed a solid $100 of chips to the center of the table. The pot was already at $80. Therefore, the new total of $180 was more than most of the remaining players had in their respective stacks. Everyone had engaged in a pissing contest before the flop. This was going to be a make-or-break hand for the players involved.

"Get 'em!" barked Craig Foxx, who had been eliminated from the game earlier. He and his friend Big Trace leaned against the bar separating the dining room and the kitchen, drinking scotch and chatting intently.

Craig was a strapping white man in his late 30's, his arms decorated with various banded tattoos, his white tank top thinly covering a broad body rippling with muscle; he was a manager of a local construction company. Big Trace Onwudiwe was even larger than Craig, less boisterous but more intimidating, a quiet black man of high fashion, standing out among the crowd in a bright purple satin shirt and glittering black jeans.

"Psst, do they usually just... hang out here?" Brody whispered to Jimmy. The plum-colored fedora he wore cast a shadow over his dark, sunken eyes.

Jimmy glanced back at Craig and Big Trace. He made quick eye contact with Craig. Craig winked and grinned wryly.
"Well... they're friends with Manny, so..." Jimmy said as he flipped the edges of his cards with his fingers.

Anvil folded, mucking an unfortunate hand of low cards. An interesting trend among this group of friends is that they often played bad hands hard, these ego-driven "A-types" often refusing to let go of bluffs, or in Jimmy's case, practitioners of the Daniel Negreanu school of play, in which lower hole cards were of equal value to the player as high face cards. Jimmy had more to play for than the others. He wasn't made of money, being an underpaid and unappreciated pro football mascot, "Sailor Smash," the obnoxiously nautical rhinoceros who represented the Columbus Discovery, one of the new Patriot Football League's teams... of which Naev Broadnax, his good friend, was the unlikely starter of next week's game; a backup quarterback staring chance and fate in the eye.

Jimmy stroked his light brown beard and opted to call Trevor's raise. The call put over half of his remaining stack into play. He glanced over at Brody, the small, enigmatic hipster with a blow-over haircut, whom most of the guys had just met today. Brody called without much to-do. It was hard for them to get a good grasp of Brody and his playing style. The new guys were always the wild cards, unpredictable, and out for an excellent first impression. Manuel folded after triple-checking his cards. He leaned back, smirked at his luck (or lack thereof), and watched the proceedings with interest. Anvil reached for the deck to deal the turn. Trevor MacKenzie held out an arm to stop him, and Anvil slid the cards to the side.

"You know what, boys... I'm feeling lucky tonight. I think I'll throw in something you would almost want to take home to your mother!" Trevor shouted, spreading his arms wide. He reached into his black leather coat pocket and pulled out a small candle, the label reading, "*Cowtown Candles:* Ohio Made since '88." He slammed it on the table with a clunk. Every player raised their eyebrow or looked curiously at this simple vanilla candle. Craig and Big Trace gathered around the table as well.

"You cray, brah," Big Trace grunted. "How you get that? You can't afford that."

Trevor winked. "A magician never tells his secrets, fair Nubian."

"Nigerian," Big Trace said. "You *do* realize that Nubia is a specific region and does not work as a catch-all term for all Africans, right?"

"I miss when the pandemic was going on, and I couldn't hear you from the other side of your got damn face shield," Trevor said. Awkward chuckles ensued around the table.

Trevor pushed the candle in with his chips. Big Trace shook his hand back and forth perpendicular to his own throat as he glared at Trevor.

"Yo, that's like me calling you a Minnesotan or something. But I ain't simple like you. I know you're Canadian. We ain't done with this conversation, Trevor," Big Trace continued.

"Oh, I think we are," Trevor said. He tilted back the wooden chair he sat in with a cringe-inducing creak.

Brody glanced at Trevor. "How much is this candle converted into chip form?" he asked in a quiet, formal tone.

Jimmy groaned as he leaned back and shook his head. "You're kidding me. A *candle*?"

Trevor spread his arms wide. "$50 worth of chips. Gotta throw in to go in, fellas." He gazed at Jimmy, his eyes unfocused, his lazy eye seemingly focused on something on the wall behind him. "Or, if you have as little chips as Jimmy, I'll even take cash to match this bet."

Nobody reacted when Brody promptly threw in the requested amount. Jimmy's fingers drummed across the table uncontrollably.

"What the hell? You people are actually going along with this?" Jimmy had the $50 to match but wasn't about to put in this much money for a damn candle.

Brody nodded. "It's a nice candle, mate."

Craig gestured from the other side of the table. "Top of the line. I've been friends with Country, the guy that runs the candle shop, for a while. That's one ballin' wick, brother."

"Go all in, Al. You know you want to." Trevor said smugly. "Come on. What do you have to lose, another $250?"

Jimmy's face reddened. He slammed his fist against the table a couple times, drawing the glances of everyone in the room.

Trevor leaned forward once more, all four legs of the chair coming to rest on the wooden floor. He folded his arms and rested his red-bearded chin on his cupped, freckled hands.

"Come on, Al. When you bust out, just re-buy. I... appreciate your donations. Or, should I say, Meggy-poo's donations?" Trevor chuckled, and his quip brought on some quiet laughs from others in the room.

"You're just jealous because I have a sugar momma," Jimmy said in jesting reference to his girlfriend, Megan Painter. "And trust me, brother, I earn my keep... if you know what I mean."

"Sure..." Trevor said. "Tell me, Jimbo... Meggy go on any more overnight *crisis shifts* lately?"

"Enough," Anvil said to them both. Jimmy's face maintained its redness as he slumped into his chair.

Jimmy reached for a pale green beer bottle from the ice bucket next to the table. He cracked open the Rolling Rock and took a long drink. His breathing had picked up in intensity since Trevor had started running his mouth again. Craig walked over behind him, flashing a sleazy grin and thrusting his thumb in Jimmy's direction, as if to say, "Get a load of this guy!"

Trevor shook his head, grinning crookedly. "Delay of game, #53, James Glencroft. Got a flag to throw, Naev?"

Anvil just chuckled, shook his head, and glugged down a Rolling Rock of his own. He must've been on his ninth already. Jimmy was frustrated, anxious, and tired of holding up the game over this nonsense. His armpits grew soggy with sweat. He groaned, pulled out a $50 bill, and threw it in the middle of the table.

"This better be worth it," Jimmy said.

"Congratulations on your interest in Cowtown Candles," Trevor grinned widely, wrinkles forming in his face as he leered, reminiscent of The Grinch Who Stole Christmas. "Naev. Flip the turn."

The turn presented a nine of spades. Jimmy immediately checked, knocking on the table. Brody glanced around, blinking more than a man should really blink. The bystanders gasped collectively as Brody pushed his chips to the center of the table. He was all-in. Brody had played the entire game meekly, perhaps overplaying mediocre hands when he did play... He had to have something big this time. It was now or never.

Trevor called immediately and pushed an extra few stacks to the center as well. "This... is your Destiny Stack, Jimmy," Trevor said. "The whole game I've been matching your stack with this one, special-ordered just for your gay ass. So, tell me. What's it gonna be?"

Jimmy took a deep, audible breath.

"Really again with the homophobia?" Jimmy said.

"Really again with the bitch-assed...ness?" Trevor snarked.

"That's not a word..."

"Suck me... or call me. I don't give a fuck. I won't call you back, either way."

The whole table laughed.

Trevor stared wildly into Jimmy's eyes. Well, mostly. His right eye kept twitching all the way right, back to center. All the way right, back to center. Just watching the damn googly eye made Jimmy sweat bullets. He set aside his beer and stood up. He looked right into Trevor's wild, piercing, googly gaze and didn't flinch.

"I call." Jimmy pushed his stack to the center. Everyone at the table stood up.
"We got an all-in moment!" Manuel yelled at Craig and Trace, who came over to the table to watch.

"Naev," Trevor said with nerve-grating confidence, "If you could be so kind as if to show the final card. That would be much appreciated." Jimmy swayed. Brody held his breath. Naev discarded a "burn" card, Manuel held a hand to his mouth, and Trace pulled at his gold neck chain. Trevor remained still, grinning crookedly.

The "river" card was flipped. Jack of diamonds.

Trevor removed his earbuds and stared at Jimmy. "Show me your losing hand. Bitch."

"I regret," Jimmy said shakily, "That my winning hand is not more kick-ass." He flipped over a jack of spades and a queen of spades. "Uncle Jesse says hi. Full house, jacks over tens... bitch."

Brody sighed and mucked his hand, scooting back away from the table unceremoniously. Now every eye in the room was on Trevor MacKenzie.

"Oh... well... that's too bad..." Trevor said as he began to muck his hand slowly. Jimmy let out a whoop and pumped his fist. Anvil patted Jimmy's back as Jimmy reached for his winnings.

"...Because I have four of a kind!!" Trevor flipped over pocket tens, completely dominating Jimmy's hand.

Jimmy fell back in his chair and watched in disdain as a cackling Trevor hugged the massive pile of chips, cash, and the candle in close, sliding them to his side of the table. Anvil shrugged sympathetically, and Manuel shook his head in pity. Jimmy watched the last of his bankroll fall into the clutches of an arrogant Canadian with googly eyes.

Jimmy took a chug of his Rolling Rock. "At least the defeat doesn't taste as bad as this beer does."

Later that evening, Jimmy sat on the porch, smoking a Marlboro No. 27 Blend, staring absent-mindedly into the humid Columbus night. Not too far away, he heard the dull song of occasional drivers on I-270, the sky hazy-yellow, stars washed away by the light of the city. Jimmy felt his phone vibrate; Megan was texting him yet again. He ignored the phone. Whether he came home early or stayed out late, it would be the same story every time. Poker nights were supposed to be his escape.

The screen door slammed behind him. Jimmy jumped, startled by the noise. He looked up to see Brody Marlowe, the new guy, the wild card. Brody sidled over to him and remained quiet. Jimmy scooted over and patted the stoop next to him with a raised eyebrow. "Have a seat, man."

"Hello, James, how are you, man?" Brody said.

"'Bout as good as you are, I imagine. Neither of us made it to the money," Jimmy replied. He flicked his cigarette into the driveway.

"Bad for you," Brody said. Jimmy glanced at him. Brody stared up at Jimmy awkwardly.

"Tell me somethin' I don't know, dude." Jimmy loosened up his sweater jacket. "What brings you here anyway? Never seen you around before."

"Social networking," Brody said, perhaps a bit too excitedly, his voice cracking a touch. "I'm online friends with Manuel, and he said he had folks over to play tonight, so naturally, I, as you say, let myself in on this." Jimmy shot a glare at Brody, who he presumed to be mocking him. Brody shrugged his shoulders up and down as he finished his statement.

"Oh," Jimmy replied. "How do you know Manny?"

Brody sat back a little bit and threw open his arms. "Brody knows all your bros." Judging by Jimmy's expressionless face, Brody realized he wasn't amused. "Sorry, man, new to town and not sure how ya'll jive turkeys waddle."

Jimmy shook his head and laughed under his breath. "I seem to know all the weirdos. You'll fit in if you come back, I reck..." There was a crash from the dining room, the window of which was overlooking the porch. Both Jimmy and Brody stood and walked over to peek in and see what the hubbub was about. Brody and Jimmy shared a knowing glance with one another. *MacKenzie.*

The front door crashed open as Jimmy and Brody jumped back to see three bulky bodies tumble out of it. Craig and Big Trace had done what few could do this time of year: gang tackled Naev Broadnax. The burly, shaggy-haired Naev struggled and kicked about. Craig and Trace weren't football players, but were of the size and build to do some damage. Trace put his face close to Anvil's.

"That's that shit I don't like!" Trace grunted. "Don't be pullin' that around here, now. Get out 'fore I end your career."

Craig and Trace got off Anvil, who sat up near the steps, rubbing the back of his head. Brody and Jimmy looked on in shock as Craig went back inside, and Trace adjusted his purple satin shirt, following close behind.

"What, Naev?! What? Whatcha gonna do?! Bring it, man! Who you finna try! Who you finna try?!" Trevor MacKenzie jumped around inside the house, "making it rain" with his poker earnings, throwing bills around. Anvil sprang back up and started to run at the doorway before he got leveled by the bottom of Craig Foxx's boot.

"*Big boot! BIG BOOT!*" Trevor yelled from inside.

Craig knelt over Anvil, making sure he didn't get back up. He motioned for Big Trace to attend to Trevor. Trace thundered into the home as Trevor's voice faded away, saying, "What?! What I do, man? What I do?!"

Craig got off Anvil, but not before giving him a light kick to the side. He nodded towards Brody and Jimmy. "Jimmy, can you give Naev a ride? He's had too much."

Jimmy walked over, offering Anvil a hand to help him stand. "Too much? Of Trevor, or of the Rolling Rock?"

Brody snickered, but Craig wasn't laughing. "Get him home. Now."

Jimmy gestured inside. "I need to get my keys."

Craig glanced at Jimmy, keeping a straight face. Craig reached into his pants pocket and slung a Discovery lanyard towards Jimmy, who awkwardly caught it.

"Here, now get Anvil home. Now."

CHAPTER TWO

I-71 would snake through the middle section of Columbus, Ohio, a heavily used segment of the interstate. Connecting all three major cities in Ohio, hundreds of thousands of people spent time on the road daily. During the day, it was jammed, shoulder to shoulder with impatient vehicles jostling to and from work and school. At night, it seemed serene, literally a 'night and day' scenario, even as steady streams of cars still traveled to and fro. The green 1997 Pontiac Grand Am was far from the only vehicle on this massive road tonight. To the driver, though, he felt isolated. He was surrounded by chaos and felt it burning from within as well. The portly bearded man gripped the wheel with sweaty palms, his eyes struggling to stay wide between bushy brows on top and dark bags beneath.

Jimmy Glencroft knew he was in some deep trouble.

His phone was on low battery, and he couldn't find his charger. He would feel a buzz in his pocket once every few minutes. Sometimes it was a series of sustained buzzes, signifying an incoming call. His girlfriend was relentlessly trying to contact him, yet he could not bring himself to answer her calls or texts. He knew it was just going to start more trouble.

"So, eh, Jimmy... was wondering how far off we were from Marysville, mate," Brody inquired from the passenger seat, glancing up at the focused Jimmy. Jimmy tried to ignore him, fighting off the fatigue brought on by mild alcohol consumption. Anvil was sprawled out amid old McDonald's bags, a dusting of napkins, coffee cups, and empty cigarette boxes in the backseat, snoring obliviously as he zoomed down the highway at over 70 miles per hour.

Jimmy was frustrated with Brody now. As they helped the drunken and delirious Naev into his car, Brody admitted to Jimmy that he needed a ride home. Thinking it wouldn't be a big deal or a far drive, he agreed. *It couldn't hurt to help a guy and make a new friend, right?*

Brody revealed that he lived all the way in Marysville, a small town northwest of Columbus, a half hour one way from where Jimmy lived. What didn't make sense to Jimmy is that not only did Brody ride his bike all the way from there to Dublin, but that Brody's bike was stolen not long before the poker game in broad daylight. Also, why didn't Brody just ask for a ride from Manuel Rezendes, the only one there he knew? Jimmy's buzz was killed, he knew a fight was waiting for him at home, he lost a significant amount of money tonight, and he had an awkward hipster as his main company during this unnecessary series of drives. Good times being had by all.

Jimmy mentally broke through the tunnel vision he was experiencing to glance around. The Columbus skyline loomed above them as they left I-71 in favor of I-70, heading west.

Brody stared out the windows. He hadn't talked much to Jimmy or the others about what really brought him here. He didn't want to explain much. It wouldn't make sense to them. Then again, in life... should anything make sense? His time to make an impact would come soon. For now, he didn't want to bug Jimmy much more. Life had a way of working itself out.

Jimmy gazed at the rearview mirror to see Anvil resting. The potential for money and fame, the pressures were starting to creep into Naev's life. Jimmy had often wanted to ask Naev for a favor, maybe to go on a road trip together, so he could see more of the world. Cross the Mississippi. Pass the Great Plains. See the Pacific. Scale the Rockies...

But he couldn't ask Anvil for anything. Jimmy was a proud man. He didn't ask for much that he couldn't get himself. It just so happened to be that everything he could get himself, he really had to work for. That, and he would often get help from his live-in girlfriend, Megan. Megan was great. Well, that's what Jimmy continually tried to convince himself of. The relationship started out perfectly. Jimmy was coming out of a rough patch in job-hopping and learning the big city dating game when he happened upon her. It had been too long now, and the cracks in the relationship were beginning to show. Every night, another fight. Every day, more complaints. Jimmy saw the relationship as an investment. He'd put too much in.

Leaving Megan would rob him of his security, having someone to come home to, someone to love. But is always walking on eggshells and second-guessing every word of every conversation *truly love?*

They had almost broken up once. Jimmy and Megan had lost all hold on any healthy communication. Jimmy couldn't stop texting other women – nothing necessarily malicious, no cheating – and Megan couldn't productively articulate her mistrust. One wrong Snap session went awry, Jimmy didn't set boundaries, and Megan wouldn't listen. Jimmy ended up with a smashed smartphone, a broken heart, and a half-full suitcase of clothes.

If he didn't drunkenly pass out on the living room floor that night, he would have been gone.

The next day, the lockdowns began.

Ten days to stop the spread gave way to two masks to stop the spread. Jimmy lost his job. Megan doubled the hours at hers.

A global pandemic, political unrest, and a world in turmoil.

Eventually, Jimmy and Megan learned to find comfort in one another once more.

But that was short-lived.

The Columbus skyline receded into the rearview. Jimmy took the exit off I-70 onto Hague, making a few quick, calculated turns through abandoned side streets, silent and eerie in the moonlight. Anvil's home was drawing near. Jimmy turned to Brody. "We'll just stop here for a few minutes, then it's homeward bound. You'll be home within the hour."

"Glad to hear, mate," Brody responded. *Mate? What's up with his word choices? Brody was one puzzling dude,* Jimmy thought to himself, as he turned onto 5th Avenue. Jimmy began to wonder if he could even make it home. He didn't live that far away, over in Hilliard. It wouldn't be a bad drive if he was just going straight there. But, no... Toss an hour onto the trip for taking Brody home, and Jimmy had himself one long drive.

The first stop came into view: Faraway Stay Apartments. Jimmy was roommates with Anvil there a few short years ago. The complex was a series of three-story buildings wrapped around a quarry lake with a few tennis courts thrown in. These medium-level apartments in the village of Marble Cliff Crossing, between the suburbs of Grandview Heights and Upper Arlington, housed many memories for Jimmy, both good and bad.

"Wake him up for me," Jimmy told Brody, as Jimmy hooked a right into the "gated" community. Advertised as secure, the gates were always open. Honestly, anyone could get into Faraway Stay. Many nonresidents have played, and some have perished, on the 30+ foot tall cliffs that wrap around the quarry lake.

Brody poked at Anvil with a window scraper he found beneath his seat. Jimmy shook his head. "That's not gonna wake him up. Fella looks like he got done rolled over by them Rolling Rocks," he said, trying to remember which building to go to as he drove towards a speed bump.

Jimmy smirked over an idea. He accelerated sharply, ramping the speed bump, the car going just a few inches into the air before it landed. That was all it took, and Anvil's 250-pound body slammed into the front seats, waking him up.

"Whaddafuckathingafucker..." Anvil mumbled as he clambered back onto the seat, half-conscious. His eyes were unfocused, his curly crown of hair matted and frayed, his eyes a slight red. "Home?" he asked in between snorting and grunting noises.

"Yeah, Naev, we're here," Jimmy said as he pulled into the parking lot. The time on the clock read 2:12 AM. Anvil rubbed his eyes and laughed. Brody looked at him timidly.

"What's so funny, mate?" Brody asked. Jimmy glanced at them both. It amused him to look at them side by side: 6'4" pro football quarterback beside a pale dude with a fedora who couldn't be more than 5'5".

"Man, I gotta be at the stadium at 8," Anvil said as he pulled open the car door.

Jimmy nodded towards the apartment. "Mind if Brody and I come in, grab a soda, maybe check out what you've done with the place? You know, recharge before we hit the road again?" he asked.

"Nah, dude," Anvil slurred, "Dana would be pissed if you came in. She's probably trying to sleep. Maybe tomorrow after the game. Plus, don't you have a girl to get home to?"

Jimmy glanced at his phone. 4% battery remaining. Nine unread messages. 17 missed calls. One set of rolling eyes and a deep, knowing sigh.

"I guess I do, man," Jimmy concurred. "I have to be at the stadium early too. Guess I better get out of here. It's been real." Fist-bumps ensued.

"Nice meeting you, sir," Brody said to Anvil.

"Yeah," Anvil said as he slammed the door shut and stumbled across the lawn towards his apartment.

Jimmy sunk in his seat a little bit and closed his eyes. His eyelids settled, his thoughts loose and effortless.

"We gonna make it okay, man?" Brody asked.

Jimmy leaned forward, wrapped his hands around the steering wheel, and flexed his fingers.

"I am the fuckin' *highway*, bud."

Brody Marlowe sat in relative silence as Jimmy sped northbound on I-270. Every now and then, they would try to break the silence with a short-lived, awkward conversation. The two were secretly stereotyping one another in the back of their heads, which added to the stifling atmosphere. Brody thought Jimmy was a stereotypical American and doubted his general intelligence. Jimmy just thought Brody looked like a deformed Macklemore with worse teeth. Jimmy reeled at the time and realized he had another half-hour or so with him. He had to make better conversation.

"You like Floyd? I got Dark Side if you wanna get trippy. Maybe get the Led out?" Jimmy asked as he pulled out his little black CD folder. One eye on the road and the other on the CD folder, he flipped through some of the titles in front: Boston, Journey, Van Halen, and other classic rock artists were the most prominent. Jimmy passed the CD case to Brody.

Jimmy watched Brody out of the corner of his heavy eye while he drove. Brody flipped through the folder, spending just a second or two looking at each page. He looked unimpressed.

"You got any uh... Pavement? Or, Neutral Milk Hotel?" Brody asked. Jimmy raised an eyebrow.

"You're gonna hit the pavement if you ask a question like that again, dude," Jimmy said, laughing. "Neutral Milk? What is that, another term for sperm?"

Brody wasn't laughing. "Neutral Milk Hotel was a prominent indie band in the mid..."

Jimmy had to cut him off. "I know who they were. You sound like you just read their Wikipedia entry before this conversation."

Brody's words sharpened. "Maybe if you broadened your horizons a bit, you'd realize..."

"Dude, my horizons are broad enough. I've tried it all. I know what I like. You can tubthump your Chumbawumba back to Shrewsbury; I don't want to hear anymore. Now let's just jam to some B.O.C. and get your weird little ass home," Jimmy said.

Brody didn't laugh or respond; he just stared out the window. Rain fell lightly, small drops appearing on the glass, not enough moisture for Jimmy to turn on his windshield wipers. Blue Oyster Cult played on Jimmy's sound system, the opening strains of "(Don't Fear) The Reaper" falling as gently as the raindrops. Jimmy took a tight turn right onto what felt like an eternal off-ramp as they passed from I-270 onto Route 33, which ran northwest out of Columbus, toward Marysville and beyond.

Jimmy slumped in his front seat and used the loud music to keep himself awake. Whether it was driving in the car, on headphones at home, or in public, he meditated on every note and pondered every word. His eyes began to slump shut...

Brody whacked him in the arm. Jimmy snapped his eyes open and glared at him.

"I'm not going to let you sleep. My life is in your hands. At least put your seat belt on if you're going to be risky. God damn," Brody said, annoyed.

"I can't wait to drop your ass off," Jimmy replied. Against his will, he clicked his seat belt in tightly. The Pontiac pressed into the night, the left side of the highway flanked by warehouses and industry, the right side cuddled up to a blanket of fields. The haze of the city gave way to starlight.

Jimmy sang along softly to Blue Oyster Cult. "Laaaa la la laaaa..."

The voices faded into an eerie guitar arpeggio with the snap of hi-hat drums. Jimmy shivered as the car was gradually illuminated in a flood of bright light.

"Brody," Jimmy said with a tremble, looking to his reluctant companion.

Brody blinked rapidly before he glanced towards Jimmy with widened eyes.

"Look," Jimmy whispered. "Are we being followed?"

Jimmy eyed his rearview mirror. He saw a set of bright headlights gaining on him quickly. They appeared to be on a truck or an SUV, accelerating towards them.

"Christ, we are..." Jimmy muttered. He slammed his right foot down on the accelerator and sat up straight.

"Come on, come on, come on..." Brody said as he watched the headlights gain on them. The vehicle behind them turned on its high beams, the light beyond unbearable.

"What the hell do they want?!" Jimmy yelled. The speedometer crept upward as the engine of the old Pontiac screamed like a jet preparing for takeoff. 80, 85... 90 M.P.H.

"Do something, Jimmy!" Brody pleaded.

"Like what? What can I *possibly* do?" The SUV matched Jimmy's speed increase. The black vehicle drew alongside them to the left, and its front right bumper swept to the right, clipping the Pontiac's left rear quarter-panel. The Grand Am went into a sideways skid as its tires squealed.

The next thing they saw was spinning starlight. The car careened off the road as a loud, dull explosion of noise deafened them. Jimmy screamed as he tucked his arms in against his torso. The car went through the grass a few meters before it caught a ditch and was sent flying. Brody closed his eyes, Jimmy screamed hoarse as the car barrel-rolled a few times, crumpling the vehicle's metal like a can.

Jimmy's world went black.

The devastated green Grand Am finally came to a halt on its four bald wheels, a smoking husk of chewed up metal. Brody let out a heavy "thank God" when he realized he was still alive, then smiled when he reached up to find that his fedora didn't fall off. He glanced up to see taillights from the SUV in the distance. Brody slid out of the car without even checking on the motionless Jimmy. He didn't bother shutting the passenger door as he pulled up his pant leg and drew the .38 Special from its holster. Brody took cover behind the front right quarter panel of the car and scanned the area. He watched intently for other assailants, focusing on the wood lines and the highway. No other cars passed; no headlights in the distance. He holstered the gun and looked to the sky, slumping against the car and breathing heavily.

"Mother fucker!" a nearby voice shouted. Brody jumped to his feet.

The voice belonged to Jimmy, who had stepped out of the car. His hat had fallen off, he had a bold red gash across his forehead, and he was covered in shards of glass from the driver's side window. The glass fell off Jimmy in flakes as he walked to the front of the car, shaking himself off. Brody observed crystalline shards of glass caught in Jimmy's beard.

"Brody, man, I might not like you, but I'm glad you made it, bud. Are you okay?" Jimmy offered Brody a steadying hand.

"Yeah," Brody said with a long sigh. "I guess. You're bleeding, mate!"

Rivulets of blood flowed down Jimmy's face. Brody reached into the car and grabbed a microfiber cloth from the wrecked Grand Am's backseat. Brody then applied heavy pressure to Jimmy's forehead wound. Jimmy grunted a thank you and stared at the wreckage.

"Black SUV," Jimmy said. "A Black SUV hit us and just drove off... Why would they do this?"

Jimmy shivered. Brody dabbed the cloth on Jimmy's forehead, the blue fiber growing a deep purple as it absorbed the blood. Brody glanced about the car quickly to assess any signs of danger. There were no flames under the hood. Globs of motor oil fell rhythmically from the undercarriage, but thankfully no open flame anywhere to spark it. In the dim light, Jimmy could see giant, muddy ruts in the ground showing where the car had slid and flipped.

"Keep pressure on this," Brody said to Jimmy, leaving him with the thick cloth. Brody shook free shards of glass from his own shirt, flexed out his stiff and sore right arm, and staggered about to shake out a leg cramp.

Brody limped a circle around the wreckage, looking for any signs of people. Across the highway, beyond fencing, he observed buildings from one of the businesses on Industrial Parkway, but they were likely closed for the night. He felt around for his phone. Not in his pocket, perhaps it was still in the wreckage. He limped over towards Jimmy, who was pacing about and kicking the air.

"What happened back there, mate?" Brody asked.

"What happened," Jimmy started, "is that life decided to *fuck me again!*" he yelled as he pulled his cell phone out of his pocket, flipped it open, and tried to dial Megan. That's when he realized the screen was shattered, several buttons and the battery missing. Jimmy hauled off and threw it out over the highway. Brody watched in awe. Brody's mouth slacked open as he listened to Jimmy's launch into a fiery rant.

"I suck at being a mascot. I suck at being a boyfriend. I suck at poker. My phone is broken, I have no insurance on it. My shitty car, mind you, my *only* car... was wrecked by some bozo. It doesn't have insurance either! It's like 3 in the fucking morning, I'm stuck with some weird stranger, I have work in a few hours, and my old lady is going to *kill me.*"

Jimmy impulsively patted his pockets, rolled his eyes, and threw back his head. "I can't find my damn cigarettes either!!"

Brody watched Jimmy cautiously. Brody edged towards the wreckage as Jimmy continued ranting. Brody opened the passenger door and dug around for his own phone. No sign of it anywhere. He searched the grass where the car had slid and flipped. No sign. Brody came to the slow-burning realization that he hadn't lost it in the wreckage. He had lost it at the poker game. Brody took a deep breath and leaned against the Pontiac head-first with a light *thunk.*

Jimmy paced around, flailing his arms around helplessly in frustration. He turned to Brody. "If your ass drove instead of wanting to *go green* and ride a bike every damn place, I wouldn't be out here. I'd be in bed, I'd be rested for work, and I wouldn't be stuck in a damn field with you!"

... "You got a phone?" Jimmy amended his rant with this question in a more respectful tone.

Brody shook his head. "Lost it."

"...Lost it?! Not in the car anywhere?"

"It's not in there. Honestly, I think I lost it at the poker game."

Jimmy sat down cross-legged on the ground. "Bro," he said as he shook his head incredulously, "we are so *fucked.*"

Brody glanced up towards the somewhat distant haze of the city. "Maybe not."

Headlights illuminated the liminal space of the empty highway. Jimmy looked up to see the headlights and sprinted to the shoulder, flailing his arms again and yelling. Brody trotted behind.

"Hey! Hey! Slow down, we need help!" Jimmy hollered.

An eighteen-wheeler truck roared past. The wind of its draft whipped the two men's clothes and blew back their hair. It didn't stop nor slow, headed west into the black.

"Fuck!" Jimmy yelled. He paced around on the shoulder, shaking more glass out of his clothes as they waited for another car to come by. He checked to see if he had any glass in his skin, but luckily so far, nothing. He saw the silver lining that he had escaped with a gash, a few minor cuts and scrapes, and some bruises. Jimmy was going to be okay... physically, at least.

Rainfall came again, a warm and moist mist. Jimmy's clothes were filmy from both sides, between sweat and blood and rainfall. In the back of his head, he wondered how upset Megan was going to be. She had helped him invest lots of cash into fixing up various ailments with the Grand Am, and she had been on top of him getting insurance, which he just kept putting off and putting off...

"Jimmy, another one!" Brody shouted. Jimmy turned to see more headlights, two sets of them this time. He jumped up and down and flailed his arms. One sports car whipped past without slowing. The second vehicle in the far lane, a pickup truck, followed suit.

"What's wrong with you people?!" Brody yelled. "Hit and run, nobody stopping to help..."

Jimmy sighed as he kept walking down the highway, Brody not far behind, both moving just to make sure all their parts were still together. The lack of streetlights on this part of the highway made for an eerie feel.

"Brody, dude, if nobody stops, we're going to have to walk all the way back to Dublin," Jimmy said between deep breaths as they walked.

"Hey, well, at least we still have the ability to walk," Brody reminded him.

"For now."

The two men walked in silence for several minutes, not even bothering to flag down passing cars after two, three, ten more passed without stopping. Brody stayed alert, hanging back away from Jimmy and closer to the field side of the shoulder, ready to react to any threat if needed.

Brody stopped cold and felt adrenaline rush from his torso outward as a large van barreled onto the shoulder ahead of them. Brody dove off the road, rolled, and kept a hand on his gun. He snapped his head up to watch as the van came to a steady, non-threatening stop about thirty yards away from them. Jimmy cautiously approached, holding up an arm to shield his eyes from the rain. Squinting through the glare of the van's high beams, he could see the windshield wipers swiping once every few seconds. He heard a door slam shut, but couldn't see it. A shadowy figure, a little taller than Jimmy and of a lighter build, moved into view, silhouetted by the headlights and eerie in the solemn night. As Brody focused his sight, he could not believe his eyes. This wasn't the guardian angel anyone was expecting.

CHAPTER THREE

"Well, howdy pardner, fancy seeing you here!"

Trevor MacKenzie limped forward, his crooked grin displaying snaggled teeth. He extended his hand to shake Jimmy's. Jimmy just stared, dumbfounded. Trevor wore his work uniform, a green apron, and green hat. The Cream Dream Donuts logo was emblazoned on the cap, bright red and white.

"The hell, man? I thought you were off today?" Jimmy said, his head spinning.

"Someone called off, so I'm on the job." Trevor looked to his right, saw Brody Marlowe, and tipped his hat to him. Brody quietly nodded back.

"Still a lil' drunk, but oh well. What are you doin' out here trampin' around, Al? Where's Meggy-poo?" Trevor stepped closer and saw that Jimmy was cut across the forehead, muddy, and still had a few shards of glass in his clothes. Brody didn't look much better as he staggered up onto the shoulder, a bit muddy as well.

Jimmy stared sharply at Trevor. "Dude, no time for jokes. Some asshole in a black SUV wrecked my car and drove off. I ain't got no insurance, *Meggy-Poo* is probably home worried sick, my phone's crushed, my face is bloody, and I just don't give a damn anymore."

Trevor shook his head, still grinning inappropriately. The rain picked up its pace as clouds rolled over the remaining few visible stars overhead.

"Jimmy," Trevor said, "Do you need an ambulance? You know, for your car and stuff?"

Jimmy shook his head. "No health insurance. No car insurance. I'm scared shitless, man. I don't know what to do."

"Yeah, mate, Jimmy, how are you feeling anyway?" Brody asked.

Right when Brody asked, Jimmy noticed the mild pain. He lifted his shirt to reveal a bluish-purple bruise the size of his palm on his left side. His left arm was throbbing, and when he pulled up his sleeve, there were multiple scrapes above his elbow and a fist-sized brown and red bruise on the outside of his upper arm stretching up to his shoulder. His head pulsed around the temples, and the flesh of his lower back stung.

"Damn, son," Trevor said, "If that bruise doesn't hurt now, it definitely will later." Brody nodded in agreement, and Jimmy shrugged.

"I don't want you guys out here wet and bruisy. Come on up, gentlemen. You can ride along while I make my deliveries, and I'll get you home. I only got a few more left." Trevor walked to the side of the van and opened a sliding side door. There were a few stacks of donut boxes on rolling shelves, but plenty of space for a couple people to sit.

"We will figure out what to do with your car, man," Trevor said to Jimmy. "Have I ever let you down?"

"Yes," Jimmy said coldly as he shuffled over to the passenger side door. "Several times."

"Where you goin', buddy?" Trevor asked Brody.

"My apartment is in Marysville," Brody replied, climbing into the donut truck. "Thanks for the ride."

"Any time, man. I've got a few boxes to drop off at a gas 'n' grub on 36. I'll get you home after that. Help yourself to some donuts," Trevor offered with a grin. He slammed the door shut after Brody got settled. Trevor turned around, pulled out a box of Newports and a lighter, ready to light a cigarette. He looked up to see Jimmy, just standing there by the passenger side of the truck.

"How do you still have a job?" Jimmy asked. "Giving donuts away, working drunk on no sleep, and giving people rides in the company van... I don't get it."

Trevor pulled a small red-orange and yellow bottle out of his apron pocket with his free hand and winked. "Five Hour Energy. When you gotta get stuff done."

"Well, I know how you work drunk on no sleep, but..."

Trevor cut him off with a wave. "Get in the truck before you get soaked. You can have shotgun. I'll even give you a square."

Trevor climbed into the driver's side and started up the Cream Dream Donuts truck with a rumble. Jimmy looked at his wrecked car in the distance one last time before opening the other door and stepping in. Both doors slammed, a couple smokes were lit, and the two frenemies rode off across county lines with a few dozen donuts and a mysterious, vaguely foreign hipster in tow.

"What the hell, man," Jimmy Glencroft said to himself as he leaned onto a stained ceramic sink, looking at himself in a cracked gas station mirror, the fluorescent light flickering on and off, the floor sticky as he shifted his feet. His blue eyes tinged with a light red, drooping grey bags beneath, stubble formed along what was an otherwise well-trimmed beard. His forehead gash had stopped bleeding a while ago. It didn't seem deep enough to require stitches, but it certainly was too big for a band-aid. Jimmy had busted his head a few times before, recalling various football and wrestling incidents. The rest of his forehead was marked here and there with a few old telltale battle scars. He decided to grin and bear it without really grinning. He didn't have much to grin about right now.

Jimmy took off his shirt, a grey sport shirt with a blue, red, and yellow Discovery logo on the front. The shirt was matted with sweat, rain, and stained with blood. He shook it out completely, shards of glass quietly tinkling as they fell to the floor below. Jimmy surveyed his body for any other shards; and examined his bruises. He didn't feel them yet, so he knew he would be one sore individual tomorrow. He groaned in disgust as he slid the shirt back on.

Jimmy sighed and wondered what Megan was doing right now. What was she thinking, what was she feeling? Was she still awake? Had she fallen asleep while waiting for him? Did she just finally give up on him being reliable on his time frames and promises? No matter which way he looked at it, he knew he would be in trouble with her. Every week he did something wrong. He couldn't stay on top of the ever-changing, challenging landscape of a modern adult relationship. Jimmy didn't just want this relationship, though. He needed it. He needed Megan more than she needed him. This much was for certain. Looking at his messy, sleepless, bloody, and disheveled self in the mirror, Jimmy promised to himself, and to Megan, that he would be a better man. A better boyfriend. A better person in general. Losing the car would be another nail in his proverbial coffin, if not the last one.

Jimmy was jolted from his reverie by loud pounding upon the bathroom door. "Jimmy! Come on, man, time to hit the next stop," Trevor said dimly from the other side. Jimmy didn't respond. He turned on the faucet and slapped some more of that not so pure Union County water on his face, rinsing his wound once more. He patted himself dry with a gritty paper towel.

There was another knock at the door, lighter this time. Jimmy slowly opened it, expecting to see Trevor.

24

Brody Marlowe peeked in. "Hey, you doing okay?"

Jimmy laughed. "Dude, I bet you think I'm an absolute mess. Great first impressions, right?"

"I've seen worse," Brody said. "If that's any consolation."

Jimmy stepped out of the bathroom and shut the door behind him.

"Oh, I've seen much worse too. Most of my life and my friends are just messes born of messes."

"You going to be okay, man? I feel like you're stressing about a lot. Anything I can do to help?"

"Loan me a few grand and get my girl to chill out?" Jimmy said with a laugh.

"Well... I can't say I can't help you with both eventually, but right now? No such luck."

The two men strode around the gas station idly as Trevor cleaned up the donut station in the corner.

"Why are you worrying about your girl so much anyway?" Brody asked.

Jimmy shrugged. "She's done a lot for me, man. She takes care of me. It's hard to make it on your own as a mascot, you know?"

"Yeah? What's that pay?"

"Pay? Ha! I get $150 per game. So, the hourly rate is legit, but unless I get booked for special appearances, I'm lucky to work two days a week. And at this point in time, Columbus is a Brutus town. Sailor Smash doesn't get shit."

"No side gigs?"

"Well, I just... Nah, honestly, not really... Poker is my side hustle. Why?"

"I just figured a guy with so few hours a week would keep busy with a second job or a side gig, that's all," Brody said.

"Yeah, poker normally does that for me, but it's been getting harder for me lately. Megan's fed up with it. She doesn't like that scene. She's gonna be putting her foot down if I lose too many more checks."

Brody nodded sympathetically. Then his eyes widened, and he looked up at Jimmy. "Let me know if you're ever looking for extra work."

"Ah, really? What is it that you do?"

"...Distribution."

"Like, warehouses and shit?"

"Yes, sir. We're always looking for temps and under-the-table guys. Just let me know, alright?"

"You bet. That could be a life-saver. Thanks, man. I'll get you my number once we get our phones back," Jimmy said.

Brody and Jimmy shared a fist-bump. They walked out of the gas station with Trevor, the doorbell dinging behind them as Jimmy took a deep breath of the chill morning air. Trevor and Jimmy hopped into the front of the donut van and slammed the front doors almost simultaneously. Brody drug Trevor's dolly to the back for him, and clambered in.

"Another square?" Trevor asked Jimmy as he turned on the engine with a rattle.

Jimmy nodded. "So, you never did tell me why people call cigarettes 'squares'..."

They sparked up a couple more Newports as the van turned out of the parking lot and drove towards the rising sun.

Night gave way to early dawn as Trevor MacKenzie drove between various gas stations and convenience stores across Union County. Brody Marlowe caught up on his own sleep, laying on a pile of empty donut boxes in the back of the van as Trevor made his deliveries. James Glencroft would go into the stores with Trevor. Jimmy refilled the same Styrofoam cup with coffee at each location and chatted with the clerks and customers about the Columbus Discovery. He didn't reveal to anyone that he was the mascot, using his anonymity to get an informal survey of how the fans felt about the team. He was pleased to hear that they all approved of his friend, Naev "Anvil" Broadnax's playing style, some comparing the unlikely football hero to Ben Roethlisberger or Daunte Culpepper.

Jimmy also took his time to get some treatment for his cuts and gashes, buying bandages, gauze, and medicine from a pharmacy to patch himself up. Jimmy didn't talk to Trevor much but made sure to let him know that he appreciated his kindness with two packs of smokes bought with the little money he had left from the poker game.

There were several times where Trevor offered to let Jimmy use his cell phone to call Megan, or "Meggy-poo," as he snidely called her, but Jimmy declined. He wasn't ready to hear anything from her knowing how bad the lectures were going to be. The whole day, a sense of dread nested uncomfortably within him. Jimmy winced once as he thought of the idea of yet another thrown mug, a shattered glass, another verbal beating.

Jimmy expressed concern about the authorities finding his wrecked car, tracing it back to him, and charging him for driving without insurance. When he told Trevor this, Trevor promptly called Craig Foxx, who had not yet slept either.

Craig was kind enough to personally drive over to the charred wreckage on Route 33 with two of his employees and pick up the wrecked Grand Am with a flatbed truck. Craig said he would store it at one of his warehouses in Dublin until Jimmy decided what to do with it. Jimmy asked Craig how much he owed him, but all Craig said in return was that he just may need a favor someday, and Jimmy would be the first man he'd call. Despite his wrecked car and tumultuous relationship, Jimmy was pleased. He was thankful he had helpful, albeit shady and unpredictable friends.

Jimmy looked out the donut truck window as it rolled around the flat, nondescript Union County countryside. As they traveled towards Trevor's last stop for the morning just outside of town, Jimmy had some not-so-fond memories of this area. Before the Discovery, before the pandemic, he lived with Megan at an apartment in Marysville. The only reason Jimmy agreed to live in the area was because of the low cost of living, with him being broke and bouncing around between jobs at the time. For his taste, Jimmy never found much to do in Union County, spending most of his time reading, listening to music, working when he could, and spending time with Megan. He was glad he was back in Columbus and away from this dull area.

After some dull puttering through town, Trevor's donut truck pulled into Engelbert's Gas 'n' Grub, a small family-owned convenience store with faded signs in the windows and cracked cement wreathing the building. Trevor showed signs of fatigue, yawning here and there, taking more time before getting out of the truck after every stop. He looked in the back from his perch in the front seat to check on Brody, who was still asleep.

"You wanna grab the front door for me, man?" Trevor asked Jimmy.

"Sure," Jimmy said as he popped out of the passenger seat. "What else have I got to do, write the great American novel?"

Jimmy opened the swinging glass door in front of Trevor, who walked in with three boxes of donuts in his arms. Trevor walked over to a Plexiglas case by the cappuccino machines to fill up a few shelves of sugary treats. Meanwhile, Jimmy walked over to the counter's magazine rack, adjacent to a bathroom door. He popped open a fantasy football magazine to check out the latest power rankings. He sought out Anvil in the Patriot Football League quarterback list. It read:

"Naev Broadnax, QB, Columbus Discovery. #13. 6'4", 253 lbs. Quarterback Ranking: #27. Our editorial staff here at *Fantasy Freakout* was shocked to see Broadnax this high, but we expect to see some big things out of this big man over the next few weeks. His two touchdown, two-interception performance as a substitute against Knoxville last week was inspired yet uneven. More snaps will bring more rhythm, and we expect him to break out soon. The highlight of the game, and his career thus far, was a 25-yard touchdown scramble complete with several broken tackles."

Sounds about right, Jimmy thought to himself. He turned the page and began looking for more Discovery colleagues to read about when the bathroom door beside him creaked open. A man about Jimmy's height but a bit wider and more muscular came out. He wore a plain blue shirt, jeans, boots, an Indianapolis Colts hat, and a small handheld radio was strapped to his belt. Jimmy saw the well-trimmed mustache and recognized this man immediately.

"Finn!"

"Jimmy!"

The two men engaged in a "bro hug" that started out as a handshake. Finn Aittokallio was a firefighter with the city of Marysville. Jimmy's high school friend from down in Nawakwa, separate paths brought them to the same town.

"How ya been, man?" Finn asked as Jimmy put his fantasy football magazine back on the shelf. "Looks like you got in a fight with a dinosaur," he said, commenting on Jimmy's array of patches and wraps that held gauze and bandage on his cuts.

"Uhh, got jumped at a poker game," Jimmy said, laughing it off. Finn raised an eyebrow.

"Who did it?" Finn asked. "It wasn't Foxx or that Trace guy, was it? I've always thought they were up to something."

"Nah," Jimmy replied, committing to the lies. "Some dudes they invited that I hadn't seen before. Thought I was stacking the deck. I called them out on marking cards. They thought they could get anything by a new scene. We all know I'm slicker than that. They didn't take too kindly to my observations."

"Think they'll be back? If so, I'll come along and help you show 'em some Mothmen pride," Finn said as he smacked his own bicep.

"Nah," Jimmy said again. "I got enough of a piece out of 'em myself that they won't be back for a while. Kicked some ass for the working class."

27

"A true Heartland Hero," Finn said with a laugh, referencing Jimmy's old wrestling persona. "Say, how's Megan?"

"She's Megan," Jimmy said indifferently. "I'm kinda worried she may dump me sometime soon."

"What?!" Finn said, shocked. "She's not cheating or anything, is she?"

"Megan wouldn't do that. Nah, man, I've just been a shitty boyfriend lately. Staying out all night, not really responding when she tries to hit me up, gambling too much... you know. Just being reckless."

"Reckless ain't the word for it, bub." Finn shook his head. "You gotta prioritize, Jimmy. What's more important to you?"

"Really, dude?" Jimmy asked testily. "I know what's more important."

Finn sighed. "Jimmy, man, the cards are never going to treat you as good as Megan does. It's okay to play, but man, you gotta take a break sometimes. You getting jumped should be telling you something. You're getting in too deep. Get out before you lose too much money, or lose Meg."

"It's like Ron Swanson said. 'Never half-ass two things. Whole-ass one thing.' You gotta go all in, bud."

"I may start looking for some new income. I'm not sure what I'm going to do yet. But it's time to branch out. Maybe Meg will appreciate it," Jimmy said.

Finn nodded towards Jimmy's Discovery shirt. "By the way, man, don't you have a game to mascot in a few hours?"

"You know what, I guess I do. Been a long night."
"If you need to blow off some steam, shoot some guns, watch some racing or some shit, you know where to find me," Finn said.

"Bet," Jimmy replied. "I'd love to see your dog again, too. Homer's the best."

Jimmy was in the middle of a farewell handshake with Finn as, but the sneering Trevor MacKenzie strode over to say hi.

"Look at what the cat dragged in," Finn said with a laugh. "What's up, MacKenzie?"

"My bankroll after beating this dude in cards last night," Trevor joked, nodding towards Jimmy. Jimmy glared at Trevor.

"Hey Trevor, let's get going man, I gotta go home and get ready for work," Jimmy said urgently.

"Don't rush me, bro; I wanna tell Finn all about it!" Trevor turned to Finn. "So, no shit, there I was, playing with Rezendes, Anvil, this new hipster guy..."

Jimmy pushed Trevor towards the door. "Just Skype Finn later or something, dude," Jimmy muttered to him.

Jimmy waved to Finn. "We'll catch up later. I'll drop by next week, maybe."

"Maybe," Finn replied. He watched Trevor and Jimmy squabble as Jimmy tried to get them out the door as quickly and honestly as possible. They piled into the donut van, still arguing even as they did so. Unbeknownst to Finn, Cecil Engelbert, the shop's owner and proprietor, had walked up near him, wiping out a coffee pot.

"Like a married couple", Engelbert said, the shrewd, short fellow chuckling. Finn flinched, surprised by his presence. Finn watched as the donut truck sped away.

"Like somethin', alright." Finn turned to Engelbert and flashed a grin. "So how about that free coffee for firemen?"

Fifteen minutes later, the Cream Dream Donuts van finally rolled into the parking lot of Brody Marlowe's nondescript brick apartment complex. Brody invited Jimmy and Trevor in, but both men declined, running on fumes and ready to call it a day.

Jimmy's eyes were transfixed to the digital clock in Trevor's donut truck the entire drive back to Columbus. The closer they got to I-270, the more the knot of nervousness grew in Jimmy's stomach. Trevor tried to ease Jimmy's tension, joking about poker and sports and telling stories about days gone by. Jimmy could only half-listen to Trevor. He was too busy mentally preparing himself, scripting what he would say to Megan when he got home.

Jimmy continued to stare at the clock on the donut truck dashboard. *8:07 AM*. He had to be at Ohio Stadium in less than six hours to get ready for work. Naev Broadnax was already there, or at least he should be. Jimmy wondered if Anvil was going to be able to perform with a hangover. *Probably*, he thought... professional football locker rooms had a chemical solution for any problem floating around.

Jimmy had been awake for nearly 24 hours now, and he felt like he had lived 24 years in a single night. Jimmy's breaths came ragged as Trevor drove down I-270 southbound toward the Cemetery Road exit, not far from the home Jimmy shared with Megan.

"So, eh, why did you lie to Finn about the poker game?" Trevor asked as he drifted the donut truck across several lanes of interstate without a blinker. "You embarrassed, bud?"

"Well, see... Finn's a fireman, you know. He's always got that little radio on him. If he knew I wrecked and had Craig pick up the car rather than call authorities, he'd have some annoying questions. I just wasn't feeling it," Jimmy explained.

"*Sure*," Trevor teased. He scratched his arm as he rested it on the steering wheel, staring ahead at red-light traffic atop the exit ramp.

"So, what exactly happened between you and Naev?" Jimmy asked, referencing the conflict from the poker game. He hadn't seen what started the fight, just how it had ended, with Anvil being thrown through the front door by Craig Foxx and Big Trace.

"Sucked out on him," Trevor explained. "He had top top, and I called his all-in on the flop. Running spades put him out. I may or may not have talked too much trash when I won, but he got his panties in a bunch and wanted to swing on me."

"Go on," Jimmy said, still only half-listening despite his best efforts.

"Little did he know that I can handle my own," Trevor said with a snicker. "I may or may not have rock-bottomed him through a table."

"No way."

"Well, maybe not through the table..." Trevor shrugged. "I just slapped him in the face a few times. You know how it goes."

"Not sure I do, man," Jimmy said with a sigh as he stared out the window. "And you had a problem with *my* lying."

They hooked a right turn off the exit ramp after the light turned green, exiting onto Cemetery Road.

"So, this black SUV. No clue who it was?" Trevor asked.

"If I knew, they'd be dead by now." Jimmy said. Even as he said it, Jimmy doubted it himself.

"It's a *conspiracy*!" Trevor said enthusiastically.

Jimmy rolled his eyes. "Everything's a conspiracy with you, dude."

"I'm just saying, I'm sure something doesn't add up, bud. Just ask questions. Follow the answers."

"What if they lead me to Bigfoot? Argentina? Jimmy Hoffa? That place in New Mexico with the alien labs?"

"Now we're getting somewhere!" Trevor said as his eyes widened. "Did you listen to Clark the Snark talk to that guy who worked at Fort Sproat? Rumor has it there's, like, a terror cell in the woods near the West Virginia border! Remind me to send you a link..."

"Clark the Snark is bad and you should feel bad for still listening to his bullshit," Jimmy said. "Stay off those podcasts, man. Last time you got into them you legit started believing in QAnon."

"You don't think there's a sinister cabal controlling world governments and covering up sinister trafficking rings?!"

"I believe it about as much as I believe anything else you say, man." Jimmy took a deep breath. "I don't feel like talking about this right now. I've just got a few minutes to try and relax."

"Alright, bud. Suit yourself," Trevor said as the truck puttered down the road.

Jimmy didn't say much more. He closed his eyes slunk down in the passenger side seat, said a prayer in his head, and took deep, swelling breaths. Jimmy was clenching and unclenching his hands to keep his mind off the surge of fright within him. He had almost gotten himself completely calm when Trevor's voice cut through the silence.

"We're here."

CHAPTER FOUR

Megan's silver Sunfire sat in the driveway, the first reaches of the morning brightening its sheen. Jimmy Glencroft glanced in its passenger window as he walked by and noticed the fake plush red rose she had tied around her rearview mirror. He had gotten it for her on their first Valentine's Day from a gas station when he barely had any money to his name. It was an unsuspecting reminder of all Jimmy needed to make up for, and yet simultaneously, the charade that their relationship had become. He shook his thoughts aside and silently unlocked the door.

Jimmy kicked off his muddy, water-logged Reeboks and fell immediately onto his couch. He held a pillow close and shoved his face into the side of the couch arm, breathing in and out in huffs.

There was a knock at the door. Jimmy rolled off the couch and ran over to see what was going on. He looked through the peephole to see Trevor MacKenzie's crooked face looking right back at him. Jimmy cracked the door open slowly and whispered to Trevor.

"Trevor. Get out of here. Why are you knocking?"

"Sorry, just remembered. I wanted to see if you could float me some gas money for driving you around," Trevor said.

"*Gas money*?!" Jimmy felt his face redden. "You drove me around *on company time*. You were on the clock the whole time, dude! You already got paid to drive me! Besides, you won at least a grand at poker last night, *and* I was in a car accident! I bought you two packs of Newports! Get the fuck out of here!"

"Whatever, dude, you owe me," Trevor said. Before Jimmy could respond, a firm and calm female voice did so for him.

"You owe me, too." Megan Painter stepped out of the bedroom. Just under Jimmy's height, the young brunette wore one of Jimmy's blue Discovery t-shirts and bright pink pajama bottoms. Her hair was up in a messy bun; her bright blue eyes were offset by dark circles and smeared mascara. She snuffed out a cigarette in the glass ashtray she held.

Trevor stood in the doorway nonchalantly as Jimmy leaned against the frame, his heart pounding. Jimmy absent-mindedly let go of the door knob, letting the door swing slowly open with a creaking sound, revealing the full form of the smirking Trevor.

"I don't even know where to begin," Jimmy said with a tremble.

"I do," Megan snapped. "Why the fuck are you cut up, where the fuck were you, and why the fuck is this crackhead in my house?" Venom rang in her every word.

"Technically, I'm not in your house. I'm on your porch," Trevor replied as he lit a cigarette. He fumbled with his overused lighter, caught flame, inhaled, and exhaled a raspy, "So why the fuck are you bitching at me?"

"I'm asking the fucking questions!" Megan yelled. "Why the fuck aren't you leaving, and why shouldn't I call the cops?"

Trevor inhaled and flicked ash onto the carpet. "I'm not breaking any laws. Meggy-Poo, why are you such a c..."

Trevor barely dodged the glass ashtray as it flew through the doorway. The ashtray shattered on the sidewalk outside.

"Don't fucking ash on my floor!" Megan demanded as she looked around for another object to throw.

Jimmy went to restrain her, but Megan gave him a firm shove. "Why aren't you getting him the fuck out of here?!"

Jimmy stuttered out an explanation, but she cut him off. "Bullshit. Jimmy, just make your junkie friend leave before I do."

"Don't need to tell me twice!" Trevor exclaimed. He turned back around and flicked the remainder of his burning cigarette inside of the apartment before he yelled, "Cute makeup, whore!"

Jimmy grabbed the burning cigarette and tossed it outside. He pulled the door shut as he glanced atMegan. She stood in silence, glaring at Jimmy as he sat on the couch and looked straight forward, staring at nothing. They heard the rumble of the donut van's engine come to life, tires squealing as Trevor peeled out and on down the road. His engine faded into the distance, and they were finally together, alone, in silence.

"What the fuck, dude," Megan said. She crossed her arms and glared down at Jimmy.

"...The car is totaled," Jimmy said blankly.

"What?!" Megan threw her arms down and clenched her fists at her side. "You crashed your car? Where?"

"Route 33," Jimmy responded. "I wasn't drinking. Not much, anyway."

"James Glencroft," she said, "How could you? What were you doing out there? Where's the car?"

"One question at a time, please." Jimmy sighed. He cracked his knuckles and leaned forward. He supported his elbows and forearms on his thighs, looking down at the mottled tan carpet. "I was giving a friend of mine a ride to Marysville. I didn't think it would hurt, considering I knew how to get there and back pretty fast. When I was driv..."

"Who is she?" Megan interrupted.

Jimmy ignored her question. "I was driving my friend on 33 westbound, near Glacier Ridge when..."

"Who were you fucking, James?"

"I wasn't fucking anyone, Megan." Jimmy paused for a minute, waiting for a rebuttal from her, but she remained silent.

"I was hit by a black SUV. Hit and run. They spun me out. I flipped the car. We escaped with no major injuries." Jimmy paused again. "Thanks for asking about my friend, by the way."

"I don't give a fuck about your friend," Megan said. "I'm beginning to wonder why I even give a fuck about you. Where's the car? Did you go to the hospital? Were you charged with anything? How did..."

"I wasn't hurt enough to go to the hospital. We had a friend pick up the car in a flatbed. He's keeping it at his warehouse until we figure out what we're doing with it."

Megan stared at Jimmy, slack-jawed. "What kind of shady friends do you have? Who the hell just has a flatbed and a warehouse and willingly stores people's uninsured wrecks there?!"

"Craig Foxx, to be precise," Jimmy said with a shrug. "It's over off Industrial Parkway, not too far from where we wrecked. I can show it to you if needed."

Megan sat down on the other end of the couch.

"Who the hell is Craig Fox? You didn't even call me... I lost track of how many times I called and texted you."

"Phone was shattered in the wreck," Jimmy said. "Completely inoperable."

Megan shook her head. "I had been texting since 9 last night. I just wanted to know where you were. That's all I needed from you. Did you even read my texts?"

Jimmy sat in silence. Megan stared at him as she shook her head back and forth. A tear slid down her cheek, blackened by her smeared mascara.

"It's so erotic when your makeup runs," Jimmy said with a half-smile. Megan's jaw dropped.

"Porcupine Tree? Porcupine Tree!? Are you fucking quoting a song lyric? Fuck you, dude. Fuck you."
Jimmy shook his head and sighed in defeat. Megan stood and walked towards the hallway that led to their bedroom. Jimmy started to get up, but she waved him off.

"No. I don't want to see you. I don't want to talk to you. I don't know why I put up with your shit. Don't fucking talk to me, don't come to bed, just don't," Megan said.

Megan stormed down the hallway, slammed the door, and threw something against a wall with a shatter.

Jimmy felt heavy all over. His eyes, his head, his chest; everything had a weight about it. He felt the bruises from the wreck. He felt the stress tear away at him. He kept his eyes shut and prayed for comfort as he pulled a weighted blanket over his sore form.

Jimmy opened his eyes to see Megan softly shaking him.

"Hey," Megan whispered. Her eyes were red and puffy, but she had cleaned off the smeared mascara from her face.

"Hey, what time is it?" Jimmy asked. He winced as he moved his arms and legs.

"It's noon. You've only been asleep a few hours. Come to bed with me. It's hard sleeping without you," Megan said with a sad smile as she peeled the weighted blanket off Jimmy.

Jimmy smiled back and tried sitting up. The pain was more significant than he imagined, and tears sprang into his eyes. He shut them quickly, groaned, and breathed through the pain.

"What hurts?" she asked.

"Side, left arm, lower back, and head," he whispered in one breath.

"Wait here," Megan ordered. She rushed into the kitchen and pulled down a bottle from the cabinet above the dishwasher.

Jimmy heard running water and sat up slowly, clenching his teeth. Megan came back with a Pink Floyd *Dark Side of the Moon* collectible cup half-filled with water and handed it to him.

"Take these," Megan ordered, holding out her hand.

Jimmy grabbed the pills and immediately knew what they were. Senior year, Mrs. Livingston's computer class, last period at 2:45 PM without fail, Trevor MacKenzie would crush up two with a borrowed ruler and snort them off his red folder.

"They're left over from the root canal I had last month, remember?" Megan asked.
Jimmy remembered everything about the surgery except the pills. The few days Megan was out of commission because of the surgery had brought them closer together. Jimmy spoon-fed her yogurt and water, changed her gauze, and held her when the pain became unbearable. She refused to take the Vicodin and took twelve Aleve a day instead. When Jimmy asked her about it, Megan merely stated that they don't help, and Jimmy left it at that. Megan milked Jimmy's attention in that week, but Jimmy didn't care. He was happy to show her what he would do to take care of her, and she took notice. Jimmy sprang on opportunities like this to patch up the many holes in their life, to keep the anger at bay for another few days, to make it feel like he had put forth his minimum effort.

"Meg, while I appreciate the gesture, you know how I feel about taking drugs, especially ones with street cred," Jimmy said. He glanced at the Vicodin, then back up at Megan. He smiled.

"Maybe I should just flip these bad boys on the street? That will help our money issues," Jimmy said with a laugh. Megan didn't return the humor.

Jimmy stood up quickly as if to show Megan he was fine, and immediately regretted it. Tears ran down his face. His body shook as it tried to adjust to the sudden movement. Jimmy clenched his fists and stood still until the waves of pain subsided.

"Jimmy," Megan said, "Take them and don't argue, please. I am still so incredibly mad at you, and you owe me whatever I ask of you right now."

"Just once," Jimmy said. He took one at a time as Megan watched him intently.

"Good, now call the stadium and leave a voicemail. I already took tomorrow off. I'll call Brandon while you're doing that to fill in for you. I remember him wanting extra hours anyway," Megan said, stretching out her arms.

Jimmy closed his eyes.

"Meg, I have to go to work. I can't miss this, and I'll need you to take me. I have to be there by two. Please," Jimmy opened his eyes and looked at his girlfriend.

"James Glencroft, you are in no position to be running around in a mascot costume. You can't move without crying, for God's sake." Megan looked down at the floor and shook her head. She closed her eyes, and the two lovers stood in silence for a moment.

Megan's head snapped back up.

"Who are you fucking, Jimmy?" she asked through her teeth.

"What?" Jimmy asked in surprise. "How did you even come to that assumption, Meg?"

Megan stepped forward and leaned in towards Jimmy's face until their noses were practically touching. "Lies after lies, James. You probably already called off, spoke with Brandon, I can't believe..."

Jimmy gently grabbed Megan's face and kissed her before she could react. She tried to pull away, but he resisted against her and deepened the kiss. When he pulled away, tears were falling from her eyes.

"Megan," Jimmy said softly, wiping the tears from her eyes, "I love you. I know you don't trust me, and you have no reason to, but believe me on this, it's you. That's it. I only want you, babe. You'll be dropping me off at the stadium. Stay and watch."

"But you..."

"No, Meg," Jimmy interrupted, "Think about it. My phone was destroyed; I couldn't have contacted Brandon, or the stadium, or anyone. I'm not smart enough to think of a plan like that. Besides, no one else will have me, except you. We go together like no one else can," Jimmy said with a small smile.

Megan's expression softened, but she remained silent.

"I feel better from the pills," he stated truthfully. His body was beginning to loosen up, and the pain was slowly diminishing.

"I'll only be giving 10 percent, and I promise to take more tomorrow. Megan, all I need now is to hold you while we nap," Jimmy said.

Megan let out a long breath and hugged Jimmy. He sighed as he hugged her back.

Jimmy's body felt heavy yet relaxed from the Vicodin. He was mentally drained from arguing, he was exhausted from dealing with the wreck, but he still couldn't sleep. Megan drooled and snored as she slept on Jimmy's chest, and he didn't care. He could control the next hour before dealing with the world again, and that is all he could ask for.

Jimmy just remembered he hadn't checked his social network in a few days. He wanted to take care of a few things, maybe see if anyone was posting about last night's events. Perhaps he would even look up Brody and send him a friend request. He shifted a little, feeling some pain, but thankfully not as much as he had been earlier. The pills were doing their job. Jimmy managed to free himself from Meg, who stayed asleep as she slumped down onto the bed and off Jimmy's chest. Jimmy leaned over the side of the bed to grab Meg's touch-screen tablet so he could check his social network. He noticed the smashed Pink Floyd mug shattered and strewn about the floor in the corner. *Go figure*, he thought. These mugs were Meg's favorite things to throw and smash while they fought, as they were gifts from one of his exes. He only had one left.

Jimmy shifted into a more comfortable position and adjusted his body, so the pain from his injuries was lessened. He turned the tablet on. The device played obnoxious start music, and Jimmy almost dropped it, trying to turn down the volume. He looked over at Meg to see if she had awoken. She slept on and snored even louder than before.

Jimmy powered up his social network and began browsing around. Brody had beaten him to the friend request, which he accepted right away. Despite their differences, Jimmy had grown to be okay with Brody by the end of the night. Tragedies and trials had a way of helping people bond, after all. Jimmy flicked through his notifications:

Trevor MacKenzie: krazey night duuuuuuude

Craig Foxx: So about the money it ain't even funny

Megan Painter: this is getting old.

Jimmy sighed at her update. He looked over at his sleeping lover and again swore to himself things would change. He kept scrolling through his friends' updates.

Sloth Hopkins: Stoop nasty gig last night. Dropping that new single soon! Don't forget to vote for Readymade on CD 92.9's website for "Best Local Band!" Peace, love, and chicken grease.

LyTz de Rueda: I'm so done with this life. Someone get me out.

Milson Pisatini: Philly cheesesteak pierogis, steamed artichokes, and an original Sangria recipe. Now I just need someone to share it with.

Jimmy rolled his eyes. It was more of the same old-same old on the networks. He was about to shut off the tablet when he noticed there was a new name among the usual updates. *Lytz de Rueda*. He hadn't seen that name in a long time. He clicked on the link to her profile with a quick touch. Jimmy didn't notice the smile creeping onto his face.

How did she show up on my notifications? I didn't even think she had social networking, Jimmy thought as he pulled up her profile. The profile picture showed a thin-faced girl with long straight black hair. A longish, thin nose and a light smirk completed her features. Jimmy noted dark makeup and signs of profound weight loss since he had last seen her. He scrolled down the profile and saw "Friend Request Pending." He accepted with no hesitation. He didn't remember seeing the request notification pop up.

Jimmy looked at her current location. *Columbus, Ohio*. He grinned. Jimmy and Lyndsey "Lytz" de Rueda were friends in high school. He stopped talking to her just before he had started dating Megan and missed her immensely. He had no clue she was in town and realized he wanted to see her. Another realization quickly dawned on Jimmy: He had to pee.

Jimmy set the tablet down and sat up. Megan stirred lightly beside him. He got up carefully as to not wake her up. He staggered down the hall to the bathroom.

After finishing his business and returning to the bedroom, Jimmy arrived to see Megan reaching over the bed's side to pick up the tablet.

"What are you doing, Megan?"

Megan grinned. "I want to play Apple Smash. I forgot I haven't played in a while. My trees need to be planted, and I need eight more Core Combos to advance to the next level!"

Jimmy groaned. He watched Meg flick on the tablet screen. Her mouth slackened, and her eyes widened. Jimmy had forgotten to close out of his social network. Megan could see that he was viewing another woman's profile. His gut sank.

Here we go again.

"So, this is the skank you're fucking?!" Megan tossed the tablet across the room at him. He stepped to the side as it fell to the floor.

"Megan, please. I can explain."

"I don't want to hear it," she replied tersely.

"... You're gonna hear it!" Jimmy said with an edge of aggression.

"Or what? Or what are you gonna do? Cheat on me?!"

"No! You know I wouldn't do that. Listen to me. That girl is an old friend of mine. All I did was accept her friend request."

"And fap to her pictures, I'm sure," Megan said before she quickly twisted her body so she was facing away from Jimmy. She pulled the blankets and quilt over herself in a tight ball. "Leave me alone. I don't want to be with you."

Jimmy felt a tear slide down his face. His skin grew hot. "Megan, please. You have to understand. I haven't seen her in years."

"How am I supposed to know that, you shady bastard?" Megan pulled the blankets entirely over her head. "Leave."

Jimmy turned around with a heavy, shuddering sigh and stepped towards the door. "Oh, I see how it is, *don't fight for me,*" Megan muttered from under the blankets. Jimmy threw his hands up and groaned. He couldn't win. He stepped out of the bedroom and strode toward the kitchen. He had to be at the stadium soon, and between being awake for so many hours, the heartbreak, and the injuries, he knew he couldn't perform at a high level.

Jimmy pulled open the refrigerator to see two Red Bull energy drinks. He looked to his left to see his coffee maker, with today's grounds already in the filter and ready to brew.

He brewed his morning coffee with Red Bull instead of water.

Jimmy Glencroft fidgeted as his girlfriend drove him through a series of side streets, trying to evade pre-game traffic. Both of their faces were gaunt, black beneath their eyes. Jimmy gazed at Megan Painter as she drove. They shared an intense silence.

They turned onto Lane Avenue, just down the road from Ohio Stadium. For today's game, streetlights up and down the road had blue, gold, and red banners hanging down with the Discovery logo. Even several miles back from the stadium, throngs of fans walked towards the stadium, bedecked in their jerseys and hats and novelty gear.

Amazing we still have fans, Jimmy thought. *The team barely gives them anything to root for. Pandemic recovery went too slowly – that just makes it worse.*

The silver Sunfire pulled close to the stadium. The sidewalks were now thick with fans, and cop cars were everywhere as officers directed traffic and kept a watchful eye on the crowds. Megan pulled into the stadium parking lot as her back right wheel hopped the sidewalk corner on accident. Jimmy felt sleepiness sink back in, weary from the roller coaster of stimulated awake and then tired. Caffeine-fueled awake, and then tired. He slumped against the passenger window, eyes half-open, staring straight forward.

"Jimmy, are you checking her out?"

Jimmy didn't even realize he was looking at a girl, his sagging eyes too unfocused to see a shapely tan girl in shorts traipsing past. He spun, suddenly all too awake, eyes wide to see a red-faced Megan, the blush of anger swallowing her faint freckles.

"No, why do you always think..."

"Get out," Megan commanded.

"Why? I mean, I still have a few..."

"Get. OUT!!" Megan exclaimed as tears ran down her face, her frayed, matted hair sticking to her wet cheeks.

"But Meg, let me explain..."

"Get out. Get out. Get out get out get out get out! GET! OUT! GET! OUT!"

At this point, Megan screamed at the top of her lungs. With every word, she would slam the Sunfire's steering wheel with both hands. He obliged, backing out of the door, still leaning in and trying to bargain with her. She reached over and slammed the door shut in Jimmy's face, the door nearly catching his hand as he tried to stop her from doing so.

He watched numbly as she sped forward. Suddenly, the car came to a screeching halt. Jimmy sighed as dozens of fans in the parking lot turned to watch. Megan slammed the car into reverse and halted with a squeal right in front of him. A masked gentleman yelled in fright as he dove aside to dodge the silver Sunfire.

She rolled the passenger side window down with the automatic controls on her side. Jimmy trod up to the door and bent in to speak. Jimmy couldn't duck as Megan hurled a bottle of Vicodin at him, the pills smacking off his sore face and rolling down the concrete. His forehead stung with pain, his wound aggravated.

"Fuck you, Jimmy. I should've never dated you." Megan said.

Jimmy stammered a response but couldn't get it out as Megan threw a full can of Red Bull at him, smacking him in the teeth.

"Meg, what the hell?!" Jimmy yelled as he grabbed his mouth. "My teeth!"

Megan shrugged and slammed the car into gear. She sped off and nearly mowed over a cluster of fans. Jimmy looked up to watch her go. An invisible fist gripped his heart and refused to release. His lips and fingers went numb as the world streaked around him like a hyperspace jump.

Megan Painter's middle finger thrust high, her arm straight out of the driver's side window, she disappeared into the distance.

CHAPTER FIVE

Jimmy Glencroft struggled with perceived invisibility.

People rarely said hello to him when he was pumping gas, buying groceries, drinking at the bar, or going for a stroll. He was an out-going guy, never hesitant to say hello to a friend or offer a helping hand to anyone nearby, even when folks didn't always do the same for him. He knew as a mascot he was disguised; he would never gain the fame and face recognition someone like Anvil Broadnax would experience. Jimmy wasn't out for fame. However, today he was going to do his best to feel like somebody.

He could see the coach's son now, his rival for so many years in school. His words hung in his head, the memory stark and clear as day, through the fuzz of fatigue, Vicodin, and anxiety. "You'll never do anything with your life, Jimmy," Ren Yancey said. "You'll never make it to the League."

Life moved in slow motion for Jimmy as he made his way down the corridor. He wondered if it was the cocktail of Vicodin and energy shots that made everything seem this way. He didn't mind much. Jimmy felt epic and determined as he took huge, loping strides. He felt the soft smack of his fuzzy mascot boots. He flexed his jittery hands open and shut in the wide Mickey Mouse-style gloves he wore. He exhaled sharply, the hot breath fogging in the cool underground tunnel, making it hard to see through the white mesh teeth. His body was unnoticeably sore; he felt heavy and light all at once.

Jimmy was motivated. Jimmy was ready. He was done taking his dream for granted. Today, he was not James Glencroft. Today, he was Sailor Smash, and he was out to prove he was the best damn mascot in the upstart Patriot Football League.

There was one person he didn't mind revealing his identity to. Jimmy had kept it a secret this whole time, a giddy little thrill to himself. He walked up to a security guard and tipped his massive plush rhino hat up long enough to reveal his face.

"Hey, coach's boy," Jimmy said arrogantly. "Look who made it to the League."

Jimmy and Ren Yancey locked eyes a moment. Jimmy flipped him off, flexing out the comically oversized middle finger. He slammed his head down and kept his determined stride down the hall towards the field. Jimmy laughed as Yancey yelled, "It doesn't count! You're a mascot!" Jimmy didn't care. It was good enough to him.

In the distance, he heard cleats banging off the hard floor of the corridor. The Discovery players jumped around, getting psyched for the game. Jimmy turned the corner, and Old Jerry held a furled Discovery flag, resplendent in navy blue and crimson with golden yellow trim. Old Jerry nodded encouragingly to Jimmy.

"Remember, Sailor... Make your mark. I believe in you," Old Jerry said with a wholesome smile. "If I didn't, I wouldn't have hired you. Make me proud, son."

Jimmy jumped and landed in a boxing stance. He spun his clenched fists around in concentric circles. Jimmy fist-bumped Old Jerry, seized the flag and took off running. Jimmy could see the huddled mass of players and coaches at the end of the hall. He didn't stop; he was at a dead sprint, going as fast as the 30-pound costume and his weary frame would let him go. A player saw him and shouted, "Sailor Smash!"

Jimmy leaped into the giant, sweaty pile of blue and crimson. The players cheered and smacked Jimmy around. He felt like one of them. Jimmy could barely see through the foggy white mesh teeth, but he didn't need to. He was starting to get used to the routine, the exact path he would take as he sprinted on the field. Jimmy pushed through the players. He got smacked and tapped in weird places, but being a former player himself, he knew that's just

39

how they were before games. Jimmy strode to the front of the group, the light of the Sunday afternoon just a few yards in front of him as the hard floor gave way to field turf.

Jimmy looked to his left to see two of the team's captains. #14, Kip Kazdorf, undersized wide receiver, long-haired lothario and parkour hobbyist who utilized the art of movement to be the most lethal special teamer in the Patriot Football League; and #73, Napoleon DuPlessiss, the muscle of the offensive line, a bruising right tackle, known for his intimidatingly dirty play.

Jimmy looked to his right. One of his best friends, his old roommate, a partner in crime for years now, #13, Naev Broadnax, flashed the "rock on" horns at him. #70, "Freeway" Obie Hill, a veritable wall, an immovable object, smacked them both in the head, grinning white teeth from behind his cage facemask.

Head Coach Bill Kurlen walked up from the tunnel. Kurlen was a stout man in his mid-60's, wearing huge bifocals, a navy-blue visor, and a matching fanny pack. He looked at his team with a wild grin.

"Great day God gave us for some football, right?!" he shouted to the Discovery. The team cheered back their agreement.

"I want to be the first to say that the articles are rubbish. We're not a bad team. We're a new team. We've had our growing pains this year, and I know moral victories don't put us in the playoffs. But I was hired by this organization to do one thing. The same thing all of you were hired to do. That was to win."

Kurlen took a beat to gaze at his captains, the team, his assistants, and the obnoxious-looking mascot in their midst as well. "Today, we will make our mark. Today we will... Discover... what it feels like to be true victors in the League."

Bill Kurlen pointed towards the field. "There are 6.9 million high school football players in the United States. 10,800 are lucky enough to play at the top collegiate level. Only 2,200 people in this entire nation are talented enough to call themselves professional football players at the highest level. Out of them, we are only 52. You are blessed to be in this position. Let's prove we belong. Let's get our first win and show we are for real. Today will go on paper as only one victory when - not if, but WHEN - we win."

Kurlen took off his glasses and took his time to look into the eyes of every player nearby. "To me, it's not going to be one victory. To me, it counts as a victory to each and every human soul here. To me, it's 52 victories when we win today. Go out, and win not only for yourself but for the fans. Win for the city. Let's prove there's more than just one big-time team that belongs in Columbus."

A lithe intern wearing a team polo and thick-rimmed glasses ran up to Kurlen, holding a crackling walkie-talkie. He muttered something to the head coach. Kurlen nodded, turned to his team, put on his glasses, and grinned widely.

"Game time!"

Suddenly, Jimmy heard the distorted opening strains of Muse's "Map of the Problematique." A churning blend of electric guitar, thundering drums, fuzzy bass, and spacey piano blended into a tense fury. He couldn't believe it! The sound guy took his recommendation for a new entrance song. Jimmy's heart thundered in his chest as he unfurled the flag. After letting the song build for around 40 seconds, Muse cut into a terrifying riff. Jimmy took off into the light, becoming Sailor Smash, with the Columbus Discovery sprinting in his wake. With an unbelievable roar, 85,000 fans split the air with a hearty welcome.

Jimmy ran full bore across the turf, between rows of shimmering pom-poms as the cheerleaders lined the field. Pyrotechnics on either side of the cheerleaders went off, a loud blast of smoke and sparks thrusting into the air every few yards, going off as Jimmy passed each row. He sprinted as hard as he could to prevent the players from overtaking him. He could feel and hear them just a few yards behind him.

Through the foggy mesh teeth, Jimmy could barely make out a man dressed up as a cowboy, complete with hide vest, spurs, and a ten-gallon Stetson hat. His coworker and backup Brandon Brooks, dressed as a Western gunslinger to parody their opponents today, the Fargo Rangers. Brandon stood in the middle of the field, pantomiming as if he were about to draw twin six-shooters for a duel. They had barely rehearsed this stunt this week, and Jimmy only had one chance to make this happen.

Jimmy planted his left foot, took a massive stride with the right, and jumped off it, throwing himself off to the right as he cleared the two rows of cheerleaders. In midair, he threw the flag at Brandon as if it were a spear, trying to lead him. Jimmy landed hard on the turf and rolled to the side to prevent himself from getting trampled. He felt as if his throw was off; he closed his eyes and waited for the players' thunder to pass. A swell of nerves ran through him as he staggered to his feet. He raised his head to see that the stunt had worked. Ranger Brandon lay in the middle of the field, the Discovery flag planted in the crook of his armpit, waving in the wind as fake blood spread through his cowboy outfit. Jimmy thought to himself, *this is legitimately the coolest thing I've ever done.*

Jimmy took off down the sidelines and tried to launch himself into a cartwheel. He misjudged his landing and tumbled onto his bottom. He heard players and crowd alike near him laughing uproariously. *Not the best way to make a mark,* Jimmy thought. He brushed himself off and loped towards a secure gate that led to the stands.
May as well ride the wave of the painkillers by mixing it up with some fans, he thought as he took a few deep breaths and staggered into the crowd.

Naev Broadnax jogged towards midfield with Kip Kazdorf, Napoleon DuPlessis, Obie Hill, and the kicker, #19, Anton Treptak. Naev was getting over his hangover gradually and was now weathering nerves and soreness from the fight last night. Naev took off his helmet to feel the mild early October wind brush across his face. He glanced over his shoulder as he jogged to see his pal Jimmy botch a cartwheel. Naev shook his head, smirked, and turned his attention back to the coin toss.

The Discovery captains were the first ones to midfield. The referee and a CBS camera crew met them for the coin toss. Kazdorf stood beside Anvil and nudged him.

"Fargo, eh?" Kazdorf grinned. "We may actually beat these guys."

"Should beat them," Anvil said. He kept his hands wrapped in the white towel looped through his belt. Naev eyed the other sideline. The Fargo Rangers were in their 2nd year in the Patriot Football League as well, and like the Discovery, they were experiencing some struggles early. Whereas the Discovery had never won, Fargo had won twice, once the previous season en route to a 1-15 campaign. They sat at 1-4 on the year thus far. Anvil scanned the other players up and down. The Rangers didn't have much explosive, premier talent on their team. The closest thing they had to a star was the outspoken, brash J'Shia Beverly, a 1st round draft pick out of Oregon State during the expansion year. Anvil couldn't find Beverly's #10 jersey. He was easy to miss. Standing at 5'8" and weighing only 178 pounds, he was undersized, much like Kazdorf, but had even more explosive speed and a reckless headhunting style. He played multiple positions, not unlike Chris Gamble, Kordell Stewart, Keyshawn Johnson, or Deion Sanders. Wildcat quarterback? Check. Downfield wideout? Check. Late-game defensive back sub? He even did that. J'Shia earned every bit of his contract.

"There he is," Obie Hill said, pointing towards the Rangers sideline. J'Shia Beverly emerged from the wall of white and maroon jerseys. J'Shia left his helmet on when he came to midfield and danced around, keeping loose and warm.

The referee gestured towards Beverly. "Are you the only captain for Fargo?"

J'Shia Beverly made a clicking sound and shook his head, dreads flopping. "Nope. But I'm the only one that matters. Let's do the damn thing, shall we?"

The referee shrugged. "Fair enough. Okay, time for the coin toss. The white team is away, the blue team home. The white team captain will call in the air, heads or tails."

The referee showed both teams' captains the quarter's head side and tails side. He flipped it up in the air and let it plummet to the ground. As it hit, he looked at J'Shia, who stood stock still while the Discovery captains peered at the coin.

"I didn't hear you make a call," the referee said to J'Shia.

"I *said* heads," J'Shia replied. "Didn't you hear? Use your ears, man, come on. We'll take the ball." He turned and jogged back towards the sidelines.

"...What? He didn't make a call!" Anvil said, his skin flushing red-hot with anger. "Ref, dude, he saw it was heads and called it. That ain't right."

The referee shrugged and looked blankly at Anvil. "Defend south or north goal?"

"I'd like to flip the coin again, please, and have the away team call it properly!" Anvil yelled.

"South or north endzone, sir?" The referee asked sternly.

"Neither, I want a re-flip!" The other captains looked at Anvil blankly.

Kazdorf muttered to the ref, "We'll just take the north goal," and then made to start steering Anvil back towards the sideline. Anvil spiked his helmet at midfield, near the ref's feet, and pointed at him as his team tried to get him moving. Obie Hill grabbed the helmet for him.

"Naev, dude, they don't wanna play the same game we do. Just settle it on the field. We gonna earn this respect." Obie pulled his own helmet down. "C'mon now."

Anvil snatched his helmet from Obie and stormed towards the sideline, surrounded by the other Discovery captains. He turned and yelled at the ref, "You will rue this day!"

Kazdorf sighed and shook his head. "Jimmy is rubbing off on you, bro. Let's go play some football."

Meanwhile, on the other sideline, J'Shia Beverly skipped around between his teammates intensely, repeating the words "We got this ball, we got this ball, we got this ball," under his breath. He went out of his way to go over to a CBS reporter who was unoccupied.

The reporter was taken aback by her unexpected guest. She motioned for the camera to start rolling and turned to face it with a microphone. "We are here with Fargo star J'Shia Beverly, and..." before she even got a chance to finish her question, J'Shia grabbed the microphone from her. Not even considering the camera, he said, "Yo. J'Shia is about money. Know what I mean? Shout out to the haters. I'm finna run this back. Watch now. I'm on my flex." He tossed the microphone down before skipping erratically back down the sideline, leaving a reporter perplexed and millions at home entertained.

Jimmy Glencroft maneuvered his way through the first few rows of the stands, high-fiving fans and signing a few items with a black Sharpie marker. Jimmy still hadn't developed a unique Sailor Smash signature. He mixed it up, sometimes signing the whole name, or writing two sharp side-by-side S's for smaller items. A middle-aged woman wearing a white #14 Kazdorf jersey held out a child, blocking his way as he worked his way up the steps.

"Sign my child," the woman demanded of Jimmy, holding a drooling kid who was too old to be involuntarily drooling. The kid had matted, unwashed hair, and his white Discovery shirt was stained with nacho cheese. Jimmy gave a thumbs-up, pulled his sharpie out from under his sleeve, and attempted his double-S signature. The drugs and caffeine were not paring well, and the S's blurred together. He flashed another thumb up and went to tramp up the stairs.

Jimmy didn't get far before he felt a pull at his tail.

Probably a kid, he thought, as he woozily turned around.

Kids were always pulling his tail, sometimes they succeeded in pulling it all the way out, and he hated chasing them around to get it back. He may have been messed up on Vicodin, but he wasn't messed up enough to deal with this. He was shocked to see the woman whose child he had just signed, sans child.

"Hey, I'm Dorothy," she said. "Remember me? You just signed my child."

Of course, Jimmy thought to himself, *how could I forget the weird kid I just signed 10 seconds ago?*

"You signed my child with Nazi propaganda!" Dorothy said in a shrill voice loud enough to make a few passersby turn around and look on, amused.

Jimmy didn't even react with a cartoonish shrug like he usually would in these situations. He just looked at her blankly, unmoving.

"I demand an explanation!" Dorothy insisted.

Jimmy had a policy that he had to abide by where he couldn't talk as Sailor Smash. He lazily made a zipping motion across his giant white rhino smile with one hand.

Dorothy grunted in disgust, and from out of nowhere, thrust the child back in his face. Jimmy's first instinct was to knock the kid out of her hands, but he couldn't exert that kind of effort. He turned around to walk away.

Dorothy yanked his tail again. "Re-sign my child! I can't bring him home to his father with the Schutzstaffel logo on his shirt!"

Jimmy turned around, annoyed. He never even thought of the Nazi S.S. when he developed the sharp, lightning bolt-esque double-s signature. In fact, he saw it as being closer to the KISS logo. Jimmy uncapped his marker again and put a "K.I." in front of the "S.S." It looked a lot like the classic rock band's logo. Jimmy chuckled proudly and flashed a thumbs-up to Dorothy again.

Dorothy looked at the child's new KISS shirt, then looked at Jimmy, slack-jawed.

"You want me to kiss you now?! You sex beast!" Dorothy yelled as she slapped Jimmy.

Jimmy didn't feel the slap because of the thick plush padding, but he wasn't going to tolerate this today. He tried to walk around the woman, but she stepped in front of him, trying to block his path. Jimmy held up his hand to try to block her vision, but he moved his hand too quickly and accidentally palmed Dorothy in the face, pushing her and the child off to the side.

"SECURITY!" Dorothy screamed.

Jimmy bumbled to the wall separating the stands from the field and awkwardly utilized a parkour jump that Kip Kazdorf taught him last year. Under his woozy state, Jimmy failed and landed awkwardly. He proudly remembered to "roll through it." He knew he was hurting himself, but he couldn't feel it. Jimmy finally understood how Trevor MacKenzie could take so much Vicodin.

Jimmy rose and loped down the sidelines. Wolfmother's "Joker & the Thief" blasted as the teams prepared for kickoff. He strutted to the guitar rhythm and arrived at another stadium gate. Jimmy decided he'd give the fans another chance. He wasn't going to let one bizarre woman and her drooling child ruin his day.

The security team unlocked the gate for Jimmy, and he clambered up the stairs. He high-fived a few people as he walked up the stairs, leaning on the railing to support him. His shoulders drooped and his steps slowed as the weight set back in.

Jimmy noticed a large, balding man in his late 60's sitting on the edge of a row, eating nachos and cheese. Jimmy plopped down next to him, offering a knuckle-bump. The man obliged and nodded to him.

"Hey Sailor, how's it going?" the man asked.

Jimmy flashed him a thumbs up.

"Want some nachos?" he asked, extending the plastic container towards Jimmy.
Jimmy's stomach growled in response, and he realized how hungry he was. The only thing he ate when he woke up was two pieces of burnt toast. Jimmy shook his head, and the burly fan chuckled.

"I get it, lo-carb diet, right?" the old man asked, dipping a nacho into cheese.

Sure, we'll go with that, Jimmy thought.

"Not for me," the man said, taking a bite.

I didn't ask you, Jimmy thought.

"Say, I got a question for you," the man said.

Well, ask it, Jimmy thought. *I'll be glad to speak through my mesh mouth and answer. Haha, Mesh Mouth. Good name for a band.*

"Why don't you go ahead and take off your head for the Star-Spangled Banner?"

Jimmy slowly pulled his head back and opened his mouth. *What was he expecting? Do other mascots just freely respond to bullshit questions like this?*

"See, I think even mascots need to take off their heads for our National Anthem. Too many heroes have died for this country to see disrespect like this. Try doing that from now on for me, alright?"

Jimmy didn't react right away. After a beat, he stood up and shot the man a thumbs-up.

"Say, answer me a question," the man began, "...You Democrat or Republican?"

Libertarian, Jimmy thought.

"Thumbs up for Republican, thumbs down for Democrat."

Jimmy wondered to himself, *what do I use to respond if I'm anything else?* He decided to throw a lava. He intertwined his fingers and moved his arms up and down in a horizontal wave motion.

"The hell you say?" The man asked, laughing maniacally. "Hey, get a load of this guy!"

He nudged a massive woman next to him. She looked stuck in her seat, and the pink tank top she wore did a terrible job at holding her cleavage in. He spaced out as he stared into this new great beyond.

"Hiram, I'm trying to watch the damn game!" the woman said. Jimmy snapped back into focus.

Jimmy chuckled at the scenario, saluted Hiram, and turned back towards the field.

"There he is!" he heard a woman scream. Jimmy turned and looked up the stands about twenty rows to see Dorothy, the over-reactive fan from earlier, still holding her child. Standing with her were two security guards, one being the guard he encountered before the game, Ren Yancey.

"He assaulted me! The Nazi elephant assaulted me!"

"Lady, I'm a rhinoceros, not an elephant. The Nazi rhinoceros assaulted you!" Jimmy yelled from behind his mask.

"Hey, he ain't so bad!" Hiram turned and yelled at Dorothy.

"He assaulted me! He's a sex monster and a socialist!"

Hiram turned and looked at Jimmy. "You don't say?"

I'm done peopling today, Jimmy thought.

Jimmy jumped the wall to get back to the field and landed awkwardly. A stiff, sharp pain went up to his knees and into his back. He tried to roll with it but fell over instead. He closed his eyes and winced.

Maybe I'll just lay here a minute, he thought. One *minute won't hurt.*

CHAPTER SIX

Bill Kurlen paced up and down the sideline. Usually calm and collected, the coach shook off some new jitters. Kurlen was known as a bit of a traditionalist when it came to offensive plays. He leaned on Anvil to be a game manager more than a superstar under center. A backfield by committee, Kurlen rotated two fullbacks and two tailbacks in various full house or Wing T formations. Ohioan born and bred, Kurlen learned by watching Woody Hayes growing up, idolizing his "three yards and a cloud of dust" philosophy. Kurlen was both criticized and applauded as a conservative coach, specializing in ball control and minimizing turnovers.

Today, this was going to change.

Kurlen leaned forward and watched with bated breath as Anton Treptak teed the ball for kickoff. Treptak raised his hand to signify readiness. The referee blew his whistle, so the game began. Treptak jogged forward and swung his leg back to boot the ball deep as five special teamers flanked him on either side, all itching at the chance to put J'Shia Beverly on the turf.

Treptak kicked the top of the ball from the side. The onside kick caught the Fargo wedge by surprise, the ball skidding across the turf and then taking an awkward bounce into the air. Kip Kazdorf leaped up to grab the ball, but a Ranger front lineman met him in midair. Kazdorf could only get one hand on it and swatted the ball back towards his Discovery teammates.

Anton Treptak ended up in the right place at the right time to recover his own onside kick, catching Kazdorf's volley. Per League rules, the kicking team cannot advance the ball whenever they recover their own kick. As Anton wrapped the ball in his arms, possession signified, the referees' whistles blew the ball dead, but that didn't stop J'shia Beverly.

The whistle blew as Beverly was in a dead sprint. Rather than halting himself, he threw himself at Treptak. Beverly caught the kicker off guard and sent him sprawling to the turf. It wasn't a dirty hit, but yellow flags flew all around him.

Beverly walked deliberately around the fallen Treptak in a wide circle, shaking his head back and forth. As the offenses and defenses subbed onto the field for the special teams, Beverly performed his trademark skip to the sideline.

Bill Kurlen strode deliberately over to Naev Broadnax as soon as he saw Treptak stand up safely. Kurlen grabbed Anvil by the facemask before he could get out onto the field. Anvil could tell the usually clean-cut, by-the-book Christian man meant business when he looked him in the eyes and said, "Naev, today you send Beverly back to Hell where he belongs. At. All. Cost. I've had enough of this."

Anvil was taken aback. Kurlen was trembling. Anvil nodded to his coach and jogged onto the field to commandeer his huddle. He heard Kurlen yelling to the sidelines. "That ain't football! Let's not take this lying down! Man up, Columbus!"

Through Anvil's earpiece, clear against the buzz of the riled-up crowd, he could hear the offensive coordinator, Tim Adder, give the first play of the game.

"Bullet Lazer 43 post right."

Anvil relayed the play to his team, and together they moved to the line of scrimmage. Anvil put his hands beneath the broad haunches of his center, R-Qwan Wallace, and surveyed the defense. Fargo wasn't known for its defense. They were huge but had below-average game intelligence. He knew he could exploit them for a significant gain. Their linebackers played a

46

bit too far off the line of scrimmage, but the defensive line was positioned too well for him to risk calling a run. He decided to call a pass audible.

"Clear! Clear!" he shouted his code word for Kazdorf, who was in the left slot. "Rambo, Rambo! Clear Rambo!" Rather than a post, he was having Kazdorf run a drag, hoping he could catch on the run and turn the corner on these out-of-position linebackers. He glanced at the play clock. Just one second left before a delay of game.

"Hut!"

Anvil faked a handoff to his fullback, the burly Andrew McCluskey, who blocked a blitzing linebacker on the left and bought Anvil a minute. Kazdorf got jammed by his defensive back and had difficulty achieving separation. Anvil peeled out to the right, running an impromptu bootleg to buy Kazdorf some time.

Kazdorf couldn't get open. Every step he took, the defender mirrored him. One of the deep linebackers crept forward, spying on Anvil to prevent a run. Anvil sensed his running back, Leon King, running to the flat. Anvil looked to his right to find him.

That's when he saw Jimmy fall out of the stands. It isn't every day one sees their mascot friend crumple to the ground after a ten-foot fall. He spent a second too long watching Sailor Smash tumble. A Fargo lineman cleared DuPlessis' block and blindsided Anvil, his helmet dislodging the ball from the quarterback's hands as he was slammed to the ground.

Anvil cursed in dismay as he watched the ball tumble away into a pile of white and maroon. Yet another turnover on the season. Anvil staggered up, his arm stinging from the impact, angry with himself for the bad audible as well as the lack of focus.

Anvil trudged to the sidelines. Bill Kurlen was already waiting for him. Anvil brushed past him tersely. "I know, coach. Messed up the audible."

Anvil slung off his helmet and slammed himself on the bench. He sat alone, frustration evident in his snarl.

Bill Kurlen stood in front of Anvil, arms crossed over his clipboard. "When I said, 'at all cost,' that doesn't mean to cost us the game, Naev." Kurlen shook his head. "You know better than that. A soft cover 2 is still a cover 2. You can't expect to beat their spy when you run a 5.0 40 and play on a hangover every weekend."

Anvil stared at Kurlen.

"Don't think I don't know," Kurlen said. "You're not in college anymore, kid. It's time to prove you belong in the League. It's still early. Get out there and get us a touchdown next time, okay? Come on, you're better than this." Kurlen smacked Anvil's shoulder pads with his clipboard and walked away, pulling down his headset to discuss the failed play with the coordinator.

Anvil looked back over his left shoulder from the bench to the sideline, where a small gathering of Discovery workers and a couple interns were tending to Jimmy. They sat the giant white rhino up and tried to pull the head of the costume off, but Jimmy resisted. He wondered if it was part of an act and watched a bit too long, missing a change in possession after Obie Hill's sack led to a punt and a decent return. Kurlen was on top of him with another clipboard smack and a stern command.

"Wake up, son! What did I tell you? Go show you belong! Go run your offense."

Anvil slammed on his helmet and dashed onto the field. He saw that his personnel for this series was Cardinal. Four wide receivers and running back Leon King were his playmakers. Tim Adder came in on the helmet speaker with a crackle.

"No huddle, Naev, no huddle. Start it out with Cut Rocket Cross Louie. Don't get cute out there again."

Anvil broke his huddle and directed them to the line. He stepped back five yards behind his center R-Qwan Wallace, settling into a Shotgun formation, King in a two-point stance to his right. Kazdorf was in the left slot, Pete Myer in the right slot, C.S. Agnew and Faizaun Dodgson on the flanks. Anvil scanned the defense. No sign of a blitz, linebackers playing man up on the slots. The Discovery held a speed advantage with this matchup.

"Hut!"

Anvil faked a handoff to King. King took a pass-blocking stance as Kazdorf came around for a reverse. Anvil again faked the handoff to Kazdorf. DuPlessis scrapped with a Fargo defensive end, holding him up and leaving an open lane to the flats as Myer and Dodgson sprinted across the field, crossing left. There was no pressure; Anvil had some time. Kazdorf and King dashed right, up towards the line of scrimmage, having several yards' separation from the linebackers assigned to defend them. The pocket collapsed, two huge Rangers rushing Naev from the middle. He launched a tight spiral out right towards Kazdorf. Anvil had no sooner got the pass off when the Rangers linemen hauled him to the ground. Anvil's head smacked off the turf and he winced in pain as the 300-pound monsters rolled through the tackle and over his body. Anvil sat up to see the result of the play.

The crowd unleashed a thunderous roar, and Anvil scrambled to his feet to see the referee's hands in the air, arms parallel to one another. Touchdown. Kip Kazdorf ran vertically up the goalpost base and backflipped off it in his trademark parkour-themed celebration. The score was Columbus 6, Fargo 0.

Anvil ran over to congratulate Kazdorf. His friend and teammate launched himself in the air at him, and Anvil caught him in a big, swinging hug. The crowd continued to roar as they disengaged and jogged back to the sideline as the extra point team came onto the field. Anvil ran over to Bill Kurlen and slapped him on the shoulder, grinning widely.

"Great coaching, sir!" Anvil's hangover had been erased by excitement and adrenaline.

Kurlen winked at Anvil and nodded toward the field. "You ain't seen nothin' yet, my boy."

At the 2-yard line, the Discovery settled into their extra point formation, Anton Treptak preparing to kick from a hold by backup quarterback John Black. Fargo lined up huge linemen, their tallest defenders in the center, to block a low kick. They brought out a couple speedsters to rush off the edge, one of which was the ever-elusive J'Shia Beverly. Anvil stood watching beside Kurlen, with various players coming by to give him a congratulatory pat or slap for his touchdown throw.

Long snapper Ron Adams hiked it to Black. Treptak took a couple strides forward to kick the ball, then suddenly both he and Black rolled to the left, Treptak a few yards back and to the left. They were faking the kick, trying for a bonus point on the conversion attempt.

The crowd cheered the brave move. Black ran straight off the left tackle, who seemed to have Beverly secured. Suddenly, the undersized star shook free of the block and was hot on John Black's heels.

J'Shia latched onto Black's legs just before he got to the goal line. His momentum stalled, unable to cross the plane, he tossed the lateral off to Treptak. Treptak caught it with his fingers inches from the ground, and with a few yards' separation between him and the next Fargo defender, he sprinted for the corner pylon. Meanwhile, J'Shia twisted as he pulled Black down, obviously trying to injure the backup signal-caller.

Just as Treptak's tall, gawky frame crossed the goal line to score the two points, a Fargo safety named Malcolm Lynch dove for his legs. Treptak didn't get a chance to brace himself, and Lynch's helmet connected with his right knee while locked straight. Treptak felt a pop, immediate burning pain, and collapsed to the ground with a yell. Yellow flags showered the turf as the Columbus training staff, Bill Kurlen, and a few assistant coaches rushed the field to tend to Treptak, who was lying on his back with his helmet undone.

The Discovery sideline sharply descended into chaos. Nearly every player was swearing and yelling over the cheap hit as the crowd booed. This was the 2nd time the kicker, the most vulnerable player on the field, had ended up with the ball in his hands. It was also the 2nd time he had been hit after the whistle. At this point, it was obviously intentional, and a heated energy brewed in Ohio Stadium.

John Black limped straight past J'Shia Beverly after the whistle, ignoring the player who had tried to hurt him. All Black cared about was taking care of the man who took out his kicker. He walked up behind the #29 white and maroon jersey of Malcolm Lynch.

Before Black could do anything, his teammate Napoleon DuPlessis was upon him. DuPlessis pushed him back, the lineman dominant in strength and size.

"He's not worth it, man," DuPlessis said. "Let's get him on the field. Get on outta here. We'll take care of him."

DuPlessis kept pushing Black to the sideline until the backup turned and stomped away. The Fargo Rangers on the field jeered him, throwing various below-the-belt insults at him to try to draw a penalty from him too. Black reluctantly took to the sideline, ripped off his helmet, and chucked it against the stadium wall.

Bill Kurlen strode deliberately back from the endzone, his face pale. A green and yellow John Deere cart emerged from the stadium tunnel. Anton Treptak wasn't walking again today, let alone kicking.

In traditional fashion, most players and coaches on both teams had taken a knee while Treptak was down, a sign of respect while he was attended to. Anvil scanned the sideline as he took a knee. There were only two Rangers who weren't kneeling: Malcolm Lynch and J'Shia Beverly. Not only were they not kneeling out of respect, they were shuffling back and forth in rhythm, whipping extended arms side to side.

They were "flossing."

"Fortnite dances... you're kidding..." Anvil muttered.

Bill Kurlen stomped back and forth up and down the sideline as Treptak was loaded into the cart. Kurlen threw his clipboard, laminated papers flying everywhere as he screamed.

"The first person to take out Lynch or Beverly gets ten grand. I'm so sick of this! This ain't football they're trying to play. They're turning it into a street fight. Well, let's beat them at their game!"

He pointed at their sideline. "Ten grand. Bring me back their helmet to redeem your prize." There was some mild cheering from the players, some too afraid to react, others enthusiastically responding to the challenge.

Anvil stood and ran over, waving his arms and shaking his head. Another team in another league had faced severe penalties for having a bounty program, and he didn't want to see this happen to the otherwise honorable Bill Kurlen.

"No, no, no," Anvil said to Kurlen. "Think about this; you know what you're saying here?" Anvil could've sworn he seen a tear welling up in the corner of one of Kurlen's eyes. Kurlen was trembling.

"Naev, I'm sixty-six years old," he said softly. "I haven't won a game as a head coach in 21 tries. Management already told me I'm probably not coming back next year. I have enough money to retire. On top of that, no team in either League will want to sign someone with my record." He took a long pause before continuing. "I want to leave behind a legacy not of just losing, but of change. I want to cleanse this 'hood' perception from professional sports. Especially before it leaks across the PFL. That's why this league was started. No kneeling, no social justice warriors, no trendy liberalism. Teams like this need a good dose of old-school justice. Before I leave, I want to ensure these changes are made."

Kurlen offered his hand out for Naev Broadnax to shake.

"For you, Naev. Twenty-five grand."

James Glencroft opened his eyes. He was in a bright white-lit room. He squinted to shield his adjusting vision from the fluorescence blinding him. He realized his mascot outfit was heavy, soggy with sweat. Jimmy exerted effort to sit up, and as he did so, his entire body erupted with pain. The Vicodin had worn off.

Jimmy realized he was sitting on what felt like a hospital bed. He panicked. He couldn't remember coming in here. He plopped to the ground, heavy mascot feet slapping the floor, trying frantically to recall everything. The last thing he remembered was some shrieking woman and that bastard Yancey chasing after him.

Jimmy looked around for his mascot head and recognized his surroundings as he limped about. He was in the training room, where he typically changed and came in for breaks. There were usually a couple trainers in here during the games that he chatted with, but today, the place was empty. Jimmy found Sailor Smash's rhino head beside the bed he had been lying on and grabbed it, stretching out his other arm and getting ready to go back outside.

The door flung open, and a gaggle of the team trainers pushed their way in, clearing space on a bed across the room from Jimmy and preparing supplies. They were followed by two interns, who held between them a limping, wincing football player. Jimmy immediately recognized the player. Between the #19 on the jersey, the thick nose, and the shaggy, unkempt hair, it was clear that the injured athlete was "The Leg of Lipetsk," Anton Treptak.

Treptak lay upon the bed and let out a guttural yell. Two trainers peeled back his pants to get a better look at his injury.

"One to ten, how bad is it?" one trainer asked, touching his knee.

"Don't touch me," Treptak said. "That's how bad." He howled as they prodded his knee more.

Jimmy wandered close, standing on his tiptoes, trying to get a good look. One of the interns came over and grabbed Jimmy's arm.

"Sir, you shouldn't be in here," the intern said.

Who is this guy? Jimmy thought. I've never seen your ass around here before.

"This is where I break," Jimmy said. "I gotta stay in here. Do you know who I am?"

"Yes, and you can't be in here. We have an injured player."

"No shit, Sherlock," Jimmy noted how portly this intern was. He smacked the intern's gut. "Or should I say, Spurlock?"

The intern's rotund face reddened as he pointed at the door. Jimmy sauntered over and opened it, giving way to a lobby where Discovery field staff and stadium workers could take breaks and watch television. Mounted in the corner was a large H.D. T.V. on which live CBS coverage of the game was showing. Jimmy watched, feeling a bit detached as he did so. God, I need a nap, he thought.

Jimmy grabbed a remote control sitting on a nearby table and turned up the volume on the television. CBS showed replays of what appeared to be a fake extra point conversion. He heard the excited, near-yell of a hyper male commentator.

"This was a bold move by Kurlen. Absolutely a risky move, as we can see. It paid off as far as getting him an early lead and getting into Fargo's head. But watch this. This is what happens when you put the ball in the hands of a fragile player, an important player, someone you shouldn't be so unprepared to lose."

Jimmy gazed in awe as the screen showed a slow-motion replay. John Black, inches from the goal line, twisting and falling, chucking an awkward lateral to the lanky Russian kicker. The replay showed a miraculous fingertip grab, and Anton Treptak looked every bit a hero as he galloped into the endzone.

"And right here. Right here, you can see almost the exact moment his season, and I pray not his career, is likely ended by Malcolm Lynch."

The coverage switched cameras to a shot from the side of the endzone. Treptak had planted a leg completely straight in mid-stride when he was hit by Lynch's helmet. In fact, Lynch led with his helmet a solid two seconds after the play was over. In nearly a frame-by-frame pace, the camera showed Treptak's knee cave in, the leg bending in the wrong direction, a sickening, buckling motion indicating that essential parts of his knee were impacted.

The camera switched yet again, showing a slow pan of the Discovery sideline. Rows of players in blue jerseys were jumping up and down, yelling, getting ready for battle.

"After multiple cheap shots on vulnerable players early, it appears that the Columbus Discovery sideline is out for blood. Unfortunately, I think you can take this literally today. And now for a word from our sponsors, brought to you by..."

"Jimmy."

Jimmy immediately felt a cold freeze of fear in his chest. The voice was stern, perhaps a bit too quiet, yet it cut through the lobby and sank Jimmy's spirits immediately.

"We need to have a talk, Jimmy."

The sweaty, bruised, and disoriented man in a soggy, stained rhinoceros costume turned around to witness Old Jerry, stadium staff manager, standing in the lobby with his arms crossed.

"Jerry, I..."

"You'll have your chance to speak. Come sit down in my office."

Old Jerry turned and walked away down the hallway, moving at a rapid pace. Jimmy remembered Old Jerry's words from earlier, and as he scrambled to remember what happened between being in the stands and waking up in the training room, he could feel his heart gallop out of control.

Responsibility. Pride. Being smart. Making your mark.

Jimmy strode quietly, slowly down the hallway. His breath tightened, and cold sweats replaced the hot ones he felt previously. Old Jerry's office door was open; he was already seated at his desk. Jimmy meekly stepped in to an immediate, urgent demand from his superior.

"Shut the door."

Jimmy slowly pushed it shut and let go of the handle. The door, even more slowly and with a squeak, swung open a little bit more.

"Damnit, kid, you can't even shut a door right, come on," Old Jerry said as Jimmy got it shut with a second, more aggressive try. Jimmy put his Sailor Smash hat to the side and sat down, feeling like he was in the principal's office in high school all over again.

"I warned you," Old Jerry said, his expressionless face glaring at Jimmy from the other side of the messy desk. He leaned forward and clasped his hands.

"What?" Jimmy said. His thoughts flitted between football and Megan and money and the car wreck; even Lytz's face came to conscience.

"You aren't doing a very good job today," Old Jerry said pointedly. He sighed. "I thought about getting the tape, but honestly, it's not worth the trouble and for your sake think I should destroy the evidence."

"...What are you talking about, sir?"

"Look, Jimmy. I know you're fucked up. I know you had a wreck, and I appreciate you toughing this up. But whatever you did to help the pain, it ain't workin'. You need to get ahold of yourself out there."

Jimmy nodded. He didn't reply.

Jerry stared intensely into Jimmy's eyes. Jimmy struggled to maintain eye contact. It was hard with eyelids heavy, thoughts webbing out and his anxiety fueling the madness. He almost felt like a kid who was caught sneaking in late, facing his parents, trying to hide the fact that he was stoned or drunk.

Might as well be with all the Vicodin I took and only a few hours' rest.

"I understand taking extra breaks," Old Jerry said. He sighed again. "I understand not doing a lot of tricks or walking around much, you know? We all have our off days." He leaned forward, closer to Jimmy.

"What I don't understand is pushing around fans, especially ones holding kids... What I don't understand is leering over people, looking down shirts, and falling over walls like a common clod. You're better than this. You rocked this shit when you were with that baseball club. What's wrong with you?"

Jimmy didn't respond.

"I said, what's wrong with you?"

"Well," Jimmy said, "I've got so much going on. I'm sore, and I want to be honest, I may have taken too many pills. I'm not trying to be messed up. I love this job, and I don't know why I acted that way, sir."

Old Jerry nodded. "I appreciate your honesty, and despite the fact you've slacked a lot, you've done some good things here as well." He gestured towards the phone on his desktop.

"I can give Brandon a call and have him get in the backup costume," Old Jerry said. "If you'd like to take a half-day and get to feeling better, I'd understand."

Jimmy shuddered. "No, sir," he said, trying to sound firm. "I'm going to finish what I started. I was born to be a professional mascot. I want to go out there and be a part of our club's first victory."

Old Jerry let himself smile a little bit. "I'm glad to hear that. Listen, kid, if you think you can do this, take your time before going back out there. Drink a little water, stretch up a little, just make sure you're sound of both body and mind. We can't have you acting like an asshole and pissing off our fans. With how we've done lately, I'm surprised we're still packing the house. Now get on out of here, and be the mascot you were born to be."

Jimmy smiled through his nerves, the nerves that were still shot despite this somewhat encouraging meeting. He grabbed the rhino head and was on his way out the door when Old Jerry called him back.

"Jimmy," Old Jerry began. "By the way. This is the second talk we've had today. I've never had to have three talks with any of my employees in a month, let alone in one day."

Jimmy nodded. "I'm going to go make my mark now, and I won't let you or Columbus down."

Old Jerry nodded and smiled once more. "Good. Now get out of my office and never come back," he said with a joking tilt, smiling a little bigger as Jimmy slammed on the head and went jogging down the hall. He leaned back a bit in the chair and clicked on his monitor to check e-mail, the time, and the game's score. Suddenly, his office phone beeped. He grabbed the handset to answer.

"Jerry Hickle, Discovery grounds manager."

"Old Jerry, it's Paul," a low-tone, raspy voice came on the line. It was the Discovery owner, Paul Czaplewski, a gentleman who made a fortune from investment banking, someone who meant business with every word of every conversation.

"Yes sir, what can I do for you?"

"The mascot. We spoke about him earlier, yes?" Czaplewski asked.

"Yes sir, I just had him in my office."

"Did you do it?" Czaplewski's near-growl never shifted in volume as he spoke.

"No, sir, I couldn't do it." Old Jerry let out yet another sigh. "I got a soft spot for him. But he's probably going to strike himself out. I don't need to push the matter. Maybe he can go down well."

"Maybe he can, maybe he can't. I'm going to say he won't, actually." Czaplewski's voice increased in urgency. "He's a liability. That woman he struck wants to sue. I can't be having that."

"Understood, sir," Old Jerry said, feeling his own anxiety seep in.

"When I want someone fired, I want someone fired. I pay the bills and sign the checks around here. I'm going over your head on this one, Hickle. I respect what you do, but I respect the business more.

"Listen," Czaplewski beckoned. "I want you to go find Glencroft and tell him to go home before he messes up again."

"But, Mr. Czaplewski, we're not even in the 2nd quarter, and..."

"I've already spoken with Brandon, and I'm promoting him to head mascot on Tuesday. He's on his way to pick up the second suit now."

"You've already told Brandon this? Sir?"

"Yes, and that's the last I'll speak of it. Now, if you'll excuse me, I have to call the training staff and check on my kicker. That's a million-dollar leg that I can't afford to lose. Go fire Glencroft."

The phone clicked off before Old Jerry could offer any more rebuttals. He groaned and rubbed his wrinkled, sun-weathered forehead.

In the hallways of the lower level, Old Jerry Hickle chased down his mascots. The team never put out two Sailor Smashes simultaneously, and Jerry wanted to avoid this confusion.

Meanwhile, out on the field, the Discovery was on a chase of their own: a chase to pin down their first-ever Patriot Football League victory.

Playing perhaps a little too hard, many a defender for Columbus whiffed on the more diminutive, nimble Fargo Ranger playmakers as they juked, jumped, and dove their way to multiple field-spanning, clock-crunching drives, each of them ending in the end zone as Fargo pulled ahead 14-8.

Every time Naev Broadnax led his offense down the field to strike back, an unfortunate turnover, penalty, or lousy play call would negate any progress made at that point. One drive, Napoleon DuPlessis was called for holding on what would've been a 40-yard touchdown by C.S. Agnew. On another play, Leon King had made a run downfield, only to drop the ball while ten yards from the closest Ranger defender. These minor blunders added up, the tension was palpable, and Columbus struggled to find their way back to the lead.

As the first quarter gave way to the second, it was apparent that the Discovery's initial strategy of trick plays and unexpected conversion attempts was cracked by the cunning Fargo coaching staff, led by defensive coordinator Hal Tremont. This week, most of Bill Kurlen's improvised playbook relied on fake kicks, onside kicks, no-huddle formations led by the special teams... All packages that involved the talents of Anton Treptak, all packages rendered irrelevant by his gruesome knee injury early in the 1st quarter. An error in oversight, Kurlen did not practice these packages with any other player, so he abandoned these pans in favor of his standard style of run-heavy, pitch-driven offense. The punter, Jay Orem, was set to pull double duty. This made players and coaches alike nervous as his leg was unproven when kicking from tee or hold.

The bounty thus far had been unclaimed as J'Shia Beverly was elusive when handling the ball and had not nabbed any interceptions or fumble recoveries. When a stray Discovery lineman went out of his way to block J'Shia, the undersized athlete utilized his quickness and agility to evade the attack. Frustration mounted among the Discovery bruisers because nobody could get a good, clean hit on J'Shia before the whistle. Despite Kurlen's bounty, he still preached class and urged the players to at least pretend to be sporting about the whole thing.

Late in the 2nd quarter, the Discovery offense huddled together for an inspirational word from Coach Kurlen.

"So, before any of you get carried away about the whole bounty thing or talk to the damn media, I just want to make it clear that was a 'heat of the moment' kind of thing, and I don't really want ya'll trying to kill J'Shia or Malcolm." Kurlen paused with a smirk. "Well, I do, but I'm not going to encourage anything other than fair play and sportsmanship from here on out, okay? I think we can win this game, and I want to make sure I'm here to coach us to the playoffs."

Kurlen looked over the group of players. All shapes and sizes, these gridiron warriors dripped with sweat and reeked of physical effort.

"We're going to run our Wildcat no-huddle formation for the rest of the half once we get this ball punted to us. I want to beat Fargo at their own game." Kurlen turned to Anvil. "Broadnax will be playing in the slot, with King and Kazdorf split out wide. McCluskey will play tight, Dunbar at back, and Black taking the snaps. We're going to move the ball, we're going to protect the ball, and we're going to take the lead. Who's with me?"

The offense led out a hearty cheer. Kurlen thrust his hand between the assembled players.

"Now remember, team, no more of that bounty business. That was a joke, okay? Let's bring it in and get a 'Pride' on three."

"1! 2! 3! PRIDE!" The offense broke the huddle and prepared for their drive as a booming Fargo punt trickled out of bounds. The drive would start with the Columbus Discovery on their own 7-yard line. They had 93 yards to span in just over two minutes. Anvil slapped on his helmet and went to trot out onto the field when he was stopped by Bill Kurlen. Kurlen leaned in and spoke lowly to Anvil.

"Naev, you and I still have an agreement. There's a reason I'm putting you in the slot."

Kurlen's blue eyes were sharp as steel as his voice dripped with malice.

"Thirty grand."

Anvil responded with a nod and jogged onto the field.

CHAPTER SEVEN

Jimmy Glencroft meandered his way through throngs of fans in the lower bowl. He signed autographs, danced along to music played between drives, and played peek-a-boo with youngsters. He was fueled by the smiles on the fans' faces. He wore the Discovery uniform with pride and felt a renewed energy.

Even with constant thoughts of Megan, Lytz, money, and his car dancing through his head, he felt more optimistic. The drugs were wearing off, and the pain of his bruises and cuts were stark, but the fuzz had lifted. It was about halftime. He was going to finish out this game on a positive note and deal with life later.

Jimmy was strutting back into the concession corridor when he turned to the left and saw the last individual he expected to see at this juncture in the game. A second Sailor Smash was strutting around as well, fist-bumping, high-fiving, and even posing for a picture with a family. Jimmy watched in awe. *What was Brandon doing in the backup costume? They never ran two Sailor Smash costumes at the same time!* Jimmy froze in place.

"Mommy look! Two rhinos!"

A small kid shouted and pointed from a nearby pretzel stand. Brandon looked up and saw Jimmy. The two mascots locked googly eyes. It was time to improvise.

Jimmy popped, locked, and then sunk in a sumo wrestling stance and beckoned to Brandon in a "Just Bring It" hand motion, a la The Rock, urging him to fight. Brandon spun down the open corridor in his slightly smaller, slightly brighter Sailor Smash outfit, flailing his arms and legs around in ninja moves.

Jimmy bowed to Brandon, and he bowed back. Suddenly the two mascots were embraced in a standing head-tie, amateur wrestling style. Jimmy just wanted to get close enough to speak with Brandon, and his understudy took the cue well, the two plush rhino heads locked side by side. The crowd cheered on as they circled for position on one another.

"What the hell, man?" Jimmy said, his voice low and muffled as the two grappled with one another.

"Jimmy," Brandon said in a hush, "I didn't want you to be surprised. You're going to be let go tonight."

Jimmy felt his gut drop lower than it had in the last 24 hours. He felt sick and more anxious than he did when he wrecked his car, lost nearly $500 in poker, or endured either of his two fights with his girlfriend.

"Dude. But why?" Jimmy put Brandon in a head and arm lock.

"I don't know, man. I told them not to. I'm not ready to be #1 yet. But old man Czaplewski told me earlier to suit up."

Jimmy breathed heavily. He felt Brandon jab at him with pulled elbow strikes. A drunk redneck screamed, "Kick the donkey's ass!"

"No chance of redemption?" Jimmy's left arm was tingling.

"None," Brandon said. "Old Jerry is probably trying to find you to fire you now. I don't want you to go out like a bitch, though. Make your mark. Start with me."

Jimmy took the cue. He felt adrenaline surge as if he were in a real life or death fight. Jimmy pulled away from Brandon, put a giant plush shoe in his sternum, then turned around and delivered a falling three-quarter face lock... a Stone Cold Stunner.

Brandon sold the finisher with a backflip and landed inches away from the gathered fans. He laid motionless as Jimmy got up and turned around to look at him. *What a good sport.* Jimmy dusted off his costume.

"Smash!"

He looked up in the distance to see a thin, short man wearing a Discovery cap and bright blue lanyard dashing his way.

Shit, Jimmy thought. *Jerry.*

Jimmy turned and bolted in the opposite direction. He had to get to the field one last time. Jimmy couldn't give this job up yet. Every minute he could evade Old Jerry was another minute on his paycheck. Every corner turned brought a new opportunity to make his mark. Every night, when he previously worked for a minor league baseball team, he gave the local press something to talk about. This afternoon, he wanted to give the national media something to talk about, a goal he had failed to work toward the whole two years he represented the Discovery.

If there was anything Jimmy was great at in life, it was pulling off absurd successes at the last minute. He was determined to make this afternoon another case of winning against all odds.

The bright setting sun and a horseshoe-shaped wreath of blue and crimson shirts filled Jimmy's mesh-filtered vision as he turned the corner and ran down the bleacher stairs towards the field in Ohio Stadium for the last time.

"Hut!"

John Black took a shotgun snap from R-Qwan Wallace. Kip Kazdorf screamed at an all-out sprint from the left flank, taking the handoff from the backup quarterback. Kazdorf's legs churned hard over the turf as he turned upfield and shifted the ball from his left arm to the right, away from the closest Fargo defenders.

Up ahead, Kazdorf saw the #13 jersey of Naev Broadnax, the quarterback putting a hand on a Ranger linebacker, stymying the imposing defender, and buying Kazdorf a little extra time. Rather than tuck in behind Broadnax's block, Kazdorf took an angle towards the sideline, anticipating secure blocking from the reliable Leon King. Kazdorf made the mistake of not looking both ways before choosing his direction and felt a player come at him low from the side. Kazdorf tried to hurdle the defender, but they caught him hard in the shins and sent the Discovery star flipping in midair.

Kazdorf landed on the turf hard back-first. He rolled through the impact to the side and came to a knee, looking over to see Malcolm Lynch performing a celebratory dance. Kazdorf looked back to the sidelines, seeing that he had cleared the first down marker.

Who celebrates tackles when giving up a first down? Kazdorf thought as he ran back to the line, John Black shouting out commands, trying to snap the ball before the two-minute warning came.

Wallace shot the ball back to Black just as the game clock came to 2 minutes remaining in the half. Kazdorf sprinted across the field again, taking another handoff from Black. This time, Anvil, McCluskey, and Dunbar were all pass blocking, picking up on a zone blitz. Kazdorf flipped the football in his hands as he looked downfield, seeing Leon King sprinting down the sideline, Malcolm Lynch matching him step for step. Kazdorf glanced left, seeing John Black lurking in the flats, wide open. An enterprising Fargo lineman read Kazdorf's line of vision and started strafing towards Black, cutting off one of his lanes downfield. Kazdorf pump-faked down the sideline and caught a glimpse of DuPlessis blowing yet another block, a mean Ranger defensive end bearing down on him hard.

Kazdorf stepped right, a feint step as he countered back left, the defensive end just a yard behind. The linebacker stepped towards the line of scrimmage between Kazdorf and Black, who was accelerating up the left sideline. The linebacker made the decision to blitz Kazdorf. Kazdorf leaped into the air and fired off a sidearm pass, the wobbly throw going around the linebacker's arm and into the hands of John Black.

A lane of wide-open turf lay before Black. He sprinted, ball in his left arm, tucked in tight to his body. He ran down the Discovery sideline, his teammates erupting in cheers as he sprinted past the 20-yard line, the 30, the 40.

J'Shia Beverly gained on Black, the fastest of the Fargo defenders by far. The nimble defender caught up to Black just as he crossed into Ranger territory. Black thrust out an arm, pushing to fend off Beverly. Beverly stuck with Black and grasped at his jersey to slow him down. Black slowed but kept going, grinding his cleats into the turf to keep the momentum moving forward. Beverly, unable to complete a proper form tackle, reached up and clasped a gloved hand around Black's face mask. The crowd's boos deafened all in the stadium as Beverly pulled down Black by the face mask from behind, his neck at an awkward angle as they landed.

Several Discovery players rushed towards Beverly, but their more level-headed teammates stepped in front of them, putting up a monumental effort to hold them back, cleats ripping at turf as they stayed their ground. Black lay still, a limp husk. J'Shia Beverly did not just walk back to the huddle or sideline; even as referees rained down yellow penalty flags around him, he jeered the Discovery sideline, skipping around and making tugging motions toward Discovery players at his crotch level.

Anvil and a few other players walked over to check on Black, who was being tended to by the training staff. He was sitting up now, obviously stunned and sore, rubbing his neck and looking up at his teammates and trainers, dazed, his eyes unfocused.

The boos among the crowd gave way to cheers as Black was helped to his feet. He staggered to the sideline, unable to walk in a straight line. Bill Kurlen walked deliberately up to Anvil.

"Broadnax," he said, "I'm putting in Agnew at Wildcat now. Not only is Beverly a pain in my ass, he's shitting all over my game plan. First Treptak, now Black."

Why would Kurlen keep sticking to this game plan when the backup quarterbacks and critical players were dropping like flies? Anvil thought. He didn't remember Agnew taking any snaps practicing the Wildcat under center, let alone ever throwing the ball in practice.

"Coach, I want under center," Anvil said urgently. "I can make this happen. Give me a chance to throw the ball. I haven't been able to get a lick on Beverly at all."

Kurlen eyed Anvil curiously. "We didn't practice with you under center in Wildcat this week."

Anvil shook his head, his voice rising in volume as his frustration boiled within. "Coach, forget the Wildcat. Let me heave it. No more tricks, it's just hurting our guys."

Kurlen glared, his head tilted sideways. He threw his papers up in the air and spat to the ground. "Have it your way, Naev. No huddle, shotgun with Cardinal. Start things out with Rocket Cross Louie Ziplock. Bring me back a touchdown or bring me Beverly's head."

Anvil nodded and turned to jog back out to the field. "Naev," Kurlen said shortly. Anvil turned back around.

"Forty grand." Kurlen glared as he upped his offer. Kurlen spat to the ground and pointed to the field. "Two-minute warning's up. Do something."

Anvil jogged over to his huddle. The appropriate substitutions were made as the Cardinal personnel lined up around him. Anvil put his arms around DuPlessis and Kazdorf, leaning in close.

"Hurry up offense. Rocket Cross Louie Ziplock. We got thirty yards to go, and we score, got it, boys? Let's do this. Ready, BREAK!"

Anvil looked left to see Kazdorf and Agnew line up, Kazdorf in the slot, and a yard off the scrimmage line. He glanced right to see Myer and Dodgson position themselves accordingly. King was immediate to Anvil's right. King leaned in so Anvil could hear him over the buzzing crowd and shouts of the defense.

"Ay yo, Naev," King said excitedly. "I think they're zone again. Send Myer and Dodgson up deep, I follow, you get it to me, that's *six*!"

Anvil shook his head. "Leon, that ain't the play. Block for me here. I'll need you."

King shook his head, didn't respond, and stepped over to his proper position. Anvil stomped the ground, urging the snap back to him. He glanced left as he stepped back, seeing Kazdorf cut towards the left sideline as Agnew sprinted right. Their defenders stuck to them like glue, no open throwing lanes. Anvil looked right. Dodgson had one safety over, one safety under. Myer was nowhere to be seen. Anvil glanced around, panicking, nobody open. The offensive line was buying him some time. He had no more check downs.

Suddenly, Anvil saw King sprinting down the right sideline. With the Rangers only blitzing four, he had nobody to block. King had a bit of cushion, no defenders nearby. Anvil, frustrated at King for abandoning his assignment, reluctantly gave him what he wanted and hurled a spiral down the right sideline.

Anvil lobbed the pass high, leading King deep, the running back sprinting underneath it. Both Malcolm Lynch and J'Shia Beverly were covering deep. They were racing behind King, closing on him more the longer the ball hung in the air.

King did not have a single eye on the defenders. He held out his arms and cupped his hands. He was not aware that Lynch was right there waiting. Lynch stuck in an arm and batted the pass up into the air; the ball lobbed ten feet high.

King stopped in his tracks and spun, eyes on the ball, trying to reach out and grab it. Lynch hugged King's arms tight to his body and slammed him to the turf. This gave J'Shia Beverly the chance to catch up. Beverly ran under the ball and caught it before it plummeted to the ground. Interception, Fargo.

J'Shia had a wide-open lane down the left sideline, the Fargo sideline, being cheered on by his teammates. The shifty star took off, fluidly putting one foot in front of the other mere inches from the edge of the sideline. He saw a wall of blue jerseys closing in up ahead, so he planted his left foot and changed direction out to the right. Agnew tried for a tackle, but Beverly spun off the weak attempt and kept moving. Myer sized up for a tackle but was hurled through the air, a victim of an impactful Ranger block. Beverly ran back to the right, looking for open field.

Beverly looked behind him, seeing Kazdorf hot on his heels. He kept watching Kazdorf, running hard as he could, ball held loosely in his left hand. Kazdorf gained ground, just a few yards back.

Beverly was so distracted from watching the pursuant Kazdorf that he did not see Naev Broadnax upfield. The quarterback had backpedaled a bit instead of running forward to pursue the interceptor. Anvil had strafed himself into an optimal position to make a hit. He loped ahead a bit as Beverly drew close.

Beverly turned his head to look forward. He noticed Broadnax far too late to dodge him. The enormous quarterback lowered his head, legs set in a robust base. Broadnax thrust his helmet under Beverly's own, leveling him with a helmet-to-helmet hit. Beverly's body fell limply to the ground as the football rolled out of bounds.

Anvil spat upon Beverly's body as the crowd fell hush in shock before erupting in a massive thunderous cheer. A pool of red seeped from Beverly's motionless shell. Yellow flags came down like rain.

Before Anvil had a chance to do anything else, a wall of maroon and white descended upon him from the sideline. Three Fargo defenders gang-tackled him and began swinging. Dozens of other Rangers ran forth and mobbed him. Broadnax's blue jersey could not be seen amid furious opponents.

Not long after that, the cavalry arrived. Discovery teammates shoved, pommeled, and threw hands aside Fargo players, engaged in full-on combat. The ring of blue swelled as the benches emptied. Suddenly, white jerseys scattered and spread out. Anvil had surged up out of the middle.

Anvil kicked one Ranger in the gonads, leveling him. A smaller defender leaped upon his back. Anvil spun and threw him down with a shoulder toss. Another smaller player jumped into his arms and tried to reach under his helmet.

"I'll beat a motherfucker with another motherfucker!" Anvil yelled as he swung the player off him and into Malcolm Lynch, who was felled by the blow.

Larger Discovery combatants had fought through the fray and gotten to Anvil. Thanks to his teammates, the mob had broken up into many one-on-one fights rather than one giant mass. He caught a moment to breathe and scanned the area, seeing an all-out riot between maroon and white and blue. He spied referees and security mixed in, zebra stripes and bright orange trying to break up the carnage.

Anvil shoved through a few of his teammates and tried to escape to the sideline. After ducking between DuPlessis and Obie Hill, he ran straight into a vast Fargo lineman. The lineman ran into him hard, lifting him up into the air by the throat, about to slam him hard to the turf.

Kazdorf slid in out of the mess, using a capoeira leg sweep to fell the massive foe. Anvil managed to stumble instead of getting slammed and nodded his thanks to Kazdorf. They joined hands and ran through a Fargo defender, clotheslining him as they escaped the weakening riot.

"Let's chuck the deuces and save our cabooses!" Kazdorf shouted. Anvil nodded, and they ran for their sideline.

The crowd roared as a giant plush rhinoceros vaulted over the wall separating the public from the field. Anvil and Kazdorf looked at one another in shock, then looked back at James Glencroft as he sprinted towards the brawl, his battle cry audible through the mesh.

"Jimmy, don't!" Anvil yelled as he tried to get in Jimmy's way. Jimmy sprinted past, straight for the fight, lowering his head and getting on all fours, looking as much like an actual rhino as he possibly could.

"Dammit, we have to go back in there and save his ass," Kazdorf said as Jimmy galloped into the midst of the action, ramming an unsuspecting Ranger in his legs and bowling him over.

Jimmy hyperventilated, the combination of exhaustion, strain, drugs, and anxiety forming a lethal whirlwind of ill-advised actions.

Fame, he thought as he rammed a Ranger in the hindquarters, sending them sprawling to the turf. He was going to make his mark, one highlight at a time.

Success, Jimmy got to his feet and leveled a helmetless player with a crunching right hook. He was going mad with power.

Women, He had lost his lover and his job, more than likely. He had a story to tell unfolding on national network television. Jimmy roundhouse kicked a Fargo player in the back of the head, the surge of fear and adrenaline sharpening his abilities.

Damn, Jimmy felt the plush head ripped from his costume. A breeze of fresh air accented the sudden exposure. He turned around to see Malcolm Lynch holding the head of Sailor Smash, who had plucked it off from the back. Jimmy heard the gasp of the crowd and felt a dull thud as the Fargo player swung the head into his face. The impact brought Jimmy to one knee. Lynch stomped on the back of his head, feeding Jimmy a mouthful of turf. All Jimmy could do was lay there and take it while Lynch repeatedly hit him with his own mascot head. Jimmy wept, closing his eyes, praying for it all to end, the ultimate embarrassment for a mascot befalling him just as he made his mark.

Malcolm Lynch tossed aside the Sailor Smash head and turned to find another fight, finished with the weakened mascot. Three security guys tried to apprehend him, grabbing at his jersey and positioning themselves in a circle around him. Lynch shoved back, freeing himself, jogging backward to get away. He was entirely oblivious to Kazdorf, on his hands and knees behind him. Lynch tripped over Kazdorf and fell flat on his back, startled, gasping as the breath was pushed from him with the impact.

Naev Broadnax took a running start, hopped into the air, and delivered a crunching Hulk Hogan-style leg drop to Lynch's upper body. Lynch rolled over in pain, unable to get to his feet and defend himself. Anvil cupped his hand around his ear, urging the crowd to roar even louder. Kazdorf thrusted his pelvis at the melee, chopping at his thighs with his hands, taunting the other team as the swarm of referees and officials began to clear up the mess.

Two referees had witnessed Anvil and Kazdorf's participation in the brawl and grabbed them by the arm. "Come on," a referee said, pulling at the reluctant Naev.

"Don't resist, man, it's over," Kazdorf advised as he walked with the other referee towards the tunnels on the sideline. Anvil watched the last bit of the brawl.

"I may have made some mistakes," Anvil said quietly. The referee tugged at his arm again. Anvil turned his head to the sky, unable to look any fans or coaches in the eye as he walked away.

"Naev!"

Anvil looked back down, turning to see the source of the voice. James Glencroft, looking every bit ridiculous with a human head and an anthropomorphic rhinoceros' body, came running up. Jimmy's face was caked with blood and tears. Eyes red, beard unkempt, Jimmy pushed through the officials to his friend.

Anvil hugged the disheveled and sobbing Jimmy. Anvil then shared a fond look with Kazdorf, who also came up and put an arm around them. The referees tried to separate them and keep urging them to the locker room, but Anvil waved them off.

"Jimmy? You okay, man?" Anvil asked.

"Thanks for everything, Naev. It was an honor working with you," Jimmy gasped in one clear sentence between the sobs.

"What are you talking about, bro?" Kazdorf asked. He kept his head on a swivel, watching out for any rogue Fargo assailants.

"I'm done. I'm fired. I won't be a part of the Discovery for sure now."

"Now, I'm sure it's not all that bad," Anvil said.

Jimmy didn't respond as his body went limp, slipped out of Anvil's embrace, and slumped to the ground.

CHAPTER EIGHT

"Bro, I can't tell whether this is bad or good for business," Big Trace Onwudiwe said. The bearded man reclined in a leather armchair with his feet up. He wore the blue, crimson, and yellow Columbus Discovery home jersey with a matching fitted hat and spotless, shining blue and crimson Nike shoes. Trace wore designer sunglasses inside, a single gold chain around his neck, a fat marijuana blunt lit and smoldering as it rested between his thick fingers, his bright and gaudy rings contrasting his dark skin.

"You'll be finding out tonight," Craig Foxx said, leaning on a nearby doorway. He sipped from a red plastic cup, his tan, tribal tattoo-laden arms exposed, wearing a white tank top and jeans. A flaming razor blade across the front of Craig's neck was the most striking tattoo of them all.

Onscreen, the referees and security officials had broken up the giant melee, the screen displaying J'Shia Beverly's blood-caked, still face in 1080 High Definition.

"Homie gonna need some Space to fly outta that pain," Trace said as he took a slow, deliberate draw of his blunt, wriggling his toes inside his shoes as he did so.

"You're right," Craig said. He walked into the den and set down the cup of his cough syrup-laden concoction on a coffee table. Craig faced Trace as he hoisted a leg over a leather ottoman and sat atop with crossed legs. "Are you making the deal tonight, or am I putting Manny on it?"

"I'll do it, mang," Trace said as he put out the last portion of his blunt in an ashtray on a table beside him. He leaned forward, grinning wide, his eyes tinged red. "I'm feelin' some kind of way right now."

"Me too," Craig replied with a grin.

Craig closed his eyes a moment before he continued, "We're getting a big shipment in from PharmaScenticals tonight. Country will be picking up his storefront share tomorrow, and after that, we will have our biggest stock yet, even after our regulars take their share. I was talking to Obie before the game. Guess who's going to be in town."

Trace looked at Craig. "Dunno, who?"

"Montreaux Pickens," Craig said as he leaned forward, his eyes gleaming in excitement.

"West Coast Gold?! No shit!" Trace exclaimed and grinned.

"Yeah, he has an operation already in place, and Obie tells me he likes to party, if you get my drift. Don't know if he's Spaced yet. You should hit him up tonight, see if he'd be interested in what we have."

Trace shook his head back and forth as if to snap himself out of a trance.

"Them guys keep racks on deck!" Trace wrung his hands.

"Yessir," Craig said. "I've bought this huge shipment primarily on credit. So, getting the cash on hand will allow us to pay that off pretty quickly. If Montreaux knows people who know enough people, we could really scale up this operation."

Trace leaned back again and looked at the ceiling fan. He watched it for a moment before he spoke. "Tonight could spark our biggest deal yet," Trace said.

"Trace, my man. You secure the deal tonight; I'll get you out."

Trace sat back up sharply, looking Craig directly in the eyes. His grin shifted to a look of concentration and gravity, his hands clasped in front of him.

"You mean it?" Trace asked Craig. "You'll buy me out?"

Craig nodded. "Your daughter needs a daddy around. I've got no kids of my own, so I don't want to risk losing you any more than I do now. I'll finance your clothing line. You'll be free to follow that course long as it will take you. And if that ever falls through, you can come back and work it off. You've done well for me, Trace. I want you to know that."

"Bro. You ain't gotta offer me that. But I'll take it. We've made some money. But I just need that extra to cut loose. I'll do you some good," Trace said. He got up with a creak and walked over to Craig, who stood back up as well. They clasped a handshake and came together in a hug.

"I got you, bro," Trace said as Craig patted him.

"I hate to interrupt," a sharp voice cracked through the warm fuzziness. Craig and Big Trace disengaged to turn and face a short, thin man standing in the kitchen, leaning on the door frame. He wore a dirty, oversized purple-striped button-down shirt, untucked over a pair of even more soiled khakis, various stained shades of brown and green. The man wore thick bifocals, had thinning hair, and a thin dusty-brown mustache over a toothless mouth.

"Aw shit, what the hell is it, Landers?" Big Trace asked. Landers grinned, flashing his gums, causing Trace to wince and look down and away from him.

"The phone. Brody Marlowe," Landers said, holding up the small Android smartphone. "I got it cracked. Took me one whole minute." Landers held the phone at an angle for Craig and Trace to see as his colleagues approached. The glint of the light revealed the greasy patterns of Brody's fingers in a triangle shape.

"As you can see, the fool swiped his lock screen. All I had to do was tilt it to see what his pattern could've been. Four swipes, and I was in. And this cat isn't who he says he is."

"I'm more concerned as to what you've been doing for the last few hours when you say this only took you a minute," Craig said, his burly arms crossed as he looked down on the skinny, sloppy I.T. guy.

"Frankly, you should be more concerned about his texts, but no matter. I spent the last few hours changing all the warehouse passwords for construction, PharmaScenticals, and Cowtown Candles; calibrating the security cameras, spot-checking the recordings, and re-encrypting our database. I've been busy." Landers grinned. "Even found time to fit in a little *Grease and Ambition*."

Craig sighed. "How serious are these texts? Let's get to business. I knew this kid wasn't to be trusted."

"You are correct," Landers replied as he held up the phone to show off the contents. "It's strange that he has only three contacts. Each of these people also has an oddly similar name. Brody Marlowe, of course. Cody Barlow. Jody Giancarlo. Zoey DiNardo. I mean... really?!"

"Code names, for sure. Brody isn't this guy's real name," Craig observed.

"Correct," Landers said as he flicked through the phone's contents. "No pictures, no apps, no porn, just business. Kid didn't have this burner for very long. As you can see... the only searches were for Manny's address, poker tips for beginners, and, interestingly, searches for Foxx Construction, Cowtown Candles, PharmaScenticals, and random Columbus Discovery players."

Big Trace's brow furrowed, and lines formed in his expansive forehead. "He onto us," Trace said. He spat into a nearby trashcan before he looked over at Craig. "Who are these people?"

"Wish I knew," Craig said morosely as he walked by the other two and sat at the nearby kitchen table. He gazed out the back door window for a moment.

"Landers, do you have any leads on their identities? Also, let's get on with these texts," Craig urged.

"I tried calling each number. Check it out. I'm trying Cody Barlow first," Landers said as he swiped through a couple screens to get to the address book. He dialed the contact and switched the cell phone to speaker, so everyone could hear it.

After a single ring, an automated voice message said, "The number you are trying to reach is no longer in service. Please hang up and try again."

Craig raised his eyebrows. He looked back and forth to Trace and Landers.

"They're slick. Once our friend realized his phone was gone, I bet he warned them," Craig said as he drummed his fingers on the tabletop.

"Indeed," Landers said. "I ran a Google search on all four names. All four had a Facebook profile on the front page. I tried to access the profiles, but they were all deleted. These guys acted fast. I can tell Marlowe used to have the Facebook app downloaded, but it was removed before we got a hold of this phone.

"As far as the texts, I have reason to believe we may be either compromised or on the verge of being so. Every text Marlowe sent was a group text to the other three. Basic stuff in low detail, but enough that I'm certainly suspicious. And I quote: 'The candles are real. I saw one earlier.' 'The host is close with them.' He texted Manny's address and the names of everyone at the table, even the unaffiliated ones, like Glencroft and MacKenzie."

Craig looked up at Landers, his face straight and tone firm. "I need you to realize, Landers, that we must treat MacKenzie as if he's affiliated. He's one of our biggest day-to-day users. He knows his connections, who we are, all that stuff. MacKenzie is also the one who came along and screwed everything up for us when he picked up our target before we could even get there."

Landers nodded, nonplussed. "Craig, I need you to realize that MacKenzie is an unpredictable and unreliable meth addict and will screw things up for himself before he does us. I'm not overly concerned about him or the Glencroft guy. In fact, I feel kind of bad for Glencroft getting caught up in all this. He's worthless, but I'm relieved that he wasn't killed in that accident. We don't need that collateral damage, and I feel like we should let make things right for him."

Craig furrowed his brow deeper. "I need you to realize that you are the I.T. guy. You don't make decisions as to who's a concern and who's not. I don't need to tell you again... Know your place, Landers. Besides, I'm working on a deal with Glencroft. He's going to need money, and we're going to need bodies."

Landers nodded, wringing his hands around the cell phone. "I'd like to learn more about your roles. Especially if we nail this deal and get Big Trace out."

Craig raised an eyebrow. Big Trace looked back up with a start.

"How did you know I'm tryna get out?" Trace asked.

Landers flashed a toothless grin, causing Trace to look away again. "You weren't using your inside voices. Even if you were, I think you forget I have every room bugged. Remember, if I.T. can't trust you, you can't trust I.T."

"You motherfucker," Craig said, returning his grin. "I guess you're right. Go play your game, Landers. You did good work today. I'll go figure out what to do with this Marlowe kid and the others. Come on, Trace, let's take a ride."

Landers nodded and then held up the phone once more. "Very well. But before we go, I want to breach one quick discussion of intel."

Craig nodded, his expression straightening up once more. "Go on."

"I have reason to believe that this may be a move by Dayton's very own Dirty D Posse. We have never dealt with them directly, no?"

Craig frowned. "No, not directly, but I have a passing familiarity. Dirty D? Aren't they a brother posse? Trace, did that kid look like a brother to you?"

Big Trace shook his head. "Nah, fam... How do you figure he's Dirty D? Kid was white as snow."

Landers gazed out of a window, considering what he knew carefully before he spoke. "My dark web contacts in the area have indicated a recent... ah, expansion. Dirty D is losing out on some customer base between here and Dayton that have traditionally bought from them. London, Urbana... Marysville..."

Craig crossed his arms once more. "Marysville? Dirty D considers that their territory?"

Landers nodded.

"God damn," Craig muttered as he leaned against the door frame. "I bet this leads back to Captain Galactico."

"Indeed," Landers said. "I think we should have tightened up Galactico a bit. Undoubtedly his, ah, integration of our candles into his sets has caught some unwanted attention. I recommend we cut his sourcing until we can get a handle on this Dirty D threat. I have no clue how long they've been on our tail, but I do know this... It's early, and we can probably get ahead of this now."

Big Trace shook his head. "Are you sure it's Dirty D? Sounds like a whole lot of reachin' to me, man. There's no smoking gun."

Landers held up the phone and wriggled it around. "This is as close as we're going to get. Just put everything together. Strange foreign-looking young guy. Rave scene. Galactico. Marysville. Missing candles. You saw how hard he went for that candle at the poker game. They're here. And we need to be vigilant."

Craig strode up to Landers and gave him a quick embrace, the taller crime boss dwarfing the skinny I.T. guy.

"Look, this helps a lot, thank you. Go play your game. You earned it. Take a night off."

Landers shrugged. "Thank you, but I'm not so sure a night off is a good idea. We should post our guys up, get to work. I don't want anything popping off."

Craig pointed to the other room. "Go on, man. Enjoy yourself. If it does end up popping off, there won't be any nights off for a while. I'm letting Barclay and Troyer enjoy themselves tonight too. Trace and I will go run this deal by Pickens. Manny will run the route, and I'll give Beekman and Stowe protection assignments on Country and the candle shop. Hauerchuk and Wainwright are already at the facility. It's all gravy, baby."

Landers nodded. "Yes. Indeed. Gravy. All right, good luck tonight, boss. I'll enjoy my night off."

Big Trace and Craig Foxx both shook hands with Landers before the scrawny tech guru slunk off into his office with the intention of playing video games for several hours.

Manuel Rezendes sat in the front seat of an idling black 1987 Buick Skylark, chain-smoking Marlboro Lights as he gazed out the windshield over the Scioto River and downtown. Nightfall crept over Columbus, and traffic had thinned. The clouds hung low, and rain sprinkled on and off throughout the evening. The setting sun cast an eerie orange haze over the city, lights going dim in the skyscrapers as people closed shop for the night. The occasional distant siren, the rare blast of car stereos, the low hum of passing cars – although the city was dying down, the night was coming alive.

Manny's shift was just beginning. Riding shotgun was a briefcase that contained rows of unmarked non-sequential bills. Behind him, strapped in the backseat, were rows of candles in two different color-coded pallets. The Buick seats had faded with age, ripped in some areas, speckled with cigarette burn holes. The car had a gritty, acrid smokers' odor. There were two pistols in the car – One unloaded in the glove compartment with an additional magazine, another loaded under the passenger seat.

Manny's cell phone buzzed. He unclipped it from the side of his belt and swiped the screen to reveal the caller, Craig Foxx.

"This is Manny," he said as he addressed his boss.

"Manny, my boy," Craig said. There was also a low "Whassup?" from Big Trace in the background.

"Yes?" Manny said. Although he had been dealing candles for Craig for some time, he still felt a pinch of nervousness in his stomach. In this kind of business, one had to expect the unexpected. Manny preferred having control over his surroundings and comfort. He often wondered why he kept going, but then Craig would sign over a four-figure check for minimal work. Manny's debts were almost paid off. Maybe soon he could buy a new car or get a house. He had to keep going.

"I've received some disturbing news," Craig said. "It appears that hipster kid that showed up to your place for poker the other night isn't who he said he is."

"I knew that. I thought you knew that. Isn't that why you drove off to wreck him and Glencroft?" Manny asked.

There was a pause on the other end. Craig continued speaking, his tone terse.

"I had other motivations," Craig said. "I'll explain everything to you later. But for now, I need you to run some product over to MacKenzie."

Manny sighed in relief. Trevor MacKenzie was one of the syndicate's regular customers. He purchased product at least once, if not twice per week. Beyond business, they had known one another for over a decade.

"Fair enough," Manny replied. "He call in an order yet?"

"Nope," Craig replied. "Spot him a Nova candle. Let him know it's from our... Rewards program. That's all."

Manny shook his head. "Craig, there's something else, isn't there? What else is going on with MacKenzie?"

Craig laughed in response.

"I have reason to believe that Brody Marlowe may have acquired one of our candles. We do not believe he is the type of individual we need to have around one of our candles," Craig explained. "When you are in MacKenzie's residence, keep an eye out for another Nova – Cowtown branded, guise vanilla. Once you get a chance to look around, call me. Whether you see it or not."

Manny nodded. "Will do, cap'n. No actual sales there?"

"Correct," Craig affirmed, "Unless he has cash on hand for more, and you can spare the product. Otherwise, stick to your normal Saturday. You should have Marcum, Phillips, Sivanathan, and Polowicz tonight."

"Right you are, boss," Manny replied. "Say, what are you and Trace about to get into?"

Manny could hear Craig smiling in his voice as he replied.

"We're getting a big shipment; we're securing a big deal. Some good things are on the horizon. We're gonna try to do enough to get Trace out. Keep putting in that kind of work, Manny. I'd like to have you move up in the organization soon."

A wide, yellow grin displayed under a bold black mustache as Manny smiled. "Thank you."

"Oh, and by the way, Manny. Keep your head on a swivel. Let me know if you see anything suspicious."

"It's the meth, isn't it? Is Trevor using again?"

"It doesn't matter. I don't care who else he buys from or what he does as long as he spaces out with us. I just need to make sure he has that candle and that nothing else weird is going on. Got it, Manny?"

"Yes, yes, Craig. Good luck on your deal tonight."

"And yours. Goodbye, Manny."

"G'night, boss."

Manny re-clipped his phone, closed his eyes and sighed. He opened his eyes and gazed at the skyline for a moment before he set his Buick into motion and rolled away into the twilight.

The Skylark rattled to a stop outside of an off-white duplex in the neighborhood of Columbus Hilltop. The neighboring home to one side had wooden planks nailed up over the windows, the door decorated with bright orange zoning and dereliction notices. The home to the other side was a burned-out husk. It caught on fire over a year ago and had not yet been repaired or demolished.

Manny swung his legs out of the car, stood slowly, and cracked his neck before he unloaded a suitcase and slipped a loaded pistol into his waistband, careful to pull his sport coat over the bump it formed. He shut the door quietly, kept it unlocked, and crept toward the duplex.

One side of the home was dark, whereas the one to the right had some sign of activity. The upstairs window glowed light blue, with occasional bright flashes and some muffled laughter and noise. MacKenzie and his deadbeat roommate were probably playing *Grease and Ambition*, Manny concluded. He crept to the front door and knocked on it – three sharp raps. He waited a moment after no response before knocking again, this time a good bit louder. Another moment passed, but there was no response. He sighed and walked to the side of the home, easing between it and the burned-out abandonment next door. He popped open a rusty gate latch at the short fence and walked around back, hearing the laughter and commotion continue from upstairs.

The back porch, damp to the touch, was slick from the day's rains. There were multiple black trash bags out, a couple of which were presumably ripped open by local vermin, fast food bags, and cigarette boxes strewn around them. The rest were tied shut, with no sign of damage.

Manny pulled open the screen door and knocked on the wooden, weather-worn door behind it. It was not shut all the way. It slipped open with a creak.

"Hello? Trevor? Sean?" Manny hollered inside. He waited a moment... No response again. He stepped into the house after a cursory glance over his shoulder.

The back room served dual purpose as the kitchen and dining room. To say it was a pigsty was an understatement. There wasn't even a trash can. There were about a half-dozen garbage bags set sporadically atop broken-up and moldy tile in various states of fullness. The light was off when he entered, but it would flicker on and off randomly, accompanied by a clicking sound every time. Fast food bags adorned the counters, sauce and liquid spilled all around, empty liquor bottles and full ashtrays all about. There was a pungent stench in the air and a stale quality about it. Manny coughed back a gag from the feeling – as if the moisture was sucked from his throat. He reached into the inner jacket of his sport coat to produce his old pale blue face mask. He wrapped it around his ears and gleefully pressed his nose and mouth into the familiar fabric to subdue the aroma.

Manny looked for any sign of the candle Craig Foxx had mentioned. He brushed aside bags from every major chain; McDonald's, Burger King, Wendy's, Taco Bell. Manny flipped over an empty case of Natty Light and shook it before he tossed it aside. He even opened the fridge, seeing naught but spoiled milk, empty egg cartons, and several beers. No luck. Manny came upon a White Castle bag, and as he moved it, even through his mask, he caught a whiff of onion and jalapeno. Realizing he hadn't eaten since he watched the big game earlier, he felt hunger pangs in his stomach. He fished into the bag and tossed aside some trash before he found several uneaten cheeseburgers. Manny pulled down his mask and let it dangle off one ear. He smacked back a bit of drool before fishing out a cheeseburger. Manny closed his eyes and went in for a bite.

A white-hot flash of pain exploded in the side of Manny's face, and the next thing he tasted was tile and grit. Blood poured from the corner of his mouth. He looked up to see Trevor MacKenzie, the Canadian's googly eyes bloodshot and wildly unfocused. Trevor brandished a black pistol and waved it toward the back door.

"Get out, bud. Go on. I don't want you in here," Trevor snarled.

Manny hadn't quite caught his bearings. He sat up, his jaw throbbing in pain. He spat out blood and ran his tongue across his teeth to make sure none fell out.

"Trevor, dude, it's me. Manny. What the hell?" Manny reached for his suitcase.

Trevor kicked the suitcase to the side, keeping the pistol trained on Manny.

"I know who you are. Get out. I didn't call you here," Trevor said. "Am I stuttering?"

Manny knelt up, gesturing toward the suitcase. "Craig sent me. He wants me to spot you a Nova for..."

"I don't need your charity!" Trevor screamed at Manny. Trevor picked up the suitcase, hauled off, and struck Manny in the back of the head with it, sending the taller man face-down yet again. Manny yelled and rushed Trevor on all fours. Trevor dropped the suitcase and pistol, caught Manny in a headlock, and dragged him forward, ramming his head into the refrigerator. Manny slumped to the ground and moaned in pain. Trevor delivered a swift kick to the ribs and stepped back. He stood imposingly over the trembling Manny.

"Get out, bud. Go on. More where that came from. Worse where that came from, I could say."

"Dude, what's *wrong* with you?!" Manny screamed as tears welled in his eyes. "Are you on fucking *meth* again? Jesus Christ!"

Manny crawled toward the back door. His head was throbbing with pain while his mind raced with fright and anger. He reached for his waistband to grab his gun. He was going to try to "negotiate" with Trevor in the worst way. With a grip of panic, Manny realized the pistol wasn't there. It must have slipped out during the fray. He turned, planted on his right hip, his vision blurring...

Trevor wielded Manny's loaded pistol, his eyes wide, and his crooked grin wider. Trevor flipped the safety, having realized his good fortune. The only clarity in Manny's vision was the barrel of the loaded gun as it focused between his eyes.

"Manny, Manny, Manny... my gun wasn't even loaded. What a great gift you've bestowed me. What a great gift you've bestowed... Us..."

Manny felt tears well up in his eyes. "Trevor, what's the meaning of this? Dude, put the gun down! I'm not even trying to sell. I'm here to give..."

"And given you have done," Trevor responded as he pressed the cold steel against Manny's sweat-soaked forehead. "Give me your phone."

"It... the phone... it's in the car..."

"Then leave your keys. Go. Walk. Begone from here."

"Trevor, please... Craig... He will know. He will find you..."

"You really think I worry about... Craig? Manny, Manny, Manny..."

"Don't shoot..."

"You really think I'll... pull the trigger?"

Trevor released his grip and lowered the gun. Manny let out a heavy sigh of relief, slumping to the floor, tears and blood flowing. Trevor put the gun down on the counter and gazed at Manny.

"My old friend... You deserve better than this. I'm sorry," Trevor said. Manny put his throbbing head in his hands and sobbed openly.

"Trevor, you're my friend..." Manny said. "How could you attack me like this?"

Trevor shook his head and looked at the ground, facing away from Manny.

"What the hell's this?!" a creaky voice snapped.

Another man entered the room. His brown hair was cropped short, his bone-thin body covered by a white tank top and baggy jean shorts. The man's scrawny arms were mottled with pockmarks, scars, poorly applied tattoos, the ink black or a faded blue.

"Sean... look who came to visit us," Trevor said to his roommate, friend, and partner in crime: Sean Doan.

"Who's this guy?" Sean squinted his bloodshot eyes, leering closer to the prone and wounded Manny, hooking his thumbs into the belt loops on his shorts. He spat off to the side.

"Manny. He's one of Craig's dealers. Supposedly Craig wants to spot us a Nova," Trevor said, shrugging towards Sean. "I told him I didn't want his charity."

"So... you beat the shit out of him?" Sean said incredulously. "You know we don't say no to free drugs."

Trevor nodded. "But don't you think there's something fishy about that?"

"Still, man, you don't do this to someone just because you disagree with them. Worse yet, you don't do that to someone from a *drug empire*."

"That's where you're wrong, kiddo," Trevor replied.

Sean eyed Manny, whose breathing had finally leveled and whose bleeding had slowed.

"Actually, this dude was hella sloppy. Guarantee he's not their top guy. He's disposable then. Bet you Craig won't miss him," Sean said.

Manny and Trevor shared a quick glance, then looked up at Sean.

Trevor knelt and looked into Manny's eyes. "Old friend. I hate to do this to you. But I'm cranked out of my ever-living mind right now. And I want your drugs. All of your drugs." Trevor leaned in closer, nose to nose. "Your sweet, sweet candles. Your dust and dro. I'm taking it all. And it's going to be so, so sweet to me."

With that, Trevor stood up and stomped heavily on the back of Manny's head three times, hard as possible. Manny laid still, unmoving. Trevor and Sean watched in anticipation as finally his torso rose and fell, almost subtly, the man still alive but wholly unconscious.

"Shit, Trev, I can't believe we finally pulled this. What do we do now?" Sean asked.

"We flip the merch and go straight," Trevor replied. "I know this dude's rounds by heart. Marcum, Phillips, Sivanathan, Polowicz. I know all of them. We just deliver for him, then finally go off the grid. Get outta here."

"You must not be too cranked if you're talking about going straight!" Sean exclaimed. "Come on, man. Why's that even a thought? Just think about how spaced we can get with all the shit in his car!"

"Well, Sean," Trevor responded, "I really want to do independent film. It's time to finally split and make those shows I've been telling you about. I think we can make some badass stuff. Especially if we're spaced! Come on, man, let's partner up. Make something real."

"Flipping the syndicate's shit out of your donut truck hasn't made you enough?"

"Sean, my friend... have you seen my student loan statements?"

"Student loans. Ha. Look where those got you." Sean gestured broadly at the squalor around them.

Sean looked back and forth between Trevor and the prone Manny Rezendes, then back behind him towards the central part of the home, then back to the door, then back to Trevor. He sweated and distractedly pulled at his own clothing before clapping his hands once in epiphany.

"Compromise. Let's get really cranked, then we'll work from there." Sean said.

Trevor sniffed and looked around, then nodded. "Deal. I'll get his pallets in a minute. Meantime, what should we do about him?"

Sean paced around for a minute and swung his arms back and forth. He gazed at the ceiling and then leaned on the counter, running his bony hands through his thinning, short-cut hair.

"I got it!" Sean exclaimed. "Look, we need to get rid of the dealer, and we need to get rid of the bitch. I think this could be one of them get two birds stoned at once things. We can't get our prints on this any more than we already have. We can't get caught dumping or killing this fool. The bitch has been running interference on too much lately, and I'm bored with her. She'd do anything I say. Maybe with her out of my hair, we can get really cranked up and maybe even rock with your idea and split this town."

Trevor leaned against the refrigerator with his eyes closed for a moment. He turned to Sean, nodded with a snaggly grin, and his reddened eye googled almost to the point of no return.

"Perfect! Let's throw him in the trunk, grab his candles, cell, and crank, and have your old lady drive him to the river. We'll put a call out on her, maybe through Barclay or Troyer, that will be that, and we'll get really cranked tonight. Tomorrow we'll split for Nawakwa or Slade City," Trevor said with uncharacteristically focused eyes.

"Yes sir," Sean said. "I still have some buddies up in Youngstown who can help us if things go sideways. Now, let's get this dude loaded up – and then *we* can get loaded up."

CHAPTER NINE

Lyndsey de Rueda sat at a makeshift desk in a basement, made of a fold-out card table with her laptop computer and all manner of general clutter atop it. She was cross-legged in a steel chair, noise-canceling headphones wrapped around her dark-haired head, the gloomy tones of rock band Porcupine Tree filling her ears. She could not hear any of the commotion upstairs that occurred between Trevor MacKenzie, Manuel Rezendes, or her boyfriend, Sean Doan. Lyndsey, encumbered by the weight of these hustlers and their schemes, was finding any escape she could from her own mind and her drifting reality. Tonight, she listened to one of her favorite albums via stream and looked through online galleries of treasured lost memories.

Now that Lyndsey had finally befriended Jimmy Glencroft again on social media, she could see all their old pictures together, ones in which she had previously been untagged. One of she and Jimmy atop an old Ferris wheel at an amusement park on the coast, the neon lights bright in the background. Another yet was of them with their old high school journalism class, a formerly tight-knit crew that has since separated far enough to span the entire globe. She looked through the dozen or so pictures fondly, recalling how close of friends they used to be before his girlfriend drove a wedge between them and Jimmy had not the heart to fight, continually frustrated with Lyndsey and her choice to maintain a relationship with Sean Doan, whom Jimmy had seen as an inferior partner for her.

Lyndsey reflected about Sean for a moment, running her hand over a bruise on her upper arm. She caught a reflection of herself on the computer screen. Her eyeshadow and mascara style had been adjusted to account for a small cut and bruising below her eye.

I'm overdue for an escape. This thought punched through the reverie, and Lyndsey closed her eyes, imagining what her life would be like if she hadn't gone through these years of abuse, addiction, and resentment.

Just as she had nestled comfortably into the music, Lyndsey heard a thundering boom at the door behind her, and she fell out of the steel chair, her laptop clattering against the floor beside her.

Lyndsey winced as both Sean and their disrespectful junkie roommate, Lyndsey's childhood friend Trevor, burst into the basement. *They're here for trouble,* she realized as she saw the wild-eyed expressions on their faces.

"We got a score, dollbaby, the biggest score yet," Sean said as he flared his arms out.

"What our dear friend means is that we have *found* a score; I don't want him to imply with his poor enunciation that we *gotta* score, which means that we *have* to score, which we will anyway..." Trevor rambled, white foamy bits coming out of the corners of his mouth.

"Shut the hell up," Sean said as he tossed Trevor against a wall. Trevor slumped against it with a crooked grin on his face.

Lyndsey staggered to her feet, using the folding table to steady herself, glancing to her laptop. Thankfully it was not damaged when it fell off the table. Her gaze turned back to Sean.

"Look, baby, it's great; we came upon a bunch of those candles and some crank! We're gonna flip it and dip back home. Or just do a ton of drugs. But I don't know. Isn't that exciting, though, baby?!" Sean went to embrace Lyndsey, and just as she had become accustomed to, he was overly aggressive and intrusive. He slapped her posterior before clutching her tightly, rocking back and forth, his skin filmy to her touch as she passively returned the embrace.

"Yeah, Sean, that's great..." Lyndsey said flatly. In Sean's current state, he couldn't read her tone. Otherwise, he would realize that she really was not that into this revelation.

"We just need to run an errand real quick. A favor, see. I got you, dollbaby. Do you think you could help us out?" Sean said. He grabbed Lyndsey's cheeks and pressed his nose to hers. "You love me, right? You'd do anything for me?"

Lyndsey meekly nodded. *I'd only do anything for you so you wouldn't hurt me again.*

"Yes, green bean, I'd do whatever you needed of me," she replied.

Sean smiled at her widely.

"Baby, I need you to hide a car. Destroy it. Something. Anything."

Lyndsey raised her eyebrows. "You stole a car?"

Sean shrugged. "Stole. Came upon it. Have it. Shit don't matter. It's hot, though. Can you do this for me, baby?"

Lyndsey sighed. "We're both on probation, babe. We can't be doing this. We have to get out of this lifestyle before something happens."

Sean paced for a second before he came back forward, putting his face up against Lyndsey's again. He put a hand to her cheek, kissing her nose before he looked in her eyes once more.

"Listen, babydoll. I won't do all the drugs. Maybe a little crank to keep me going, maybe light one candle. It's all good. I was doing that tonight anyway. But if you do this for me, I promise you this, we go straight. Finally. No more drugs, no more crime, no more fighting, no more rehab. You get rid of this car, we go straight, it's over. We can start a family; we can get married. Let's do this, baby. Let's get out of this," Sean pleaded.

"We can do some independent film," Trevor muttered from across the room, to no acknowledgement.

Lyndsey sighed more deeply this time. "Sean, I don't know. You've said this before. We've tried schemes like this before. It never works. It always ends the same. You either go to jail, go broke, overdose, or hurt me. How do I know this is the last one? How do I know you are telling the truth? Why can't *you* do this?"

Sean threw his arms wide and paced in a slow wide circle, shaking his head. "Why can't I do this? *Why can't I do this*?!" Baby, it's a *SUNDAY*! I'm cranked out of my goddamn skull! Besides, if you get caught, it's only thirty days minimum. No big. If I get caught, I'm off to the stir. I can't do this, baby. That's cold turkey. That's awful, that's two years, I can't be out two years! What about you, baby? How would you get on?"

Sean stopped pacing and walked over to Lyndsey, looking her right in the eye, tears welling in his own.

"You wouldn't leave me, baby? *You* wouldn't hurt *me* like that, would you? Please don't leave me, I'd kill myself without you! You know that!"

Sean flinched once, then stepped back and kicked the steel chair across the basement. Lyndsey winced, and Trevor fell over.

"I'd fucking kill myself and take everyone with me, baby. I'm nothing without you, and you're nothing without me. We're a team. We need to keep fighting."

Sean walked back to Lyndsey and put his arms around her softly, cooing, "Shh, shh... it's okay, baby... listen. Just one last go. I promise. I'll sell some of these drugs; I'll buy you a diamond ring. I'll get that job, and we'll go straight. Come on, baby, one more try?"

Lyndsey blinked away a tear, at first reluctant to embrace Sean, before she gave up and fell into him, her makeup smeared.

"Yes, green bean... but you have to mean it. This has to be my last run," Lyndsey acquiesced.

Sean smiled wide and smacked her shoulder.

"WHOO! That's my babydoll! That's my ride or die. Hell yeah. That's why I love you. You always come through. Thank you, darlin'!"

Sean reached into his pocket, fished out the keys to Manny Rezendes' Buick, and thrust them into her hands. He closed her hands around it and kissed her hard on the forehead.

"Now go, baby. Ditch these wheels and make your green bean a happy man!"

Lyndsey returned a single kiss, then nodded at Trevor and turned to rush up the stairs.

Trevor staggered up. "Wait, Lytz! Hold up a second," he said as she stopped at the bottom step. He lurched forward as he reached in his waistband.

"It's dangerous to go alone. Take this," Trevor offered as he handed over his pistol.

Lyndsey looked at the gun, then back to Trevor, then at the gun, and back again.

"You know, the last time I used one of these, it was trouble," Lyndsey said. "Are you sure about this?"

Trevor nodded. "No serials. Just ditch it if anything gets hot, and you can make it safe without. Now be safe... *babydawwwl.*"

Lyndsey stared at her friend for a long moment before muttering a thank you, tucked the pistol into the back waistband of her sweats, and trotted up the steps.

Sean turned to Trevor after the outside door had been slammed shut.

"Trev, get ahold of Barclay. He'll be the one to take care of this. Manny's his boy. He'll wipe everything clean one way or another." Sean said.

Trevor raised his eyebrows. "Sure he won't say anything to Foxx or Trace?"

Sean shook his head. "Manny's his boy, like I said. He will keep this under wraps. Where do you think she will take the car? Downtown, the country, where?"

Trevor leaned forward, putting his face down into his hands, thinking as he recalled all the bodies of water he had seen, been to with Lyndsey, knew that she knew would be secluded...

"Barclay's actually the right man to call. I'll get him now. He should be down at the pub," Trevor said.

"Oh, I see... the quarry, right?! I know ya'll hung out there with Glencroft back in the day," Sean recalled.

"Yes, yes... it's a little too easy to hide shit there, trust."

"And Trev... the gun? We're in trouble if Barclay gets hurt, or worse."

Trevor grinned his wide maniacal grin, teeth all a-snaggle as his eye twitched involuntarily.

"Unloaded. She's up crime creek without her paddle," he snarled.

Sean slapped Trevor's shoulder with a triumphant whoop. "All right! Now call Barclay and get your lighter, man. We've got candles and crank to light up!"

"You're not going to believe this, Boss," Mirko Pavlovic said as he leaned down behind the console of his navy-blue Ford Taurus so as not to be seen. He breathed heavily, having had to dash back to the car after his cover was nearly blown.

"What? What could have possibly gone wrong?" a sharp, tinny voice barked back from the other end of the cell phone.

"It's not necessarily wrong. But the dealer I'm following? He got beat up and thrown in the back of his own car. His first customers whooped him and took his work. Now they're sending this girl to dispose of him and the car, it seems." Mirko replied.

"Shit." A long pause. "Thank you, Cody. Stay on the girl and the dealer. What did the thugs do with the drugs, eh?"

"I couldn't hear much, but it sounds like they're going to do some of them, then take the rest and sell them. I think they're going to skip town."

"Smart on them, eh?" the voice said on the other end. "I'll put Jody on their tail to keep an eye on them, maybe see if they can intercept some of the work. Discreet, of course. We can't go loud just yet."

Mirko nodded. He peered over the console to see Manuel Rezendes' Buick backing out, lights turning on, then slowly turning onto the road.

"Boss, I have to move. The girl's driving off now. Any chance of interference?"

"Absolutely zero. Good work, Cody. Now don't run any interference of your own. Just watch. I appreciate you."

The phone clicked off, Mirko Pavlovic turned the Ford's engine on, then followed Lyndsey de Rueda from a distance, thinking as he drove.

I really wish they gave us cooler code names...

Not even a block behind Mirko Pavlovic, codename Cody Barlow, a similarly European and similarly titled Brody Marlowe ignited a Prius and pulled out to tail the tail. Real name Drago Zupan, he was on the phone with the very same boss as Mirko had been a minute before.

"Brody, my boy, we would have never had this opportunity without you," the boss said, with a warmer tone than he used when addressing Mirko.

"Thanks, Boss," Drago said. "You're the one that pinned Rezendes as the easiest in. This is your doing too."

"I appreciate you giving Cody the lead on this one. He's green and needs to fly solo for a bit. But we can't let him completely out of our sights. I just can't help but feel his instincts are a bit flawed, and my hunch is that he could blow a simple tail job. Don't let that happen, and if it does... clean it up."

"Will do, Boss. Jody and Zoey... what are their assignments tonight?" Drago asked.

"I'm rerouting Jody from surveilling the candle shop to an intercept job on the junkies. Zoey is trailing Pinky and The Brain right now. She's got eyes on them outside what could be a big meet. Will probably follow them or this new target, Swiss Cheese. Big money guy. I'll have intel on this for you tomorrow."

"Perfect," Drago responded. "We're about to get on the interstate. I'm going offline. I'll get ahold of you."

"Thanks again, Brody," the boss said as Drago flipped his new burner phone shut. He had barely gotten it in time to call the boss and set up this mission. *Who would have thought buying a prepaid phone from a convenience store would be such a hassle?*

Rezendes' Buick, driven by Lyndsey; Mirko's Ford, and Drago's Prius formed a spaced out and unwitting convoy as they hooked a right onto I-70 West from the downtrodden Hilltop neighborhood. The Columbus skyline was now resplendent in shades of bright white and orange as night had taken hold.

Winslow Barclay tilted back the giant mug of beer and chugged heartily, rivulets of foamy alcohol spilling out from the sides, getting sopped into his brown whiskers. He slammed the mug down on the counter, shaking his head and grinning heartily. 6'5", brawny and bearded, the enormous Barclay wore a white t-shirt two sizes too small, under an unzipped hoodie two sizes too big.

"Thanks for the round, kid," Barclay said to a younger man beside him. "It's been so long; your dart game really needs some work."

"Gee, thank *you*, Barc. Say, speakin' of which, you hear about the football game earlier tonight?" he asked.

"Nah, I couldn't care less. I'm not into watching other people's jobs. I'm into doing my own."

"This was different, though. I guess a big fight broke out between the two teams."

"Still couldn't care less. I'm not into watching other people's fights. I'm into having my own."

"You're a tough nut to crack, Barc."

"That whole sentence made me feel like a giant friggin' squirrel," Barclay replied. "Don't call me Barc again, or you'll get the next round, win or lose."

Barclay's pocket buzzed. He excused himself from his friend and pulled out his burner phone. *This is my off night. I'm trying to catch a different kind of buzz. This better be good...*

"Barclay?"

"...Trevor?"

"Yeah, man, it's me," Trevor MacKenzie said on the other line. "I don't mean to bug you, but it's about Manny."

Barclay paused, eyes widening.

"Deal went south. Some bitch knocked him out, threw him in the trunk, and drove off," Trevor said.

"You're kidding me!"

"No, dude. Trust me on this. We think she's going to dump him in the quarry after she takes his work."

"Shit shit shit. Did you let Craig or Trace know?" Barclay asked.

"They'd probably come for me for letting it happen, but she's crazy. She pulled a gun on me. I'd hurry. She's probably almost there. I'm worried about Manny."

"Me too. Thanks for letting me know. I'm down the road. I'm on my way."

Half-buzzed and wholly floored by the news, Winslow Barclay dashed from the front of the pub. He knocked into a couple patrons and spilled someone's beer, but didn't stop nor care. Within a few seconds, he was in the drivers' seat of his little two-seat truck, engine rumbling to life as he peeled out of the gravel lot and onto the main road, cutting off traffic and squealing into the Columbus night.

Lyndsey de Rueda's heart felt like it was going to beat right out of her chest. Her hands were firmly grasped around the wheel of Manuel Rezendes' Buick Skylark. The stench from Manny's chain-smoking made her gag, despite her own smoking habits.

Little did she know that in the trunk, Manny was stirring. He was groggy and in severe pain, a concussion evident as head pains wracked him and his ears rang incessantly. Gagged, blindfolded, and bound, he tried to thrash against his bonds but to no avail. They were weakly tied, as the drug-addled Trevor and Sean were not exactly boy scouts in behavior nor in knot-tying talents, but Manny's injury kept him from fighting at full strength. He could barely form any coherent thoughts. He had a vague concept of painful existence, and all he knew was that moving around would keep him alive and give him a fight.

Lyndsey pulled up to the gates at the Faraway Stay apartment complex. Usually, these gates were flung wide open, but tonight they were closed. She stopped the car at the top of the turn-in, halfway on the main road, looking behind her as one by one, two cars came to idle. First a Ford car, then a Prius. She cursed in frustration, then walked up to the Ford to see if they had a key card.

The window rolled down, and Lyndsey came eye to eye with Mirko Pavlovic.

"Excuse me, sir, but do you have a key card?"

"Koliko za jedan sat, devojko?" Mirko replied with a grin.

"What? English, please?"

"Govorim bosanske besmislice namerno. Nisi ništa mudriji."

"UGH!!" Lyndsey tried to pantomime a key card by sliding her flat hand back and forth, but Mirko just grinned at her. The Prius honked at them repeatedly to get them to hurry. Lyndsey pantomimed the keycard to the Prius driver, who just looked on and furiously honked some more. She threw up her arms in exasperation as a truck pulled in behind the line of idling cars too. Lyndsey turned and ran back to the front of the Buick. She slammed the car in reverse, nearly hitting the Ford Taurus behind her as she peeled off and away from the apartment complex.

"Of all the nights! That gate is almost always wide open. Damn it, damn it!" Lyndsey yelled as she accelerated down the road and onto a bridge over the Scioto River.

That's it. The river. Drive the car into the river. The current will suck it under! Nobody will see it there!

Lyndsey was so excited by her sudden revelation that as she peeled left onto Riverside, she didn't notice the two operatives trailing her, and shortly behind them, a half-drunk drug dealer in a pickup truck determined to recover his friend.

Moments later, she pulled into a loop road in a city park. Not seeing headlights ahead, she made her move. Unfortunately for Lyndsey, she had not seen the cars remaining shortly behind her due to a rise in the terrain. Just as she passed two low brick buildings and just out of eyesight of the road, the convoy emerged.

Lyndsey shut off the headlights and drifted between the two buildings on either side of the loop, idling the car down a descent and alongside the Scioto River. She kept slow, creeping the vehicle along, looking for opportunities to push it in. Lyndsey thought about a ramp beside a boathouse but was afraid it would be too shallow. She continued to search as she drove upstream, the river wide to her left and an embankment to her right, lines of trees separating the view from the road.

Mirko Pavlovic turned into the park, dimming his lights as he edged forward. He drew a pistol from the glove compartment and silently followed suit. Mirko could not see Lyndsey and the Buick yet, knowing to keep enough distance. He would catch up with her in due time. Mirko eyed parking lots as he drifted past, considering parking at a distance and then running to catch up. He decided against the matter; he wanted to get as close as possible, as soon as possible. He drove on.

Drago Zupan drove onto the park lane next. He dimmed his lights sooner than the others. Having been stationed by the Posse in Marysville for some time, he had been by this area a few times to play disc golf. He mostly knew the lay of the land but had forgotten one detail that apparently both Lyndsey and Mirko had overlooked: the two buildings at the top of the drive were patrol houses.

Griggs Marine and Reservoir Patrol sat atop the rise overlooking the dam and were responsible for night patrols both on the water and along the trails. Drago cursed as he surveilled the area, seeing several parked patrol cars and trucks and even a dry-docked patrol boat. He promptly pulled into a nearby spot, killed the engine, and flipped open his phone to contact Mirko. *This is risky, but I'd imagine he has his ringer off now. But then again, the idiot missed driving by a patrol station.*

"Dra.. er... Brody? What do you want? I'm on a job," Mirko said.

"I know. So am I," Drago replied. "Look, you idiot. Boss had me tail you. He knew you weren't ready."

There was a massive sigh on the other end. "Shit. Well, what the hell do you want? I have this under control, brother."

"I don't think you do," Drago said. "Both you and the woman drove through a patrol station. This park is monitored. Neither of you are safe right now."

"The woman? What, wait... how long have you been following me?"

"All night. I'm in a Prius. I'm parked by the patrol station. I'll keep my eyes on it for you. Just make sure the woman doesn't spot us. We need this to play out, but we need to know what happens with the body... and the woman."

"...Gee, thanks, Brody. I could not have done this without you," Mirko said with a heavy dose of sarcasm as the phone clicked off.

Drago turned his attention to the rearview mirror. He watched intently, looking for any sign of movement or life, sighing in annoyance at the situation as he waited.

Meanwhile, Barclay didn't even slow down for the first parking lot. He was intimately familiar with this stretch of road, the river, and the city park. So many times, he'd sneak down to these parking lots and trails to smoke a bowl or get to know women, literally and in the Biblical sense. He sped up, planning to cut Lyndsey off at the dock by the bridge. Barclay blew past red lights and gunned the truck down an incline to the dockside parking lots. Lights still on, he pulled up to see a thin brunette woman in a t-shirt and sweats, leaving a Buick Skylark backed up to the top of the ramp. She looked up at the truck, shielding her eyes, her mouth slacked open as she stood frozen at the open door.

Mirko watched from behind his parked car on the far end of the lot. He cursed under his breath and watched the truck squeal to a stop seventy yards ahead, its lights on. He flipped open his phone, immediately dialing Drago, struggling to contain his breath as it sped up.

"We have company," Mirko said in a hush.

"Just watch. See it play out," Drago replied. "We cannot get involved. Keep me on the line, feed me updates."

"Any sign of 5-0?"

"No life yet. Just stay kept."

"Some guy is getting out of the truck. I'm muting your voice and trying to get a little closer. Stay tuned," Mirko said as he tapped a button on the phone and snuck closer to the confrontation, keeping to the grass along the knoll and keeping a hand on his gun. From this vantage point, dangerously close, he could see and hear almost everything.

Barclay slammed the door shut on his truck and came barreling towards Lyndsey, barking at her, having at least a foot in height and 150 pounds on her.

"WHERE'S MANNY?!" Barclay screamed as he hoisted Lyndsey into the air and up against the windshield awkwardly. She whimpered as her body hit against the body of the car, looking up at Barclay.

"I don't know, where *is* Manny?" Lyndsey asked.

"Where's Manny?! Where's my friend? Is he in the trunk? Don't make me ask you again! No funny business!"

Lyndsey trembled, her skin turning pale. She didn't respond this time.

"Don't move!" Barclay demanded before he shoved her across the front of the Buick, where she crumpled down on the other side with a thud against the concrete. The car was in park, right above where the boat ramp started its decline. Barclay moved around the back and knocked on the trunk.

"Manny? Are you in there, bud? Knock if you can hear me," he said as he put his ear to the trunk. No response. Barclay rushed to the front of the car, reached down, and popped the trunk lever. He nearly slipped and fell down the ramp as he sprinted back to the rear of the car and opened the trunk.

Manuel Rezendes lay still, gagged, blinded and bounded, unresponsive. Barclay leaned into the trunk, openly crying at this point, and held his fingers to Manny's neck. It took a moment, but he felt a pulse, faint and infrequent.

"Can you hear me, Manny? Are you okay? It's Barclay... Listen, I'll get us out of here..."

Lyndsey, ignoring Barclay's warning to stay down, rolled over and slumped against the side of the car. She could still feel the pistol tucked into her back waistband. *I need to get out... This will be my way out...*

Lyndsey staggered to her feet, reached behind, and drew the pistol. She felt around it to look for what she thought was the safety and changed its position, assuming it was ready to fire. She was careful with putting her finger on the trigger as she aimed the pistol at Barclay, the towering man still rummaging for Manny.

As Mirko watched Lyndsey get thrown across the hood of the Buick, he felt a red-hot seething rage surge through his skin from the chest outward. A thousand memories of his abusive family overseas flashed all at once as his vision tunneled on Lyndsey. She was an unwitting pawn in this game. His only thought was to stop Barclay and keep him from hurting Lyndsey more. He had no ideas of retaliation, politicking, escalation, territory, or anything more significant. Mirko wanted to be the hero. He slunk behind a light pole, ducking down behind the concrete base, his own pistol drawn and safety off.

Barclay looked up as he worked on freeing Manny, who was now awake, groggy, and entirely out of sorts. He felt a kick in his chest when he saw Lyndsey standing at the front of the car, fumbling with a pistol. *The one thing more dangerous than an experienced criminal is an inexperienced criminal*, he thought as he reached inside his hoodie to draw his own pistol, stepping forward, setting stance, and pointing it directly at Lyndsey.

"Get on the ground!" Barclay yelled, raising the barrel to point at her face. Lyndsey shook her head, crying, now wrapping her finger around the trigger.

"I said get on the ground... *bitch!*"

"Nobody calls me a bitch!" Lyndsey yelled back in defiance.

"You're damn right, they don't," Mirko said as he came walking up, behind and to the left of Lytz, hoisting up his pistol towards Barclay's face.

Barclay instinctively turned and shot Mirko in the face, a spray of red splattering behind him as he fell to the ground, dead on impact. Ready for Lyndsey's response, he ducked low and ran into her, tackling her before she could shoot. They fell to the ground hard, Lyndsey's head banging off the concrete, Barclay taking her breath away with his weight and force. Her pistol clattered to the side.

Both individuals breathed heavily, stunned at the event. Barclay rolled off Lyndsey, commanding her to stay on the ground, as he went to go check Mirko's body. The now-faceless man was dressed in a nondescript black dress shirt and matching slacks. Barclay looked him over and patted his body down, careful not to look too much at what used to be a human head. No wallet, no identification, nothing else was in his pockets... except for a phone.

"Cody? Cody?! I heard a shot. Everything okay?" a voice was yelling on the other end. Barclay held up the phone and put it on speaker so he could hear it more clearly.

"Cody. You have to get out. 5-0 is moving. You have two minutes, tops. Meet me at my place. GO. GO!"

Barclay turned around and threw the cell phone into the river with a splash. He looked south downriver towards the patrol office, listening for anything breaking the silence. Barclay then heard the whine of police sirens echoing over the river, momentarily transfixed by the sound. He leaned down over Lyndsey, whose eyes were wide with panic.

"I don't know who you are, and I don't care. Get out of here. I never want to see you again," Barclay implored.

Lyndsey looked around in wide circles and staggered to her feet. Barclay nodded toward Mirko's parked car in the distance.

Lyndsey took the cue, turned, and sprinted for the parked car in the near distance, the sirens growing louder. There was a brief feeling of relief as she heard its engine still running. She threw open the door and promptly threw the Ford Taurus into gear, squealing into drive, initially heading back in the direction in which she came. She saw the blue and red lights throbbing about a half-mile downriver and realized she was heading in the wrong direction. She spun the car around in a wide circle, nearly going off the pavement and into the water before she remembered that the road continued under the bridge and back to Riverside She gunned the accelerator as the world became a blur around her. Lyndsey nearly clipped Barclay's truck as she churned over bumps and rises, getting airborne and almost losing control multiple times, her knuckles white over the steering wheel.

Barclay hefted Manny out of the trunk and over his shoulders, the barely conscious man tall and heavy, burdensome for even the colossal Barclay. No time to act or reason, Barclay threw Manny in a fireman's toss into the bed of his truck, scrambling back around to the front. He glanced over his shoulder, seeing the red and blue lights now refracting off trees and water. He figured he had less than a minute. Now thinking somewhat more clearly, Barclay picked up Mirko Pavlovic's corpse, the smaller man much easier to carry than Manny.

Barclay went to the front of Manny's Buick and used his foot to pry open the driver's side door, which was not fully closed shut. He tossed the body awkwardly into the front, Mirko tumbling into the passenger side, upturned, his feet to the sky. Barclay turned the key to the engine, rumbling to life after a considerable rev. He quickly rolled down the driver's side window before leaning across the corpse, doing the same to the passenger's side. He shifted the car into neutral and backed quickly out of the driver's side door as the car rolled backward into the river.

Barclay glanced back downriver. He could see the form of a single police car now coming into view. He heard two sets of sirens, one immediate; another one in the far distance, coming from the direction of downtown. Barclay looked back towards the Buick. It was mostly in the water, starting to tilt backward, caught up in the shallows. It wasn't sinking all the way, rather conspicuous as it listed at a 45-degree angle. Barclay ran at it, leaping into the air, giving the front fender as hard of a shove as he could before he fell at its resistance, finding himself splashing into the shallows of the river and smacking his knee hard on the pavement of the boat ramp.

Furious, scared, hurting, and soaking wet, Barclay stumbled back up, slogged towards his truck, and hopped in.

Barclay shifted it into reverse, careening back into the parking lot and turning, looking ahead in the direction that Lyndsey sped off to. There was a dull thud as the unsecured and unconscious Manny tumbled in the truck bed.

I hope that didn't make things worse... Hang on, Manny.

Barclay sped off as fast as the truck would allow, looking up in the rearview mirror to see a cop now hard on his tail. He was paying more attention to the pursuit than the road ahead. Barclay drove off-road, the truck bouncing over the grass as he veered to the right. He shifted his focus to the ground ahead. Riverside Drive was just ahead, between two trees. The knoll flattened out the further he got from the dock and bridge and could now be safely crested.

Barclay drove between the two trees, one ripping off his right-side rearview mirror, but the truck escaped otherwise unscathed.

The cop wasn't so lucky. The patrol car clipped the tree to the left with force, sending the vehicle spinning onto Riverside, now with traffic closing in from both directions. The cop, unharmed, corrected the car's path, but by this time, it was impossible to see Barclay's truck

85

due to vehicles passing in both directions, several of which slowed down nearby to watch the proceedings and check on him.

Lyndsey de Rueda got away, speeding down Riverside Drive and into the night. She passed cop cars heading in the opposite direction, and every time she did, she would gasp deeply and nearly pass out from the sheer panic that consumed her mind and body. Yet, she sped on her way, no direction known, just striving to escape it all, to get away from the crime and the murder and the drugs and the law.

Winslow Barclay got away, bringing the truck to a stop once he felt the coast was clear, parking it behind a familiar bar near campus where he would sell product and where he could trust most people who could potentially see him. He climbed into the back of the truck, rushing to check on his dear friend. Barclay hugged Manny close, the large bearded man crying genuine tears, realizing the amount of pain and trouble Manny was in, constantly checking his pulse and breath, knowing he couldn't take him to a hospital, knowing the syndicate's veterinarian was on the other side of town.

Manuel Rezendes slipped away, dead from head trauma and oxygen loss, in the embrace of his sobbing friend. When Barclay felt Manny's pulse stop, he performed resuscitation, pressing on his torso in contracted rhythms and repeatedly checking his heart. After minutes of fruitless CPR, Barclay gave up and laid his head down on Manny's chest, his tears sliding into Manny's plaid shirt.

Drago Zupan was not so lucky. When the lone stationed patrolman took off towards the riverside skirmish, Drago took a silent and distant pursuit in his Prius.

When Drago saw the cop chase Barclay into the distance, he pulled up close to the dock. He abandoned the car and ran to the edge of the water. The Buick had sunken more quickly after Barclay drove away, the open window allowing water to rush in and pull the vehicle down. Now only the edge of the rear bumper was above water.

Drago's head spun as for the first time since his earliest days of running party drugs, he felt panic and fear. He spied a handgun lying in the grass close by. He picked it up to inspect it, maybe hide it... but then he looked at the parking lot beyond the tip of the barrel.

A splash of red blood, shattered bone, and smeared gristle decorated the concrete not far in front of him. Mirko was nowhere to be seen. All at once, the wail of sirens and the flashing of lights closed in from all directions, the slamming of car doors and the yelling and pointing of guns, the confusion, and fear and weight of the world coming down.

Drago fell to his knees, put his hands behind his head, and let the pistol fall to the ground. He voluntarily planted his face to the grit of the blacktop, closed his eyes, and prayed for the end.

And the 1987 Buick Skylark slipped away, as close ashore, rights were read, and questions were asked and empires hung in the balance; the rear bumper was finally eclipsed by water and darkness, dragging Mirko Pavlovic and his memories and his secrets to the recesses of time eternal.

CHAPTER TEN

The Bierstube was a small pub in the Gateway district of Columbus, Ohio. Tucked between a larger bar, a carry-out, and an apartment complex, the pub was easy to miss when driving by, even while strolling down High Street. The dive did not draw much of a crowd; college students and young professionals were more likely drawn to the polish and pomp of clubs up the street. Dimly lit by not much more than the big-screen televisions broadcasting sports coverage and with classic rock hits from Billy Joel and Bob Seger dominating the jukebox, the little crowd it did draw were typically hipsters seeking a retro throwback or neighborhood folk who wanted to avoid students. For these reasons, Naev Broadnax preferred "The Stube." He had been a regular there since he was a player at nearby Heartland State.

Anvil sat amidst his fellow regulars, slumped over the bar with a glass of Guinness in his hand. He wasn't intoxicated yet, just sipping away to take the edge off his sadness over the events earlier in the evening. He sighed and took another sip as SportsCenter played on the big screen. Usually, Anvil enjoyed watching highlights of himself, but he wasn't particularly looking forward to what the press had to say after the fight. Hell, he hadn't even seen the replays yet. He took a big drink of his stout.

One of the Sportscenter anchors turned to a close-up camera. "How about that fight in Columbus?!" he exclaimed. A graphic appeared on the screen's left-hand side, a picture of Anvil standing over the motionless J'Shia Beverly, with the caption "FootBRAWL" in bold white text beneath it. Anvil kept his gaze steady as he felt all the eyes in the bar turning towards his sulking form.

"With tensions mounting in their game against the Fargo Rangers, the Columbus Discovery were burdened by multiple cheap shots by Fargo players," the anchor started. Suddenly, the jukebox in the corner came to life, blasting "Jack and Diane" by John Cougar Mellencamp, the music drowning out the coverage. There was a collective groan from the bar regulars, and Anvil spun on his stool to see who was responsible. A man in a bright green hoodie was putting more quarters in.

"Hey, what the hell man, we were trying to watch the highlights!" Anvil yelled at the man. "What gives?"

The man looked up at Anvil. A black eye, a forehead gash, a big smirk, and a light brown beard. It was James Glencroft.

"Jimmy, you gonna come in here and not chill with me, dude?" Anvil walked over and gave Jimmy a hug. "How you holding up?"

Jimmy shook his head. "Let's get drunk." He went straight to the bar, and Anvil followed, the men seating themselves in front of the TV as it showed the slow-motion replay of Anton Treptak's leg injury – the gruesome injury contrasted by the chipper nostalgia of the jukebox.

"I'll have your finest Rolling Rock," Jimmy said to the bartender. He turned to Anvil. "I turned on the jukebox so you didn't have to hear the talking heads run us down. Trust me, man. Sometimes you just don't wanna see yourself or hear what they have to say. I'm sure you'll hear enough from the front office this week." In the background, The Coug extolled the virtues of sucking on chili dogs outside the Tastee Freeze.

Anvil nodded. "I get what you're saying, man. What are you gonna do about finding a job? You gonna go back to Dice Stop?"

Jimmy shook his head. "I'm not ready for that world again. I'm not ready to even talk to Meg yet. I'm sure she's heard the news. Hell, I wouldn't be surprised if one of our dingbat friends has already hit her up about it. Who knows? I ain't got a phone right now."

Anvil nodded and took a gulp of his beer. He glanced at the TV to see himself level Beverly with the helmet-to-helmet hit. "Hey, I actually look kinda badass here Jimmy, what's up?"

Jimmy shook his head as the wave of Rangers descended upon Anvil in the replay, swinging on him indiscriminately before a large lineman tossed him to the ground by his facemask like a 250-pound Olympic hammer throw.

"From badass to baby back bitch. It's all good, man. I didn't fare much better," as the screen focused on Sailor Smash elbow-dropping the pile. "I can't watch the next part; let's go out for a smoke."

The two men rose from their stools and strode to the front of the pub. Anvil kept peeking at the television screens, but Jimmy continued to urge him forward. They stepped out into the night.

Jimmy pulled out a pack of Marlboro No. 27 Blends and a lighter. He offered a cigarette to Anvil. The two sparked up and leaned against the building, watching college students stroll up and down the street. The air hung low and stuffy with collected moisture.

"You think you'll get any kind of fine or suspension for this?" Jimmy said as he flicked his first ash to the ground, gazing down the street absently.

"Fine, yes, suspension, probably not." Anvil coughed before he continued. "They can't suspend every player on both teams, can they? But they sure as hell can fine us. If anyone should be suspended for all this, it should be J'Shia and Malcolm, but you know they won't do it. Those two are money for Fargo. Mon-*ey*."

Jimmy sighed. "Hey, at least we still got poker. Maybe we can make an extra buck or two next week."

Anvil shook his head. "I don't know if I wanna go back. Craig keeps getting shadier and shadier; everyone's more into getting messed up than playing cards... and I don't know if I can take any more of Trevor. If I want to gamble, I can afford to just go to the casino now. I've been meaning to check it out again since it re-opened all the way."

Jimmy nodded understandingly. "Trevor has been a... handful, to say the least."

Anvil pointed toward the road. "Hey, check it out, ain't that Kip?"

Jimmy looked up. A shorter man wearing a light brown jacket with a black hood flipped up walked toward the pub. His hands rested in his pockets as he moved quickly. The man was relatively under-dressed, but Jimmy could see how Anvil recognized him. The hooded man walked around puddles deliberately, wearing dark brown, thin-tipped dress shoes with a luxurious shine. Jimmy laughed.

"Yo, Kip! Whassup?"

The man looked up at Jimmy and then looked back and forth quickly. He loped towards Jimmy and Anvil, making a throat-slash motion toward the two.

"Hush, hush, fellas," Kazdorf said with an unusually straight face. "Listen, listen, don't want the normal folk knowing I'm over here; I don't wanna answer any questions about tonight."

Anvil shrugged. "Everyone in the place knows me, and nobody's bugged me. They've been pretty respectful."

Kazdorf sighed and gestured towards the street, then back toward the apartment complexes nearby. "I don't mean the folks in the bar, man. Normals. Passerby. Don't want them knowing I'm out here tonight. So, don't say my name."

Jimmy raised his eyebrows. "All I said was 'Kip.'"

Kazdorf shook his head. "How many Kips are there? Come on, now. Plus, I'm a celeb, a celeb with a weird name. That's like you saying, 'Yo, Shaq!' You're playin' with fire, bro."

Jimmy leaned back against the building once more. "You're letting your fame go to your head, broski. Besides, there's tons of famous Kips. Maybe they'd think I was talking to Kip Winger or Kip Cameron."

"*Kirk. Kirk* Cameron. Level up, bro. Let's go in and have a drink. I wanna see the highlights."

Jimmy shook his head. "I don't think it's a good idea, fellas. Let's go somewhere they don't have ESPN on."

Kazdorf laughed. "That would also be somewhere I'd be recognized, somewhere with ladies. I'm a sex addict, Jimmy. That would be bad. I'm trying to recover over here. I'm an addict."

"I heard you the first time," Jimmy replied. "Naev, what do you think? Are you ready to watch the highlights?"

Anvil nodded. "I ain't got a problem with the highlights. Yeah, I got thrown, but you got the worse end of it. I should be asking you, Jimmy, are you okay with this?"

Jimmy shrugged. "Eh, I ain't got anything to lose at this point. Let's head in. Maybe it'll be worth a laugh, right?"

Anvil patted him on the back. "That's the spirit. Let's make a drinking game out of it. Every time they show one of our highlights, take a shot."

Kazdorf grinned, perhaps a little too excited about getting inebriated. "Two shots every time it's in slow motion."

The three men shared a hearty laugh. "Deal!" Jimmy said. "And if the anchor gives you a corny nickname, you buy the whole round."

Kazdorf couldn't get in the bar fast enough. "I don't care who buys; I'm just tryna drink!"

"You ever notice... that nobody ever *really* wins drinking games, after all... *hic!*" Jimmy mused to Kazdorf, slurring his words as he leaned on the bar, staring at the last slurp of his Guinness.

Jimmy wasn't expecting so many highlights of himself to be shown, let alone in slow motion. He folded his arms beneath his chin, feeling the muscles in his face droop as he gazed absently at the screen. Jimmy's thoughts rushed, and he felt physically removed from the bar he was leaning on. Jimmy choked back bile as he watched ESPN return from a commercial break. The SportsCenter anchors were just now beginning to run through the night's Top Ten.

"For tonight's FootBrawl out of Columbus, we will actually be doing our nightly Top Ten entirely out of highlights from the fight! Not just the game, but the fight! It was hard picking ten 'best' shots, let alone putting them in order. You can always debate the outcome on your mobile device or computer at our website!"

Kip Kazdorf looked towards Jimmy, grinning from beneath his hood. "Bartender, we're gonna need some more shots over here."

The bartender walked over with a bottle of Jamison. "You sure about that? Your friend looks like he's had enough."

Kazdorf slid a crisp $100 bill across the bar top toward the bartender.

"Ben says he hasn't."

The bartender shrugged, took the bribe, and poured enough shots to make LMFAO blush.

The drinking game had taken a massive toll on the three men. Anvil grinned absently while leaning on the bar and looking around with wide, red eyes. Kazdorf sang obnoxiously, making less than kind remarks toward the few women in the bar, goading them into paying attention to him. Jimmy was entirely out of sorts, choking back bile every now and again. He had a hard time controlling his actions and words, finding himself questioning every move.

At least they didn't give me a nickname, Jimmy thought as he lurched off his barstool and staggered toward the bathroom. Anvil had been referred to as "Devastatin' Naev" and "Naev the Gravedigger" during the top ten alone. There were some highly amusing shots of Kip Kazdorf using capoeira and parkour to deal and dodge the damage. The SportsCenter anchors coined his combat style "Kipoeira" and were already making jokes about him having a future in cage fighting.

Jimmy was most depressed because SportsCenter had to give out his real name while playing his brutally embarrassing highlights. *Why couldn't they have just said "Sailor Smash" and left it at that, rather than calling me "James Glencroft, the man who portrayed Sailor Smash?"* The entire nation now knew his name and his humiliating plight. Again. It was only a matter of time before the National Anthem crap from high school came back up again. He swung open the bathroom door to go puke out his sorrows.

After hurling out orange-brown acidic vomit on his knees for several minutes, Jimmy came to a standing position in front of the mirror in the cramped bathroom. He gained his bearings, turning on the water faucet, splashing his face, and cleaning out his re-opened wound, jagged across his forehead. Jimmy spat a few times, sweating profusely. He noted this was the third time he had looked at his wounded, exhausted face in the mirror while cleaning cuts and pondering life's deeper meanings in the last 24 hours.

After his extended stay in the bathroom, Jimmy swung open the door and made his way back to the bar. *I've mostly been awake for 36 hours,* he thought to himself. Jimmy plopped down next to Kazdorf, sweat coursing down his face. Kazdorf had just tapped out of a call on his cell phone when Jimmy took his seat.

"Ay Naev," Kazdorf said, "Party at Obie's. How's about we get up out this place and turn up?"

"I'm not about that life," Anvil said, shaking his head. Kazdorf smacked him in the shoulder.

"Come on, Naev. Married Naev. Don't be so married. Let's go mix it up."

"For some reason, I'm not feeling like this is a good idea," Anvil replied.

"Come on," Kazdorf continued. "Let's ride. If you don't wanna hang, you can chill in my whip with ol dude over here," he said, nodding toward Jimmy.

Jimmy raised an eyebrow. "Why do I have to chill in the whip? Why can't I go in?"

Kazdorf shook his head. "Exclusive shit going down tonight, brah."

"Mind explaining?"

"Actually," Kazdorf said, "I do mind. Maybe they can let you in, but you can't be doing stupid stuff. Come on boys, let's mount up and get movin'."

"Wake up, Jimmy, we're at the spot."

James Glencroft had no clue how long he had been asleep. He must have needed the rest. He sat up in the back of Kazdorf's white Lexus sedan, rubbing his eyes and wiping off the film of sweat on his forehead, which was beginning to seem omnipresent. Jimmy looked around and couldn't get a grasp of his surroundings. He just knew he was in front of a massive brick house in an isolated, dark area, possibly in a gated subdivision.

"Where are we?" Jimmy asked as he looked around. Anvil was slouched in the passenger seat. Jimmy looked down at his green hoodie, the one piece of clothing he had on him from today that wasn't caked with some combination of sweat, dirt, and blood. The scent of stale alcohol caught his nose sideways and forced him to choke back another retch.

"Obie Hill's pad," Kip said as he swung open the door of his Lexus. "You sure you don't want to keep sleeping, dude? People in here are going to be alpha, and you look like a bum."

"Man, you know I don't care. I just need somewhere softer to lay down. I need to keep my mind off things, too."

Anvil sat up and looked back. "Maybe you can get a lap dance!" he said with a chuckle.

"...A lap dance?! What? What is actually going on tonight?" Jimmy asked as Anvil got out of the car. Jimmy pushed open his own door, feeling pain in his side even with the casual motion.

"Look, after every game, Obie has a party. You know that, you've even been invited. But you never show up because Megan," Kip explained as they walked toward the house. Jimmy limped and Anvil stumbled as they walked among a makeshift parking lot in the house's big yard. There were Rolls Royces, Ferraris, and Jaguars by the dozen.

"There's usually strippers and dancers here. You know, the works," Anvil said. He stepped into a small pit in the yard and tripped over. Kazdorf kept walking ahead while Jimmy checked on Anvil.

"You alright, bro?" Jimmy asked.

"Yeah," Anvil replied. "I'll be alright by next week. We play Austin at home on Monday night. If I even get to play."

"But are you alright now?"

"Fine as I'll ever be."

"Now, about these strippers," Jimmy said, his voice hushed. "I can't be here. Hell, you can't be here. We have girlfriends."

Anvil sighed as they began walking again. "Everyone has a girlfriend here. I'm not cheating, I'm just enjoying the scenery. Maybe you could do with one of the two since Megan has surely dumped you at his point."

Jimmy had a reply, but it was forgotten as he looked up to see Kip Kazdorf sitting on a Lamborghini.

"Kip, what are you doing, man?! Get down from there," Jimmy said, jog-limping over. "You'll get shot doing that."

"Nahhh, he good," came a voice from inside the yellow Lambo. Jimmy didn't even notice someone was inside. He looked inside to see R-Qwan Wallace, the Columbus center. R-Qwan was in his late 30's, one of the most experienced members of the team, a mass of a man, and one of the few who could actually start for one of the more established programs. He rocked a thick beard, a fashionable silken black cap, and even wore sunglasses at night. Kip slid off the roof of the luxury car and stood beside Jimmy.

"I was just reminiscing with Qwan about when he first got this. We were JuCo in the 'Yay Area,' so to speak, back in '07..."

"Rough year," R-Qwan said in his baritone voice.

"Yeah, it was. I barely played, and the guys in front of me weren't that good themselves. Anyway, I barely played, and neither did Qwan here, because of an injury. So, we had some extra off time, he had some money, and we started messing around with cars on the reg," Kazdorf explained.

"This is the car I taught Kip how to ghost ride in," R-Qwan said with a big smile.

"Ghost ride?" Jimmy asked incredulously.

R-Qwan smiled up at Kazdorf, and on cue, they sang together.

"When you get a new car," R-Qwan started.

"And you feelin' like a star," Kazdorf said in a call-and-answer fashion.

"What you gonna do?"

They both looked at Jimmy, grinning big as they sang the next part together.

"GHOST RIDE IIIIT! Ghost ride ya whip!"

Jimmy stood there with a blank face. Two wealthy athletes were singing a song about ghost riding. *Am I really seeing this, or am I starting to hallucinate from being awake and messed up so long?* Jimmy thought.

"That didn't really explain anything," Jimmy said to the two.

Anvil stepped in to help, singing as well. "Pull up, hop out, all in one motion. Dancin' on the hood while the car's still rollin'!"

Jimmy nodded. "I get it now. Sounds dangerous. People do that? Am I the only one that doesn't know about this?"

Kazdorf laughed. "Pretty much. Put down the Rush every now and then, bro. Now come on in, Qwan has some people coming in from the Bay soon, and Obie said he has a surprise for us. Let's go."

Jimmy looked around apprehensively as he walked into Obie Hill's mansion. The stench of potent marijuana was ripe in the air, a smoky haze lingering in the halls. People were packed almost shoulder to shoulder, holding personal liquor bottles. Jimmy recognized many of the people there as being Discovery players, but there was a high number of folks that were unfamiliar to him. He could feel eyes following him wherever he roamed, the stout unkempt guy in a dirty green hoodie standing out against the sea of Prada and Gucci. Almost impulsively, Jimmy reached for the pandemic-era mask that he no longer kept in his hoodie, still not quite re-accustomed to crowds in social situations.

Jimmy found an open seat in the living room and collapsed into it with a sigh, his arms slumping over the side, kicking his legs out as he fell into the cushion. Discovery players and scantily clad women danced together to the thumping soundtrack spun by a DJ on the other end of the room. A vertically challenged rapper expertly spat verses between hype beats and casually segued into call-and-answer stanzas that apparently everyone in the room knew but Jimmy.

"What's my favorite word?!"

"BEEEEYITCH!"

"Why ya'll gotta say it like Short?!"

"BEEEEYITCH!"

Jimmy was so exhausted, he would have likely fallen asleep, even with the bass and music, if it wasn't for an incessant rhythmic blasting of whistles.

Kip Kazdorf was drawn into the mix of people and soon found himself sandwiched between two women, hands in the air as he danced to the beat. Anvil found McCluskey and DuPlessis, catching up with his blockers over a few shots and a lot of laughter. Jimmy didn't have the desire or patience to mix with anyone, dirty and tired and of different socioeconomic standing; he felt out of place. He got up and moved to the hallway, exploring the area, looking for the door.

Obie Hill stood at the front door, the mountainous clean-shaven man wearing his own #70 jersey, gold chains draped around his neck and a solid gold chalice in his hand. He saw Jimmy looking for a way through and called him over with a grin. He had company, two smaller women, and a couple other defensive linemen from the team. Jimmy dropped his jaw when he saw a familiar face beside him, not a player from the Discovery, but someone he had seen on television before, Bay Area socialite Montreaux Pickens. The dapper, velvet-robed Montreaux puffed on a massive cigar, his rings glinting through the darkness.

"Hey mascot dude, that you? Get on over here a minute; why you leaving?" Obie waved Jimmy over with his chalice. Jimmy meekly walked up to the group, catching himself looking at Montreaux. Montreaux noticed Jimmy and grinned widely at him, nodding a welcome.

"Hey Obie. I'm exhausted. Been a long few days. I was just going to go to Kip's car and sleep it off," Jimmy replied meekly. Obie and the others all nodded or smiled.

"I feel ya, lil guy. You went hard in that brawl earlier. I think you need to relax. Things been all kinds of crazy for you today. Come on upstairs. We'll find you something to make you feel right."

Jimmy reluctantly followed the small crowd up the stairs. *This sounds shady*, Jimmy thought, *but... it's not every day you get to spend time with viral sensation Montreaux Pickens*. The upper halls of the house were significantly less packed than downstairs. Only a few individuals milled around outside of various doors. The halls were lined with different pictures of Obie and his abundant awards from his time not only on the Discovery but also for college and high school. Jimmy stayed near the end of the group as Obie directed them towards the end of the hall.

The three football players, reality TV star, two women, and the exhausted, drab guy in a hoodie walked into an expansive marble-floored, marble-walled room with a unique set-up. Pricey vases and pottery sat on pedestals that broke up the flow of the walking space. These vases were colored blue and green, and purple. A shallow hot-tub bubbled and steamed in the center of the room, donut-shaped, with a marble island prominent in the middle.

The men disrobed, and Jimmy averted his gaze as to not see anything. Despite his years in a locker room, he could never get used to seeing others nude. He only lifted his gaze when he realized the women were stripping down too – that's when he made eye contact with a partially submerged Montreaux Pickens, who winked at Jimmy and flashed a huge grin.

"Don't be a stranger. Come on in, it's okay to look – come, take a swim."

Jimmy breathed out a heavy sigh. He removed the hoodie and his jeans, stripping down to his boxers. Jimmy was conscious of every ripple of fat and every shameful stretch mark he had as he slunk into the water amidst the professional athletes and attractive women. His heartbeat picked up from a trot to a canter.

Obie Hill gestured towards Jimmy, smiling warmly. "You look like you need help relaxing, my brother. What has you so wound up?"

Jimmy shrugged apathetically. "I got fired today."

"Aw man, I had an idea that was coming after the fight. It's one thing if we do it, another if it's the warm and fuzzy," Obie replied. "You hang in there, though."

"Well, trying my best," Jimmy said as his head pounded. He closed his eyes and sunk deeper into the tub, paying close attention to how the bubbles and the warm water felt against his skin. It helped to a degree, not necessarily relaxing him but making him realize more and more just how exhausted he was.

"I was actually fired before the fight," Jimmy said as he opened his eyes once more. "My running down there was good timing, heat of the moment stuff. I just wanted to make my mark before I was shown the door for good."

Montreaux grinned as he lit another fat cigar. "I been watching the League for years; I never seen a thing like that. You could do serious work in entertainment anywhere. I was watching from the airport... *nothin' like it.*"

"Thanks, Montreaux," Jimmy said with a smile. "Sure is nice to meet you."

Montreaux raised the cigar and nodded at Jimmy. "Man, *you* are more famous than *me,* if only for tonight. Relax, my brother, enjoy it. Everything will sort out tomorrow and in the days to come."

"I can't quite get there," Jimmy said. "I think I just need to sleep everything off. I've had a crazy few days."

Montreaux nodded towards the two women sitting nearby. "Maybe one of our lady friends here could help you relax?"

Jimmy felt the color rush from his face as the two women grinned at him and dipped underwater, slowly making their way to him. The chilling mix of fear and anticipation drove him to sit back up awkwardly against the back of the pool, his hand instinctively sliding down to cover his crotch as he nearly fell out backward.

"Oh? I misread you. Maybe... *I* could help you relax?" Montreaux flashed a feisty grin.

"I'm uh, taken," Jimmy said. "Well, I think. We're fighting. But uh, I can't be here."

Obie stood up too, calmly putting his big hands on Jimmy's shoulders and smoothly guiding him back down into the water.

"Relax, man," Obie said, gold chains glinting in the moonlight coming in from the window. "It's cool. We don't know her. We won't rat."

"Snitches get stitches and get thrown in ditches," Montreaux said with a laugh.

"Doesn't make it right," Jimmy said as he sighed and tried to relax once again.

"Look, I can tell you haven't dealt with fame much," Montreaux said. "Once you figure out the... *rules* apply differently to fame, you'll be able to... *relax* more easily, be it with women or the finest... *indulgences* this world has to offer."

"Well, I had a brush with fame once," Jimmy said. "Remember about ten years ago? The national anthem kid?"

There was a pause among those gathered in the tub. Suddenly Obie grinned ear to ear, teeth brighter than his bling.

"Yeah! I know you! You're the one those coaches yelled at but never got in trouble for. Dude, you had some *stones* to do that!"

"Oh, Jimmy *GLENCROFT!*" one of the girls said in sudden recognition. "I don't necessarily agree with the direction of our country, but you standing up for what you believe in... kind of sexy!"

Jimmy laughed. "I'm not here to stir up old ghosts, but I don't believe in our country as much as I did as a teenager. It's cool. I mean, I support the troops and all, but our government is ten kinds of awful."

Montreaux nodded, grinning. "You get it, man. You get it. While I'm happy to have made a great living, these taxes has got me *wrecked*," he said. "I've lost so much of what I earned to tax. I still owe more. I'm rich, but I can't *live* rich the way I want to. Government always up my ass and shit. That's why I like to keep myself incognito. Off the grid. Live my life, Nah mean? Side hustles, brother! Keep yourself some side hustles." Montreaux took a deep drag of his cigar.

Jimmy couldn't contain his grin. "Now that's more my speed. I feel you, Montreaux."

Montreaux shook his head a bit. "Don't get me wrong, I don't mind paying my fair share. But when I realize my share that these pigs is hounding me with is going towards so much imprisonment and death for young black men just trying to make a living, these people just trying to live their lives and break the system, doing their thing... it ain't right."

"Preach, my brother!" Jimmy exclaimed.

Obie laughed. "Jimmy, my dude, you ain't got the right to call us brother yet."

"I'm so sorry, look, I didn't mean it that way..."

"Jimmy, bro. We're messing with you. Take it easy, hold up," Obie said.

Montreaux nodded to Obie. "Look, I think our *brother* needs a little help relaxing. I think we need to give him some... space."

Obie smiled wide. "Space!"

One of the other linemen nodded. "I'm tryna blast off."

Jimmy raised his eyebrows. "Pardon?"

Montreaux reached into a bag beside the Jacuzzi and pulled out a small candle, no larger than a whiskey tumbler, colored bright red. He sat it on the marble island in the middle of the tub.

"What's the deal with these candles?" Jimmy asked. "I've seen and heard my friends talking about them quite a bit. Do they... like, *do something*?"

Obie took the lighter from beside Montreaux. "Ha! Do they *do something*?! We're taking you into orbit tonight, son. Just you wait."

Montreaux pulled out a couple other candles, arranging them on opposite ends of the pool. "Doors and windows closed, Obe?"

"Yezzir," Obie said enthusiastically.

"Wait," Jimmy said. "Could these candles get us in trouble? Like... are these drugs?"

Montreaux shook his head, leveling his gaze at Jimmy. "Look, kid. For someone who hates the government, too, you worry about them too damn much. Look, like I said, I don't believe in snitchin'. This shit here? It's a... *pharmaceutical approach* to optimal relaxation and awareness. There's a reason your friends dig this shit. Now I know you ain't ever seen nothin' like this. Trust us... this will be the trip of a lifetime."

"Don't get me wrong, I don't mind the occasional thrill, but I'm just trying to avoid the stir," Jimmy said.

Montreaux nodded towards the others. "Look. We all have secrets. I want us all to be on the same playing field if we're going to blast off together. Let's share some shit. Trust exercise. Let's go around the circle. I'll go first. I just blasted off for the first time earlier. I'm still elevated. I'm a mental warrior on the warpath, and I'm conquering my own goddamn conscience like the man I am and am meant to be. I'm about to be a junkie on this shit, and I want to take you through this time warp into the great beyond."

"My secret is I can't wait to be on this," one of the other players said, grinning wide. "Sounds like some good stuff."

"Hell man, I don't even like football," said another. "I'm just here for the money and drugs while I can be. I'd rather be a mailman or some shit."

"I'm a spy," one of the girls said. "That's my secret," she continued with a wink towards Montreaux.

"Well why don't you come on over here once we enter orbit and be the spy who shagged me?" Montreaux said as everyone laughed around him.

Jimmy leaned back and slid further into the water. "Alright ya'll, I guess I'm in. I'm fucked up enough as it is. Let's ride the tiger."

Obie took a moment to light each of the three candles. The three football players, socialite, two women, and Jimmy Glencroft sat in a silent circle, gazing at the central candle, waiting in anticipation.

A solid two minutes passed before Jimmy broke the silence. "Um, is something supposed to happen?" he asked. "They're just... burning. I don't even smell anything."

Obie shook his head, keeping his eyes closed. "Just wait for it. Close your eyes, and it will come."

"Breathe deep, my brother," Montreaux said, his own eyes closed as well. "Let Space come in and become you."

Jimmy closed his eyes and sunk even deeper into the water, just his face and head above the surface now. The warmth of the water embraced him. He propped his feet up against the island. He could feel the grit and texture of the tiny grains of rock and concrete between his toes.

I feel like I'm high, Jimmy thought. *Just like a marijuana high. Oh, so high-O. High in Ohio. So high, though. High as a silo.*

"Bro," Obie said lowly beside him. "That's a trippy song."

"What?" Jimmy asked, snapping out of his thoughts.

"That song. High in Ohio. How's it go?"

"What song?"

"Boyyyy, you were just singing it."

"Oh. Wow. I thought I was thinking it," Jimmy said in wonder.

"Sing the song," Montreaux said, flicking Jimmy with a splash of water. "My sirens over here want some tips," he said to some excited giggles from the two women.

"Alright. One, two, three..." Jimmy counted himself in. As he started to sing, Obie joined in immediately, matching him word for word, the two of them on the same page both in rhythm and in word, the melody making Jimmy think of old campfire songs he heard from the movies or even the viral sea shanties from Tik-Tok.

Oh, so high-O. We're high in Ohio! So, so high, though. High as a silo.

Oh, so high-O. Me, oh the my-O! No need to lie though, we're high in Ohio!

Jimmy turned to behold the gazes of the others in the tub. Montreaux was slack-jawed, staring him wildly in the eyes. Montreaux laughed suddenly, a deep throaty robust laugh, guffawing until he cried. He leaned against the edge of the tub and repeatedly coughed until he settled down. Then he turned to face Jimmy and Obie.

"Hol-eeeeeeee shit, boys! One time for the one time. Let's do this again. We got a hit on our hands."

Yet again, Jimmy and Obie sang the song, but this time Montreaux jumped in with a rich tenor. Jimmy wasn't much of a singer, but this felt about as close to harmonizing as he had ever felt.

Oh, so high-O. We're high in Ohio! So, so high, though. High as a silo.

Oh, so high-O. Me, oh the my-O! No need to lie though, we're high in Ohio!

"This song has got me so wet right now," one of the women giggled out.

"Baby girl, we're *all* a little wet right now," Jimmy said as he flicked her with a splash of water. Everyone in the tub started laughing together as if they were all the oldest and dearest of friends. Jimmy, like Montreaux, laughed until he started crying openly. He ducked under the water consciously to clear his face and hide the tears, embarrassed that they were letting loose.

As Jimmy rose from the water, it became clear that the high was going to a whole new level. The plain dark of the room had given way to a light purple. The moonlight and stars outside the window had taken on a kind of effervescence, popping and twinkling. Jimmy was moving his mouth, but he couldn't feel it or hear anything coming out.

"I feel like I'm living in a champagne bottle," a lineman said in reverence.

"I feel like I'm living in a bottle of Faygo," said the other.

Meanwhile, Obie was humming the "High in Ohio" song, and the two girls were now flirting and frolicking with Montreaux, and Jimmy closed his eyes to enter his own fantasy.

"Awaken the wind and ride with it, my child," an accented voice had seeped in from the far reaches of his conscience and echoed inside his mind.

"Carlos Santana? Is that you?" Jimmy said in shock, and, oddly enough, a dose of fear.

"Yes, my child," he said as in Jimmy's mind, Santana appeared before him, outlined in neon green and purple, cowboy hat low over his head and guitar in hand.

"What brings you here?"

"I just thought you could use some vengeful Latin rhythms," he said. Sure enough, in Jimmy's mind, rich and overwhelming, he could hear the tempo and percussive beckoning of maracas, bongos, and drums.

"I'd love this... nothing more than this... but... the others? Are they okay with it?" Jimmy whispered out meekly.

"They are more than okay. This is your own personal trip, and I am your guide. Destination? Rhythm." Santana whispered out.

"Mr. Santana... I'm glad you're here, but dare I ask..."

"Say no more... say no more."

"...No kidding?"

"No kidding. They are here. Just like you wanted."

Over the distant horizon of Jimmy's recessed mind, a low moon had hung over the jagged outlines of the buttes of Monument Valley, the iconic landscape of the West. The stars took on a bold yellow hue, the colors of the atmosphere swirling around them as if to copy the image of Van Gogh's *Starry Night*. Rising from behind the craggy peaks and valleys, in full resplendent Vegas-style neon, Carlos Santana played arpeggios on his guitar, slowly and hauntingly, as if an invitation. Rising behind him and towering above them all, two white men, one with curly hair and a bright scarf at a keyboard, and one, with a blowout afro and a giant Fu Manchu mustache, with a guitar of his own, and they began to play along. The keyboardist's tones were the warm Hammond B3 organ, churning and rollicking, echoing and rolling. Together, Santana and the other guitarist played tones that wove and tangled and interplayed, harmonizing, dueling, flirting, and tangoing.

Jimmy grinned wider than he ever had for anything before. Carlos Santana, Gregg Rolie, and Neal Schon, all in bright neon, played exotic jazzy music high above the American West's unfettered skies. Jimmy began dancing, only vaguely aware that he was dancing, his arms feeling to him like they had separated, fluttering off and exploding into the sky like a million fireflies. His legs pulsed and contorted, up and down, the motion feeling like a stork picking its way through mild quicksand lined with landmines. One of the mines exploded, and a million white crystals exploded into the sky as well while the neon Santana played on, and Jimmy danced through the desert and into the great unknown.

"Aha! They're in here," Kip Kazdorf said excitedly as he popped open the door with his foot, beckoning Naev Broadnax to come in behind him. Anvil put his hands on Kazdorf's shoulder as they both opened their eyes and mouths wide with shock at the scene playing out before them.

"Naev, bud... is this life right now? Like... am I dreaming?" Kazdorf asked.

"I... don't think *you're* the one dreaming..." Anvil responded as they crept into the room slowly, careful not to clomp across the stone floor to disturb the proceedings.

Obie Hill stared directly at the ceiling, almost completely submerged in the donut-shaped jacuzzi tub, his tongue out of his mouth rolling around, to and fro, back and forth. Montreaux Pickens sat on the other side, laughing uncontrollably, a woman on either side of him, both laughing as well. They weren't even doing anything X-Rated, they just kept hugging one another and cackling like they were watching the funniest comedy show on Earth, but their gaze was unfocused on any one thing. One lineman had disappeared entirely, the back door to the two-story deck hanging open in the light breeze. Meanwhile, the other one, stark naked, lurched up to Kip and Anvil in a hurry.

"I. Am. Watercress! I seek naught yet to be sought, my mind taut with the thoughts it had been taught," he said with every ounce of absolute seriousness to Anvil and Kazdorf.

"That uh... actually makes sense," Kazdorf replied.

"Stay woke," the large man said as he bent down and kissed Kazdorf gently on the forehead, before turning and sprinting outside the house without another word, his hindquarters billowing in the moonlight.

"What the actual..." Anvil said.

"I can't even," Kazdorf responded. "Good God. Look at Jimmy."

In the center of all the disjointed activity was James Glencroft, dripping wet and wearing only boxers, standing atop the marble island in the center of the Jacuzzi. He moved around without any focus or reason, and it was only as Anvil and Kazdorf walked around to look at him from the front that they realized he was trying to dance. Jimmy had a lit candle in one hand, drumming his stomach with the other.

"Jimmy, what in the world is this?" Anvil asked. "Give me that candle, man, before you drop it on Obie," Anvil said as he took it from Jimmy and took a sniff. "Oh, well, hey, it's like the one Trevor had the poker game."

"Be careful huffing that shit, Naev," Kazdorf said as he grabbed the candle back from Anvil and put it on a windowsill. "It's that psychedelic everyone has been raving about, pun intended. 'Space,' they call it. It's consumed in an aromatic form."

"Oh, no shit? Do you think we'll get high from that?" Anvil said.

"Not like these guys," Kazdorf said as he nodded to Jimmy and the others in the hot tub. "I wouldn't huff it again, though. The door's open, which will help."

Anvil turned back to Jimmy. "Jimmy, man. What's wrong with you? Are you okay?"

Jimmy turned around and gazed at some point far off behind Anvil's right shoulder as he replied.

"I am the Sensei of Magnitude, and these are my most glorious chronicles. Sway with me as we embrace the zephyrs of unparalleled Latin rhythms, bestowed upon us by the kings of Monument Valley," Jimmy said, mumbling out the words, enunciating just enough to be heard and understood.

"What. The. Hell. Did you just say?" Kazdorf asked.

"The souls of a thousand virgins take flight as if puffed from the pipe of the finest opiate one could imagine, unchained to take root where they please," Jimmy replied with slightly more distinct, dramatic enunciation this time.

"That's... beautiful, man," Anvil said. "I mean that."

"The Earth has music for those who will listen," Jimmy replied. He went back to his absent-minded, half-speed dancing atop the marble island.

"Dear God," Kazdorf said. "Dude, should we bring the guys in to watch this? Or maybe like... videotape this?"

"Maybe Clusk and Nap will get a kick out of this. But I don't want to embarrass Jimmy much more than what he's dealt with here lately," Anvil replied. "Let's leave him be for a bit."

Naev Broadnax and Kip Kazdorf took one last amused look at the tripped-out denizens of the Jacuzzi before they turned and walked back to the party, careful to shut the door behind them.

As night gave way to morning, long after partygoers had passed out or paired off, having bid one another farewell or having ducked away anxiously into the dark, or in the case of two wealthy athletes, having passed out naked in the woods behind a subdivision; the chill autumn dawn was cloaked in grey as a cold front had moved in, the winds more bitter than usual. The resplendent leaves of deciduous trees were ripped from branch and bough as the sun's muted rays struggled to peak through the ominous cover. A dense fog's tendrils wrapped tight around trunk and treetop alike.

Out of the Spaced-out trippers in the Jacuzzi tub, one of the women was the first to awaken. She was the shorter and more diminutively built of the two. She looked to her left to see the other woman, who she never met before last night, asleep on Montreaux Pickens' chest, who was snoring lightly. Obie Hill slept against the side of the tub, and James Glencroft was out as well, draped across the marble island and snoring louder than anyone else present, his shirtless body occasionally shuddering and heaving with some great unconscious terror.

The woman slipped out of the pool and quickly wrapped a nearby towel about her person, head on a swivel to ensure nobody could see her up and moving. None of the folks in or around the tub stirred. There wasn't anyone else around. The door to the back deck hung wide open while the entrance to the house was fully shut. She realized then just how cold it had gotten outside, and her body shook with a significant tremor of chill.

Barefoot and wearing naught but a towel, she ducked outside and ran down the two flights of stairs to reach the ground floor of the double-decker cabin-style porch. She peeked through the not-fully-shut blinds of the ground floor window to note that nobody was within view of her; the kitchen was still devoid of life. The porch light wasn't even on, allowing her to move discreetly by shadow.

She found her duffel bag stashed just within arm's reach of a hole she had kicked into the skirting of the porch's bottom floor. She quickly changed into black sweatpants and a matching layered hoodie, pulling on black tennis shoes, head constantly on a swivel as she rushed into warm clothing. She slid a 9mm handgun into her back waistband, covered it with her hoodie, and tiptoed back up the steps and into the house once more.

She smacked her tongue inside her mouth, working her way through the simultaneous inconvenience of cottonmouth and a bitter aftertaste, a dull pain constant in the right side of her head. She nabbed the burned-out candle and put it slowly and silently into her go-bag, careful not to awaken any of the slumbering partygoers. She tiptoed around the hot tub room, deftly flipping through clothing and bags and personal effects to gather what she needed. In Obie's discarded clothing, she found another candle, this one unburned. Straight into the bag, it went.

She turned and ducked out of the patio door, careful to shut it completely, gently, and with little noise. She scurried around the mansion and past the sports cars parked in the drive and on the lawn. Once she was clear of the mansion, having successfully gotten out of earshot with the candles, she pulled a cellphone from her bag and made a quick call.

"Yes, this is Zoey. Candles acquired. I've hooked an even bigger fish too. More details to come. Requesting extraction."

She put the cell phone back in her bag, sat down on the subdivision's sidewalk, leaned back, and gazed skyward into the fog.

CHAPTER ELEVEN

South of Columbus, city streets and skyscrapers gave way to outlying neighborhoods. Just as one would pass the outer belt, U.S. Route 23 was cloaked naught by building and bustle but by crops of corn and soy. Every now and again, an intersecting state route would be framed by a few gas stations or chain restaurants; rarer still were the cities along the way. Eventually, 23 would lead to some small towns like Circleville, Chillicothe, and Waverly. After Waverly, but before Portsmouth at the Ohio River, an eastbound road called State Route 808 took travelers deeper into the hills to more nondescript Appalachian burghs, such as Nawakwa. Beyond that, and flanked by Ohio's lone proper mountain, Mt. Massie, lay Slade City.

An old red Ford Ranger truck rattled down U.S. Route 23 among the agrarian plains. It lacked a front bumper, but to compensate, a wooden plank had been bolted to the frame, the license plate drilled into it. There was no back bumper either; the license plate instead taped to the turtle shell's back window atop the truck bed. Inside the truck bed, there was a felony quantity of industrial-strength hallucinogens, manufactured in secret and trafficked to consumers in the guise of a candle that looked at home in a Cracker Barrel, branded as *Cowtown Candles*, now within the radar of the DEA and drawing the attention of regional drug mafias. That's not counting the heroin, cocaine, and marijuana that were also stuffed among the pallets in the back.

A Slavia United operative was very much aware of what was within. Not far behind the red truck, but always keeping at least one car between them, was an old Corolla with false tags. A well-built bearded man named Robert Nenkovic was behind the wheel, his seat leaned slightly back. Adorned in the black and white striped jersey of FK Partizan and with a clove cigarette between his fingers, his essence of chill contrasted with the loaded Micro-UZI submachine gun beneath a blanket in the passenger seat, its back handle poking out a bit for quick access. A Bluetooth earpiece blinked in his ear with a ring. He reached up and tapped the button on its side.

"Jody."

"Brody," Drago said from the other line. "How goes the tail?"

Nenkovic took a drag from his clove before responding. "Slow. They are driving so slow right now... it's hard for me to stay up to legal speed."

"That's a pity. Are you going to try to ice them or not?"

"Yeah, of course, that's the plan, right? I just haven't had a chance."

"Do you have a plan?"

"I'm not going to do a drive-by in the open. I'm going to wait until they stop, no matter where they stop. If it's soon, good. If it's in Nawakwa, good. I can't do anything to give us away."

Nenkovic flicked his cigarette out the window. It tumbled erratically down the pavement before being run over by a Denali about twenty car lengths behind them. Unbeknownst to Nenkovic, the Denali contained two plain-clothes federal agents, watching Nenkovic as intently as he was watching Trevor and Sean. The very phone call Nenkovic was on played through the speakers of the Denali.

"Yes, Nenko, I would hate for you to give us away," Drago said. "Be safe out there, and call me if you need me."

"Yes, brother. I'm glad you made it through the other night. Have you found out who shot brother Mirko yet?"

"Not yet, but we have ears to the ground. Stay well."

"And you."

Drago clicked off the phone and looked up and around him. His eyes were sunken – he had not slept in over 24 hours. His clean face was now lined with stubble, and his normally-styled hair was unkempt from all the rubbing and scratching he had been doing.

DEA Agent Gabriel Contreras, a barrel of a man, flashed a thumb up to the rest of the room.

"Got it! Premeditation!" Agent Contreras shouted.

"Christ, keep your voice down," a woman said back to him. She stood behind the seated Drago, a hand on his shoulder. DEA Agent Sophie Browning was a short woman with a sharp face, her light brown hair pulled back tight in a bun. She patted Drago's shoulder before walking around the room, gazing at the ceiling.

"You did well, Drago," Agent Browning said. "You did the right thing by offering yourself to us."

"That's because I did nothing wrong," Drago said. "I was just at the wrong place at the wrong time."

"Yeah, that's what everyone says," Browning replied. "If a dog lays down in the dirt, he sure as hell ain't clean. We've ID'd you with Slavia United, Mr. Zupan. The connection is clear, and your only way out of this is to help us. Nice touch with switching to real names in the middle there – that will help us convict. Thank you."

Drago sighed and looked down at his hands, folded in front of him not far from the phone handset. Contreras worked on his laptop, headset on, and eyes forward. Browning muttered a few things to two other agents sitting on the other end of the table.

"Okay. Okay, I didn't tell you everything," Drago said.

Browning turned around sharply, thin eyebrows raised. "Pardon me, Mr. Zupan. You were saying?"

"I can't wait to get to Nawakwa and get started," Trevor MacKenzie said, staring out the window at the passing countryside as the red truck rumbled down U.S. 23 South. His head rested on one hand while the other twirled around with an empty can of dipping tobacco.

"I know. You've told me like eight times. Come up with something new," Sean Doan said. He had a striped beanie pulled down low over his forehead, his skinny frame swallowed up in an oversized olive-colored hoodie. He sniffed deep and then hocked a loog, which he spat into an open Styrofoam milkshake cup.

Trevor stared out the window for a few minutes. He tapped on it excitedly, turning his head to look at Sean. "Hey bud, we're coming up on South Bloomfield. Let's stop at that gas station coming up on the right. Could suck on a chili dog."

"A... chili dog. I thought you couldn't wait to get to town and sling? And you want to stop for a chili dog?" Sean said.

"I'll just be a minute. Actually, I might not want a chili dog. Maybe one of those pepper jack taquitos."

"See, that's your issue," Sean said. "Then after you pick up a taquito, you will put it back on the grill because you want donuts instead. Then you will buy a scratch-off, win a dollar, then 50 minutes later I'm bored as hell, while you're telling some bullshit story about hockey to a trucker who could not possibly care less."

"Dude, I promise. In and out. Taquitos. That's all," Trevor pleaded.

"Alright, fine," Sean said as he flipped on his right-hand blinker. "I could go for some nachos."

"You ever notice that picking a taquito flavor is like playing roulette, man? Seriously. Even when there's only one type of taquito on the roller, it's like a 50/50 shot that it's labeled correctly."

"You eat too many gas station taquitos, man."

"I don't think either of us are in a position to judge what we put into our bodies."

"*Pfft*. I guess you're right."

The red truck with the missing bumpers pulled into the far right-hand side of a bright orange and midnight black-colored Dice Stop gas station, pulling parallel to the storefront before pulling into a spot, partially taking up the spot next to it as well. Trevor threw open the passenger door and leaped out with a swing of his legs. He walked inside immediately. After a moment of closing his eyes and sighing deeply, Sean started to open his door but was cut off by a silver Corolla that slammed on its brakes with a squeal. Sean's mouth tightened. He watched as a large black-bearded man in a soccer jersey climbed out, turning to look straight on at him.

"Hey, what gives?" the bearded man yelled as he shut his door and walked around the front of his car. Sean shut the truck door fully and rolled up his window. He kept a sliver open at the top of the window.

"What do you want?!" Sean yelled back. He put a hand down to feel for his pistol in the bin by the door.

"Watch what you're doing, man! Your door almost got taken clean off," Nenkovic yelled. His front passenger side window was all the way down. He spun his head around in a circle. He leaned his arm into his car, grasping for the SMG under the blanket, keeping eye contact with Sean.

"Re-think that move, son," a voice spoke from behind them. Nenkovic had lost focus on the world around him as he prepped his mind for the shot and had not noticed the black Denali blocking both vehicles alongside the Dice Stop storefront. A mustachioed man in sunglasses in a dark peacoat had emerged, flashing a laminated badge. "Agent Doyle, Drug Enforcement Agency. Step away from the gun and put your hands over your head."

"Shit..." Nenkovic said as he stepped back. "I didn't do anything. I don't have anything. The gun is registered."

"Just like your Corolla is?" Agent Doyle asked. "These tags belong to someone else. Now put your hands above your head and fall to your knees, Mr. Nenkovic. You are under..."

He stopped speaking, holding up his badge with his left hand while his right hand pressed against his ear, listening to a transmission coming in over his earpiece.

Sean watched wide-eyed as his would-be assailant obliged the federal agent's orders, kneeling before a small crowd of onlookers who came out of the convenience store. He looked to the right to see a man clothed similarly to Agent Doyle open the passenger side door of the truck and get in, holding up a badge.

"Agent Rosh. You're going to sit still, now... Hold up a second, will you?" He also pressed a few fingers up to his right ear for a quick moment. He looked back at Sean after.

"Stay here," Agent Rosh said. He hopped out of the truck just as quickly as he had boarded. Sean watched in the rearview while Rosh went around back and conferred with Doyle, who nodded to his remarks. Both agents turned and opened the front doors to their Denali and climbed in.

As this whole exchange played out, a dark green Humvee without tags pulled up to the Denali, drawing parallel to it. Its dark-tinted passenger side windows, front and back, both rolled down simultaneously. Nenkovic turned around and scrambled for cover, diving in front of Sean's truck and skidding across the sidewalk.

The vicious rolled report of Uzis echoed throughout town, jarring all those near enough to witness and all within earshot. The windows of the Denali shattered, and Sean couldn't see the federal agents any longer. He could not discern if they were hit or if they were ducking. After the Uzis ripped through the first magazine, the assailants reloaded, and a third shooter on the other end popped out over the top of the Humvee, peppering the storefront with fire as well, glass shattering all around. Trevor MacKenzie spun around just in front of the trucks, inside the store – he dropped his slushie and chili dogs, then turned tail and sprinted for the back door of the Dice Stop.

Sean threw the truck into reverse, gunning the accelerator. The back end of the truck jarred the back of the Denali, and then he shifted into gear. Sean drove over the edge of the sidewalk, clipping a petroleum display and hurtling over a divider before erratically driving through the field behind the store. He disappeared into the neighborhood beyond the other side of the field.

The Humvee's assailants waited a moment, then lit up the Denali from the windows down, bullets ripping into the vehicle and puncturing metal and tire alike. After they realized no movement from the Denali, the Humvee sped off, heading north. Sirens filled the air around the Dice Stop, drawing closer.

Robert Nenkovic scrambled up from the sidewalk, having evaded the fire from the anonymous Humvee assailants. He opened the side door to the Denali, and Agent Doyle's bloodied, ripped body fell upon the sidewalk. He yelled aloud and backed up quickly, tripping and falling into the entryway to the Dice Stop, plummeting into shattered glass shards that shredded his skin. Around him, frightened witnesses and victims screamed and scattered, tending to one another or bolting for either their cars or the edge of town. Nenkovic stood up, looked down to see the glass shard sticking out of his palm, and as he suddenly he felt his pulse throb around the wound, he realized his pain for the first time.

Nenkvoic dashed through the store. He slipped through an unexpected pool of blood by the bathrooms in the hallway leading to the back and fell hard into the tile. Instinctively, he put his wounded hand down and shrieked in an unearthly pitch as he drove the large shard further into his flesh and bone. He clambered to his knees to see a Highway Patrolman and two EMTs run into the building.

"Help! I'm a victim!" Nenkovic yelled. He grabbed his wrist and writhed.

One EMT rushed ahead with the Patrolman to survey the store and administer aid. The other one stooped to help Nenkovic directly, setting to assess his wound.

Behind the store, Trevor MacKenzie had made it about a quarter-mile away. His breath came in ragged gasps as his pale face gained a new shade of red, sweat beading around his wispy blonde locks. He keeled over, his hands on his knees, looking around, seeing cops and ambulances swarming the front of the store. Even in the calm autumn air, he could feel the heat permeating through his skin. He took to one knee and stared at the ragged grass beneath him.

A truck horn blared. Trevor shot his gaze up to see Sean Doan pulled up to him at the roadside. Trevor scrambled for the old red truck and pulled himself into the passenger side. He hadn't even fully gotten seated before Sean sped off with the door still open. Trevor fell out of the vehicle, rolling along the pavement, the tiny white and gray houses around him spinning in his view as he tumbled. Sean squealed the brakes, threw the truck into reverse, and barely missed plowing into Trevor as he came back to pick him up. This time, Sean waited a split second longer to allow Trevor to seat up.

Trevor inspected his right arm, the top layer of skin shredded and tendrils of blood seeping through. "Damnit Sean, what the hell happened back there?"

Sean breathed heavily and gunned the engine harder, barely making the manual shifts. His clunky shifts would rock the truck hard, and the whole thing seemed like it was on the edge of control.

"Sean? You okay, man?" Trevor asked.

Just before the truck got back to the main road, a dark green Humvee emerged from a driveway and completely blocked the road. Sean downshifted hard and squealed through the brakes, the smell of tire smoke filling the air. They stopped about ten yards short of the Humvee.

The Humvee's doors opened, three of them, and three men emerged. One bald man with a neon green bandana tied over his head, a white t-shirt, and cut-off jean shorts. Another man, dreadlocks falling out from under his neon green trucker hat, wearing a green tracksuit. The third man was wearing a green soccer jersey with a yellow cross emblazoned across the front. All three were holding submachine guns.

"Get out of the truck!" the bald man yelled, pointing his Uzi towards the windshield. Sean and Trevor obliged, both stumbling as they took to the pavement. Trevor even put his hands above his head.

"Put your hands down, fool! We're not the feds, damn. I know you're not going to try anything," the dreadlocked man said. "Jason, take the truck. Go back to HQ."

The guy in the soccer jersey obliged and hopped into the driver seat. He looked around inside, checking the console and the glove compartment. He looked at the slot inside the door. Jason looked back up at everyone in the road, waving Sean's pistol around with a crooked grin.

"Get out of here!" the bald man yelled, waving his gun back. "This place is gonna be crawling soon!"

The truck shifted into gear. Jason accelerated away with the drugs and gun now in his possession. Sean paled, sweating profusely and fidgeting. Trevor was more stoic than he, his lips taut together and his forehead wrinkling under his wispy hair as he looked around at everything.

"What gives?!" Sean yelled. "Who are you?"

"Who we are is none of your business," the bald man said. "You had our drugs, so we took them back. That's all. Now get out of here and lie low. One of our guys will stop by soon to sell to you. Just look for green."

"No, those aren't your drugs; those belonged to Foxx and his crew; how did you know we had..."

Sirens filled the air more loudly than before. Police were on their way into the housing development.

"Silence. Get out of here. You're on the radar now. Keep your heads down for a while. We will be in touch."

The two men walked back over to the Humvee and climbed in. Before the Humvee pulled away, the driver rolled down his window, finally showing himself. A thin-faced older man in a pale blue shirt, red tie, and a tan pageboy hat gazed at Trevor and Sean from behind aviator sunglasses. He tilted the sunglasses down, pointed his left index finger and middle finger at his own eyes, and then pointed at Sean and Trevor with both fingers. He rolled up the window, turned, and drove away with the armed men inside the Humvee.

Sean stood dumbfounded in the middle of the street. Trevor looked around. He saw an older woman a few houses down open her front door to see what the hubbub was. Trevor grabbed Sean by the arm and jerked him towards the sidewalk.

"Come on, dude, we gotta get outta here; you have warrants and shit!" Trevor yelled. Sean snapped out of it, looked at Trevor, and looked behind him to see a cop car turning onto the street a quarter-mile away. Sean and Trevor both turned sharply left, dashed between two houses, clumsily climbed and then fell over a wooden plank fence, and then ran as hard and as quickly as possible through a mottled and muddy field. They faded into the trees on the far edge of the field, flanking the Scioto River, and escaped from view as the cop cars slowly drove through the subdivision, looking for the shooters.

CHAPTER TWELVE

James Glencroft sighed deeply, his ragged breath heaving out of him loudly enough to draw stares of those around him.

Slouched over a computer desk at a public library, Jimmy wore massive noise-canceling earphones over his black beanie, pulled low over his forehead. His brow furrowed in concentration as he scrolled through job listings, face pressed up close to the monitor. His eyes were tinged red, dark half-circles beneath them, sweat visible even through the armpits of his dark gray hoodie.

To the left of him, a middle-aged white man sat wearing a loose untailored tan suit. This man had several days of stubble and a messy ring of hair around his balding head. He would sit in absolute calm for several minutes at a time before spontaneously bursting out with loud, angry curses. He was yelling at an online poker game and would be just as loud whether he won or lost hands. Jimmy couldn't help but periodically get distracted by this man. He would lean over and glance at the screen, letting his attention wander away from his job search. The man continued to be disruptive despite multiple admonishments from library staff.

I relate more than you could ever imagine. Jimmy thought about the man as he reflected over his own poker losses over the years. How many thousands of dollars had he lost since he started playing? When the number in his head reached five digits, he winced and continued to scroll aimlessly through Monster and LinkedIn listings.

That's when the kids beside him to the right began to yell and prance about. Two young kids, maybe no older than 7 or 8, played *Grease and Ambition* on the computer. Jimmy raised an eyebrow, surprised that the public library permitted that with its internet filters, and further surprised that the kids weren't in school. It was a Monday afternoon, eight days after the FootBrawl.

In the week that passed after the chaotic events that rocked the lives of Jimmy Glencroft and his friends, he sought comfort, peace, and recovery. After returning home to an emptied house, a nasty letter from Megan, and a world of doubt, Jimmy pumped the brakes on life for the first time in years. Jimmy took the time to downsize his bills: slowing down his internet, canceling ConnecTV, keeping the heat off during the chill late October nights. He put together a budget, pulled together his savings, and sold a few inconsequential items on Marketplace. While waiting for his unemployment application to clear, he spent his days catching up on books, music albums, and movies he had always wanted to consume, all while calling Megan in between. She would never answer.

Jimmy also hurriedly took out a payday loan while still technically employed by the Discovery to pay off exorbitant lot fees on an old Dodge Caravan. The Caravan had been impounded for a couple months for a parking violation; Megan had refused to bail Jimmy out of that one. Jimmy further realized his mistakes when he finally read the terms and conditions of the payday loan. This triple-digit APR interest would surely deplete what little was left in his accounts if a new job wasn't obtained soon enough.

Additionally, some pieces of news weighed heavily on his mind. In particular, a Dice Stop store that he had worked a few shifts at in the past had been shot up, resulting in the deaths of two men that were later revealed to be federal agents. A foreign man was found dead in a sunken car upriver from Jimmy's old apartment. Naturally paranoid enough as it were, Jimmy was extra worried due to his erratic sleep cycles and recent drug-induced trip. The world was all a blur of delirium and spectacle to him anymore. Besides – the car that the one guy died in? The Buick? It looked awfully familiar...

Jimmy sighed, annoyed by the loud distractions on either side of him, and frustrated with the lack of well-paying job leads he was finding. He clicked on an ESPN link and read through commentary on FootBrawl.

No players involved in the colossal FootBrawl were suspended, as the damage done to their bodies and wallets by the event was more punishment than enough. Anton Treptak's knee surgery was successful, putting him on a healing timeline that may keep him out of action for a full calendar year. J'Shia Beverly wasn't so lucky, being dealt a significant setback with a concussion diagnosis, ruled out indefinitely until he could be cleared by League doctors.

Kip Kazdorf was fined $50,000 for his involvement in the fight, and Naev Broadnax forfeited two game checks to the Patriot Football League as punishment. Anvil's coffers were a cool $140,000 lighter as a result. The fines levied to Fargo and Columbus because of the brawl broke the League record for the most fines and penalties given on one play. The League called the game early and awarded both teams with a loss – a first in PFL and professional football history - a decision that had been costing the League money and reputation already in the week since.

This first click led him through a rabbit hole as he continued to obsessively read every article about the event he could find, doing so for the first time since it all happened. His eyes widened as he counted how many times his name was coming up connected to the event. Five, ten, twenty... he lost count, sweat pouring down his face as his breath became shorter and his face flushed a brighter shade of pink.

Maybe this is why traditional employers aren't calling me. My name is all over the place in the news. Thankfully nobody has brought the National Anthem issue yet...

Just as soon as Jimmy had those thoughts, he decided to Google his name. He began drumming his left hand furiously against the desk while he scrolled through search results with his right, his bottom lip curled inside his mouth deeply.

Breitbart: *TURNCOAT PATRIOT JIMMY GLENCROFT: THE SECRET INSTIGATOR OF FOOTBRAWL!*

Buzzfeed: *TAKE OUR FOOTBRAWL QUIZ – WHICH EMBARRASSING JIMMY GLENCROFT MOMENT ARE YOU?*

TMZ: *JIMMY GLENCROFT, INFAMOUS MASCOT – BROKE AND LIVING LIFE OF SADNESS!*

TMZ really does get everything right... Jimmy thought. He glared at the screen for a long moment, still furiously drumming his fingers.

"Excuse me, sir, you'll have to quiet down," a meek elder library aide said as she put her hand on Jimmy's left shoulder.

Jimmy jerked his arm, taking the library aide aback. His glare shifted to her as his pale pink face flushed to a darker red.

"*Me,* quiet down?! Lady, *damn*! This old coot and these two little twerps can yell and scream all they want, but *I'M* the one that's too loud?!"

Jimmy observed people all over the library turning to look at him, and subconsciously he may have realized he *was* getting too loud. Still, any embarrassment or self-awareness he had was already out the window.

"Sir, please. If you don't stop, I'll have to ask you to leave," the aide implored.

"FINE! You don't have to ask me shit, lady. I'll leave on my own." He flung himself up from the desk and kicked over the chair as people flocked over to watch. Jimmy was dimly aware of camera phones in the air, and one young man called out, "Oh my shit, is that Jimmy Glencroft?!"

The aide beckoned for a security guard across the main area to come over, but his ambling was no match for Jimmy's frustrated speed-walk. Jimmy burst out of the library and into the chill fall air, the near-freezing temperatures stinging his ears and nose, making his face redder yet.

Jimmy lost track of time as he had just walked and walked until he could calm down. He even stormed right past the parking lot his purple minivan was in. When he finally snapped out of his embarrassed rage, he realized he was close to German Village. Collecting himself and tying his gray hoodie even tighter around his face, Jimmy continued his walk down a brick road, lined on either side by historic homes, well-maintained with still-green yards void of leaf or obstruction. He would pass occasional people out jogging in their pastel Fabletics outfits or UnderArmour uniforms, or well-coifed urbanites walking purebred dogs with bright coats and gamely paces.

When Jimmy turned a corner in the labyrinth of narrow roads and clean alleys, he found himself outside a coffee shop that looked like a small house. The steps leading up to the door were crooked and aged concrete, edges hewed and worn, pebbles strewn about the front and sides. The door was chestnut brown with a bright bronze knob. The building itself was paneled in a creamy yellow. The window frames were a weathered brown wood, with the textures - rivulets and crevices - a much darker shade. The roof came to a perfect point, not leaving much room for any kind of 2nd floor – perhaps just an attic, one small window halfway up from the beginning of the point with a lit candle in the sill.

The brightest part of the façade was the sign. Clean white etched-wood letters stood out against the pumpkin-orange board, a foot or so above the doorframe of the café, reading in cursive letters, *Full Nest Café*. Jimmy gazed at the sign for a long moment before the sting of the wind against his cheeks and the stirred-up soreness of his bruises beckoned him in. He opened the door, letting in a burst of cold air before he shut it, trapping himself into a sudden embrace of warmth and delight.

A row of eight wooden stools sat alongside a wooden bar top, clean and smooth, stained with swirling rich tones of umber and tawny. A thin woman sat at the far edge, asleep over an open computer with wraparound headphones over her long messy black hair. To his right was the counter and register, on the short end of an L-shaped bar top, the register lined on either side with two cases of fresh-baked goods, one with cookies and brownies, and the other with coffee cake and tiramisu. The long end of the counter had more stools. Behind the counter, a short female barista washed a pot. Her auburn hair was pulled up in a tight knot underneath a hairnet. The wall behind the counter was lined with racks that held dozens upon dozens of mugs of various sizes and colors. Several tall stainless-steel brewers, espresso machines, and various other mechanisms lined the counter that sat alongside the wall.

Jimmy leaned over the main counter and looked around at the coffee shop. Further back, beyond a sitting area with a handful of tables and chairs, stood a small elevated stage in a condensed performance room. A single amplifier sat behind a tall stool. A few beanbag chairs and low-to-the-ground cup seats dotted the floor near the tiny stage.

"What will you have?" the barista asked Jimmy after she put away the pot.

Jimmy pored over the paper menu for a moment. "I'll keep it simple today. Dark blend, black – with a shot of espresso."

"Long night?" she asked as she entered his order into the register.

"Long week. You have no idea." Jimmy responded. He fished out a wrinkled $5 bill from his pocket and put it on the counter. "Keep the change."

Jimmy put his head down between his arms as he awaited his order. After a moment, a feminine voice called over – "Bad mood, Jimmy?"

Jimmy lifted his gaze and felt his heart jump into his throat as he locked eyes with Lyndsey de Rueda, who had looked up from her computer and removed her headphones with a smile. He returned her smile, left the counter, and walked quickly over to her, throwing open his arms. She tossed her headphones down on the table and fell into him, pressing her face against his chest as he put his face into her hair, their embrace lasting several long seconds as they swayed back and forth. Finally, they disengaged and sat down on stools beside one another.

"Lytz! How have you been? Why are you here? Why do I always have moments like these in coffee shops?" Jimmy asked.

"Jimmy, you never did answer me! Are you in a bad mood? You always order black coffee when you're in a bad mood. Some things never change, I swear!" Lyndsey said.

"Well, if you must know... I'm not necessarily in a *bad mood*, I'm just... in a weird place right now. Have you seen or read the news?"

"Honestly, no... I've had enough on my own plate recently. It's been a weird week or so for me."

"How so?"

"If I told you, you would never believe me. What about you? What's going on in the news?"

"If I told you, you would never believe me."

The two old friends shared a laugh as the barista walked by and delivered Jimmy's coffee on the bar top. Jimmy and Lyndsey continued to look at one another. Both smiled wide through their otherwise apparent exhaustion. Lyndsey's eyes were mildly bloodshot, and her dry facial skin had a slight sag to it. The creases in Jimmy's face seemed more profound than they had ever been.

"What brings you to this part of town?" Lyndsey asked.

"Well, I went to the main library to job hunt and maybe pick up a book or two. Long story short, I'm unemployed right now. People were too... ah, loud... at the library and I couldn't concentrate. I was on a walk to clear my mind. What about you? What brought you here?"

"The exact same thing!" Lyndsey laughed. "I had only been here for like a half hour before you. There was this guy playing poker at the computer there that got under my last nerve."

"Ha! Wow. Maybe fate brought us back together," Jimmy said. "Are you still with Sean?"

"It's complicated," Lyndsey replied. "And you? With Megan, right?"

"... It's complicated." Jimmy said. "Are we living the exact same lives or something?"

"Haven't we always?"

"Well, I never... well, I think we went off course here lately. But here we are."

"Right, right... well, where are you staying right now?"

"Hilliard. I was renting a house with Megan off Cemetery road. Still am, I guess. But I don't know what her deal is. What about you?"

"...Jimmy, if I could be 100% honest with you, I think I'm homeless right now." Lyndsey sighed.

"Again? Lytz, dear... why? How? Everything ok?" Jimmy said as he reached out and put a hand on hers. She lifted her thumb and placed it over his hand in return.

"Yeah, well... getting better. Sean is just... something's wrong. He's gotten deeper into the drugs than I ever did. I think he's going to get in trouble soon. I just grabbed what I could from the house while he was gone the other day, and I'm pretty much living in a car. But yeah, you won't believe who our other roommate is!"

"Who? I have no idea," Jimmy said.

"Trevor!" Lyndsey exclaimed.

"No shit? Wow. I've been playing poker with him again lately, and I had no idea."

"And I had no idea that was going on either. He must just talk about completely different things when he comes home."

"Like what?" Jimmy asked.

Lyndsey stared into her coffee for a moment before taking a sip. She pushed it back on the counter and sighed before she looked back to Jimmy.

"We have a lot to catch up on. Not only over the last couple of years, but here lately. I need a nap. I've been so exhausted... Let's go out tonight. Let's go run around town like we used to back in the day. I'll take a nap and meet you somewhere."

Jimmy smiled and then sighed. "That sounds great. I'd love that. But I'm not sure what Megan would have to say about this."

Lyndsey laughed. "It's complicated, right? No need to *make* it more complicated on your end. Is your number still the same?"

"My phone got damaged recently. I can't be reached by phone right now. What about you? Maybe I can contact you?"

"I'm a bit out to lunch on that myself. How about we just agree to meet on the Broad Street bridge, by downtown. How's that sound? Maybe 5:30?"

"5:30 works. I look forward to catching up with you."

"You too, Jimmy." Lyndsey threw back the rest of her coffee, closed her laptop, and leaned in to give him a quick hug. She smiled, waved, and turned around to exit, walking quickly. Jimmy watched her leave and stared at the door for a moment after she was gone. He sat back down and took a sip of his coffee. It was already lukewarm.

CHAPTER THIRTEEN

"I want to get lost, you know? I want to feel like a tourist in our own city. I want us to just be completely, anonymously. *Happily*, in this moment," Lyndsey de Rueda said as she leaned over the rail along the Scioto River, her eyes clear in the sunlight, her long black hair whipping across her face in the breeze. She wore a waist-length electric-blue blazer over a white blouse and a black skirt that loosely fell about her legs.

Jimmy Glencroft stood alongside her, clad in a brown and orange plaid shirt tucked into his jeans, squinting against the sun as it hung above the Columbus skyline, the dipping sun's light refracting against the sides of the skyscrapers and making the view even brighter. Despite the painful glare, Jimmy gazed on, taking in the magnificent architecture before him like he had so many times before.

"What do you have in mind?" Jimmy asked.

"How much do you have in your pocket?" Lyndsey smiled.

"I have 37 dollars."

"Mmmmm... where'd you get *that* kind of money?" She turned and smiled wryly at him.

"Oh, girl, you have no idea. What about you?"

She flashed a blue credit card. "Let's live it up, courtesy of structured debt."

"So... the girl who's living in her car and hasn't had a real job in forever has a credit card. A'ight, that's cool. That's not a red flag or anything. Okay, let's commit to this. From this point forward, everything's going to get weird."

"Deal!" Lyndsey turned around and loped down the sidewalk towards Broad Street and the bridge across the river.

A new bar had opened recently in the shadows of the iconic LeVeque Tower, the cream-colored Art Deco spire that marked the highlight of Columbus architecture. The bar was on the ground floor of a neighboring high-rise, a bright pink and blue flashing marquee indicating that *Mixx Midtown* was open for business. Jimmy and Lyndsey shrugged and smiled at one another before entering, flashing IDs to the disinterested doorman and wandering into the establishment.

Mixx Midtown's open floor plan had plenty of room for dancing and mingling, spinning blue and pink lights flashing across peoples' faces to the rhythm of electronic indie music. On a weekend evening, a place like this would be brimming with young professionals and college students prowling for a good time. This was no weekend evening, though; this late Tuesday afternoon found Jimmy and Lyndsey with minimal company.

"Corona with lime," Jimmy said to the masked male barkeep. Lyndsey slapped the blue credit card face-down on the table.

Lyndsey snickered, wrinkling her nose. "Corona? Really? Come on, Jimmy. Bottomless tab on me."

Jimmy smiled. "No, really, thanks. I don't want to drain you. We should take it easy."

Lyndsey lightly kicked Jimmy's shin with her flat. "Go on. I don't care." She smiled at the barkeep. "I'll have a Long Island."

Jimmy sighed and then smiled and waved back to the barkeep. "Better add a Jaeger Bomb with that Corona, friend."

"That's more like it!" Lyndsey said. "I'm gonna go check out the TouchTunes since there aren't many people here. Let's take it over like old times."

"Alright, I'll catch up. You know I need to hear some shitty alternative rock, Lytz!"

"You got it," Lyndsey said as she sauntered away.

The barkeep dropped off Jimmy's shot and beer. Jimmy turned his attention to the TVs for the time being. He powered through his Jaeger Bomb, wiped off his mouth, and tuned in to what the evening news anchors were discussing, reading the closed captioning as Lyndsey's music choice ("The Distance" by Cake) warbled through the bar.

Jimmy's relaxed attention on the television became markedly more intense as the lead story played through. The anchors were discussing reported gang violence flaring up in Columbus. Jimmy's face drained to a light pale behind his beard, and he held his cold beer against his furrowed forehead as he watched the video coverage play through.

Two federal agents were murdered in South Bloomfield. No arrests were made, authorities looking for a green Humvee without plates. Dice Stop closed until further notice. Police are looking for a person of interest, Robert Nenkovic, 30, of Beavercreek, Ohio. A reward line has been set up with any information on the whereabouts of Robert Nenkovic.

Body of Mirko Pavlovic, 27, of Dayton, Ohio – recovered from a sedan sunken in the Scioto River at Griggs Reservoir. Pavlovic was killed by gunshot wounds before the car was intentionally disposed of. One person of interest is in custody. Columbus Police are looking for the owner of the sunken sedan, Manuel Rezendes, 29, of Columbus, who has also been named as a person of interest in Pavlovic's murder.

Rezendes has been reported missing by his family, and a multi-district search operation is underway. Again, here is the Columbus Police Crimestoppers reward line – any information related to his whereabouts? Call this number.

"You okay?" a bartender asked Jimmy. This one was a woman – the male bartender earlier was busy with another patron. Her question spooked Jimmy, and he dropped his beer, the Corona flowing all over the bartop.

"Oh my God, I'm so sorry," Jimmy said. "Here, let me get..."

"Don't worry about it. It's okay," she replied as she pulled out a large rag and cleaned the mess. "Want another?"

"Yeah, yeah, sure..." Jimmy said, still processing the information he saw on the TV. "I'm sorry. I just, I just found out on the news that my buddy went missing."

The bartender drooped her eyes above her bright pink mask. "I'm so sorry, honey. Tell ya what. Next drink you get, I'll make it strong for you. What do you want?"

Jimmy shook his head, sighing. "I appreciate the offer. Uhhh... I'll have a Jack and Coke, then. Thanks, ma'am."

The woman laughed. "Ma'am? Honey, I'm not old enough for that yet. Alright, so do you want it on your tab?"

"Yeah, sure. It should be under de Rueda. Thanks."

The bartender turned to ring up the drink. Jimmy looked back up at the TV, hoping to see more information on Manny's disappearance. The news had already moved on to a local interest piece about a child entrepreneur. He sighed and drummed his fingers against the bar while he awaited his next drink. After a moment, the bartender returned, shrugging.

"Sorry, hon, I don't have a card under de Rueda," she said.

"Ummm... well, what about Doan?" Jimmy asked.

"Let me check. Hold on one second, hon." The barkeep turned to the computer monitor at center-bar and scanned through the names.

"Well, there are only two other folks on the tab right now – and I know them both. Are you... Pav... Pavlicheck? Polachek?"

"Come again?" Jimmy lifted himself out of his chair.

"Pav... no, I'll spell it... P-A-V-L-O-V-I-C. That you or your friend?"

"Oh God."

"...Hun. Everything okay?"

"oh god."

Lyndsey trotted back over to Jimmy, smiling as she sipped her Long Island through a straw. "So I have Cake, Collective Soul, and Beck coming up and... Jimmy, are you okay?" she stopped midsentence as she looked up to see all color drained from Jimmy Glencroft's face.

"...Mirko Pavlovic? Please tell me this is a coincidence." Jimmy muttered.

Lyndsey dropped her glass. It shattered. One of the bartenders let out a muffled groan.

"Jimmy, I know you probably have a lot of questions..."

"He's dead. Why do you have a dead man's credit card?"

Lyndsey glanced over her shoulder to see that both bartenders and a fellow patron were looking on in interest. "Not here. Not now."

"Then where? Then when?"

"Jimmy, please. I think I'm in danger. We need to go."

"Am *I* in danger? By talking to you? By being in public with you? What the hell is wrong with you?"

"Jimmy, please."

"Lytz, no. God damn!"

Jimmy turned on a heel and walked quickly out of *Mixx Midtown*. He threw his arm up in front of his face to conceal himself from any cameras. His other arm held his stomach instinctively as his breaths came ragged. He pushed past other pedestrians and ran down the sidewalk, the dimming twilight and the concrete of the city and the grey of the rain-streaked sky all blurring in his vision as he ran.

"Jimmy! Wait! I need you more than ever. Please," Lyndsey yelled out to him as she ran behind him. Jimmy ignored her and pressed forward, back across the bridge over the river. Cars around them slowed to watch as she screamed for him. Lightning cracked the sky.

After what felt like a half-marathon, Jimmy reached the surface parking lot about a block down the bridge, where his minivan awaited him. He knelt over to catch his breath, eyes shut as he processed everything running through his head.

"Jimmy! I'm begging you!"

Jimmy jogged towards his minivan. Time slowed all around him as he realized a Cream Dream Donuts truck was parked right beside him. Sean Doan walked around from the truck's passenger side wearing a baggy Cream Dream uniform, a tire iron clutched in both hands. Trevor MacKenzie popped out from the drivers' side, a beanie pulled low over his head, similarly in uniform.

"Whoa, Trevor! What the fuck are you doing here? Oh God. Oh no," Jimmy gasped as he saw Sean Doan.

Sean walked right past Jimmy. Jimmy turned to follow Sean's stern gaze and screamed when he saw Lytz walking up the sidewalk not far away. He dug his feet in and tried to run for Sean, but Trevor wrapped his arms around Jimmy from behind and held him close.

"Dammit, Trevor!" Jimmy yelled. He threw a sharp elbow back into Trevor's ribs. Trevor maintained his grip through the successive two jabs but could not hold on as Jimmy dropped to one knee and rolled into a face lock takeover, tossing the taller Trevor over his shoulder. Jimmy popped Trevor in the face with his fist, rolled and staggered up, and sprinted after Sean.

Lyndsey gasped when she saw Sean, clenched her fists, and froze in her tracks. As he approached, she turned and ran back towards the bridge. A sidewalk led down towards a wider greenway trail that ran parallel to the Scioto River to the right. She slipped down the embankment, and Sean bore down on her, getting a grip on her.

"You stupid bitch! You fucked everything up for us!" Sean screamed into Lyndsey's face.

"Sean, no! Please, go! Lyndsey screamed. Rain poured down from the closing clouds above, soaking Sean's oversized, *Trevor*-nametagged uniform.

"Fuck you! Fuck you!"

Before Sean could raise the tire iron to strike Lyndsey, the wail of sirens broke his rage. Red and blue reflected across the white of the bridge. He left Lyndsey and turned back up the embankment just as Jimmy Glencroft was running down it. The tire iron fell from his hands as Jimmy tackled him to the ground, and they slid down the muddy knoll. Jimmy brought his fists down upon Sean's head and face with force, rocking him with repeating blows, Sean's attempts to block weakened by his surprise and prone position. Jimmy drew blood as he smashed his fist repeatedly into Sean's eyes, nose, and mouth.

"Columbus P.D.! Put your hands in the air!" a shout came down from above.

Jimmy finally stood as Sean scrambled off, past Lyndsey and down the greenway at a full sprint. He disappeared from view. Jimmy numbly raised his hands in the air, staring listlessly after Sean, and his gaze shifted to Lyndsey. She mouthed *thank you* and turned to run off in the same direction as Sean.

Jimmy didn't see the police officer. He couldn't bear to turn and look. The officer grabbed his hands and held them behind his back as he slipped cuffs around his wrist and clicked them into place.

"Am I under arrest?" Jimmy asked.

"Come with me," the officer said and jerked his arm.

"Am I being detained, or am I free to go?"

"I said *come with me!*" the officer barked.

"Am I being detained, or am I free to go?" Jimmy repeated.

"Save me the bullshit, kid. Say that one more time, and you *will* be detained. Now *come with me*, and we will take care of you at the station."

The cop pulled Jimmy along with him, and they walked back up the embankment towards the bridge, where two cop cars had blocked off traffic going in either direction. Jimmy started to walk towards one of them, but the cop jerked him back in another direction. There was an unmarked black car, its only police identification the whirling red and blue lights tucked between the windshield and the hood. The cop opened the door for Jimmy and guided him in to sit comfortably as possible with the cuffs on. Jimmy looked to the ceiling of the unmarked police car and whispered a prayer as the cop shut the door, walked around to the drivers' side, and climbed in himself. After he closed the door and dimmed the police lights, he took off in the opposite direction of the bridge. They rolled past the gentrifying neighborhood of Franklinton and off to the blight of The Bottoms as the sun sank, dimmed, behind swirling rain clouds.

CHAPTER FOURTEEN

Jimmy Glencroft stared straight ahead at the wall. He sat at one end of a long table in the dimly lit conference room of an unmarked and nondescript business, deep in the reaches of an outer-ring neighborhood. The best he could gather, the little strip mall business used to be some kind of payday loan place or bank – he saw a teller window from the back hallway as he had been ushered into the room by the unidentified officer who had cuffed him and hauled him away from the riverside.

Jimmy sat in the conference room for over an hour by himself. His right arm was cuffed to an office chair and was cramping. No matter how he squirmed, he couldn't get the cramp to relax, but at least he found a way to kink his arm to where it didn't get worse. Jimmy's right and left ankles were both cuffed tightly to the office chair to keep him from pushing around. This further complicated his efforts to seek comfort, as he was careful not to haul himself down to the ground in an ugly pile.

The door to the conference room finally opened. Three figures walked in: a short and matronly woman with her hair in a tight brown bun, a larger man with close-cropped hair and olive skin, and the officer who brought him here, an older fellow with a ring of grey hair around his otherwise bald head. They carried with them a few dark manila folders filled with papers. A fourth man entered shortly thereafter, a stocky white man with his white hair in a short ponytail. He looked like he would be more comfortable wearing a tie-dye dancing bear t-shirt than the crumpled bargain-bin suit he wore – ugly gold and brown, a look straight from the Dwight Schrute collection. He took a seat next to Jimmy.

"James Jackson Glencroft," the shorter woman said as she looked straight into his eyes with her own steely blues. "Detective Sophie Browning of the Drug Enforcement Agency. I'm here with Agent Gabriel Contreras of the DEA," – the large olive-skinned man nodded – "and Lieutenant Lewis Carew of the Columbus Police Department, Missing Persons Unit."

"I'm your lawyer, kid. The name is Gerald Uhlrich," the ponytailed man next to Jimmy said as he passed him a card. Sure enough – *Gerald Uhlrich, Public Defender*.

"I... I don't have a lawyer?" Jimmy said.

"Oh, we know," Detective Browning said with a smirk. "We got you one. It's hard to afford one with thirty-seven dollars in your bank account and facing homelessness, with no employment prospects. Have you heard from Megan or heard back from that job application with Metro?"

"I, er... what? How... Oh," Jimmy stammered.

"Yeah, kid, they're the government; they know everything," Gerald said. "You don't have to answer anything they ask, for the record."

"We would be interested in hearing more about your friend Manny Rezendes," Lieutenant Carew said. "It would probably be in your best interest to talk about him."

"Or maybe your friend Brody Marlowe?" Agent Contreras asked. "How's he doing? You hear from him?"

Jimmy stared over Detective Browning's shoulder at the wall. His heart flurried as blood rushed to his head.

"Don't worry, kid, you're not in trouble... yet," Detective Browning said. "We could have got you for assault today, but the witnesses split. Or maybe fraud – after all, you were drinking on a dead man's dime."

"Poetic..." Jimmy muttered. Gerald nudged him with a sharp elbow.

Jimmy looked back and forth to all three law enforcement officers before he turned back to Gerald.

"I... I guess I'm willing to talk to you guys, but I don't know what you want from me. I just... I guess... I don't want to get in trouble for anything I say?" Jimmy said to everyone.

Gerald leaned forward across the trouble and whispered to Detective Browning. Browning nodded and turned to face Jimmy.

"The federal government can work on full immunity in return for anything you tell us. You're a witness and not a person of interest," Detective Browning said.

Gerald stood, reached across Jimmy, and pulled up the chain at his right arm while he glared at Browning. Browning sighed and rolled her eyes.

"Okay, so maybe you're a person of interest," she said.

"What?!" Jimmy exploded. "Are you kidding me? For what? What did I do?"

"Sounding awful guilty there, buddy..." Agent Contreras said.

"Again, Jimmy, silence is golden..." Gerald growled.

"So is compliance," Lieutenant Carew said. "Let's start with Rezendes. Since our interests with him are mutual across the board."

Jimmy nodded. "Sure. Start with Manny. Where is he? Is he okay?"

The three officers exchanged glances with one another. Jimmy squirmed. Gerald elbowed him again.

"Better if they ask the questions," Gerald said.

There was an uncomfortable pause before the conversation continued.

"Manuel Rezendes. You played football with him and have maintained a friendship with him throughout adulthood. What can you tell us about Manny?" Detective Browning asked. Agent Contreras reached across the table with a recording device. He planted it in front of Jimmy and clicked a button.

Jimmy regarded the device with a moment of curiosity, and then he spoke.

"Alright, so... Manny Rezendes. Yeah, we graduated together. Been friends for over ten years. Um, he works hard; we lost touch for a few years because he went out west to work oil fields or drive a truck or something. We play poker and sometimes party together."

"Party together, eh?" Detective Browning said. "Can you tell me more about that?"

"Well, see, nothing crazy. Like, high school house party style partying? I dunno. Just beers and stuff."

Jimmy looked up. Gerald was glaring at Lieutenant Carew. Carew turned to Jimmy.

"The City of Columbus can work on immunity too. Please elaborate on your parties with Manny. Did you... see or do anything weird with him?"

Suddenly, Jimmy's mind clicked. *The candles. This is about the candles. Oh shit, they know about them.*

"No trouble? For me or any of my friends?" Jimmy asked.

"No tro-" Agent Contreras started. Detective Browning stamped on his foot.

"No trouble for you. Your friends have their own troubles. You control your own destiny," Browning said. "I can't guarantee anything yet. But work with us, and we will work with you."

Gerald nodded for Jimmy to continue.

"Okay..." Jimmy took a deep breath. "Do you have any water? I haven't had anything to drink in hours, and my head is pounding. It's been rough."

Contreras nodded and produced a bottle of lukewarm generic-brand water from his bag. He looked to the other officers and offered them bottles too. They declined.

"Thanks for asking me, Gabe," Gerald said.

"That's Agent Conteras to you," Agent Contreras said. Jimmy took a swig from the water before breathing deeply once more and starting his story.

"Okay. So... I see that honesty is my best policy here. Manny Rezendes... okay, so we have gotten drunk a lot together. We've smoked some weed – and I've seen him do pills. Not sure what kind of pills, but I can't imagine that these were prescribed to him."

In addition to letting the recorder capture everything, Detective Browning and Lieutenant Carew jotted notes on small legal pads. Browning nodded for Jimmy to continue.

"I... I don't know what it is some of my friends are up to. I feel I've always been kept on the edge or outside of something they have going on. Manny is probably involved, to be honest – but not the leader."

"Okay, we're getting somewhere," Browning said. "If you could pin any one of your friends as the leader, who would it be? And why?"

Jimmy sighed. "I don't want to be some kind of snitch here; I really don't."

Contreras nodded. "I understand that. Believe me. But Jimmy – I don't think many of these people are really your friends. You're always going after them, but how many of them go after you? Think about it."

Jimmy stared absently at Contreras.

"Gabe has a point," Browning said. "Does it feel like you're the only one who visits the others, the only one who makes the first call? Friendship is a two-way street. I'm not asking you to rat out any true friends, Jimmy. If cutting off the head of the snake prevents other people from getting bit, wouldn't you do it?"

Jimmy laughed. "Sounds like U.S. foreign policy."

"Sounds like you're not in a position to make that observation," Contreras said. He tapped the table. "Come on now, buddy. We need some names, some locations, something."

"I don't think these guys are bad people. I really don't want to see anything happen to them."

"Jimbo," Browning said, "these guys *are* bad people. They've been dealing drugs and committing petty crimes like theft and assault for a very long time. It appears to be recent that they've escalated to murder and grand larceny. Even before the murder, people *have died* directly because of your... friends. You can save lives by talking."

Gerald nudged Jimmy and whispered. "You really don't have to say anything, kid. You're safe either way. You're not the one they want."

"Never said he was safe," Browning said. "But he could be."

Jimmy nodded and sat silent for a long spell. Detective Browning kept her eyes transfixed on him while Agent Contreras leaned back and stared at the lights above. Lieutenant Carew shuffled through papers as they all waited for Jimmy to say something, anything.

"I have an idea," Jimmy said at last.

"Go on," Browning replied. Gerald leaned forward in interest and clasped his hands under his bearded chin as he leaned his elbows on the table.

"Okay, so... I'm certain the ringleader of this whole thing is Craig Foxx, Foxx Construction. If you guys are any good at your jobs, I'm sure you already know about him. I don't know why he's mixed up in dealing drugs when he owns a construction company, especially one that always seems to have projects," Jimmy said.

Browning smiled. "This is the kind of stuff that can help. Thank you, Jimbo. Please, by all means, go on..."

"I'm glad. Well, I don't think I can go much further until something gets done on my end. See, I'm broke and unemployed and running out of options and time. I don't want to end up falling in with guys like this, you know? But... I owe Craig Foxx a favor, and I'm sure I can negotiate with him to where I can do some work for him," Jimmy explained. "Here's what I'm thinking. You give me a chance to go on a job with Craig Foxx and earn a little money – I'll wear a wire. Or a secret camera. Or I'll just let you know what happened. I need something, I need help... I don't like saying this, but I'm up against the wall here."

Gerald put a hand on Jimmy's shoulder as Jimmy wiped a tear out of his eye. "I'll keep them to their word," Gerald said. "You get them some inside intel on Foxx and his operation, and we will see to it that your life gets better."

"This will get us closer to finding Manny," Lieutenant Carew said. "Your point of contact moving forward will be Browning – CPD will get necessary info through her office. We will give you some breathing room to operate."

Detective Browning nodded. "Jimmy, let's get you on the phone with Foxx and his people here in a minute... and we will get Gabe to fit you with a wire. I'm sure we can arrange a per-diem for food. Let's move this forward."

Jimmy sighed, closed his eyes, and waited as the law enforcement agents shuffled about, conversed in hushed tones, and scribbled out his fate.

An hour later, Jimmy was finally able to leave. He found himself outside of a strip mall on the west side of Columbus in the middle of the night, not an ideal situation for anyone. He sighed and stared into the misty sky above. The faintest sliver of a newly waxing moon winked at him from behind a cloud before it disappeared. He whispered some thoughts to himself as he walked, circling, hopeless in the sparse parking lot. In one hand, he held a plastic bag, in the other a half-empty bottle of water.

"They got you too?"

Jimmy jumped out of his skin. He dropped the bottle and did not watch it roll away.

Lyndsey de Rueda waved at him from under a streetlight. A cigarette smoldered between her fingers.

"Jesus, Lytz, you know I don't like surprises," Jimmy said as he strode over to her. "But you sure are a sight for sore eyes."

"I've been told that a time or two," she said as she tossed her cigarette on the ground. "So what do they have you doing?"

Jimmy raised his eyebrows at her.

"It's cool, bro, you know we're in this together," Lyndsey said. "They've got me working on Sean and Trevor. I guess I can finally get back at him by trapping him with the Feds."

"And Trevor?!"

"Jimmy, it's probably best you think about letting Trevor go. He's enabled Sean's abuse and is just as bad off. His record is cleaner than Sean's, so I'm sure he will be okay once the hammer drops." Lyndsey walked closer to Jimmy and hugged him. She nestled into his flannel and sighed.

"Lyndsey, you're just... *okay* with snitching on our friends like that?" Jimmy asked.

"Did you just call Sean your friend?"

"You know what I meant."

"You're thinking about it, too," Lyndsey guessed. "What's in the bag?"

"Oh, this? I..." Jimmy held up the plastic bag. "Okay, you got me. A wire. A couple coordinates. You know... completely normal shit."

"I'm too good, aren't I?"

"Something like that."

"Hey, Jimmy... I'm glad you ended up here too. I think this could be great. We might have a second chance. A way out," Lyndsey said. "We deserve this."

"I don't know," Jimmy said. "I don't think we can be the judge of that."

"I think we can. The gavel's in our hands now, so to speak." Lyndsey looked into the sky and smiled. "You've been wanting me to leave Sean for years. Here's my chance to finally do that without worrying about getting beaten or hurt more. Are you in?"

Jimmy kicked some gravel and muttered before responding. "At the cost of our integrity? Working with the government? There's something bigger at play here. I don't like this one bit."

"Come on, that's high school Jimmy speaking. Come on, Pastor James, let's not stress on that too much. We should probably be heading home."

"*We?*"

"Yes, 'we.' Can I crash with you, Smash? Come on. Your girl's gone, right? It will be like old times."

"Heh... which old times? I'm sure there are some I wouldn't go back to."

"Oh, you know the ones. Come on, it will be okay. There's nothing wrong with doing what you need to survive, and I'm sure we will need one another at some point."

"That's what I'm afraid of."

"I'd be lying if I said I wasn't afraid either, Jimmy. But I'm less afraid when I'm with you."

Lyndsey's brown eyes gazed into Jimmy's gray blues for a long moment, then she turned and began walking east down the street. Jimmy observed by the way she played with her blazer that she wasn't as confident as she let on.

"Come on, I think we're only a fifteen-minute walk from where you parked your van earlier. Do you still have that weighted blanket?" Lyndsey asked.

"Only if you'll still let me rub your feet," Jimmy said. His hot blush was even more apparent in the pinch of the November cold.

"See, those are the good times. I'll even let you play your music."

"Hah, the joke's on you, Lytz – I lost my best CDs when I wrecked the Pontiac..."

And so Lyndsey de Rueda and James Glencroft strode down the street in the wee hours of the morn, huddled together for warmth and more, the fuzz of optimism audible against the dirge that was their situation.

Drago Zupan smirked to himself as he watched them walk past his position, sitting on a bench in an empty bus stop. Jimmy was so wrapped up in Lyndsey that he didn't bother looking at Drago. He touched his chest to make sure his wire was secure under his own jacket, waited until there was a safe distance between them, then stood to deliberately follow suit.

CHAPTER FIFTEEN

Foxx Construction's main warehouse was off Industrial Parkway, a long two-lane road between Plain City and Dublin. A large black and white sign with the company's name stood at the end of a long, wide drive between densely aligned trees. The electronic gate opened for James Glencroft and Finn Aittokallio, the firefighter driving a rusted white pickup truck onto the property with Jimmy as the passenger. Jimmy's head swiveled, gazing at the bustling construction yard as they pulled to the front of a long, vast building. Forklifts, trucks, and all manner of heavy vehicles moved around on the other side of a barbed wire fence, hauling pipes and metal and lumber. Craig Foxx was already waiting outside, his tattooed arms crossed over his barrel chest, wearing a black company polo and khakis.

Jimmy shook hands with Finn, hopped out of the truck, and thanked him for the ride. As Finn backed the truck out to turn and drive away, Jimmy stepped toward Craig, extending his hand for a shake with him as well.

Craig just nodded at Jimmy, his face tight and severe, arms remaining crossed. Jimmy put his hands into the pockets of his black Flavortown hoodie and braced himself against the crisp autumn wind. Craig looked down at Jimmy.

"Well, glad you showed up," Craig said matter-of-factly. "Your vehicle is starting to use up some much-needed space in the warehouse. I'm excited to get rid of it."

Jimmy sighed. "I didn't mean to be a bother," he said with a slow shrug. "What do I owe you for storage? I'm sure we can work out a payment plan?"

Craig unfolded his arms and tucked his hands into his khaki pockets. He shook his head. "I told you, I don't want you to pay me anything. We're good. All I want is to cash in that favor and cash you back out."

"What do you mean?" Jimmy asked meekly.

"I've got a buyer," Craig said, allowing himself to grin a little. "One of my clients was over and saw your vehicle. They are into, I guess, 'artisanal junkyarding?' Your car fits their piece. I couldn't act without you because it's technically under your name."

"Artisanal junkyarding? I guess I've heard it all now. Whatever gets this off our hands," Jimmy said. "I guess Dale Earnhardt Jr. does stuff like this too; it wasn't him buying it, was it?"

Craig shook his head. "No, just a client. We've actually arranged to meet him at another warehouse. If you come with us and just agree we can sell the car to him, you'll get a cut."

Jimmy raised his eyebrows. "A cut? The car wasn't worth much before it was wrecked. I can't fathom how much it is now. Besides, why just a cut?"

Craig let his grin widen a little more. "Well, there's the whole storing-your-uninsured-wreck-for-three-weeks thing. My cut will cover the business costs associated with this. Don't worry, I'll get you a full invoice. Perfectly legal."

I'm being hustled, Jimmy thought. *Yet again, I've allowed myself to. I shouldn't have ever told him I'd pay. At least I can get some information for Browning...*

"How much is my cut?" Jimmy asked, feeling for his wallet in his hoodie pocket. Thin, it only had a few small bills and a near-useless debit card inside.

"We'll see after we talk to our guy," Craig said. "It will be worth our time. Now come with me – We're delivering a few things to this other warehouse. It'll be a convoy. We got room for you if you're willing to ride out Nawakwa way."

"Nawakwa? That's where I'm from, actually. I'd love to ride out that way. Let me call Finn. I thought this would be quick. I'll tell him where I'm going; he'll love to hear this. Do you have a phone I can use?" Jimmy asked excitedly.

"No, kid, calm down. It's Nawakwa. Not a big deal. Come on, follow me. Our guys are about to roll out," Craig said as he turned and waved Jimmy to follow him.

Together the construction manager and former mascot made their way through the warehouse. There were rows of stacked construction material flanking either side, whether it be logs, wood, metal, vinyl... There were many pallets of bricks and even stone. Jimmy marveled at the warehouse's size and scope as he followed close to the fast-walking Craig Foxx. Between the beeping of forklifts as they moved material and the coarse language of workers as they moved among the rows yelling at each other, Jimmy felt like this was a mix between the back of a home improvement store and the factories he once toiled in back home.

There must be a million dollars' plus of material alone, Jimmy mused as he gazed at the tall racks of material. He was so busy staring around, he bumped into Craig, who had stopped in the middle of the aisle to check his phone.

"Hey, kid, watch where you're going," Craig said as he pocketed the phone. Jimmy muttered out an apology, but Craig cut him off. "That was the buyer. He's going to be there soon. We need to get a move on."

"So, who's the buyer?" Jimmy asked. "I'm curious, Craig. Please tell me more!"

"You're sure asking a lot of questions," Craig said. He laughed. "You wearin' a wire or something?"

"Oh, you know it, snitched up from the britches up."

Craig laughed again and kept walking. Jimmy's face reddened a shade, and he patted his shirt as discreetly as possible to make sure the bulge of his wire transmitter wasn't visible through his baggy hoodie.

After several minutes of walking, the pair came outside, the chill wind picking up. Jimmy saw the crunched-up remains of his green Grand Am on a rollback. Behind it was parked an unmarked 18-wheeler and Craig's personal vehicle, an elevated Dodge pickup with dually tires, massive chrome grille, dark-tinted windows, and four doors. Jimmy stepped toward the Pontiac to get a better look at what was his personal car for such a long time. Craig's big meaty hand reached out and grabbed Jimmy's shoulder.

"No," Craig said sternly. "Nothing to see there. Get in the truck; we need to roll."

"What's the big deal? I just wanna..."

"No," Craig cut Jimmy off. "Truck. Let's go."

Jimmy ambled over to the passenger side of the black Dodge dually and went to open the door when Craig grabbed him again.

"Wrong truck. 18-wheeler. I guess I need to make myself clear. You're riding in the back," Craig said, half-shoving Jimmy toward the semi rig behind it.

"Uh, is that legal? How do I ride?" Jimmy asked.

"Uh, is anything I do legal?" Craig said mockingly. "Find something to hold onto. You're a grown-ass man Jimmy, start acting like it. Do you want to get paid or what, man? Get in the freakin' truck."

Reluctantly, Jimmy moped to the back of the hauler. A ramp slid down and he walked up, a metallic clang with every step he took. The hauler's interior was packed with pallets and boxes stacked two high and two wide through about three-fourths of the length. A single orange forklift sat at the end, its forks solidly under a pallet in the middle, lowered and shut off.

"In case you haven't figured it out, you should probably sit in the forklift on the way there," Craig said. "The product will likely shift a little bit in transit. We tried to pack it tight, but we didn't have enough weight to move. Wear your seatbelt."

Craig pulled up the ramp and pushed it into the truck, rollers sliding it into the floor beneath Jimmy. Jimmy clambered up into the forklift and strapped himself in. He turned around to ask Craig if everything looked okay, but the construction manager was already slamming the door shut.

Relative darkness enveloped Jimmy Glencroft. There was some dim light alongside the trailer from the midday sun shining through slivers in the material, but otherwise, it was black. He could barely see the forklift controls in front of him or even his own hands. He sat there for what felt like an eternity before the engine rumbled on. *I thought he was in a hurry,* Jimmy thought, slumping as much as he could in the forklift to find a new comfort.

Jimmy closed his eyes to rest as the truck rolled forward.

No rest was to be had for quite some time. The loudness of the truck's engine, the shifting and slamming of freight ahead of him as they rolled, the loud decompression of the brakes... there was too much noise for him to handle. He tried to focus on random things to keep his mind from wandering, such as football plays or video games. Too often, Jimmy would randomly think of Megan or Lyndsey or Detective Browning and the enormity of his mission, and his mind would begin to slip again, and he would panic about his situation. Jimmy clenched his eyes shut and tried to blank out his mind as they rolled. Eventually, his own thoughts wore him down, and weary of the road, despite his discomfort and nerves, Jimmy fell asleep.

The convoy of dually, eighteen-wheeler, and rollback traveled down a two-lane road in the open country. Both sides of the road were flanked by open farmland and field. Clumps of deciduous forest would jut out from the nondescript land here and there, usually when the flatness was interrupted by a gently rolling hill. On the horizon, a single mountain loomed, wide and long, its mixed forests giving way to a weathered grassy bald at the top. Just over the lowest reaches of the mountain, discerning eyes at the proper elevation and angle could see a dim city skyline.

When a significant spot of woodland came upon the convoy, the large trucks came to a slow crawl and turned left onto a one-lane road. The vehicles barely fit. The trucks brushed against branches of low-hanging trees, the leaves ripe with the gold, yellow, and red of autumn. After a minute or two of driving, the dense pocket of woodland gave way to the open field once more. There was an electronic gate with an intercom system and keypad on one side and a kiosk where a guard could stand on the other. Today, the booth was empty. The gate was opened by someone unseen, the constant red light of a security camera in the kiosk focused on the road. Chain link barbed wire fence stretched out to either side for a hundred yards, then back several hundred more, forming a large rectangle around a concrete goliath of a building.

"PharmaScenticals" was the industry's name, displayed on a black and white sign in front of the spacious parking lot to the right of the tall, imposing structure.

There were a half-dozen trailer loading bays along the building's side, elevated above the parking lot for easy access by semis. In the front of the building, a grate garage door was raised for the rollback. Craig Foxx parked his Dodge dually outside the building and walked in via the garage, with Big Trace Onwudiwe lumbering in his wake. The dually was parked alongside a black Lotus and a half-dozen comparatively nondescript cars. Meanwhile, the eighteen-wheeler backed into one of the bays.

James Glencroft was startled when the door came open, and the ramp was lowered by Craig. Jimmy's eyes took a moment to adjust to the blast of light from outside as he climbed out and stepped onto the ramp. As he came into the warehouse, his eyes had to adjust back to dark gloominess, as the few working lights inside were dim. Craig directed Big Trace into the truck to man the forklift.

"Say, I could help out with that," Jimmy said. "I used to run a forklift down-home at a factory."

"Nah, I got something else for you," Craig said, putting a hand on Jimmy's shoulder and directing him toward a ladder near the outside wall. As they walked, Jimmy glanced around at his surroundings. This warehouse was more extensive but much emptier than the one at Foxx Construction. In the far corner sat a series of large cylindrical containers and a network of pipes. Jimmy spied what looked like a conveyor belt in the distance, dormant and still. On the far side of the warehouse, hazmat suits hung along the wall with complementing gas masks atop them.

"What is this place?" Jimmy asked as they walked toward the ladder. "What part of town is this in?"

"It doesn't matter," Craig replied flatly. "I do business here. Now, we'll be busy in the office working out the deal..."

"Can I come?" Jimmy interrupted. "It's my car."

"And it's my business, so no, you cannot come. Now, do you want me to continue speaking, or are you going to chime in again?" Craig replied with an edge. Jimmy remained silent.

"As I thought," Craig continued. "Now, here's a cell phone," he said as he gave Jimmy an old, square, gray Nokia phone.

"In the contacts, there is a number saved called 'Office.' I want you to call that if anyone at all comes to the front gate. That way, I can... let them in. Is that understood?"

Jimmy nodded. He stood there looking at Craig in awkward silence.

"Are... there any questions...?" Craig asked as he crossed his arms and tapped his right foot.

"If I call Office, will Pam answer?"

Craig's expression remained the same.

"Uh, yeah, actually," Jimmy said, "Why don't you just have me call your personal cell instead of the office phone?"

"I don't know? Because I have no service on my phone out here? Because I don't want to waste my damn minutes on this? You don't get rich by spending money. You get rich by *saving* money. Write that down."

Jimmy patted his pockets and looked around in a legitimate attempt to find something to write with. Craig groaned.

"Jesus, kid, you need to learn when someone's fucking with you. Alright, look. Climb this ladder. It will take you to a catwalk. At the end of a catwalk, a door leads to an outdoor catwalk. That should lead you to another ladder. Boom, rooftop. Call me no matter what, no matter who shows up at the front gate, okay?"

Jimmy nodded. "How long will this be?"

"However long it takes me to get my money. Now get outta here. I know you don't have nothin' to do."

Craig Foxx, Big Trace Onwudiwe, Winslow Barclay, and the two drivers, Hauerchuk and Troyer, walked into the boardroom, where Montreaux Pickens sat with three of his associates. Montreaux's associates were dressed in suits and ties, wearing sunglasses and remaining exceptionally still. This was a stark contrast to Foxx, wearing a black polo and khakis, Big Trace in a black and white hoodie displaying portraits of civil rights heroes, and Barclay and the two drivers wearing generic plaid shirts and jeans. Barclay's long hair fell between his shoulders in a ponytail.

Montreaux himself wore a suit and tie. His hair was twin-braided, his face clean-shaven, his rings gleaming as he crossed his fingers, leaning forward to face Craig Foxx.

"Glad you could finally show up," Montreaux said smoothly, his sharp dark eyes glaring holes into Craig's. "I must say, this is a lovely choice of location for an exchange. Literally the middle of nowhere."

Craig nodded, grinning. "I choose to partner with only the..."

"I was being sarcastic, you smug son of a bitch," Montreaux said quickly, quietly, and coldly. "This would have been ideal for our little exchange had it not been for the fact that the motherfuckin' 5-0 was on our tail half the way out here."

Craig raised an eyebrow. "I don't understand."

"What don't you understand, man? The motherfuckin' 5-0! Staties, the po-po's! Spooks, the boys in blue!" Montreaux clapped his hands to accent each point. "We had to split up our group and then roll up here separately. I thought you said this area was off they radar."

"It is, Montreaux," Craig said, comparatively calm. "They inspected this place for safety just last week. Never a violation here. We move the weight out any time they come over, too. Completely clean."

"I'm not so sure I can trust this transaction right now," Montreaux said, leaning back. "Only reason I'm here is because when I say I'mma meet, I mean I'mma meet."

Craig sighed. "Look. 1.6 mil in the truck, both weight, and arms. One mil of weight inside that car on the rollback. I know the truck is a bigger risk, but the rollback? Hiding in plain sight, Montreaux. Half now, half later? I can arrange to deliver the truck if we need to."

"You think you can get that weight across the country without getting popped?" Montreaux said. "Look, I can tell you small time. I don't know if you ready for the big time. I'm out."

Craig stood up, face reddening. "I don't know why you're backing out now, after coming across the country!" Craig yelled. "You're letting *one* cop sighting spook you? You say I'm small-time; if you're so big time, how come you let *that* get to you?!" He slammed a fist on the table, startling the otherwise stoic associates on both ends of the deal.

Craig leaned across the boardroom table. "In the last three weeks, I lost an employee. My clients are spooked and scattered. I lost some product. There's this gang outta Dayton trying to move in on my territory," Craig ranted. "To be honest with you, we're probably not safe here no matter what. It's not hot with the cops; it's hot with another group. The quicker we make this exchange, the better."

"...The fuck is wrong with you, man... The fuck is wrong with you?" Montreaux asked. He stood up and took two steps back from the table. "For all this trouble you're putting me into, the least you could do is give me a risk discount. What do you say two mil for the whole deal? For my trouble?"

Craig pushed down on the thick table, taking out his anger on it, his large arm muscles taut. Veins popped in his neck, visible even behind the razor blade throat tattoo. "If anything, I should *raise* the price for all the shit we've been through. I'm not here to negotiate. It's 2.6 mil for the whole deal, and I'm not leaving without it."

"...Are you *threatening* me?" Montreaux Pickens stepped forward, face to face with Craig. "You're not leaving without it? You keep talkin' like that; you'll be lucky to be leaving here at all."

The boardroom door unexpectedly swung open. Both sides stood, startled, drawing pistols and SMGs, ready to engage the threat. Barclay, Hauerchuk, and Troyer all groaned and lowered their arms when the entrant was revealed.

"Glad you're all armed," Landers said as he stepped into the conference room, flashing a gummy grin, looking quite out of place in an anime character t-shirt and sweatpants. Big Trace winced at the mere sight of Landers.

"We've got company."

132

Jimmy Glencroft sat atop the roof on the edge of a catwalk. He had one arm wrapped around a support bar, his legs dangling off the edge, swinging around back and forth in boredom as they were suspended in the open air. He watched for any birds or planes, anything to take his mind off things.

The wind chipped at his exposed face. He pulled his hood down and drew it tight. Jimmy's eyes wandered around the autumn colors of the woods around the property. After a few minutes, he stood and walked around the catwalk to see more of the area. Craig told him they were going to Nawakwa, but Jimmy did not recognize this part of town at all. Having been a former mailman and resident for 20+ years, he knew the lay of the county rather well, but this area was quite unfamiliar. He looked out over the open plain and sought landmarks such as hills or structures in the distance, but no such luck.

Jimmy came back around to the front and leaned over the rail of the catwalk. He pulled out the cell phone Craig had given him. It was an old phone; it had a couple bars of signal and no customization on the screen whatsoever. Jimmy idly flicked through the text message archive and contacts, snooping for fun. There were only two contacts: Office and Voicemail.

Jimmy yawned. Although it had been a couple weeks since his hellish weekend and he had gotten caught up on rest, Jimmy had felt tired ever since. When he was awake, he was fatigued. When he got around to sleeping, it would last for over twelve hours. Finding a balanced sleeping pattern had been difficult, and his body was feeling the stress.

It didn't help matters that Lyndsey was inconsistent company at best. There one night, gone for two. Always wanted pizza, never wanted to pay, never wanted to cook. No phone, no vehicle, but always seemed to come and go with no issue. Jimmy had been giving her the space she seemingly needed, as he recognized just how much he smothered her with attention when she was around. He was also dealing with paranoia about the return of Megan or revenge from Sean. Jimmy was constantly staring out the living room window...

Jimmy sat down and folded the hood of his black Flavortown sweatshirt around to his shoulder. He leaned against the outer wall behind him and improvised a pillow out of the hood fabric. At last, Jimmy closed his eyes.

Jimmy was snapped out of his reverie by the slamming of a car door in the distance. Jimmy scrambled and hoisted himself upright by the top bar of the catwalk. He blinked grogginess out of his eyes and focused through the daylight to see two black cars in the distance. They had parked behind the electronic gate, the vehicles adorned with bright yellow livery. A man in a dark uniform shined a high-beamed flashlight into the abandoned security kiosk.

Sheriff's Deputies! Jimmy's heart jumped into overdrive as he fumbled through his pockets for the phone Craig had given him. Jimmy's trembling grasp nearly dropped the phone when he located it. *Craig is so doing something illegal down there. The candles? His demeanor? I am in so much trouble... I hope Browning holds up her end.* Jimmy's thoughts snowballed out of control as he dropped stomach-first against the dark catwalk and observed the deputies, hoping he would blend in with the metal and shadows around him.

The cell phone rang as Jimmy prepared his own call. He had turned off vibrate somehow, the pinging ringtone loud and prominent. Cold sweat dripped down Jimmy's brow as he silenced the incoming call. He looked up, seeing another deputy step out of the other car, both uniformed men looking his way. *They heard the damn phone! I am so screwed! I don't have time for this incoming call. I need to call Craig!*

Mind racing, Jimmy flicked through the phone menu until he came to Contacts. As he looked at the deputies, one of whom appeared to be talking to someone on the radio, he pressed "Dial." Jimmy put the phone to his ear and cupped his free hand around his mouth to muffle his voice so the cops would not hear him.

A massive explosion ripped through the cop cars and sent them flying haphazardly into the air, clanging and disintegrating as shredded sheet metal flew in all directions. A billowing, full plume of orange and red fire erupted into the sky, a noxious-smelling gray smoke wreathing the ball of heat. Jimmy knelt, his jaw hanging wide open, unable to move as he watched the gate, kiosk, and trees to either side become engulfed in flame. Jimmy refused to seek any sign of the deputies. If not killed on impact by the explosion or a flying car, they would indeed be burned alive.

"Holy shit," Jimmy said softly as he watched the tendrils of flame and smoke spread across wood and metal alike. "Holy shit."

While Jimmy gazed at the wreckage, he did not see that Craig Foxx had made his way to the outer catwalk as well. Slowly, silently, the taller man moved beside Jimmy, calmly leaning his tattoo-wrapped arms onto the rail as well, smiling grimly as he viewed the wreckage.

"Your first kill was a double play," Craig said as he surveyed the chaos before them. Jimmy looked up at him, eyes wide and red as tears welled up.

"We need to leave," Craig stated as he put an arm on Jimmy's shoulders and guided him to the door. "You're going to come with us, you're going to stay calm, and I am going to find you a way out of this."

Craig and Jimmy made their way to the door, into the inside catwalk, and, one-by-one, down the ladder to the factory's production floor. Jimmy's climb down was laboriously slow as he trembled uncontrollably, moving only because he knew he had to. Craig Foxx maintained a smooth demeanor as he helped Jimmy down the ladder.

"What the hell, Foxx?" Montreaux Pickens shouted as he walked across the floor toward Craig and Jimmy. He was flanked by his three silent, suit-wearing associates. Big Trace, Landers, Barclay, Hauerchuk, and Troyer scrambled to keep up behind them. Big Trace moved up to stand with Pickens, who shoved the larger Trace back with menace.

"Don't be pushing my guy like that," Craig said as he stepped forth and glared down Pickens, one hand on his hip holster and the other pointing at him.

"I told you I don't like surprises, motherfucker," Pickens yelled at Craig. "You just blew up a pair of deputies, and who here is this guy? He sure as fuck wasn't on your dossier!"

Pickens leered at Jimmy, finally making eye contact. His eyes widened suddenly when he recognized him.

"It's the crazy dude from the fuckin' hot tub. Dancin', all singin' and shit... had no clue he was one of yours. I should have known. He soft as butter, though!"

"I had to have an extra body as an insurance policy," Craig said matter-of-factly. "You need to calm down – you're being too loud. We're all in this shit together. Jimmy here wouldn't have cleared your guys. I brought him along because we kind of owe each other, and I was giving him some of my cut."

Pickens shook his head, smiling. "I know this motherfucker ain't hard! Everyone wanna be hard until it's time to do hard shit. What are you doing making him the trigger? This kid ain't ready to be blowing up twelve! You tricked him, didn't you, Craig? I know this kid don't know!"

Craig glanced at Jimmy before looking back to Pickens. "Listen, Montreaux. I'll settle with him privately later. We did the right thing here if you want to keep this operation going. Now we should probably arm up, load up, roll up, and roll out."

"Really? Really, motherfucker?" Pickens paced back and forth. Both crews stood in a semicircle around him, Craig, and the openly weeping Jimmy Glencroft. Pickens threw his arms in the air.

"I been running an operation for years, and ain't no fool lost his life, my side or theirs, yet! I come to this little backwater Podunk motherfuckin' hamlet, and you blow up two cops. You said this was straight. You done fucked up, Foxx."

Craig stepped forward, reaching out his hand for a shake, trying to plead with Pickens. "Montreaux. I know it's bad. Reacting this way ain't gonna make it any better."

Montreaux Pickens had a .45 pulled in a flash, whirling around and pointing it at Craig's chest. Trace, Troyer, Barclay, Hauerchuk, and Landers pulled their weapons too; they were met with a quick reactionary draw by Pickens' three men. Craig stood in the middle of it all, slowly putting his hands behind his head, all the while refusing to break eye contact with Pickens.

"Pulling the trigger would be a grave mistake, Montreaux," Craig said as calmly as possible. All the men's eyes shifted furiously back and forth as everyone involved tried to watch one another's movements.

"You're one to talk about mistakes, Foxx!" Pickens yelled. "They just keep comin'! I can't trust you. I should've known better than to trust you."

Jimmy stood stock still, trembling among the bristling side-arms. Limbs rubbery, thoughts numb, he watched as the criminals yelled at and threatened one another. After a moment of shock, a plan materialized in his head.

I'm the only one without a gun being pointed at me, nor am I pointing a gun.

Jimmy lifted his head to try to make eye contact with someone, anyone. *I may be depressed, but I'm not ready to die.*

Big Trace Onwudiwe was the first to glance at Jimmy. They stared intensely at one another for a few seconds. Sweat streaked Trace's cheeks. He blinked rapidly to keep it out of his reddened eyes.

Jimmy pulled the cell phone out of his hoodie pocket slowly, just enough for Trace to see. Trace didn't break eye contact with Jimmy, so Jimmy used a quick downward flick of his eyes to gesture to what he wanted Trace to see. As soon as Trace saw it, he busted a wide smile. Trace mouthed the words *I got you* to Jimmy.

"I don't know what's going on here," Jimmy proclaimed, "But I know it's a crime. I'm calling the cops!"

Jimmy whipped out his phone. Four guns turned to point at him. He heard deafening shots. He fell to the ground, his view filled with the ceiling of the warehouse. He closed his eyes and held his breath, waiting to feel the pain, waiting to feel the blood ebb from his body, saying a final silent prayer. He heard yelling and bustling around him faintly behind the ringing in his ears. What felt like an eternity came to pass, and he felt someone grab his shoulders and pull him up. Jimmy opened his eyes, looked down at himself, and realized he got through the standoff without harm. Elation flooded through his body and relieved him of his tension. He blinked several times and whispered, "I'm still alive."

All three of Montreaux Pickens' goons lay still, pools of red spreading across the hard floor from their motionless forms. Pickens himself was wrestled to the ground by Big Trace, who had disarmed him. Pickens was shot but still very much alive as he thrashed against Trace's elephantine form and swore vehemently. Craig Foxx slumped against a nearby wall with Troyer and Barclay tending to him. Craig had been shot in the abdomen. He silently clutched the wound as his employees scrambled to tear a compress out of their clothing.

Troyer motioned to Landers.

"Dude, Landers, get the vet on the line. He's losing blood fast!" Troyer yelled.

Landers sneered his toothless grin at Troyer. "I don't take orders from you."

Troyer motioned to Barclay to continue helping Craig. Troyer, a tall, thick man with a shaved head and sharp goatee, approached the smaller Landers.

"It isn't about taking orders," Troyer said sternly, "but about doing what you can to save your boss. He's in no condition to give orders right now. Now call the vet, get the truck, do *something!*"

Jimmy numbly stepped forward, still holding the cell phone. "Why don't we just call 9-1-1?"

Landers and Troyer both turned to face Jimmy.

"You're fuckin' stupid, aren't you, kid?" Landers asked.

"Go to hell, dude," Jimmy said. "And ask the Devil for a new set of teeth while you're down there."

Landers stepped toward Jimmy. He pulled back his pistol, moving as if to strike Jimmy with it. Jimmy dove to the ground. Troyer hooked Landers' arm from behind, knocking the gun from his hand. Troyer twisted Landers' arm. There was an audible crack, and Landers whimpered as he too dropped to the ground. Jimmy scooted back and got to his feet as he regarded the chaos before him.

"Enough!" Craig Foxx bellowed from the wall. "Get yourselves together. Troyer, I ought to fire you for that. A good I.T. guy needs two arms."

"Sorry, sir," Troyer said with a shrug. "He was about to hurt Jimmy, is all."

"Landers is actually a part of this operation. In fact, at this point, Jimmy is a witness and a liability," Craig continued. He tried to stand but slipped and fell again. Barclay helped him upright.

"I ought to have Jimmy shot for even being here." Craig muttered.

Jimmy's tears welled up once more as he backed up towards the wall. He scanned the area for exits and whispered a prayer.

"Jimmy! Stop, I'm not actually going to shoot you," Craig gasped out. Craig's voice softened, and he began coughing. His skin paled.

"Get it together, guys," Craig said. "The cops will probably get here before too long, the whole front gate is burning. You know the contingency plan. Blow the place. Get the drugs and money to the lockup."

"If we even get there," Landers said with a toothless sneer. He pushed himself upright with his good arm.

Barclay, Troyer, and Trace all shared a look. They turned to face Landers.

"Something clicked in my head, not long after something snapped in my arm," Landers started. "The guys from the Dirty D Posse. Diversions by cop and service are part of their trade. They sent them here first to distract us. I can almost guarantee it."

Everyone stared at Landers, who stood up shakily.

"I promise they're already here."

"Listen, man, I ain't hearin' that nonsense," Big Trace said. "We need to get to the chopper. Both Foxx and Pickens need the vet - *fast*."

"Fuck Pickens, we don't need him; why don't we just leave him with his goons?" Landers replied.

"We don't need him, but we sure need his money," Trace said. With that, Montreaux Pickens surged upward, coughing and moving to strike Trace, who countered with a swift punch to the head. Pickens tried to speak but coughed and gagged up a fit instead.

"Enough, men. We need to move," Craig urged.

With Pickens' men all slain and Pickens fading, the only resistance in getting to the rooftop helipad was their own wounds and weight. Barclay and Troyer helped Foxx into the elevator while Big Trace hefted the subdued Pickens in a fireman's carry. Landers stayed behind and commanded Jimmy to help with the contingency plan.

Landers and Jimmy staggered around the warehouse. Together they spilled gasoline out of large jerry cans, splashing the accelerant to and fro, making sure to coat cans or tanks of any kind of chemical. Landers urged Jimmy to the rooftop with the can as he took the elevator. Jimmy poured some gasoline on the ladders behind him after he climbed. He rushed out to the outer catwalk to see how the fire outside had spread.

Despite the flames being lower to the ground than they were during the initial blast, they had spread considerably. Over 50 yards across, woodland was beset by some degree of flame, and the dark smoke billowed, taken by the light breeze. It could easily be seen for miles, and the faint whine of emergency sirens carried over the distance. Jimmy found himself still and unfocused for a long moment, his gut wrenched with guilt and anxiety, his vision fuzzy and his mind hazy. Landers barked at him and snapped him out of his freeze.

"Glencroft! Up here! Now!"

Up another short ladder to the very top level of the roof, and about 70 yards to the center, was a black six-seat helicopter. Jimmy and Landers ran forward, with Landers outpacing Jimmy by about two dozen paces. Jimmy saw Big Trace hauling the slumped and staggering Craig Foxx into the front with him. Montreaux Pickens was thrown into the back by Barclay and Troyer, the athlete's hands and feet bound by rope, a shirt stuffed into his mouth as a gag. Pickens was too weak from blood loss to resist. The helicopter's blades came to life, slowly at first and then accelerating at a clip, whipping up the air around as Jimmy and Landers made their approach. Landers chatted to Barclay for a moment before turning to greet Jimmy as he arrived at the helicopter.

As soon as Jimmy went to board the helicopter, Landers pulled him back with his good arm.

"What? What's this?" Jimmy asked sharply.

"Craig's the only certified pilot here, and he's too hurt to fly," Landers said. "We're changing around some personnel. We need you to drive a rig... you can drive stick, right?"

"Yeah," Jimmy replied. "Where would I drive to? Why me? Where *are* we?"

"Look, man... Barclay was supposed to be one of the drivers, but he's the next best choice to fly this thing since he's ran drones in the Army. The more questions you ask, the longer it takes us to get out, the more trouble we may find ourselves in."

The din of approaching sirens could be heard over the whirring chopper blades.

Landers handed Jimmy a pair of keys. "You have the rollback. Hauerchuk's already in the 18-wheeler. We didn't think about it until just now, but we need Craig's truck too, so we're sending Troyer with you. Use Craig's phone and call us when you're on the dirt road heading out. We're in Perkins, right outside Slade City."

"*Slade City?!* I thought we were in Nawakwa! Shit, where am I going? I haven't been here in years."

"Back to Columbus. Hit 77 north to 70 west. Foxx Construction HQ will do, there's no heat there yet. You should get there in two hours. If you can't figure it out, just trail the others. Now go." Landers shoved Jimmy towards the catwalk with his good arm.

Jimmy ran towards the catwalk with Troyer about thirty yards ahead of him, about to descend the staircase. Three men vaulted up the steps, wearing brightly colored soccer jerseys, assault rifles in hand. It was too late for Troyer, who barely had time to react as he was ripped open by the deadly cut of the weapons' fire, sprays of red in the air as Troyer's body jerked in reaction to the shots and slumped to the ground. Jimmy instinctively slid and ducked behind a duct, barely concealed as the assailants opened fire on the helicopter, standing directly in front of him, about twenty yards ahead now.

Bullet holes ripped through the helicopter, causing aesthetic damage but not wounding anyone. Big Trace, Landers, and Barclay stepped out and returned fire upon the assailants with pistols, shooting around or under the helicopter. They were outgunned heavily by what Jimmy figured to be the Dirty D operatives.

What if this is all my fault? Oh my God, the wire...

Jimmy was out of view of both the helicopter and the assailants. He reached up into his undershirt and ripped the wire and transmitter. Jimmy grunted in pain as the tape pulled hair from his chest upon removal. He reached around the front of the duct and threw the transmitter in, and even over the helicopter's whirr, he heard the clunk of the transmitter as it fell.

Should I help them fight back? Should I get to the truck and save my own ass? Holy shit I've made it my whole life never seeing anyone die and I've seen so many today and Oh my God

Jimmy snapped out of his thoughts and ran over to Troyer's body, his footsteps drowned out by gunshots. He evaded being spotted by the three assailants, who focused entirely on the targets in and around the helicopter. Jimmy found Troyer's sidearm in a body holster. He struggled back vomit and tears as he smelled the sulfur of bullets and the searing of flesh, blood gooey on his fingers as he fumbled with the weapon.

Jimmy looked up to see the assailants close in on the helicopter, their shots now sporadic rather than sustained as the resistance ahead was weaker. Jimmy flicked off what he surmised was the safety switch on the weapon, leveled it towards the assailants, and ran forward, all outside reason and focus lost entirely, the only thought in his head being *kill or be killed*.

Barclay had made it safely into the cockpit of the helicopter. Landers and Big Trace stood their ground for a long moment before their grimmest reality set in. Landers was first to fold as he hopped into the helicopter and beckoned Trace aboard. Trace shook his head, yelling back and urging them to go on. Finally, realizing Trace was dead set on staying behind, Landers rapped on the cockpit/cabin divider to command Barclay to fly on.

Upon seeing the helicopter start to ever so slowly lift off the ground, Jimmy took his first shot. The release of the gun was more violent than he anticipated, the recoil nearly jerking the weapon from his hands. The bullet went nowhere near an assailant, and it served no purpose other than to bring his presence to their attention. They turned quickly, and Jimmy saw three rifles point towards him. He shot again twice, and one of them connected with an assailant's leg. The assailant crumpled to the rooftop and dropped his weapon.

This bought Big Trace enough time to step out from around the helicopter and take the other two down with three shots. He kept shooting, but his pistol clicked, fresh out of ammunition and unable to fire. Jimmy sprinted forward, still in his haze and unable to recognize that one operative was still alive, albeit still, lying upon the warehouse roof. Trace lumbered awkwardly back into the helicopter as Barclay kept it low for him. Jimmy was about to board when Landers stood up from his seat, yelling out of the open door.

"Jimmy! Go! Take the truck! Chuck needs backup!" Landers commanded.

"No, it's not safe here! I'm no good *dead!*" Jimmy yelled back as he considered the pros and cons of jumping onto the skid of a moving helicopter.

The last standing Dirty D operative beat Jimmy to it. The assailant limped around the back and clambered on board, clinging to the skid as he hoisted himself towards the cabin before Jimmy could react. Trace lunged forward and stomped down at the assailant's hands, arms, and face. Trace delivered one crucial blow to his opponent's forearm before the assailant reacted by sweeping Trace's calf out from under him with a swing of his arm. Trace nearly rolled out of the helicopter as it lifted further, clinging to the side with all his might.

Jimmy jumped onto the skid at the perfect time as the helicopter finally moved upward and onward, accelerating. There was a lurch with the sudden influx of his weight, but Jimmy held tight to the side as he turned to face the Dirty D operative, who was squared up to the open door. Jimmy kicked at the man's knee twice, hitting just below where Jimmy had shot him earlier, causing him to lose footing and stagger. He flailed out, grabbing at Jimmy's hoodie and just missing, before he had to steady himself on the skids and side of the helicopter. Jimmy reached up around the slide-out helicopter door and wrapped his right arm around a levering mechanism to gain bearing. He took a deep shuddering breath, closed his eyes, and lifted both legs skyward, exerting as much effort as he could against the resistance of moving air, and delivered a double-footed kick to the man's chest.

Jimmy opened his eyes to see the man fall back from the helicopter, hands unable to grasp out at anything. The assailant's eyes wide, arms flung out in desperation, he plummeted to earth outside the building and lay a limp pile of flesh and bone, lifeless after this 100+ foot fall. Jimmy felt faint, the sky fogging around him. His grip slackened and he closed his eyes. For once in his adult life, not a single thought clouded his mind.

Jimmy was suddenly yanked towards the helicopter's cabin. Big Trace clutched Jimmy's hoodie and pulled him up sharply. Jimmy flailed momentarily before he came back to the present situation and managed to crawl into the cabin. Big Trace hauled the helicopter door shut, and together they lay panting, wide-eyed, sweating, and crying.

Barclay was in the pilot's seat, focused and unwavering as he gripped the controls and propelled the helicopter forward, low and slow. Montreaux Pickens and Craig Foxx both lay silent, with Foxx clutching his wound tight and breathing lightly, and Pickens unmoving yet aware and awake, his eyes glaring daggers towards Foxx. Landers turned around from his seat, mouth open and gums blaring in the light.

"Holy shit, you guys!" Landers yelled. "We made it. I thought we were goners."

"We lost Troyer, man!" Big Trace yelled back. "This was too much. This is going to go past the local force. Feds are going to blow this up."

"Not if we blow it up first," Landers replied. "Hey, Barc, turn this bird around. We need to make sure Chuck gets out before we blow this joint."

Jimmy sat all the way up and then climbed into a seat. He leaned over and pressed his face against a window to watch as the helicopter slowly turned in a wide circle and drew parallel to the building, above it by a safe margin but still close enough to see the grounds in considerable detail. Jimmy squinted his eyes through the streaks on the window and the sunlight peeking out from beyond a cloud. He was still able to make out the speck of the man he had killed outside the warehouse and the two bodies atop the roof. The blaze of the flames had spread, now covering the woods all the way to the road.

The 18-wheel semi that Jimmy had ridden in on moved slowly as it came up to gear and ambled along to a gravel access road leading away from the warehouse and the blaze. It cleared an open gatepost and picked up a little more speed as it drove through the rest of the field before it was again flanked by woods on either side.

"Clear!" Barclay yelled.

Landers fumbled to pull out a cell phone with his good arm and hit a button.

For the second time today, Jimmy's eyes feasted themselves upon an explosion. Garage doors and windows blasted open, and parts of the roof were torn asunder as well. A plume of flame shot up from within the warehouse before settling back in. Jimmy observed plumes of fire licking around the outside of the building as well. A second blast came after a momentary pause, a large part of the roof now caving in as a billowing fire roared within.

The helicopter circled back around the blazing warehouse. The crew inside the chopper craned their necks to observe the vehicles remaining in the parking lot. Craig Foxx's prized dually, the cars of his team, and the cars of Montreaux Pickens and his crew all remained still. Jimmy smacked the window as he fixated on a startling observation.

"Guys! The rollback with my car! It's moving!"

Landers' eyes widened. "No way."

Jimmy shook his head. "No, no, you guys... do we still have feet on the ground at all?"

Craig sat up, wincing through the pain. He coughed before he spoke. "Are you sure it's moving?"

Jimmy nodded. "Yes, look down, Landers! You may be able to see it at this angle."

Sure enough, Landers cursed loudly and slammed the hand of his good arm against the cabin's side panel. "It's really moving now, boss. And no, we don't have any feet on the ground, damnit. Chucky's driving the rig, and Troyer's dead. I knew we should have brought more bodies for this."

Big Trace's knees bobbed up and down spastically, eyes kept wide. He leaned toward the cockpit, yelling at Barclay.

"Ay, Barc! Circle towards where Chucky is. We need to check on him."

Barclay nodded his affirmation back towards Landers and then leaned into the controls, pushing the chopper forward faster. After a moment of acceleration, Barclay looped down and saw the 18-wheeler straight ahead.

"Slow down, Barc – let's escort him here..." Craig said. Barclay obliged, the helicopter coming to a slow forward hover above and slightly to the side of the truck. Jimmy looked out the window.

The 18-wheeler slowed down significantly and drifted dangerously close to the edge of the dirt road's left side. The cab corrected, nearly too much, the back of the truck tilting and threatening to jackknife. It straightened back out and came to a near-crawl. That's when the driver's side door swung open, and a body tumbled out, rolling over, with arms falling limp at its side, the overall-clad man staring straight at the sky. After a few jerks, the truck came back to full acceleration as it hurtled through the narrow woodland road.

"Jesus! We lost Chuck!" Landers yelled. "Everything is going wrong. Dirty D was all over this shit! It's falling apart."

"What do you want me to do?" Barclay shouted back from the cockpit. "We can't intercept them without risking our lives and the chopper, but that's a *lot of weight*."

Everyone in the chopper's cabin turned to look at Craig Foxx. He sighed, his eyes rolling into the back of his head before he closed his eyelids. After a long moment and shuddering deep breath, he opened them again.

"Let them go," Craig said. "Me, Montreaux, and Landers need the vet. We've already lost two good men today. That's three this month. We can't afford to lose any more."

Landers turned towards Craig and raised his eyebrows.

"Boss, look... that's over $2 million in weight, *and* they killed two of our guys. We need that. We can get Beekman, Stowe, and Wainwright on it quick. We'd just leave Country exposed." Landers urged.

Craig shook his head. "We've lost too much lately. We can always get weight back. We can never get back our men. Manny, Chucky, and Troyer all in one month? This is the worst it's ever been. And it's not going to stop."

Jimmy snapped his head to face Craig. "Manny? Manny Rezendes?"

Craig closed his eyes once more as he bowed his head in affirmation. Jimmy stuffed his face into his hands with a faint cry.

Landers hollered a command back to Barclay. The helicopter banked left, now turning towards the northwest, Mt. Massie and Slade City fading into the distance behind them as they accelerated back towards Columbus. Rolling hills unfolded beneath them, the popping reds and oranges and yellows of autumn in full vigor, a picturesque quilt of color and beauty. The towering fumes from the blown-up warehouse faded away as jets of fire trucks' water and retardant rose to combat them.

Some fifteen-odd minutes of silence ensued as everyone in the chopper reflected over the battle and the losses they suffered. Landers finally broke the stillness as he turned to Jimmy.

"So, we have a regular Pinochet here!" Landers exclaimed. "For real, Jimmy, you saved our asses. Thank you."

Jimmy forced a grin. "You're welcome."

Landers leaned close. "I think I'm actually kind of starting to like you. We'll have to talk shop later. Sorry about all the shit I've given you so far."

Big Trace punched Jimmy lightly in the shoulder from where he sat alongside him. "Jimmy's cool, man," Trace said. "I've known him for a spell. Always one of the nicest dudes at poker. I didn't know he had this killer instinct, though."

Craig nodded. "Neither did I. That was impressive. Three kills today, Jimmy – you're a stone-cold gangster now. How do you feel?"

Jimmy sighed. His hands intertwined as he wrangled his fingers amongst one another fitfully. "I feel absolutely terrible. Like, my gut is so low right now. I don't know what I'm going to do. My life's going to be over because of this. Two officers, that guy on the roof? I'm so dead, guys. I can't go to jail."

Trace shook his head. "Jail's not so bad. It's prison that'll getcha!"

Craig waved one hand weakly. "Enough." He coughed and spat blood. His chest rose and fell with a shudder. "Jimmy, your hands are clean of the pigs. That will never blow back on you. As for the guy on the roof, do you still have that gun?"

Jimmy's face drained of any color that was left. "No... I left it on the roof. I'm a goner, man. The cops will be all over it."

"If they even find the gun," Landers said. "Hopefully, the evidence gets charred up enough to where if they get it, you can't get prints from it. Besides, are you even in the system? You seem like such a clean-cut guy."

Tears rolled unhindered down Jimmy's cheeks. "Yes, I'm in the system... trespassing, underage sales, assault, and inducing panic. Never spent a day in jail, but I've had a few brushes with the law."

I don't even know if Agent Browning can get me out of this one, Jimmy thought after he spoke.

The team sat in silence. As they pondered separately and individually, and as Jimmy cried quietly, the Columbus skyline pulled into view on the horizon. Barclay pulled the chopper even lower as he steered far clear of the city itself, giving plenty of distance between himself and the airport. After a wide circle around the outskirts, Barclay was as low as he could safely take the chopper, buzzing some of the taller apartment buildings beneath.

The chopper came above a small subdivision, thinner in development than the many newer mazes of roads and abodes wreathing the city. The yards were more unkempt, the houses less uniform in their size and look. Standing alone on an unfinished road off the main thoroughfare in the subdivision was the only home that could be considered a mansion. The drive leading up to it was a quarter mile or so into the field. The driveway in front of the broad, tall front door was more of a roundabout than a driveway. A pick-up truck and a van sat outside. A three-doored garage was moored along the wide part of the oval the driveway created, offset slightly from the home itself.

There was a sizeable unmarked concrete platform in the field, some ways behind the mansion and garage. It was invisible from the road due to the taller grass but evident from the skies. Barclay teetered the helicopter back and forth precariously as he struggled to land but eventually got the back skids on the concrete, just shy of the edge. The front skids came down with a thump and a cloud of dust. As the propellers decelerated, Landers left the helicopter first, jogging as fast as possible through the grass towards the house. Jimmy and Barclay helped Craig out and carried him towards the mansion. Finally, Big Trace came around, Montreaux Pickens slung over his shoulders in a fireman's carry. A man wearing scrubs waved them in hurriedly, and as Trace lumbered in last, he shut the door behind them.

"A helicopter? Are you trying to shine a beacon on our operation? Are you out of your mind?" the man in scrubs said as he walked alongside Landers.

Landers turned and pointed at Craig, who was pale and short of breath, blood having matted his clothing. "Look, Doc! This was life or death. We will pay you handsomely. You know I'm good for it. Just make sure you save Craig and this man, Pickens."

The man in scrubs looked back and forth between everyone before giving one curt nod. "I appreciate your expedience," he said. He turned to Jimmy and offered his hand to shake. Jimmy accepted.

"Doctor Landers. But you can call me Doc. Make yourself at home. We have espresso and spirits in the kitchen. I may be a while."

Jimmy turned to Landers and nodded sideways to Doc. Landers sighed. "Yes, that's my uncle. He's also a *veterinary* doctor, but he conveniently leaves that out. *Mi casa es tu casa.* Go have an espresso or some spirits with Trace. Take a nap or something. I don't care. Stay close, though."

With that, Landers followed his uncle Doc into a side room. Barclay helped Craig in before turning and dragging Montreaux into the room too. The door shut before Jimmy could get a peek at what was on the other side. He turned to Big Trace, who shrugged.

"Let's go get some spirits," Big Trace said as he put his arm around Jimmy, and they walked into the expansive kitchen sitting adjacent to the living room.

Jimmy leaned against a marble-top counter. Big Trace whistled as he gazed at the bottles of wine sitting in a large rack in the corner. Several bottles of name-brand vodka, tequila, and whiskey sat on the counter across the room from Jimmy. He let out a heaving sigh.

"Whassup, boss?" Big Trace asked. He obtained a bottle of Chateau Pape Clement Red and two glasses. "Come on, let's toast to a hell of a morning."

Jimmy ambled across the room to Trace as the large man popped the cork and poured a deep glass for each of them.

"Cheers," Trace said as he clinked glasses with Jimmy. Trace took a deep swill of his wine while Jimmy sniffed his tentatively before taking a sip.

"Holy shit," Jimmy said as he let the wine roll over his tongue and down his throat. "I've never tasted anything like this before. Whew."

"Good shit, eh?"

"I'm not sure. Different, maybe, more like."

Jimmy took a deeper swig than the first. His cheeks puffed out as he was surprised by the intensity of the flavor.

"I'm not used to this kind of wine," Jimmy said. "I've always been a two-buck chuck kind of guy."

"No shit," Trace said as he rolled the wine around in his glass. "The Landers clan might not have a lot of teeth, but they do have a lot of taste."

The men eventually relaxed as their adrenaline faded and the alcohol kicked in. Big Trace's eyes closed as he finished his glass, and Jimmy stared at the ceiling for quite some time. Eventually, Jimmy's gaze found Trace, and he regarded his friend with a degree of curiosity. The afternoon sun glinted off the ever-present gold cross around Trace's neck.

"Say, Trace... when can I expect to get paid for this whole shebang? Like, I did some baaaad shit today, man... I gotta move forward," Jimmy said.

Big Trace gave a half-smile. "Jim, my man, I know you're new to this side of the game,"

"I never wanted to be," Jimmy interrupted.

"Regardless," Trace continued, "Cash doesn't flow from the top down right away. Besides, we lost a *lot* today. Weight, vehicles, men – hell, a whole facility. There's a whole process to this thing."

"What is it?"

"Well, to simplify – earn, burn, hide, and wash. We complete the job, cover our tracks, lay low and launder the money – and once it's clean enough, we cash out."

Jimmy sighed and looked down at the floor.

"Usually a month or so, man. I'm sorry."

"I'm about to get evicted, man. I need to earn my keep. I haven't been able to get a job, and now with all this shit that happened today? I don't know if I can work again. I'm messed up over this," Jimmy explained. He sighed again, more raggedly this time, and sucked back a tear.

"Look, Jim... I got you. You're a good dude," Trace said.

"I killed like four people today!" Jimmy said. He cried out and slunk down against the wall. "I've never been what I would call a great person, but I ended *lives* today. Everything is over as I know it."

"It doesn't have to be that way," Trace replied. He walked across the kitchen and knelt beside Jimmy. He placed one big hand on Jimmy's shoulder while the other fished into his black velour hoodie pocket. Trace pulled out a money clip and put it in Jimmy's trembling hand.

"Here's a stack for you, brother," Trace said. He stood and took a step back. "I hope that's enough to keep a roof over your head until we can make up for today."

"You... you didn't have to, Trace – I can't accept this," Jimmy said. He choked back a sob.

"Nah man, I had to. You really helped save my ass and the whole operation. Look, you done dirt, but we all do dirt. Some of us is just a little deeper in it than others. We'll make it alright."

"I sure hope so," Jimmy said. He pocketed the money clip and put his head into his arms to hide the flow of more tears.

"I hate to interrupt this moment of newfound kinship," Landers said as he strode into the room. He looked Trace in the eyes and grinned his ragged grin purposefully.

"Do you ever knock?!" Trace winced. "What is it, man? Get on with it."

"Foxx is gonna make it," Landers said. "It's gonna be a rough ride for a week or two, but he's getting patched up now and getting some antibiotics. We just need to make sure he's sterile – sepsis and all that – but he should make it okay."

"Oh, thank God, man," Trace said as he touched his cross necklace. "That's my guy. I couldn't do all this without him."

"That much is clear," Landers said with a scoff. "Pickens is a little worse. I do think we should," - Landers made a throat-slashing gesture – "but there's some value to be gained by keeping him alive. Doc is about to work on removing the bullet – there's some bone damage there. No clean exit."

Landers turned to Jimmy and nodded towards the front of the mansion. "I called you an Uber, Jimmy. You should go home and get some rest. We will be in touch with work for you soon. And come by Foxx's place in a few days, won't you? We'll need to talk shop."

"Sure, Landers. I'll be there," Jimmy said quietly.

Jimmy staggered up and blinked away his tears. He avoided eye contact with Landers but nodded with a weak smile to Big Trace.

"Thanks again, brother," Jimmy said.

"Don't mention it," Trace replied. He smiled. "I look out for my people."

CHAPTER SIXTEEN

Jimmy Glencroft opened the door to his home. He smiled as he took a slow look around – he was safe another month! He threw the money clip from Big Trace down on the coffee table. He gave a deep, heaving sigh and threw himself back into the comforting cushion of the brown padded couch. He hugged an orange pillow tight and curled into it. He nabbed the corner of a blue and black Aztec throw blanket on the back of the couch and let it hang over his body. He closed his eyes tight and embraced the warmth.

In the few days that Lyndsey de Rueda had stayed with Jimmy, she had made herself quite at home. Thin black silk curtains draped across the windows; coffee tables and side tables alike were now lined with ordinary candles of different shapes and sizes, as well as incense burners, and a pink-purple salt lamp illuminated the corner of the room. A vinyl player crackled as it serenaded the room with an orchestral soundscape.

After several minutes, perhaps too moved by the warm caress of the record, Jimmy shuddered several times, his eyes clenched tight, tears streaming and soaking into the pillow, its bright orange giving way to a darker stain as the emotion flowed from him.

Lyndsey watched from behind from the kitchen bar. She wore a blue thermal tank top and an oversized heather gray hoodie that hung over the top of her black leggings. When Jimmy finished crying, she put down the cup of lukewarm tea she had been nursing and walked over lightly, careful not to startle him with the sound of her steps.

Jimmy looked up from under the blanket's edge and turned halfway onto his side to face Lyndsey as she sat down. She softly placed one of her hands on his knee from outside the blanket. She patted it a couple times as she gave Jimmy a soft smile, locking eyes with him.

Jimmy broke his gaze with her and burrowed his face back into the pillow. Lyndsey leaned over and tugged at the blanket over his shoulders. He shifted his head and looked at her once more, face and eyes alike stained red.

"Lytz... I don't want you to see me like this. Not now. Not today. Today was absolutely awful," Jimmy said softly.

Lyndsey smiled at him. For the years of hard living she had endured, she was still blessed with a full mouth of white teeth.

"You can tell me about it. Or not. I understand, no matter how bad you think it is. I'll understand," Lyndsey said. "Whenever you're ready."

Jimmy sat up and pushed his body upright against the side of the couch. He pulled up his blanket to cover his body entirely, then looked over at Lyndsey. He reached down to the bottom of the blanket and flung it up over her legs too.

"Getting what you want can be dangerous," Lyndsey said lowly. "Are you getting what you want?"

Jimmy locked eyes with Lyndsey. He half-smiled. "Not yet. I think I still have a way to go. I'm waiting for Foxx and his people to come through for me. Then I can relax."

"Why can't you relax now?" Lyndsey asked, playing idly with the blanket around Jimmy's foot. "Well, if you don't mind me asking."

Jimmy shifted, rotated, and sat all the way up. Having knocked the blanket off Lyndsey, he fluffed it back out with a flourish and then threw it back over them again. He had one leg out of the blanket, foot on the floor. The other leg was against the back of the couch. Lyndsey shifted to face Jimmy, sliding both her legs up alongside his under the blanket.

"I'm in too deep. I've done a couple things out of desperation. I've done some things without realizing what I was doing. And that's what's brought me here. I don't think there's any going back to who I used to be," Jimmy explained.

Lyndsey reached up and gently touched Jimmy's knee with her left hand, rubbing her leg more closely against his. She turned the palm of her hand upward. Jimmy's hand dropped into hers, and she held it lightly, rubbing her fingers over his skin comfortingly.

"You're doing what you have to. You're surviving. We're animals, Jimmy. That's what you have to do. Survive. And you're doing that well. You're here, after all. Alive. In this moment. Here."

Jimmy stared at Lyndsey, unblinking. She returned his gaze, smiling. She leaned forward.

"I've been in the same situation. I'm there now, after all. You'd probably hate me if you heard about what all I've had to see and do," Lyndsey said.

Jimmy shook his head. "Lytz, I'm curious. How are you so grounded about all of this? Things are going to shit for me. I don't know everything about what you've been doing, but it doesn't sound good from my end either. After all, that Sean guy? I can't unsee that, Lytz. He is so wrong for you. He's such a tool..."

"Am I Sean?" Lyndsey interrupted.

"What now?"

"Am I Sean? Are you going to hold who he is and what he's done against me? He's only trying to survive, too, after all."

Jimmy looked back at her in silence.

"After all, think about this moment. There is no Sean here. There is only you. This is only me. Allow yourself to forgive yourself, for all you have ever done, are doing, and ever will."

"Do *you* forgive *me*? For everything? For Slade City, for three years ago, for..."

"Jimmy, of course. You never had to ask."

"Why now? After all these years?"

"Jimmy, that's your problem. There can't always be an explanation for everything. There can't be timing for everything. That's why there's never been *us*, that's why the *timing* has never been here... there may never be another moment for forgiveness. There may never be another chance to clear the air..."

Jimmy shook as sweat dropped down from his hairline. His face reddened.

"I don't think you should be here, Lytz. I'm loving the feel, what you're doing with the place, but... it's still technically in Megan's name. What if she came back?" Jimmy fretted.

"She won't. All signs of her are gone. Trust me. The kitchen, the bathroom, the bedroom? All stripped clean of feminine comforts. Megan didn't want any sign of her essence to linger here," Lyndsey explained.

"How can you be so sure? Were you, like, snooping around?"

"Pfft... maybe a little, okay?" Lyndsey said. "I'm in snitch mode. It's hard to flip that off once you get started."

"Are you looking for a job? Hanging out with anyone? Hell, I... ugh, Megan used to do the same shit. Just... please, stay out of my stuff, okay?" Jimmy pleaded.

"Alright. I don't mind if you go through mine, though... just for the record."

"I have more respect for you than that."

Jimmy removed his legs from alongside Lyndsey's, kicked free of the blanket, and stood up. "I'm going to try to sleep, and then I desperately need a shower. I'll see you around," he said.

Lyndsey sighed and stared into her tea as Jimmy lurched exhaustedly down the hall and into the bedroom.

Jimmy slammed his bedroom door after he entered. He stepped slowly in a wide circle, spinning around once or twice as he glared around the room. He turned his attention to a stack of shelving built into the wall. There were still pictures of himself and Megan together lining whole shelves, along with mementos of their relationship. His last collectible Pink Floyd mug, a Sailor Smash bobblehead doll, a miniature globe, a few random souvenir pint glasses, all manner of other mementos were on the shelves too.

Everything Jimmy had been holding back for the last few weeks welled up within him. His skin reddened and flushed. His hands trembled, his vision blurred, and tears surfaced in his eyes once more. Without a second thought, he grabbed the picture frames and hurled them against the wall. The Pink Floyd mug followed next, then the bobblehead doll. One by one, every souvenir and trinket that reminded Jimmy Glencroft of his past life shattered against the wall. He threw and spiked and broke everything he could get his hands on, standing and shaking over the rubble of it all.

After a pause in the destruction, the door to Jimmy's bedroom creaked open. Lyndsey looked on at the scene before her, her eyes wide and her mouth hanging open. Jimmy turned slowly to face her, panting and sweating, the dark circles under his eyes bold against his red face. He walked over to Lyndsey and looked down at her. She looked up at him. Jimmy took her face with his left hand and pulled her close. He kissed her thoroughly as her mouth opened to accept his. Lyndsey wrapped her arms around his neck and fell into him. Jimmy put his right hand to her waist, turned around, and threw the two of them into the messy covers atop his bed. Lyndsey tangled up into him, wrapped her legs around his waist, and rolled onto him, mounted over his hips. The sheets enveloped them, the heat and stress and anxiety and anger and fury fueling the ripping of clothes and the scratching of skin and the pulling of hair, with all the surging and the throbbing and churning, everything melding into the red-hot tango of conquest and completion.

CHAPTER SEVENTEEN

Jimmy Glencroft's eyes snapped open after the deepest sleep had enjoyed in some time. He looked straight at the ceiling, completed by a sense of clarity and complacency that betrayed the complexity and danger of his current situation. He smiled and curled up into the comforter. The previous day felt like a dream from start to finish. The explosions, the helicopter, the guns... He killed a man. Well... three men.

And Lytz... Oh, God... Lytz. What was *that*? It felt like the candle trip he had at Obie Hill's, but slower and more primal, an absolute synesthesia of shared passion. Jimmy wriggled uncomfortably as his urges were awoken by these mere memories. He rolled over and lifted the lumpy comforter next to him, ready to draw Lyndsey close and have her once more.

The other side of the bed was empty. Lyndsey was already gone.

Jimmy rolled out of bed and pulled on a pair of shorts that lay amidst the wreckage of destroyed trinkets and treasures - and ripped discarded clothing. Jimmy's clothes were there; Lyndsey's were gone. He quickly moved down the hall and into the living room and kitchen, looking for Lyndsey, but she was nowhere to be found.

No note. No sign of her. Nothing.

Just a cold and empty and messy house, and Jimmy Glencroft by himself. He laid down on the couch, and his thoughts backslid into recognizing the wrong he had done. He pulled a pillow close and shoved his face into it to absorb his tears once more.

Outside of Marysville, wide-open farmland rolled over the horizon. This time of year, the harvest had concluded for corn and soy – the few active crops in the area being barley. As such, the landscape took on a withered brown and grey look to match the weather's vibe. This was a somewhat clearer day than usual – the blue sky peeked between swaths of grey.

Along the long and level two-lane roads between the fields, tiny communities would pop up now and then. These quaint villages were framed by general stores, mechanic shops, and two-pump gas stations. One such little burgh had a long grey ranch-style home set off from the road by about a quarter-mile. Its driveway was cloaked in deciduous tree cover, the last few leaves of the autumn now hanging on for dear life. A burly man exited the adjoined open garage with a thick set of tongs in hand. A giant dog pranced alongside him.

Finn Aittokallio licked his lips in anticipation as he opened his charcoal grill. Two thick bone-in steaks, charred exactly right, simmered with popping juice and flavor. Two foil-wrapped potatoes and two husks of sweet corn sat on the rack above the steak. The aroma of fresh-cooked meat filled the air with the smoke that rose from the grill. His tan-brown Great Dane, a hulking feller named Homer, barked and begged for a cut of steak.

"Not today, buddy, this is poppa's treat," Finn said as he plated his grilled goods and turned to head back up the driveway. Mid-turn, he nearly dropped the plate when he saw a purple minivan pull alongside his truck. He craned his neck to get a look and saw exactly who he expected behind the driver seat of this rusted and chipped 25-year-old vehicle.

"Jimmy Glencroft..." Finn said to himself as he walked up. Jimmy popped out of the drivers' side, wearing a teal hoodie with a pair of red gym shorts. His light brown hair was unwashed and matted.

"Hey Finn, what's up, buddy? Sorry for stopping over on short notice. You're free for a few, right?" Jimmy asked.

"Well, I was planning on consuming copious amounts of steak, but I guess I'll have to deal with you for a few. Come on in, you can have a steak and a beer."

"Well, you don't have to..."

"Shut up and come eat my food." Finn laughed. "I don't need to eat all of this anyway. I'm a fatass."

The two old friends entered Finn's house. Jimmy made sure to keep the door open for Finn as he carried in the plate of food. Jimmy flopped on Finn's low and cushy couch – one of three that were set up in the living room in a large U-shape. Finn went to the adjoined kitchen to finish divvying up the vittles at hand.

"Beer me!" Jimmy hollered. Right away, Finn chucked a can of lager to Jimmy from across the room. He caught it, cracked it, and tilted it back enthusiastically, glugging down the refreshing brew. Finn laughed as he walked back over with the two plates of grub. Finn gave one to Jimmy along with the requisite silverware and plopped down alongside him. After a few minutes of chowing down and commenting on the taste and consistency of the food, Finn noticed Jimmy had remained silent. Jimmy barely reacted when Homer came over and randomly licked his ankle.

"Everything okay, man? You seem off. You don't pop in like this much anymore," Finn said between bites of steak and potato.

Jimmy killed off the rest of his lager with a large swig. "Well..." He looked at Finn in a way that he usually would his pissed-off ex or a scolding authority figure. "I... I think I'm in too deep, brother."

Finn nodded as Homer jumped on the couch between them. He scooted over to give the colossal dog more room and petted him. "I could kind of see this coming, dude. Something didn't sit right with me yesterday when I dropped you off at the warehouse. Everything go okay with your car?"

Jimmy sank back on the couch and closed his eyes. He didn't flinch when Homer gobbled up the last bit of his steak. Finn shooed Homer off with a light smack of his Discovery ball cap.

"Craig Foxx is an arms and drug dealer. Almost everyone associated with him is, too," Jimmy said as he opened his eyes and stared at the ceiling.

"I could have told you that," Finn said. "I thought everybody knew that."

"Well, I didn't," Jimmy said. "Somehow I'm the last one to know *everything*."

"You just have to learn to pay more attention."

"You don't think I do? You don't think I try, dude? You've seen it! I've spent my whole life just... looking for the meaning behind everything, and... *nothing* clicks. There's something wrong with me. I'm broken, man... I just..."

Jimmy sighed and blinked back a tear, trying to hide it from his friend. Finn looked on without judgment.

"Jimmy, I'm sorry. I know you have the best of intentions," he said.

"I killed a man."

"WHAT?" Finn's jaw slacked open.

"I threw a man out of a helicopter. I killed him."

"...Jesus Christ, what? How? What?"

"I blew up two Sheriffs' Deputies in a catastrophic explosion."

"You're shitting me." Finn laughed. "For real, Jimmy, what's wrong?"

"I'm sure it's on the news. I'm sure it was on your fire radio or something. Dead ass serious. It happened just outside of Slade City, I believe."

"Holy shit, no, I hadn't heard anything; I spent my Kelly day out riding after I dropped you off... You better be pulling my chain."

"You know you're the first person I tell anything big like this. I don't know what to do, man. I'm not ready for this. Is this real? Are we in a simulation? What the fuck?"

"Slow down there, Trevor," Finn said as he got up and grabbed a remote. "Let's see what's on the news."

Finn clicked on a major news network after his large 4KHD television came up. The two men sat in silence for a minute, their respective minds racing as they sat through some mundane coverage about politics-this and environment-that. Jimmy's left leg bounced uncontrollably as Finn snapped at him to stop. It didn't take long for content to shift to exactly what Jimmy was referring to.

"And now we turn our attention to Southern Ohio, where details are emerging about the warehouse explosion that claimed the lives of at least seven people, including two Sheriffs' Deputies," a male anchor said as a picture popped up on the left-hand side of the screen, showing a towering blaze and several fire crews dousing it.

"The community of Perkins, a suburb of Slade City, has been reeling in horror since yesterday."

"I'm afraid to leave my home," a droopy middle-aged woman wearing a Tweety Bird t-shirt said on camera to the news crew. "This is such a quiet town. Everybody is so scared."

As coverage unfolded, Finn's gaze shifted slowly from the television to Jimmy, a bewildered look on his face. Jimmy continued to watch the coverage, his eyes glued to the screen.

"The factory that exploded is owned by a company named *PharmaScenticals LLC*. This location was used to process different chemicals into candles and other devices used for aromatherapy. The products have been sold throughout Greater Appalachia. We do not yet have confirmation from the FDA or DEA on validity or legality of their products."

"Jesus, Jimmy…" Finn said. Jimmy maintained his direct forward gaze as the TV showed pictures of the deputies he blew up – *Sgt. Lee Townshend, 1981 – 2022*; *Sgt. Robert Corso, 1977 – 2022.*

"No other bodies have been identified at this time, but Slade County authorities are investigating this as foul play. More updates to come on the hour."

Finn shut the TV off. He shook his head slowly, his stare shifting down to Homer. Homer tilted his head. His ears flopped as he let out a curious whine.

"It wasn't on purpose, Finn," Jimmy said. "Craig tricked me into pulling the switch on the officers. And I only killed the other dude because he was going to crash the helicopter."

Finn held up a hand to shush Jimmy.

"Finn, bud, I… I hope you don't think any less of me. We've been friends for years; I was just trying to survive, I…"

"Dude, shut the hell up!" Finn said. "Please! It's okay! Just shut up!"

Jimmy whimpered and fell silent. He watched as Finn stood and walked deliberately to a corner of the living room. That's when Jimmy finally saw the camera – it was small and inconspicuous, tucked away on a shelf, between a clock and a model #21 Wood Brothers NASCAR. Finn drew a pocketknife and cut the cord to the camera.

"Wait, was I – was I on camera? What?" Jimmy asked.

"Come with me," Finn said.

"I… what?"

"Don't say another word until I say you're safe. If I'm gonna know your secrets, man, you're gonna know mine. That's what friends are for. Now follow me."

Jimmy stood and struggled to gain his footing. His legs quivered as he forced one foot in front of the other to follow Finn down a short hallway to the right. Finn opened a door to reveal downward steps to his basement. Finn reached up and snipped the wires to yet another camera that faced downward from above the steps.

"How many cameras do…?"

"Dude, shut *up*," Finn barked. "Trust me on this."

Bottom of the steps – another camera. The friends turned right and entered a game room – foosball, air hockey, and poker tables were arranged neatly in the middle of a vast tan-carpeted space. Sports décor lined the walls – framed jerseys, signed balls and pucks, hockey sticks, pennants – Nawakwa High School, Slade City Snipes, Heartland State, Slade City College, Columbus Discovery – Jimmy saw his own face, his own name, his own autographs come up as he glanced around. He was jammed up on memory lane for so long, he didn't see Finn snip two more cameras in the corner of this large entertainment room.

Jimmy stood riveted by one picture in the Nawakwa High School section. In living color, wearing the navy blue and blood red of the Nawakwa Mothmen, a strikingly younger and smoother-faced (and fuller-haired) Jimmy stood on the football field in full pads. He was first in a line of smiling teens – Jimmy himself followed by Finn, Trevor MacKenzie, Anvil Broadnax, Manuel Rezendes, and then two others, a lanky lad named Dolan Boggs and a veritable mountain of a man, Reggie Peabody, nearly 7 feet tall and 500 pounds.

"We're almost safe," Finn said. "Come here. Check out my NASCAR shelf."

Jimmy and Finn walked to the end of the basement, the side furthest from where the staircase opened to the game room. A wooden shelf lined the course of the entire wall. From top to bottom, left to right, the rack was filled with mint-condition NASCAR die-cast models of all shapes and sizes. Jimmy's mouth dropped as he scanned for his favorite drivers and paint schemes from his youth. They were all there – Rusty Wallace, Sterling Marlin, Tony Stewart – and all the classics, too; Dale Earnhardt, Richard Petty, Darrell Waltrip.

"Holy shit, Finn! Is this what you spend all your firefighter money on these days?"

"This is just the beginning. Behold," Finn said as he reached up and gripped both the left and the right edges of the bookshelf. With a light lift and a firm pull, he stepped back to slide the bookshelf aside. The wheels caught a little on the carpet, but with a wriggle, Finn was able to pull it all the way to the perpendicular basement wall.

The hidden room was cloaked in darkness. Finn pulled a string on a ceiling light, and with a click, the room dimly illuminated. Jimmy stepped in and slowly rotated his gaze around the room. On the left-hand wall, a massive pegboard held no less than two-dozen guns and armaments of various ages, conditions, and applications. Pistols, shotguns, hunting rifles, semi-automatic rifles, revolvers... jackknifes, switchblades, machetes, hatchets... spotting scopes, binoculars, flares, flasks... there was enough to arm damn near an entire platoon.

"But wait... there's more!" Finn said as he stepped over to a gun cabinet, keyed in a code, and pulled it open. Bullet-proof vests, sawed-off shotguns, and a seemingly endless array of shells, magazines, and bullet boxes furnished the inside. Atop the cabinet was a pre-loaded backpack, easily two feet thick, sitting in front of three gallon jugs of water. The color drained from Jimmy's face as he watched Finn pull an Uzi from the cabinet, load a magazine, and spin the gun in a circle.

"Don't worry. Safety is on, and I didn't point it at you. Remember, trigger discipline. Don't ever point a gun at someone you don't want to shoot," Finn said.

"Pretty sure you just pointed it at me, captain," Jimmy said with a nervous laugh.

"Still not a captain, bud. Still Lieutenant. But check this out."

The room's ceiling was adorned by a black flag with two red horizontal stripes dissecting the middle, the centerpiece of which was a grey elephant skull emblem. Finn reached up and pulled down the flag from its pins to reveal a hollowed-out cubby in the space above. He withdrew a stepladder from the cubby and stepped atop it so he could root around in the area more easily. After a moment, Finn pulled out a thick and heavy tube, several feet long with two handles. Jimmy's mouth hung open as he watched Finn step to the floor of the basement.

"A... rocket launcher?!"

"Yes sir," Finn said with a smile. "Look at this. Military-grade, never been fired – I've got some shells up there with the rest of the *super* illegal stuff. I show you any more of what's in that space, I'd have to kill you."

154

"Good lord, man... I literally killed people, and I think you'd get in more trouble than me if arrested." Jimmy said.

"Maybe," Finn said. "Maybe not. I'm off the radar. Everyone I've bought, sold, traded with have been good people. Vetted Boogaloo, patriots, you name it. We're better than gold."

"Okay, Danny Gokey," Jimmy said as he mustered a smile of his own.

A rhythmic *beep-beep, beep-beep* tone came in from the main room of the basement. Finn almost dropped the unloaded rocket launcher. He glanced at Jimmy – Finn's face reddened.

"That's... unexpected," Finn said. "Get out of here. Now."

Jimmy tripped and stumbled as he rushed out of the secret room. Finn slid the shelf of NASCAR memorabilia back over the entrance to his armory. He turned and stomped over to his wall of big-screen TVs. He grabbed a remote from a caddy on the nearby TV stand. The smallest television among the wall of four, one on the top left on a swivel stand, came on to reveal live camera feeds.

Finn worked with the remote. He punched through a few buttons quickly as the television toggled through a few different camera feeds. A couple of the ones he went through were static – Jimmy assumed these were the ones he witnessed Finn cutting.

Finn reached the feed he desired, and as he did, the cycling *beep-beep, beep-beep* stopped. This particular live camera feed, in full color, displayed an image of Jimmy's chipped purple van sitting in Finn's driveway.

"The beeping was the motion sensor," Finn explained. "Sometimes Homer sets it off if he gets out. It only goes off if someone is in range, in real-time..."

Homer was not the cause of this particular alarm. In fact, the Great Dane had been in his bed near the foot of the steps, and at the sound of the *beep-beep, beep-beep* he dashed upstairs to bark at the front door.

Finn's thumb found a short joystick in the middle of the remote. As his thumb gently nudged it to the side, the camera feed on the television pivoted. Finn leaned his thumb forward, this time zooming in the camera on the side of Jimmy's van.

A tall, well-built man with a close-cut haircut in a tight black leather jacket pulled himself out from under the van. He wore dark wraparound shades and a jet black bandana across his nose and mouth. He adjusted the bandana as he sat up. The stranger's head swiveled to check his surroundings once more before he pivoted to a knee, stood, and walked away. His gait was fast but measured, and he took care to stick to the tree line along Finn's driveway.

"That's not good," Finn said.

"What the hell was he doing? What did he do to my van?" Jimmy asked.

"Best I could guess," Finn mused, "is that it was a motion tracker. The dude was in and out awful quick. I'm thankful we caught him."

"You don't think he snipped a brake line or an oil line or something?" Jimmy wondered.

"Nah. I don't think whoever this is wants you hurt or dead or stranded. I think they're using you."

Jimmy sighed. Finn eyed him curiously. Having been friends for over a decade, the two men had learned to read one another well – and Finn's frown said everything to Jimmy.

"Dude, no," Finn said, "Please don't tell me..."

"You're fine!" Jimmy emphasized. "Don't worry! I lost the wire. That's probably why they followed me and tagged me."

"Jesus, dude, I..." Finn stammered. "Who the hell did you lead onto my property?"

"DEA," Jimmy said. "Don't worry. I don't think the ATF is involved, at least not yet,"

"You're a *snitch*?!"

"I wouldn't use those words, I swear, I just fell into this!" Jimmy pleaded. "Dude, please, you have to believe me. I wouldn't willingly bring you into this. I need to get a way out of this, and I'm doing what I can, I'm trying to get all my friends cleared too, I..."

"You need to be more careful," Finn said. He sighed and closed his eyes for a moment. "I have a *lot* of work to do now, and I don't want you driving that van off my property until I figure out what they did to it."

"I get it," Jimmy said.

"You better. And I'm gonna hold you to replacing my camera system. I have to destroy it now. Dude, god damnit, and a bottle of whiskey too. I'm gonna be all messed up until I get a chance to offload my inventory and figure things out."

"I'll make it bourbon," Jimmy said. "I won't be getting paid until after we do another job or two. I'll make you whole once it's laundered back to me."

"Laundered? *Another job or two?!* Dude, Jimmy, what happened to you? What happened to getting a new job? What's going on?"

"Kind of hard to get a new job when the whole country knows me for being the mascot that got his ass whooped on live television," Jimmy said. "Nobody is emailing me back..."

"Email? Dude, what happened to your phone? I... dude, I swear to God, you're such a mess right now," Finn said.

"I'll get it together," Jimmy assured him. "Is there a way I can talk to you securely? So I can let you know you're clear with the Feds?"

"I damn well better be clear with the Feds, dude; I haven't done a thing wrong!" Finn stressed. "Look... just... if you can, meet me at Rapport Café at noon next Monday. That should give us both time to do what we need to do."

"Rapport Café. One week from today at noon. Got it," Jimmy confirmed.

"One more thing. Make sure you don't have a fuckin' tail this time," Finn said.

"I won't, man... I'll be more careful."

"Good." Finn turned off the television and walked to the bottom of the stairs. He looked up, looked back to Jimmy, and looked down at his feet. Finally, he looked back up to Jimmy once more.

"There's a dirt bike in the back of my RV," Finn said. "It's street-legal, modded – but it's unregistered. Go ahead and take that back home. I'll get your van situation figured out."

"You got it; thanks again, Finn." Jimmy smiled and extended his hand. "You're truly my best friend."

"Back at you," Finn said. "But if so, just come here and have a damn steak sometime, instead of running with tweakers and gangsters, okay? I'll keep you out of trouble."

"I hope so," Jimmy said. After a thoughtful moment, he repeated himself, almost as if to assure himself.

"I hope so."

CHAPTER EIGHTEEN

"This is where the magic happens," Landers said as he pulled back the giant InfoWars-branded banner to lead James Glencroft into his chamber.

"Magic? Whatever goes on here isn't magic, I'm sure. I feel like I'm in an incubator," Jimmy responded as he brushed against the blue and white banner and pulled one corner loose by accident.

"Precisely!" Landers spun and pointed at the ceiling. "Ideas, dreams, and machinations of the imperium divine are cultivated and incubated in this chamber. Come, let me show you…"

Jimmy stepped into the hallway and squinted his eyes against the dim blue fluorescent light. He took a deep breath.

"Ah, you smell that? Peppermint and lavender. Great for concentrating," Landers said. He pointed to a diffuser emanating steam on one shelf. "Have I told you how you can be a boss bitch with DoTerra and Essential Oils?"

"You're kidding, right?"

"…yes. Yes, I am. Come, come, have a seat. I have much to show you! I'm glad you took me up on my offer to talk shop. I've got a lot to do with Craig on the mend, but there's nothing wrong with taking a day to touch base with a new prospect!"

Jimmy crossed the threshold from the hallway into Landers' command center. A massive monitor lined the far wall in front of a window. In front of the monitor, two red and black office chairs sat with headphones hanging on either armrest. There was an unfinished dresser with myriad drawers of different shapes and sizes on the right side of the room. To the left was a corkboard with papers pinned up of various plans and ideas, most of which appeared to be abbreviated or in some kind of obscure code. Multi-colored strings were tied between different color pins, crisscrossing in no apparent pattern. There were blueprints and floorplans, lists and Venn diagrams, receipts, and pictures.

One such picture was a black and white photo of Jimmy himself in front of a doorway… that of Full Nest Café.

"What's the deal with this? That's me!" Jimmy said as he pointed at his picture. "Are you fucking stalking me?"

"Whoa whoa, Jimmy, breathe. Not everything on that board is bad. Come on, take a seat. I'll explain everything in a minute."

Jimmy begrudgingly stepped further into Landers' room. He kicked past a couple pillows and a comforter that laid unsupported on the floor. Landers reclined in one of his gaming chairs and kicked up his feet onto a TV stand in front of him, his bare feet and unkempt toenails plopped down between an X-Box One and a PlayStation 4. Jimmy took a seat next to him. He folded his hands into his hoodie pocket and hunched over as he looked at Landers.

Landers grabbed a black controller from beside him on the floor. With a chime, the X-Box One turned on and loaded onto its primary menu.

"We – we just playing video games, dude?" Jimmy asked.

"Not just any video game," Landers said as he flicked a couple buttons.

An all-too-familiar loading screen came onto the TV: one of bright pastel comic book art in four staggered panels, displaying various ruggedly attractive characters flashing weaponry. This screen gave way to the game's main menu, in which the words *GREASE AND AMBITION* sparked across a black screen in bright neon purple.

"Ah, dude, it's been way too long," Jimmy said. He leaned forward. "Mind if I take a turn on the sticks? I could use a round or two."

"In due time, brother," Landers said. "Are you familiar with the G&A modding community?"

"About as familiar as I am with the furry community," Jimmy said. He laughed. Landers didn't.

"Are you serious?" Landers pursed his lips.

"You should know – it looks like you have my life story charted on your corkboard."

"You would be so lucky if I cared that much about you. But seriously – how familiar are you with the furry community, and thereby the G&A modding community?"

Jimmy sighed. "A little bit. Passing knowledge of each."

Landers cracked a loathsome smile. "Fair enough. Check this out."

Landers loaded an online game. The camera panned over a city with a slow spin. Jimmy squinted at the concrete skyscrapers, dogged by a certain familiarity...

"Columbus! Holy shit, dude, that's Columbus! These mods have gotten outrageous since I last played."

"That's not the best part," Landers said. "Observe."

Landers' avatar looked hauntingly like Landers himself, except taller and thicker, wearing a bright red and green Hawaiian shirt. The stubble-faced man ran out of his apartment building and straight into the streets of Downtown Columbus. He knocked a bystander off their bicycle, hopped on, and pedaled away while ignoring their pleas.

"Note the realism," Landers said.

"Dude," Jimmy replied. "The ice rink is set up at McFerson Commons! There's construction at that spot on Marconi for real, too. Absolutely insane."

Virtual Landers came to the intersection of Nationwide and High. He hopped off his bicycle and produced a satchel charge out of thin air. He planted the charge on the curb and ran into One Nationwide Plaza's lobby, where he planted a detonator. AI passersby in the game looked on, alarmed – one Nationwide employee called 9-1-1.

Landers then deployed a radio control drone from the lobby and flew it through the front door, shattering the glass. The camera panned to follow the drone as it rose high above Downtown Columbus.

"Activate Tracker 12," Landers said into his headset microphone. The drone emitted a conical signal beneath it and across the skyline. A radar appeared on the bottom right side of the screen that showed city streets and buildings, big and small alike. A couple blocks to the north, a blue and red blinking dot appeared and started moving southward. Several more blocks to the south and west, three dots activated and moved towards Landers' location.

"Wow," Jimmy said. "That's the Columbus P.D. downtown! This thing is so real. Mind. Blown."

"Yes, sir," Landers replied. "What if I told you that sleeper cells of revolutionaries were using the game engine to simulate police response to acts of terror to help plan real-life sorties?"

"What?"

"Don't play dumb."

"Come again?"

"You know exactly what's going on here."

Landers' character swapped the view back from the drone to first-person. He watched from the lobby of One Nationwide Plaza as several Columbus Police Department cruisers converged on the curbside.

"I mean, I would anticipate a more impactful response if 9-1-1 was called on someone planting a remote detonator, but I wouldn't expect Nationwide agents to recognize it as such," Landers said all-too-casually as he detonated the charge.

Jimmy stared as the cop cars vaulted through the air, and a plume of flame billowed around them. Any action that Landers took in the video game from there fell upon blind eyes and deaf ears. The scene brought Jimmy's thoughts back to the catastrophic explosion outside of the PharmaScenticals warehouse.

Landers kept tooling with the video game, not paying any mind to Jimmy. He partied up with a few other players in the Columbus lobby and spoke to them as if they had all met prior. They conversed about simple life matters while they robbed banks and led police on death-defying high-speed chases. Meanwhile, Jimmy sat lost in his own mind.

After a half-hour or so, Landers bid his friends farewell, removed his headset, and turned his attention back to the silent Jimmy.

"What do you think, James?"

"I... To be honest, I haven't been paying much attention. Seems deep."

"Those guys I was speaking with. They're Boojahideen."

"Aren't we all?"

"No, no. Boojahideen is Boogaloo, but with praxis."

"Praxis? I'm sorry, Landers, I don't think I'm following."

"They actually take action. Put their money where their muzzle is."

"Oh. And?" Jimmy asked with a shrug.

"You want in?"

"Come again?"

"We need numbers. New blood. I know you're in a rock and a hard place. If you really hit a bind, let me know. I'll have my people talk to your people."

"I don't have people."

"It's a joke, Jimmy."

"For fuck sakes, dude. I don't know about this. It's a little too much too soon. I haven't gotten over the warehouse shit yet. I'm not exactly cut out for this."

"I know. But we can train you. Sharpen and harden. The Boojahideen are going to be making moves soon. The environment right now is ripe for action. You want to change history and be a patriot?"

"I'm not sure. I didn't want to shoot people and kill people, but here we are. I don't know. I'll get back to you. I'm not really feeling well right now. I should probably get on my way, actually."

"If you ever change your mind, please remember that we can make this all go away," Landers said. "You went to college in Slade City for a year or two, right? Then I presume you're familiar with Winterview State Park?"

Jimmy looked down at his hands before responding. "Yes. Yes, I'm familiar, I've been there several times."

"If things ever get too much for you, we have another, larger affiliated syndicate nearby. I can't tell you more right now. But if you need to go off the radar permanently, our fixers can pick you up. We check the Stonewall Trail Overlook every other night. Hang out there, and we will find you."

Landers' words barely sank in – like fallen leaves onto a placid pond, perhaps, floating for a moment before moving on – as Jimmy absently touched his chest and stared at the ground.

"I know you don't have shit to do, Jimbo," Landers said as he passed Jimmy a controller. "Settle down, mate. I won't push it anymore today. Wanna play a little HockeyBots?"

"Bro... that would be perfect. I haven't played in years. Let's do this."

Jimmy settled in for some gaming but could barely pay attention to Landers or his ranting. Jimmy's exhaustion and worry rendered him a standoffish and numb automaton throughout the rest of the afternoon.

As nightfall crept through the shutters in Landers' command center and Jimmy's eyes grew lead-heavy from hours of staring at the screen. Jimmy put down the controller and closed his eyes for what he thought would be a minute, but the minute gave way to minutes, and before long, he had slept through what felt like an entire round of Virtual Hockey's Highest Honours.

Landers leaned over and tapped Jimmy's face with his good arm. The clammy smack of skin on skin was fruitless in stirring the slumbering man. Landers turned off the X-Box, took one more sip of his energy drink, and slipped away down the hall.

Landers unplugged the white, orb-shaped diffuser and moved it back towards where Jimmy slept. He plugged it in atop the coffee table, topped off the water levels with the energy drink, and tossed the now-empty can into a nearby trash pail. Landers then reached into the top drawer, lifted a sock, and revealed a vial of teal liquid. He carefully leaned over the diffuser, popped the vial, and let two drops gently fall to the diffuser... before shrugging and pouring half the vial in. Landers capped the remainder, smirked, and crept out of the room. On the other side of the InfoWars banner, he pulled the folding door shut and walked down the long hallway on the upper level of Craig Foxx's otherwise empty home, leaving Jimmy alone with the fumes.

"Jimmy, wake up."

"Jimmy, these are your first steps."

"Bring back the balance, as I once did."

James Glencroft opened his eyes. The darkness did not recede. He closed his eyes and opened them once more. No change. He blinked through the rising anguish rapidly, but nothing changed, except for a rubbery sensation rippling through his skin – and a frustrating crowd of disconnected voices giving unsolicited advice.

"Seize the day, Jimmy – know, you are no good dead."

"Jimmy. This is purgatory. You haven't yet arrived but haven't yet departed. Remain calm."

"Remain calm."

"Remain calm."

"Remain calm!"

"REMAIN CALM!!!"

Sudden silence.

"Jimmy," Megan Painter's voice ebbed in from the ether, "Come home."

"Getting what you want can be dangerous," Lyndsey de Rueda's disembodied whisper beckoned.

162

"GLENCROFT! You're useless! Get off the field!" *Coach Yancey, is that you?*

More disembodied, disjointed voices from his past spiraled in together line by line until they spoke as a crowd.

"I don't want you runnin' around with no girl with holes in her face, boy! You're better than that!"

"You need help."

"You can't be afraid to ask for help."

"Asking for help is for the weak. Man up and make it happen for yourself."

"The view from halfway down…"

"Go to the petunia at once, corn cob,"

"I love you, Pooh Bear."

"Remain calm."

"Remain calm."

"Remain calm!"

"REMAIN CALM!!!"

Silence.

A purple wisp of neon floated into Jimmy's view. It flipped and fluttered around like a wayward sprite before it briefly took the image of Carlos Santana, then it flittered away once more. Jimmy saw the purple sprite move in three dimensions, the shadows of Landers' room now coming into form. Jimmy staggered up from his chair and followed it to Landers' corkboard, where his chaotic mess of criminal plans nested.

Jimmy flipped through the pictures, lists, and notes on the board. He observed the image of himself in the doorway of the Full Nest Café the day he reunited with Lyndsey. He followed a piece of red string to a picture of himself unloading the Cream Dream Donuts truck with Trevor MacKenzie. From there, a rubber band connected the picture's pin to a list, an address —

7544 Fellow Street.

7544 Fellow Street.

Where have I heard that address before?

The rubber band suddenly took on the visual elasticity of uncooked spaghetti. Jimmy tried to loosen it from the pin, but the feel was still taut. Small red and orange 16-bit explosions popped in his view as Atari-sounding explosions rang in his ears. There was a distant laughing sound.

The bottom fell out of his world.

Jimmy hit the floor on his back but felt a falling motion through the rest of his body; a vacuum-like feeling pulled at his skin and his hair. He felt a sudden tremendous itch throughout his body. An avalanche of pictures, video screens, memories, neon jazz-fusion guitarists, and chili dogs – and women and memories and fantasies and *more of these cursed memories* – all fell around him in a blizzard of painful confusion.

Silence. Stillness. Shadow.

The vacuum sensation, the falling sensation – done.

Jimmy sat up.

He had a single photo in his hand.

Lyndsey de Rueda and Sean Doan holding hands as they walked down a street.

She was wearing the exact same outfit from the day she and Jimmy had made love.

The blue tank top, the baggy gray hoodie, the leggings.

A freight train horn in a rapid crescendo. A rush of gray, silver, and metallic streaks from all directions. A distant scream, a plume of steam – bubbles all over his body, more distant laughter, a flurry in his heart...

Then nothing.

CHAPTER NINENTEEN

"So *that* is why Kaepernick shouldn't waste his time and devalue his brand by going to the Patriot Football League. The fan base doesn't even like him. Why would he sign?"

"Columbus hasn't used their second Golden Pro contract. I'm sure Kaep would rather be paid a million dollars a year than sit at home doing nothing."

"He has a Nike contract and paid speaking appearances! Columbus is below him. I want to find the blogger that started this rumor and smack him in the dental just for asking silly questions."

The spirited argument continued between Trevor MacKenzie and Sean Doan as they sat across the fire pit from one another in their shared backyard in The Bottoms. The fire pit was quite literally just a pit with a fire in it – nothing fancy – a modest flame throwing sparks and cinder into the cool autumn nightfall.

"Sean, I'm telling you, Colin Kaepernick is a tremendous competitor displaying sheer determination and resolve. He could take Columbus to the 'ship in year one. Nothing against my buddy Broadnax," Trevor rambled.

"You're missing the point," Sean said. "His profile is higher than any PFL quarterback, and one of the highest from the NFL, even though he isn't playing. He's set for life!"

"He's a maverick! He's a difference-maker!"

"If Columbus wanted a maverick, they'd just sign Tebow or something. Besides, Columbus is below him too. Why don't you give your buddy more credit? Maybe another year or two in the system, and he'd blossom," Sean said.

Lyndsey de Rueda stepped out onto the back porch, slamming the screen door shut before heading out between the piles of unkempt garbage bags. She loped over the fire pit, gave Trevor a beer, and gave Sean one as well before kissing his cheek and plopping down in a folding chair alongside him.

"Thanks, dollbaby," Sean said. "Ooh, Autumn Stout. Where'd you get this one?"

"A sampler pack at the corner store," Lyndsey said. "That one's out of South Dakota."

"And I'm stuck over here with... what's this... Misty Morning Star?" Trevor complained. "Earthen, smoky essences of strawberry with strong hemp-infused hops... *what?*"

"I figured you'd appreciate it, Trevor," Lyndsey said.

"Lytz, this isn't a beer; this is like... a god damn potion!"

Before Trevor had a chance to tilt back the craft concoction, he looked up to see a black Humvee pull up along the curb on the other side of their duplex. He dropped the beer on the ground and waved at Sean in a panic.

"Sean, look," Trevor whispered. "Is that the same one?"

"Shit! Get down!" Sean yelled. Trevor crawled through the muddy, mottled yard on his hands and knees. Sean dashed to the neighbors' side of the yard and slid beside the deck. Lyndsey stood beside the fire in a confused shrug, her eyes darting back and forth.

"What is this all about?" Lyndsey asked.

"I could ask you the same thing," Jimmy Glencroft said as he emerged from the shadows between the duplex and the neighbors. The black Humvee pulled away, and Trevor popped back up to his feet.

"Dude, Jimmy, what are you doing here?" Trevor asked as he wiped the mud from his hands off on his jeans. "Who drove you?"

"Uber," Jimmy replied without looking at Trevor. Jimmy stared at Lyndsey, who glanced to the side and played with her jean jacket pockets.

"Is Sean here?" Jimmy asked.

"I *live* here," Sean said as he jogged over to the group gathered by the side of the deck. "Why are *you* here?"

Jimmy grasped at the collar of Sean's hoodie and cocked his arm for a punch. Trevor immediately hooked Jimmy's arm and pulled it down, and Lyndsey pushed them back. Jimmy and Trevor both stumbled. Jimmy broke free and scrambled forward to tackle Sean. Sean deftly stepped aside like a troubadour and tripped Jimmy with his boot-clad foot. Jimmy fell into the deck's back steps, his head banging off the wood with a dull *thwack*.

"Calm down!" Lyndsey yelled. She stepped between Jimmy, Trevor, and Sean, the latter of whom was now brandishing a brick in his hand.

"What are you doing here?" Jimmy yelled as he cried. "You left him! How many times has Sean beat you and left you for dead? Why do you keep coming back?!"

"That's none of your business!" Sean yelled back. "We're cool, man, calm down!"

"The fuck we are!" Jimmy pushed himself off the ground with one hand, but Lyndsey walked over and pushed him back down. Jimmy grabbed Lyndsey's arm and yanked her to the ground as well, pushing past her and scrambling to his feet once more.

"Okay, now we're gonna have problems." Sean ripped off his hoodie and half of his t-shirt beneath in the process. He fixed his disheveled shirt, flexed his fingers, cracked his neck, and settled into a boxing stance.

"We've *had* problems, you piece of shit!" Jimmy took off his baseball cap and tossed it to the side. He shuffled around Sean in a looping circle, dropping his center of gravity by bending at the knees.

"Jesus, Trevor, help me," Lyndsey pleaded. She stood again, ran to Jimmy, and wrapped him up into a hug. Trevor groaned as he walked over and hugged Sean from behind. Lyndsey and Trevor succeeded in pulling the would-be combatants apart just as soon as they squared up. The unattended bonfire had shrunk in size and intensity, now a soft smoldering pile of dark wood.

"Jimmy, come with me. We need to have a serious conversation," Lyndsey said. She took Jimmy by the hand and pulled him along as she stomped to the road. As they pulled out of the conversation range of the now-quibbling Sean and Trevor, she pushed Jimmy, who tripped and stumbled as they got to the sidewalk. Jimmy turned to face Lyndsey, eyes wide.

"Are you forgetting about our little situation?" Lyndsey asked in a harsh whisper. She opened her jean jacket and pulled down the collar of her multi-colored band shirt to show the wire taped on her upper chest. "I'm working on them, Jimmy. I'm getting some good stuff for the investigation."

"I'm *sure you are*," Jimmy said. His face red with anger, he gestured to the backyard. "Why didn't you say you were coming here? We... we were intimate, and you disappeared for three days! You could have left me a note or something."

"Jimmy, please. I don't want to talk about *that* right now," Lyndsey pleaded. She adjusted her shirt and closed her jacket.

"When? We don't get to do something like that and then... *nothing*. We're better than this."

"I don't owe you an explanation or a timeline for anything, Jimmy... that's something that just, well, happened. And that's that."

"So we're not anything?"

"Jimmy, let's have this conversation after we work with our *situation*, okay? I think your priorities are a little out of whack. You're putting your dick on a pedestal like you always do. I would have hoped you'd grown up more by now. God damn," Lyndsey ranted. She walked away from Jimmy, stepping down the cracked sidewalk of the dim neighborhood, loose rocks breaking under the soles of her Chuck Taylors.

Jimmy took a long breath and followed after her. "So are you fucking Sean?"

Lyndsey ignored him and picked up her pace.

"I asked you a question, Lytz, please!" Jimmy ran to catch up. Lyndsey whirled around to face him, her dark hair falling across her eyes and face. She didn't bother to fix it as she clenched her fists and thrust her arms to her side.

"Yes, Jimmy. I am fucking him. I'm a grown woman who can do what I want, and we are *nothing*. You and I are *nothing*," she emphasized through her teeth. "I should have known you'd get all obsessive!"

"He beats you! He steals from you! He uses you!" Jimmy yelled. "You know I can treat you so much better. We don't even need to be 'anything,' I just..."

"We aren't going to *be* anything," Lyndsey said with a clap of her hands. "How do I know you'd treat me better? I know everything about you!"

"You don't know what I'm like in a relation-"

"Oh, I don't? I don't?! I've known you for fifteen years, Jimmy. I swear, fucking you was a mistake. I knew it would be."

"You don't know that!"

"I don't?! I don't?! Look at you, showing up here, looking for a fight, when you know we both have bigger things to worry about. And if we *did* date, how's it going to end?" Lyndsey asked.

"I don't want it to end, that's the thing,"

"But it will. Everything ends. Everything. You'll grow distant like you did with Megan, or you'll cheat on me like you did with Wendy, or you'll disappear like you did on Teresa."

Jimmy's shade turned pink, and he finally averted his gaze from Lyndsey. He clenched his mouth shut, kicked a loose chunk of pavement, and turned his head to face the houses and yards to his right.

"But... do you even want to try?" Jimmy said softly.

"No... Jimmy, I don't. I value our friendship more than everything. The other night? It was a mistake. I don't know why I let that happen. I just... I don't know, I've never seen you like that before." Lyndsey walked back toward Jimmy and grabbed his hoodie sleeve. "I know how you feel. I know you've always felt that way."

"I... I think I love you," Jimmy said between tears.

"I know," Lyndsey said.

Lyndsey put her hands around Jimmy's face and looked into his eyes. Her lips tilted in a half-smile as she smoothed out his unkempt beard hair.

"I don't love you," Lyndsey said, "But I love the *idea* of you. Who you could be, who you should be."

Jimmy sniffed back a sob and peeled his head away from Lyndsey's touch.

"But you're my friend. You're a great friend. Maybe we just need a little time apart while we work out everything," Lyndsey said. "I'll keep things at your place, maybe I'll be back once things settle down, once I know *you* know that we... this... it's not a thing. It won't be."

Jimmy looked back and forth, declining to respond. They had argued down a block and a half of Fellow Street. Only a few porch lamps were on, and zero street lights stood above them. The waning moon caught Jimmy's eye off a nearby Prius. He leaned against the car's passenger-side door and reached into his pocket.

"Care for a smoke?" Jimmy asked Lyndsey as he popped open a box of Marlboros with a deep sigh.

"Sure," Lyndsey said. She leaned against the back of the Prius. "I've got my own, though."

"Go ahead and light me one up, then," a tilted, vaguely foreign male voice said from the other side of the car. "We're going to be here a few minutes."

Lyndsey jumped in fright. Jimmy turned slowly to regard the voice source, and the Marlboro dropped from his lips when he locked bloodshot, sallow eyes with Brody Marlowe.

CHAPTER TWENTY

"You really need to be mindful of your surroundings," Brody Marlowe said between cigarette puffs. "Your voices carry out here. Thankfully, Sean and Trevor are too busy dicking around with the fire."

"Heat of the moment," James Glencroft said as he flicked his cigarette butt into a nearby drain. "Brody, I almost forgot about you. It's been a wild couple of weeks."

Brody nodded, looked down at his feet, and then back up to Jimmy and Lyndsey de Rueda, who also stood alongside his Prius in the night's shadows.

"That it has. We do have a bit of... catching up to do." Brody turned to Lyndsey and faced her directly. "First things first... Do you still have Mirko's credit card?"

Lyndsey blinked. "I don't know what you..."

"Don't play dumb. I'm not here to cause trouble. Unlike some folks," Brody said with a tilted nod to Jimmy.

Lyndsey sighed. "Okay, I can explain... but I need you to promise you won't do anything to me."

"Or me," Jimmy cut in.

"Okay," Brody continued. "Deal, deal, the both of you. Let's start here. My name isn't Brody Marlowe. My name is actually Drago Zupan. I was born in the former Yugoslavia."

"What are you doing in Columbus, then?" Jimmy asked.

"I've lived in Ohio for over a decade," Drago said. "I'm just as American as a lot of folks. Now come on, finish these cigarettes and let's go for a ride."

Lyndsey crossed her arms. "I should go let Sean and Trevor know we're gone."

Drago waved her concern away. "No need. They will undoubtedly find themselves occupied with other matters. You know them. Now come, I wish not to discuss further matters in open air."

Drago walked around to the driver's seat and slid in. Jimmy hopped into the passenger seat as soon as it unlocked while Lyndsey sprawled out in the back, her shoes pushed up against the window.

"Hey, careful with those," Drago warned. "I don't want to clean those windows again. This is a company car."

"What company, if you don't mind me asking?" Jimmy nodded in satisfaction as the Prius fired up and rolled onto the road quietly. "Ooh, this car rides smooth."

Drago laughed. "Yes, yes, when following people around, silence is a luxury. To answer your question, Jim, I'm employed by a... company... my uncle founded called Double Windsor LLC. We're a logistics, storage, and transportation firm out of Dayton."

Drago slowed the car to a gentle stop at an intersection.

"We also move industrial quantities of party drugs, mine and launder cryptocurrency, and provide *security* services to other firms. Simple B2B matters, really." Drago turned onto Sullivant Avenue and maintained speed just a notch below the limit.

"...By any chance, are you in some kind of turf war against... let's say, Foxx Construction?" Jimmy asked.

"Hmm, what makes you say that?" Drago laughed.

"Well," Jimmy started, but he fell silent.

"You were at the warehouse," Drago said. He stared at the road ahead. "A few of my friends died there."

Jimmy's body flushed white-hot as his heart fluttered.

"I won't hurt you, man; I know you're a pawn," Drago said. "And I don't mean that as an insult. I know you're in a rough spot."

"Warehouse?" Lyndsey sat up and interjected. "What happened?"

Drago dismissed her with a wave. "Another day, another day," he said. He turned the Prius into the empty parking lot of a little ice cream shop called the Hilltop Dairy Twist. Drago turned off the headlights and eased into a space, his head on a swivel.

"What are we doing here?" Jimmy asked.

"Sorry, folks, I'm just a little paranoid," Drago said. "I'm uncomfortable when I'm not following people right now. I just feel, as you say, on an island right now, no?"

"May I ask what's going on?"

"Okay, look. I'm working with the DEA right now," Drago said. Before Jimmy could offer a response, Lyndsey interjected.

"So are we," she said as she sat on her knees on the backseat. She popped her head between Drago and Jimmy's seats. "Working with Browning?"

"Yes, yes," Drago said. "I've got a lot riding on this, but I had to take a break. I've been in about a week or so longer than you two."

"My mic is off," Lyndsey offered, "and Jimmy lost his, I believe."

"Browning has no idea," Jimmy said with a sigh.

"I'm sure she does," Drago said.

Drago turned to look at Lyndsey. He smiled wryly.

"I tried to clean up your mess at the river," Drago said. "I followed you that night. I got busted with your gun. So snitching is how I'm trying to get out of this because otherwise, I'm a suspect in cousin Mirko's murder and Rezendes' disappearance."

"Okay, I'm starting to get some answers, but I'm only finding more questions from there," Jimmy muttered. "Lytz, you were involved in all of this too?"

"I told you that you would never believe me," she said.

"Be careful with Landers and Barclay," Drago said to Jimmy. "Something's up with those two that I haven't figured out yet."

"Why are you telling me this? What's going on, already?!"

"Calm, calm... please, one question at a time. I'm telling you this because I like you, Jimmy. Barclay's a deadeye shot, and Landers gives me fright. No good will come from them."

"He's right," Lyndsey said. "I saw Barclay kill Drago's cousin, almost point-blank. It was so awful, Jimmy; I've never seen anything like that." She shuddered and pulled her jacket together tightly.

Drago shifted in his seat and rested his arms on the steering wheel. His eyes darted to and fro every time a car would drive by. "We should probably keep driving."

"No, no, let's keep clearing the air," Lyndsey said. "Are you wired up right now?"

"No, I promise, I can disrobe if you need. I left it at home. I just feel that Browning will go back on her deal if she knew I wasn't wired. I don't trust her."

"What makes you say that?" Jimmy asked.

"Once you're in the game long enough, you start to get an instinct for these things," Drago said. "You'll learn."

"But... I don't want to *be* in the game."

"Nobody does, Jimmy... nobody does. More often than not, the game chooses you. You're too deep already. You were too deep when you were friends with these guys for years – nobody can be friends with someone that long without knowing the truth."

"I didn't, though, I swear," Jimmy said. He breathed deep and slapped his own leg. "Had no clue until the whole warehouse thing."

"Even if I believed you, the question is, will the feds? Will the courts? You're stained, brother. So am I. So is she," Drago said with a nod to Lyndsey. "Best we can do is keep washing and keep moving."

"So, what do you want from us?" Lyndsey asked.

"Like I told Jimmy, and like you were so unfortunate to see, my family has lost a few people near and dear to me. I feel guilty because I keep sending the DEA to them, I'm compromised but I keep everything moving, and... at what cost?" Drago stared out the driver's side window. "I'm barely in my thirties; I've got life left, but what is it worth if I keep pulling others down with me?"

Jimmy offered Drago a pat of understanding. When Drago spoke again, his voice came more clear and determined.

"Foxx Construction is held by the majority of my people; we call ourselves Slavia United. When we boosted everything from your warehouse near Slade City, we had a crew move on the warehouse near Dublin – the same crew that lit up that gas station in South Bloomfield."

"Sean and Trevor were there..." Lyndsey observed.

"No way!" Jimmy interjected. "I'm surprised those two have it in them to live through a mass shooting. How's Foxx Construction operating with the main hub compromised, anyway?"

"Business is operating as usual, but we have Foxx's people playing it off like we are... ah, investors, and I think it's working," Drago explained. "That leaves our central hub in Dayton weak. Little to no armed presence. That's where we are keeping the haul we stole from your warehouse near Slade City."

"That's not *my* warehouse; I don't have any –"

"Jimmy. Listen. Until we find a way out, you'll have to pretend like it's your warehouse, okay? For all purposes, you are one of them now."

"Wouldn't that make us your enemies?" Lyndsey asked.

"No, no, no... the enemy of my enemy is my friend, and all that," Drago responded. "Like I said before, you are pawns – I'm smart enough to recognize that. My friends and associates might not. The DEA understands, but they don't care. They're going to throw us all under the bus. I can just feel it."

"So... what's our move?" Jimmy asked.

"Jimmy, I want you to tip off Landers on the location of our warehouse in Dayton," Drago said as he slid Jimmy a folded-up napkin with the address scrawled on the backside.

"Won't this hurt your people?!"

"Do you listen, Jimmy Glencroft? Most everyone is at Foxx Construction. This will be an easy job for your people if you play your cards right," Drago explained. "Just be useful, do a good job, help them out – I think this will give them the momentum they need to pay you. Then we can use those resources to get the hell out of this city."

"What about us? Me, Trevor, Sean?" Lyndsey asked. Jimmy couldn't contain his groan.

"I've got plans for them too," Drago assured her. "I don't like Sean either, Jimmy, and certainly Trevor is a wild card. But – I know where we can find a stash of candles large enough to flip on the streets without being on the radar of either my family, their clients, or Foxx and his people."

"Go on," Lyndsey said.

"Ever hear of Captain Galactico?" Drago asked.

"Galactico? Oh God, I got tired of hearing about him a few years ago," Jimmy said. "Surprised, but not surprised, he isn't big yet. What's he got to do with this?"

"He uses these candles as part of his sets to get people hooked on his live shows," Drago said. "We can go to one of his shows and find a way to boost his candle rig."

"I like the idea," Lyndsey said.

"Me too." Jimmy nodded, smiling. "The syndicates won't care because that's no longer their inventory. Hopefully, that can be a smooth boost."

"We need someone on the inside," Drago mused. "Also, we may need some numbers... would you be willing to work with Sean?"

"Drago, my dude, to keep it real... I would work with Sean *so hard* if it meant never having to see him again." Jimmy turned and smiled at Lyndsey. "Full offense intended."

"Full offense taken, but understood and forgiven," Lyndsey said with a laugh.

"There's just one thing," Drago said, "How do we find someone on the inside? Do we know anyone who's just crazy and connected enough to pull this off?"

It didn't take long for Jimmy to clap his hands in sudden realization.

"I know just the guy!"

CHAPTER TWENTY-ONE

Midnight black cloaked the interior of the delivery truck, sealing the inhabitants in a tense gloom.

Déjà vu, thought James Glencroft as he sat with his legs in front of him, back flat against the walls of the truck. He felt every bump and rumble and roll of the vehicle in his spine. Sore and weary from the last few weeks, not a chance to recover emotionally or physically, he pondered his fate as the truck rumbled on, trying to talk himself into the task ahead.

Worst case scenario, you die. It will hurt at first. You will soon slip away, and you will go on to the next. Your name will go down as a criminal and a tragedy. You can't get much lower as you are now.

You get to fight again. You get to help those that have helped you. More money than you have ever had awaits on the other side of this. No more debt. No more struggle. Just one job, just this one job, and you will be free. Life begins again.

Jimmy was snapped out of his thoughts by the crackle of a walkie-talkie.

"Gear check, crew. We're in Fairborn. E.T.A. 10 minutes," Landers' voice commanded.

An electronic lantern sparked the middle of the truck to illuminate the crew and the tools at their disposal.

Winslow Barclay stared straight ahead in silence. A black beanie was pulled low over his head, eye-black smeared beneath his stern gaze and around his neck, the whites of his eyes being the only bright aspect of his visage. Barclay ran his glove-clad hands up and down a semi-automatic rifle and rubbed them against the firm metal.

Big Trace Onwudiwe was similarly clad but with no eye-black necessary on his naturally dark skin. He wore a black thermal sweater and a bulletproof vest, the only glint of brightness apart from his eyes being the crucifix chain necklace he wore. He popped open a double-barrel shotgun and loaded several shells, clicking the barrels back into place when finished.

Jimmy fumbled with his pistol, dropping it on the floor of the truck. Trace twitched, startled.

"Hey man, be more careful with that, okay?" Trace said.

"Yeah, we can't have you being a liability out there. Remember your role?" Barclay asked.

Jimmy nodded. "Stay between you and the truck. Go where the heat is. Stay out of the way."

"Easy," Barclay said. "We shouldn't have heat, though. I'll see to that." He grinned.

"How can you be so sure?" Jimmy asked as he picked up the pistol and tightened his bulletproof vest.

Barclay smiled. "I'm military. None of these clowns are, at least not that we know of. Almost all just street. I'm taking point on the way in, then Trace takes point inside. We're playing to our strengths."

The radio crackled, and Landers' voice came in.

"We're here."

The white unmarked delivery truck pulled to a curb alongside a ten-foot, canvassed industrial fence. Barbed wire rings circled the pointed tops of the posts alongside the road. Over the wall loomed a dark brick warehouse. 2 A.M. on a Thursday, and naught a soul was on this tranquil Dayton street to interfere with the mission.

Landers used his good arm to unlatch the back door of the truck and pull it up. Jimmy stood and helped open it from the inside. At the driver's seat, Wainwright leaned out the window, looking around and keeping watch. The lanky, rat-tailed, handlebar-mustachioed crew member worked a giant chaw behind his bottom lip.

"All clear, I reckon," Wainwright yelled back to them. "I'd move quickly, though. I saw headlights about a mile off when I turned in." He killed the truck's lights, putting the group into near-complete darkness.

"You scouted this place well, Landers," Barclay said as he went to the fence and pulled loose a large, pre-cut section of fence with a few firm shakes. "How do you have time for this?"

"One thing I learned from Foxx is to call in some favors when I need them," Landers replied. "Now get going. Wainwright and I will circle back to the extraction point when the coast is clear. We shouldn't have any issues."

With that command, Barclay slipped through the hole in the fence. Big Trace was next, having to squat slightly, twist his body around, and go through one leg at a time. Jimmy looked back towards Landers and Wainwright. Landers mimed a quick small circle with his hand as if to say, "Hurry up." Jimmy obliged and slunk into the hole, careful not to snag his shirt on the ragged edge. When clear, his head snapped up, and he continued along, leaving about forty feet between him and Trace, who was only slightly behind Barclay.

The three men wove between pallets, skids, shipping containers, and racks as they advanced on the warehouse. After they came free of the obstacles, it was only a brief jog from these shadows to the ones along the building. Barclay signaled for the other two to halt as he scanned the windows above them for any signs of movement. He turned and nodded them forward. He swept back and forth with his rifle, making sure he was ready for any foe from any direction. Big Trace clopped along the pavement a little more loudly than Barclay, who glared back over his shoulder at him. Trace switched his pace to a quieter heel-toe, heel-toe. Jimmy brought up the rear, clutching his pistol in both hands. They lined up in the thin shadow along this side of the warehouse.

"Ay bro, don't need to hold it in both hands, loosen up now," Trace whispered.

"Shhh..." Barclay glared back at him with a slicing motion across his throat. Trace mouthed an apology, and the three continued towards a side door. Barclay took the left side, Trace stayed on the right. Trace tried the knob. No luck; the door was locked.

The three continued along the side of the building until they turned a corner and observed that the building was U-Shaped, and they were turning the corner of one of the tips. There were loading bays along the two parallel sides of the inside of the U, with large double doors in the middle, as well as another open garage door with a small ramp leading down from it. Only one line of the loading bays showed any activity, with two rigs backed into their trailers. Neither had their highlights on, but the rumble of their engines echoed in the central lot. One loading bay was open, and the crew could observe employees inside moving about, with one forklift driving back and forth.

Barclay signaled for Jimmy to stay where he was, then he went forward with Trace. Careful to remain in the building's shadow, which was cast longer and thicker from this part of the building, Jimmy walked out a little bit to observe Barclay and Trace. They flanked the closest open bay and quickly tape-measured it. Barclay nodded to Trace, who pumped his fist. They tried to lift the bay door, then when unsuccessful, they doubled back to where Jimmy stood.

"They're not on alert. At all," Barclay said. "Not a single guard out. What kind of drug operation is this?"

"Either they don't fear us, or they're stupid... or we're getting set up," said Trace.

"I doubt Landers would set us up," Jimmy butted in.

"I'm not talking about Landers; I'm talking about Dirty D or the Euros. Maybe they put out some false info," Barclay said.

"I don't think Landers would make any plays with faulty info, either," Jimmy said.

"You suckin' homeboy's dick or somethin'? Damn, we known that freak way longer than we known you. He ain't as smart as he put on," Trace said, his voice elevating. Barclay stepped between them.

"We can argue the merits of Landers' leadership later," Barclay said. "Just because they're on low alert doesn't mean we should relax our approach. We need to find a way in to find our work. If it's not in here, we *know* it's in a more guarded joint. So, let's get in and get out; if we can get it here, we're less likely to go loud later."

Jimmy knelt on the ground beside them. After a long moment of thought, he got up and gestured across the loading yard.

"I have an idea," Jimmy said. "Somewhere out here, there's some kind of smoking patio, I'm sure. When I worked in a factory back in the day, it was around the corner from a big ramp. People would just ride their lifts out the ramp and walk around the corner from their smoke. No place out here looks like the smoke patio. It's either out back or on the other side. We can either slip in through that area or take their lift or something."

Barclay and Trace glanced at one another before looking back at Jimmy.

"Believe it or not, that's a better idea than I had," Barclay said. "Let's sneak across the way and see if we can find this break area." Trace nodded enthusiastically, and so the three men moved on, quickly walking across the front of the loading yard.

In front of the two ends of the building, an access road ran perpendicular to the lot. Barclay, Trace, and Jimmy ran along this road. Beyond, a new road expanded from the intersection of this and the loading lot, heading along canvas-lined fences to an exit gate.

As the three crew members passed through and got to the shadow on the other end of the lot without any alarm or resistance, Barclay signaled Jimmy to stop.

"Ay, Jim. Post up here a minute. I'm going to radio the truck. This is a smooth-looking extraction point. Trace, go up and make sure the gate is unlocked. I'm going to head around the corner and find a way in."

"10-4," Jimmy said.

"A'ight," Trace replied with a nod.

Jimmy turned and put his back to the wall at the exact corner of the tip of the U, so he could swivel his gaze in every direction. Trace ran alongside the fence up the main exit road. Barclay turned the corner of the building and disappeared into the shadows with no sound.

Barclay hadn't moved for long when he spied exactly what Jimmy had predicted, a break patio, with several picnic tables sitting under a bright light, and with ash receptacles and trash cans alongside them. Twin doors beckoned from the side of the building.

Nobody was outside. Barclay glanced at his watch. 2:45 AM. He slid up to where the light met the dark. He reached up and pulled the handle of the door closest to him. It opened slightly. Unlocked.

Barclay cracked the door and peeked inside. Directly ahead of him were several rows of inventory in storage, large corrugated boxes uniform in color, shape, and size; all drab brown, all considerably larger than himself. All seemed silent in this part of the warehouse. He spied a forklift in the distance, driving in the opposite direction, with the low hum of its electric engine. Barclay slipped into the warehouse, careful not to swing the door open too far. He dashed along the outer wall of the warehouse, holding his semi-automatic rifle along his left-hand side, parallel with his body. The open space Barclay ran along led to metal racks standing floor-to-ceiling, with boxes and wrapped pallets filling the rows.

The storage area across from him eventually gave way to the open loading bay area he had witnessed from the outside. One truck was already closed off and sat in the bay idle. The other truck was still open, a forklift coming by and loading in a stack of two pallets. The forklift was hypnotic to watch, as the operator's movements were somehow simultaneously smooth and robotic.

Barclay stood against one rack of inventory, pressing himself between two boxes as he watched the loading process. He pulled a spotting scope from his pack and peered through it, scanning the pallets and boxes being loaded, trying to get a glimpse of the labels or anything that would give the product away as being their own contraband.

The nearby electric whirr of a forklift startled Barclay, and he thrust the scope back in his bag, squeezing himself in between the pallets. On the neighboring section of the rack, two pallets down, a forklift thrust its skids into the pallet. The platform shook as the driver wrestled the pallet loose, lowered it slightly, then turned and whirred off to where the 18-wheeler was being loaded. Barclay backed out to the edge of the racks, then looked around. Coming from the direction of the patio door, he observed two men walking, somewhat distant at this time, but surely able to see him if they looked his way. He slid over to the empty spot between pallets and concealed himself in shadow.

Barclay stumbled on the rail and flattened his body against it. He held his breath for as long as he could, straining his neck to get a view of the two men. Barclay couldn't keep his breath longer than ninety seconds, and gasped for air. After his first gasp, he pressed his face against the closest box to keep them from hearing his breathing. They walked by without interest, so Barclay rose to one knee and then stood in full.

Barclay edged around behind a pallet and pressed up against the backside of it, watching for the two men through the gaps between the other racks and pallets. He was so caught up in that search that he neglected to listen for the forklift, which came upon his row. Barclay heard the electric whirring too late to react and was jarred by the impact. He twisted around, remaining behind the pallet as well as he could – and after he felt the tilt of the prongs to secure the load, he hopped up on the skid, straddling and hugging the box tightly.

The forklift took off to the loading bay. Barclay could only look in one direction, off to the left, unable to swivel his head as it was pressed against the box. Fluorescent lights flew through his view like streaking race cars.

Barclay regained focus and saw the two men off in the distance, not facing him. He held his breath as the forklift rolled up the ramp into the back of the open semi. He looked behind as he was enveloped in darkness. Barclay couldn't react in time as the forklift pressed him against a box and knocked the breath from his lungs. He fell, wheezing, losing his bearings. The forklift driver let out an interested grunt, pulled back into reverse, and then pushed forward again. This time he put the pallet down, putting some space between it and the next one, unknowingly crushing Barclay's arm in the process. Giving up on getting the boxes aligned, he backed up and moved on to another task, leaving Barclay stunned and breathless in the dark, pinched under one pallet and against another. Barclay finally caught his breath, drawing it in raggedly and harshly, and he had drawn blood from his own bottom lip, biting into it hard to keep himself from yelling out in agony.

Barclay managed to get his breath back under control as the forklift came back around another time. After it loaded in a pallet beside him, effectively sealing him in, he tried to pull his arm loose from the pallet pinning it down. There was no luck there – and he gasped out in pain as he tried to move. Barclay had one arm free, and he felt around along his body to take inventory. He was laying on his rifle, uncomfortably dug in against the exposed skin of his side. As he felt his radio clipped on his right hip, he whispered a silent "thank God" as he loosened the clip and pulled it up to his face.

"This is Sarge. Do I have a copy?" he asked in a hush.

"Copy, this is Luau, what's the sitch?" Landers responded.

"Man down," Barclay said. "I'm hurt and pinned inside the truck. I haven't I.D.'d the cargo. I can't get out."

"What's the call, boss?" Trace crackled in.

"Wait," Barclay said. "Silence."

The forklift came back in, pushing another pallet up against the one pinning his arm. It moved the pallet up his arm and now close to his shoulder. Barclay yelled out in pain, startled. He dropped his walkie-talkie and could hear it roll between the pallets.

"Fuck! Fuck, fuck, fuck!" Barclay yelled, flailing his legs as well as he could to try to get the radio. No success – he was now stuck, in pain, in silence, and in darkness. After another pallet was loaded on the other side of the truck, the worker pulled shut the back of the semi with a clunk, sealing Winslow Barclay into the dark completely. The wounded veteran and criminal enforcer prayed for a darkness more complete, to lift him from his pain and panic one final time.

Outside the warehouse, a scramble was on. Big Trace and Jimmy Glencroft ran to meet one another in the parking lot. Trace waved his arm towards the loading bays.

"What do we do, man?" Trace asked. "Do we rush in? What's up?"

Jimmy took a moment to answer, shaking his head to break the haze of panic. "Hey, you're the gangsta... I don't know."

"I ain't no gangsta, man... I'm just tryna feed my family." Trace's breathing intensified.

Jimmy put a hand on Trace's shoulder. "Deep breaths, man. We will get him out of here." With the other hand, Jimmy flicked on his walkie-talkie. "Sarge, if you can hear me, we will get you out of here. We will find a way."

Landers crackled in. "Smash. Channel 2. In case Sarge is in a pitch."

"10-4," Jimmy replied. He flicked over to the second channel on the walkie-talkie.

"Smash," he said.

"Loud and clear," Landers said. "Sarge, you on this channel?"

A moment of silence.

"OK, good," Landers said. "Okay. Smash, Big – going to the gate near you. We'll extract you from the main road."

"Extract? Are you serious?" Jimmy disputed. "What are we doing about Sarge?"

"He's a liability now. We don't have the manpower to rescue him," Landers replied.

"No. Fuck that. You can pick up Big. I'm going in." Jimmy handed Big Trace his walkie-talkie. Big Trace stuffed both his talkie and Jimmy's into his backpack, then picked his shotgun back up off the ground.

"I'm going with you, Jim. Let's do this." Big Trace nodded towards the idling trucks at the loading bay. "Barc's in one of those trailers. Let's get him."

The two men jogged alongside the building towards the loading bays. When they came upon the building's edge, they observed that one of the drivers had walked out from the warehouse and gave his trailer a look-over. The trailer shuddered as it was closed on the inside. He walked back around to the driver's side of the cab and clambered in.

"I'm going to pop him and drive off with the trailer," Big Trace said, raising his shotgun. He started to move forward, but Jimmy grabbed him by the top of his backpack with both hands, hauling him back with effort.

"Fuck you doin'?" Trace asked.

"You don't want to kill him," Jimmy said. "I don't think we should go loud. We need to be smart here."

"Smart? Our homie is hemmed up in there! The time to be smart has passed. Come on, we just pop him and haul outta here before everyone is onto us."

"Not a good idea, not a good idea at all," Jimmy said. "Look. Stay here. Don't move unless I yell or shoot. I have a better idea."

"What are you doing?" Trace asked.

"I'm gonna hitch a ride," Jimmy said. "Look, either stay here and watch out, or go to the gate and get with the van; I don't care. I'm going to see where this thing is going and get our boy out."

A second man walked out of the warehouse. He was taller and broader than the cab driver, well-built and walking deliberately. Jimmy and Big Trace dropped to the ground to avoid being seen. The second man's head swiveled before he opened the passenger door and climbed in.

"He must be the muscle," Big Trace whispered. "Guarantee he's strapped. Must be good ass cargo in there. Bet that's where Barc is for sure."

"Leeeeeroooooy Jenkins..." Jimmy said under his breath. He ran along the warehouse wall and positioned himself close to the loading bay, but just far enough back that he wasn't in range of the rearview mirrors. He watched the cab as he pulled a long strand of taut paracord he had fastened to his belt loop and tucked into his pocket. After a minute, the truck pulled forward. Jimmy ran ahead and reached the back of the truck while it was still moving at only 5 M.P.H. He looped the paracord around the latch poles in the center of the trailer door. Jimmy quickly slung his arm through the loop, then clutched the base of the rope behind the knot with white knuckles. He stumbled as the truck accelerated, then recovered and jumped up to the runner foothold. Jimmy crouched low and looped his legs through the footholds. Using the crook of the knee for support and holding on tightly to the paracord loop, he leaned back and took a ride away on the back of the accelerating rig.

Big Trace stared at Jimmy as he rode by. Trace's delay in reaction allowed the eighteen-wheeler to get to the gate, signaling a left turn. His walkie-talkie crackled to life.

"Biggie, is this the truck? The one about to leave the gate?" Landers asked.

Silence.

"Big, come in. Are you good?"

Big Trace finally reacted. He dashed towards the back of the truck, now about 100 yards away and in the process of turning.

"I copy," Trace said. "Smash is on the back of the truck. Repeat. Smash is on the back of the truck."

"Fuck," Landers said. Radio silence for a moment as Trace ran. "Are you close?"

"Gaining as fast as I can," Trace replied. The large man panted with exertion as he got close enough to make out Jimmy's form clinging to the back of the truck.

"Jimmy, get down from there!" Trace yelled between gasps. Jimmy either didn't hear or didn't care. The truck turned off down the city street. Trace bent over and gasped, his hands on his knees.

The white delivery van pulled up a moment later. The tires squealed as Wainwright slammed the brakes. Wainwright popped his head out, making circular motions with his arm.

"Let's go, let's go, let's go!" Wainwright yelled. Big Trace struggled to open the back of the delivery van and hoist himself in. Wainwright drummed nervously on the steering wheel as he waited on Trace to seal himself within. Finally, the back door of the truck slammed shut, and Wainwright threw the truck into drive.

Wainwright looked to his left as they took off. Two cars and a truck turned out from the employee parking lot at the warehouse. They kept their headlights shut off as they advanced.

"Shit, chief, I think we got a tail," Wainwright said as he hopped a curb and drove the wrong way down a city street. He could make out the taillights of the eighteen-wheeler about two blocks ahead. Only a right turn down the main road and a half-mile separated it from the freeway.

Landers leaned low in the passengers' seat and watched the rear view on his side.

"What's the tail? I can't make anything out," Landers said.

"A couple vehicles, I think one was a pickup truck," Wainwright said. "Headlights are out. This must be the right hauler, here – they have an escort."

"We need to get Jimmy out of there. *Now.*"

"Right, boss, but – how? He's latched in there, he's moving – Barc is in the trailer..."

"We give them a taste of their own medicine and hope Jimbo and Barclay figure it out from there," Landers said. He drew a cell phone from his pants pocket and dialed 9-1-1.

CHAPTER TWENTY-TWO

Jimmy clutched the paracord rope because his life depended on it. The cold night took a bitter bite out of his cheeks as it whipped around him. The 18-wheeler trailer accelerated up an on-ramp and onto a freeway. Every ounce of energy and effort Jimmy could muster went into staying off the rapidly passing pavement below. He felt the metal of the runners dig into the back of his knees. Every thread of paracord stood out to his grasping, desperate fingers.

After a few minutes on the highway, two cars accelerated to flank the trailer – one in each lane surrounding it. Jimmy dared not try to look at them lest he break his concentration, but the two import coupes were driven by other white men around his age, one of whom was yelling on a cell phone.

The trailer slowed, gradually losing speed. Jimmy caught his breath IN elation of relative safety, but soon realized the gravity of the situation. The cars pulled up close enough for him to see the drivers. One of the cars had a passenger. Jimmy's eyes met his, and Jimmy's eyes lowered to look into the barrel of a leveled pistol.

Jimmy threw himself backward just as the report of the shot cracked the air around him. Deafened, he tumbled on the pavement. He let his body tumble and flop to distribute the force of the impact, only taking care to shield his head and face. One of the cars slowed with him as the other drove to the front of the semi-truck, which came to a full stop shortly thereafter. Jimmy staggered to his feet as pain throbbed through his body. He stared as the car came to a stop in front of him, and both doors opened to reveal men in soccer jerseys hoisting guns. The elation Jimmy felt a moment ago had been overwhelmed by sheer fright, his body burning with a pointed urgency as he looked his fate in the barrel once more.

Jimmy had never been so grateful to see police lights. Two patrol cars screamed from the opposite direction, sirens at full tilt as they drove across the median and onto the pavement between the semi and the car.

The gun-toting men in front of Jimmy hopped back into their car at the sight of the patrolmen. One of the officers gave chase as the imported coupe rattled away, sparks flying from the back of the vehicle as it zipped into the darkness. Jimmy didn't see the developments with the other car, but the now-too-familiar *pop, pop, pop-pop-pop* he heard breaking the air was all he needed to know.

The white delivery van pulled up with screeching and smoking tires as it skidded to a stop a few yards away from Jimmy. Big Trace Onwudiwe threw open the back doors.

"Get in! *Now!*" Big Trace yelled.

"Come on, man, let's go!" Landers hollered as he rolled down the front window. "Now or never, dude!"

Jimmy took a few steps and shook his head. His body felt like it was going to explode in agony.

"I'll get him," Trace said as he hopped out of the back of the van. Jimmy put a hand up.

"Not without Barclay," Jimmy said. "Not without him. And not without the haul."

"Damnit, Jim, give it up," Trace said – but it was too late. Jimmy lurched alongside the parked trailer. As he came up beside it, he bore witness to a grisly scene, a bloodied officer with his gun up advancing on a bullet-riddled coupe. He pulled open the driver's side cab, and

183

the driver's body tumbled out into the highway. The bloody corpse barely missed him on its way down. Jimmy clambered into the cab – wait, wasn't there a second guy? *Pop, pop-pop-pop, pop. Pop.* He looked out the windshield to see him get domed by the highway patrolman in front of the cab, red mist and gun smoke in the frigid air.

The patrolman dropped his gun, staggered over to his patrol car, and put his head into his arms against the roof. Jimmy watched him for a moment, but when it was apparent the officer hadn't fully noticed him nor the delivery van, he made his play.

The truck engine was still running. Jimmy settled himself into the driver's seat, oblivious to the blood around his head like a halo. He threw the truck into gear and found the accelerator. Slowly, at first, Jimmy moved between the patrol car and the coupe. The officer looked up, gained his bearings, and gave chase on foot.

Jimmy shifted in second gear as he watched the cop run along the trailer through the right rear-view. Jimmy put his right foot down on the accelerator and put some road between he and law enforcement.

Jimmy looked up to check his rearview to his left, but it had been shot out. He was clear in the rearview to his right, and he allowed the big rig to leer rightward into the slow lane. Jimmy clenched the wheel the way he did the paracord just a few moments before and kept his eyes wide and centered. He was so focused on putting more pavement between him and the bloodbath behind him that he didn't catch Wainwright, Landers, and Big Trace flanking him in the white van.

The white van cut Jimmy off a moment later, forcing him to tap the brakes and panic-shift prematurely to a lower gear. Jimmy accidentally pushed the clutch pedal in too deep for the higher gear, and it threw the truck into a lurch.

"Been too long, damnit," Jimmy muttered as he struggled to figure out why he was losing speed and control. He then discovered he was riding the clutch – but before he could remedy the situation, he heard a horn blare from outside. Big Trace had thrown the back doors of the van open and was waving frantically at Jimmy to slow down and pull off – and Jimmy screamed as he realized he was inches from hitting Trace and his other colleagues.

The big rig trundled to an awkward, creaking stop – half in the slow lane, half on the shoulder. Jimmy hopped out as Big Trace ran to his side.

"Jimmy, you maniac, you idiot, you did it!" Big Trace panted out. "We have enough time to get Barc out; come on!"

"Trace, this isn't a good idea," Jimmy rebutted. "I'm sure that officer back there is calling for backup, there's another car out there, I... ugh, okay, let's hurry."

A mad dash ensued as Jimmy, Big Trace, and Wainwright all flocked the back of the truck. Just enough distance had been placed between them and the crime scene – for now. The police lights were still on the horizon, and the crew's heads were on a constant swivel to regard the traffic that blasted past them.

Wainwright popped the back of the trailer and stepped aside to the right as he opened the door. The trailer was only about three-fourths full. Jimmy clambered up onto the back of the truck first. He gasped out in pain as he exerted his legs, and he came to realize that his skin was flayed raw all the way up to his haunches. He stood straight as he could, gritted his teeth, and leaned against the wall of the trailer as Trace helped Wainwright in.

"Barclay? Hey bud, it's us. You there?"

Silence.

Jimmy limped over to the first row of pallets. He nodded from Wainwright to the big box before them. The two men grabbed the side and hoisted as hard as they could to move it, so they could more easily get to Barclay.

"Is there a pallet jack? Anything to help us move?" Jimmy asked, gasping through his efforts.

"Bud, I see what you see," Wainwright muttered. "Trace, you mind getting up here? Maybe you could help?"

Trace stood beneath them at the back of the trailer. He glanced over his shoulder repeatedly, his eyes wide as he panted. "I don't know how long we have, guys! The police lights just moved. Try moving the other pallet!"

Wainwright gave the neighboring box a hard tug with both hands. "Fat chance," he called back to Trace.

Wainwright pulled a mini-flashlight from his coat and stepped onto the wooden pallet so he could see into the box. He flicked on the flashlight and inspected the contents of the box.

"Jimbo, come take a look at this," Wainwright said.

Jimmy clambered onto the pallet with a grunt. He strained his eyes against the contrast of pitch black and bright light. After a moment, it came into focus.

The box was filled from top to bottom, side to side, with Cowtown Candles. Jimmy couldn't distinguish the colors of the candles themselves. Still, it was impossible to miss the characteristic red, white, and yellow label – the same one blazed into his mind whenever he recalled the trippy candle from Obie Hill's party.

"Is this from the warehouse?" Jimmy asked.

"Must be. This box alone covers a fourth of the missing inventory," Wainwright said. He stepped down from the pallet and looked out of the trailer at Trace and the highway behind him.

"Landers and Foxx are gonna be pleased," Jimmy said. "We can get paid!"

"Gotta live through this first, man, remember what I've told you," Big Trace chided. "Any way you can squeeze back there for Barclay?"

Before Jimmy or Wainwright could respond, Landers emerged from around the other side of the trailer. "No time," Landers sneered. "Every second that goes by gets us all closer to getting busted. Wainwright, Trace, get back to the van. Jimmy, you're the best driver we have right now. Get this truck back safely."

"...To where?" Jimmy asked.

"Where the fuck do you think?" Landers snapped.

"I... I don't know, dude! Our factory blew up, the warehouse is occupied, I..."

"Just get it to my uncle's place," Landers said. "Can you handle that?"

"Sure, whatever," Jimmy said as he hopped down from the trailer. Pain shot through his torn skin with the impact of his landing. He swore under his breath.

Landers nodded to Wainwright and Trace, and the three men walked quickly back to the van. Jimmy sighed and turned back to the trailer.

"Barclay, if you can hear me, it's Jimmy," he called into the darkness. "It will be about an hour. Hang in there, buddy!"

Jimmy finally heard a response from Barclay, a muted grunt. Jimmy couldn't discern what he said, but the evidence that Barclay was alive was enough to encourage him. Jimmy hurried to close the back of the trailer, run back to the cab, and get moving into the light once more.

CHAPTER TWENTY-THREE

Despite being a little over an hour, the drive back to Doc Landers's mansion was one of the longest of Jimmy Glencroft's life thus far. Despite some previous experience driving a heavy truck, it took him a while to get reacquainted with the way of the road. Jimmy endured messy shifts, double-clutches, lane drifts, a few unidentified and uncomfortable beeps inside the cab – not to mention the ever-increasing pain of road rash, an ever-present headache, and the clawing cloak of sheer panic and paranoia. Jimmy screamed out in exhilarant glee when he finally pulled onto the short road in front of the mansion. Dawn approached with the looming sun just below the horizon.

"Forget backing up. They'll have to deal with it like this..." Jimmy muttered. He hopped out of the cab, cursed in pain as the impact shot through his skinned legs, then ran to the back of the trailer. Jimmy had just made it to the trailer door when the white van containing Landers, Wainwright, and Big Trace pulled up behind him.

"Where were you guys? I lost sight of you after a bit," Jimmy said as he pulled the trailer open.

"I couldn't bear to watch you butt-humpin' that rig," Wainwright said with a laugh as he walked over. "We split up around Springfield just in case we were being followed."

"Makes sense," Jimmy said.

"We had enough time to grab some breakfast," Landers said. His tone and body posture showed that the skinny, dentally-bereft man was much calmer now than he had been in Dayton. Landers raised a greasy brown paper bag. "Sausage biscuits, hash browns in there for you," he said.

Jimmy shook his head. "I don't eat until we get Barclay out. Come on, you assholes, we put him in this spot. Let's get him out. Dude could be dying!"

Landers groaned and tossed food down on the back of the rig. He nodded to Wainwright and Big Trace. "Go on, help him out. My arm's still too jacked from last week to be moving shit. I'm gonna go get Doc, be back out in a few. Save a McGriddle for me, will you?"

"No promises, boss," Big Trace said with a grin as he hoisted himself onto the back of the trailer. Wainwright and Jimmy followed suit, and together the three men worked on moving inventory to more easily access Winslow Barclay.

After removing far too many candles from the first two boxes, Jimmy had an epiphany; he cursed himself for overlooking the pull-out ramp. After he pulled the ramp down, the three men gained more room to operate as they partially unloaded a few pallets and pulled them to the street – and repeated the process several more times.

By the time they got to the back of the trailer, the sun loomed above the trees bordering the subdivision, and the breakfast sandwiches had become lukewarm. Jimmy, Trace, and Wainwright lifted the final pallet from Barclay's arm, and the towering man crumpled down from where he had been pinned against the back of the truck with a grunt. Barclay's gun clunked down beside him, and Wainwright jumped back in fright, expecting it to discharge.

"Took you bastards long enough," Barclay said in a hoarse whisper. He sat up against the back of the truck. "I can't feel my arm."

"Doc is on his way out," Jimmy said as he knelt in front of Barclay. "Can you move it, at least?"

"Yeah, I can move it, just can't feel it," Barclay said. "The rest of me feels like shit too. Did everyone make it okay? Landers okay?"

"Yeah, he's good," Big Trace said as he shined the flashlight on Barclay so they could get a good look at him in the dark of the trailer. Barclay's long hair was frazzled and pulled about, his beard askew.

"God, I need a shave," Barclay muttered as he ran his fingers through a damaged patch of beard. "Who all got shot then? Did you guys body anyone?"

"We called the cops on the trailer," Wainwright said. "They fought with the Slavs. Don't know who killed who."

"Fuck, this trailer's gonna be hot. We should get everything destroyed or hidden. This is everything we needed, right?"

"Yup," Jimmy said as he pulled a candle out of the nearest box. "Cowtown Candles, probably a thousand of 'em."

"Any guns?"

Jimmy and Big Trace shared a sidelong glance. Wainwright shrugged.

"Damnit," Barclay said. "They have a *lot* of our guns. Well, at least we got something back. That's not as big a setback as the candles would have been."

"I know a guy that might be able to help with the guns," Jimmy said without a second thought. "Maybe I can arrange a meeting sometime."

"That would be clutch," Barclay said with a smile. "Who is it? Hook us up."

"I need to talk to him first. Make sure he's okay with everything... his inventory may be hot right now."

"Can't be having that..."

"No," Jimmy tapped his forehead, "but that means we can probably get it cheap. I'm guessing half market price, for sure."

"You really are starting to come in handy, dude," Barclay said as he ran his fingers through his beard thoughtfully. "Gimme a minute. I need to think on some things before I get up."

Barclay stood up after another few moments with the help of Jimmy and Big Trace. Together with Wainwright, they all hopped out of the stolen trailer and into the sunlight of the early morning. The outlaws stood amidst dozens of candle boxes on the edge of the unfinished road on the fringes of the subdivision.

Jimmy reached into the fast-food bag and fished out a sandwich apiece for both he and Barclay. While Big Trace and Wainwright worked on consolidating the inventory, Jimmy and Barclay ate like famished dogs.

"Mmmm, never thought I'd be so happy to have a McMuffin," Barclay said with a mouth full of food. "Then again, I'd looked at an MRE like a Vegas buffet after weeks in the field before."

Jimmy smiled between his bites. "I wouldn't know what that's like."

"Vets and civilians can sometimes have more in common than they think," Barclay said.

"I'd love to pick your brain more about your war stories sometime."

"If you can handle 'em!" Barclay laughed.

"I think you forget about all the blood I've seen and spilled this last week, man," Jimmy said with a sigh. Barclay shrugged with a smile and shook his arm around.

"Feeling's coming back," Barclay said. "Maybe I don't need Doc after all."

"Precaution is a necessary evil," Jimmy said.

"Look, dude. I need to talk to you about something. I think you're gonna want in on what I have planned," Barclay said.

"I wish that's something a credible employer would say to me," Jimmy replied.

"Ha! After seeing your face bashed in on live TV, and with all these charges you could catch any day?" Barclay scoffed. "Nah, dude, if you want paid anytime soon, you'll come to see me. This Monday, meet me at the bar by the quarry around noon."

Jimmy thought about it for a moment before he shook his head. "I've got plans."

Barclay gulped down the last bite of his sandwich, wiped his hands on his pants, and fixed his unblinking gaze on Jimmy.

"And I've got plans for you," Barclay said. "You're going to want to hear them."

"Why can't you tell me here and now?" Jimmy asked.

Barclay glanced over his shoulder at Big Trace and Wainwright, then looked around towards Doc's mansion before looking back to Jimmy.

"You need to learn conversational discretion," Barclay said. "You're useful to us, but not when you're a loose cannon."

"I guess I get it... you'll have to forgive me. I'm still new at this," Jimmy said.

"As you tell us every time. It's good, though. You'll learn."

Barclay patted Jimmy on the back with his good hand. "Alright then, Jimmy, you get on now, okay? I'm gonna go talk to Doc myself since he won't budge. Remember, noon at the quarry, Monday."

"You got it, Barc," Jimmy said. He watched Barclay walk away for a moment before he sat down against the semi-truck trailer's back tire and closed his eyes for some rest.

CHAPTER TWENTY-FOUR

"I don't know how much more I have in me, Finn. I didn't ask for any of this," Jimmy said before he took a small bite of his Italian sub and chewed slowly. Finn Aittokallio sat across the big wooden booth table from him, cutting a personal deep-dish pizza with a knife and fork.

"I bet," Finn replied. "Say, you sure this place is clear? No tail?" There were only a handful of other people in the bistro. The bright beams of high noon sun illuminated the restaurant, *Rapport Café,* on North High Street in Clintonville.

"I took an Uber. Did you drive your truck? I'm certain they've got a beat on it," Jimmy said.

"Nah, dawg. I took my bike."

"Good." Every time Jimmy considered speaking again, he would scan his surroundings as subtly as possible. "You've done nothing wrong as far as myself and the Constitution are concerned, but I know they're coming for you the day after they're coming for me."

"I knew the risks," Finn said perhaps too calmly amid a mouthful of pizza. "I'm a libertarian. Weapons are a part of my religion. This is the way."

"This is the way," Jimmy echoed. "But I have an idea that might get you clear of these dudes." Jimmy's eyes flitted side to side before he leaned in and muttered to Finn, "Everything unmarked, scratched off, or blacklisted. You'll have to unload it at 50 cents on the dollar since it's hot. I'll run it, so your hands are clean. The hardest part will be moving it without the birds chirping."

The waiter walked by to check on them. Jimmy's pale skin flushed with nerves as the waiter lingered and topped off his diet cola and slipped away. Finn laughed.

"Dude. We both know this place is clean," Finn said. "No sweat."

"I know, I know. But you know how I get," Jimmy said. He took a couple bites of his sub and let himself sink into his seat again. "What do you think?"

"Here's the thing. I don't think," Finn replied. "I know. I know this is a mistake waiting to happen. I can't just trust these guys because I kind of know a couple of them or because you vouch for them."

Jimmy sighed. He slouched and stared at his plate.

"Finn, I don't know what to tell you. I haven't heard anything from the soup bois about you, but here's what I'm thinking. It's a risk to move your stash. It's a risk to sit on your stash. But so long as you *have* your stash, it's a problem. See where I'm going with this?"

Finn stared at Jimmy for an excruciatingly long moment.

"Finn?"

Jimmy fiddled with his straw paper.

"You see yourself as one of them now, don't you?" Finn asked.

"I... don't know if I would say *that*," Jimmy said. "Do I work for them? Yes. Do I think I'm *one* of them? Well, no. I just want to be fairly compensated for my work up to this point."

"You're in too deep, man. But I don't think it's too late to step back."

"It is. I really think it is." Jimmy sighed. "There's something you should know."

"Yeah?"

"I haven't nailed it down yet, but I think I can get witness protection for everything I know. For whatever reason, they haven't gotten their green light to arrest people yet – bureaucracy, I guess, you know how it is. But... if I disappear, that's probably what happened," Jimmy explained.

"That's a lot to take in," Finn said.

"That's what she said." The friends shared a half-hearted laugh. Jimmy sat back up straight and relaxed again.

"I'll find my way back," Jimmy said. "Or I'll get back with you eventually, man. I'll let you know where I am when I can. You'll know it's me."

"Or will you?" a gravelly voice interjected from the side.

A tall, burly man pulled off his black and white Punisher-branded mask to reveal a clean-shaven face and head, and he shoved Jimmy further into the booth. Finn rose to confront the stranger, hand already on his hip, but the look in the stranger's eyes and the way he raised his hand convinced him to stand down. The stranger pulled Jimmy back up by his hoodie collar and flopped down on the bench beside him. It took Jimmy a moment to shake off the surprise and recognize the assailant, but as soon as they made eye contact, it was clear.

Winslow Barclay looked back and forth from Finn to Jimmy and back again. "Didn't recognize me with a clean shave, did you, boys? Man, you *really* need to learn to talk softer if you're going to be a career criminal, Jimbo. I'm sure half the restaurant is delighted to hear there's a fucking *spook* in their midst."

"Barclay, I... I can explain," Jimmy started.

"I don't want to hear it," Barclay said with a slam of his fist against the table. Jimmy was acutely aware of other diners staring at them now.

"But-"

"No," Barclay interjected. "You listen to me. I don't think Craig has very long."

"Foxx?"

"No, Craig Biggio – of *course,* I'm talking about Craig Foxx," Barclay said.

Finn leaned forward, eyes wide as he listened in.

"But he seemed so well last week," Jimmy said. "I thought he was going to recover."

"Me too. But I'm convinced Landers and his uncle are going to kill him. Montreaux Pickens too."

"How do you figure?"

"Landers is Craig's I.T. guy, right? He knows everything. Bank account passwords. Organizational rosters. Clientele. He knows where all goods and stashes are. For both the syndicate *and* Montreaux's operation. We've *extracted* some key information from Pickens in his vulnerable state."

"Yeah, and?"

"Can you really trust *anyone* to look all that money in the eye and not want to take it? Could you trust yourself?"

"Well, I'd really like to know where this money is because, well – I. Haven't. Been. Paid." Jimmy emphasized.

"I get it, dude, I do – you've risked your neck for the operation. For Landers, for Trace, for *me*. And I'm grateful. You're most of the reason it's still going," Barclay said.

"Then why haven't I been paid like it?" Jimmy asked.

"I'm getting to that. It's simple. Craig Foxx does not want to pay you."

Jimmy stared up at Barclay's bright grey eyes.

"I do. Landers does. But you're not going to get paid until Foxx either signs the checks or we break some locks ourselves."

"But- I've actually *known* Craig for a few years. I've considered him a friend. Why wouldn't he want to pay me?" Jimmy mused.

"He doesn't see you as a lifer. And here's the kicker... he's *right*. You're too soft. Yeah, I know you've capped a few folks and done some dumb ass shit to save us, but... you're soft. He's right."

Jimmy looked around at the restaurant, and to his relief, nobody seemed to be paying attention - nobody outside of Finn who continued to look on with rapt interest.

"Jimmy," Barclay continued, "You're in a pinch. Way I see it, you've got three options. The first is: you can snitch to the Feds, disappear to another city, and never see your friends again."

"I'll find a way," Jimmy said. "There's so much tech, social media, I'm not a dumbass, I'll..."

"No. I mean... Never. See. Them. Again. And I'll start with Fat Aittokallio over here," Barclay said with a nod to Finn.

Finn's face reddened.

"I'd like to see you try," Finn said with a fidget. "I've got more guns than you know what to do with."

"You're speaking to someone that's actually lived a fight. I did my time for ten years. I've seen more red mist than you've had hot meals. I've beaten off a whole squad of towelheads, and I'll damn well do the same to some three-buck Fudd like yourself." Barclay rattled off with a glare.

"I'm sure you beat them off," Finn said with a dismissive wanking gesture. "We all go into the same dirt when we die. It doesn't matter if there's a flag on us or not. And I'll make sure you're dead before your orc lookin', Dollar Tree Glenn Jacobs lookin' ass hits the ground."

Jimmy breathed in and out more rapidly as he realized the eyes of other people were on them again. The waiter came by and asked if everything was okay.

"We're good," Barclay said. He reached in his leather coat's pocket, grabbed a wad of cash, and stuffed it into the waiter's hand. "Your discretion is appreciated, chief."

The waiter nodded and disappeared to the back. Barclay turned back to Jimmy.

"Before I was interrupted by this citizen, as I was saying, three options," Barclay returned. "You snitch, I put your friends in a ditch. Option two, you continue to fiddle around and risk your neck while waiting for Foxx to pay you, which won't happen. You heard it here first."

"And three?" Jimmy asked. Finn glared daggers into the side of Barclay's neck as they spoke.

"Option three, you team up with Landers and me to flip the operation. We've already discussed putting you into a more, ah, administrative role. Perfect for softies like yourself."

"I'm not soft," Jimmy said softly.

"Alright. Whatever you say, killer. Look, I'll give you three days to think about it. This is your second chance since you bailed on me today. If you want to prove you're not soft, meet me in the parking lot at Dick's Den – let's say 1600 hours on Thursday? We'll do what needs to be done to secure a future for our people. For ourselves. For our future children," Barclay offered.

Jimmy sighed.

"And Jimmy?"

"Yes, Barc?"

"Stay the fuck away from the Feds until then, will you?" Barclay tilted his head forward and furrowed his brow to emphasize the request.

"Yeah... yes, yes, sir, I will," Jimmy said. "Actually, haven't seen them in a spell, to be honest. I'm kind of avoiding them."

"One last thing. Never call me 'sir' again. Hate that shit. Alright, I'll see you Thursday," Barclay said as he stood up. Barclay stared at Finn for upwards of ten seconds as he adjusted his jacket and put his mask back on. He strode out the front door as the hushed tables nearby stared in curiosity and concern.

Jimmy looked at Finn. His childhood friend shrugged at him.

"Do what you need to do. That's all I can say at this point," Finn said.

"I'll do what I must. Do you have my van?"

"Yeah. It's clean now. Had Asmir from the station park it down the road, over by that Episcopalian church," Finn replied. "Key is in the right rear wheel well."

"Thanks. I'll see you soon, friend. Stay strapped. We'll work something out to help you unload your stash," Jimmy said as he stood up. He tossed a ten-dollar bill on the table to pay for his half of the meal. He walked away from the last fourth of his sandwich as his stomach roiled in nervousness. Jimmy made a point not to look at or make eye contact with any of the diners or restaurant workers as he made his way out the door and slipped a mask over his face.

CHAPTER TWENTY-FIVE

The first snow of the season came subtly at first. Jimmy Glencroft didn't see or feel the snowflake land on the tip of his nose and melt away a second later. He focused on holding his position, rigid and unmoving on the flat roof of an unfinished home; white house wrap enveloped the exterior walls.

Jimmy raised the spotting scope to his eye. He squinted through the shadow of nightfall and homed in on his target with a twist of the focusing knob. Beside him, Winslow Barclay drew in cigarette smoke with a deep breath, a Mossberg MVP sniper rifle across his lap.

"Tell me, Barc... Do you always smoke like a chimney when you do these jobs?" Jimmy asked as he focused on the target at hand. On the other end of the block and across the street was a finished Cape-Cod style home with white exterior walls and a sloped grey-tiled roof.

"This is my first civilian surveillance job, Jimbo," Barclay responded. "Truth be told, I may be as nervous as you. Our main snoop got killed in that Slade City raid."

"I'm sorry," Jimmy said.

"Eh, I didn't know him too well," Barclay said. "But you're here, and we are rebuilding. Thanks for keeping your commitment this time, by the way. I was getting worried about you. Any movement yet?"

Jimmy's angled view revealed the side of the home, one wide window frame on the first floor, one dark upper-story window, the front yard, and part of the driveway. Jimmy zoomed out and looked around at some of the other homes for movement out of curiosity.

"Nothing. Say, Barc... lots of people are home at the other houses. This is weird. What's going on?"

"Uhhh... it's Thanksgiving. People are with their families. This may be the only day of the year our target is guaranteed to be home with his family."

"Ah, makes sense."

"Aren't you going to ask me why I'm not home with my family?" Barclay asked.

"No... didn't pay that any mind. Obviously, I'm not with mine either," Jimmy said.

"Fair enough."

Barclay grunted and shifted.

"Who's the target anyway?" Jimmy asked.

"Who said there's a target? Simple surveillance job," Barclay said.

"Do you always bring a sniper rifle on simple surveillance jobs?"

"Do you always ask so many goddamn questions?"

"You're asking a ton of questions too. What do you have to say to that?"

"You do realize I'm the only one here with a gun, right?"

"Fair enough," Jimmy said with a laugh.

"Pay attention," Barclay said.

Jimmy returned to his spotting scope. A yellow Oldsmobile Cutlass Supreme rumbled down the road to the driveway of the house he was watching.

"Scopes up," Jimmy said. Barclay raised his rifle and leaned it on the edge of the roof. Together the men watched as an old Black couple stepped out of the vehicle together. The woman carried a blue hot bag, undoubtedly filled with delectable Thanksgiving eats.

The front door of the home opened, and Big Trace Onwudiwe stepped out with a boisterous grin. He threw his arms open and simultaneously embraced the older couple. Even in the dimming light, Jimmy saw the gold of Trace's crucifix necklace.

"Uh, Barc..." Jimmy whispered.

"Shh," Barclay said as he thumbed back the safety on the rifle.

"That's Trace, that's his family, that's..."

Jimmy put down his scope to see Barclay take a deep breath and wrap his index finger into the trigger. Jimmy lunged across the few feet that separated them and kicked Barclay's left hand with the toe of his boot just as the rifle fired. A neighboring home's window shattered as the bullet ripped through it. Jimmy tumbled over Barclay as the larger man swore and jerked his arms up to trip him.

Jimmy pulled himself up in time to see Barclay clear the rifle, a spent shell flying aside. Jimmy bear-crawled quickly towards Barclay and sprinted into a complete form tackle before he had a chance to fire. Barclay's head smacked against the side of the roof as both men tumbled downward. Jimmy managed to catch the edge of the roof on his way down. He couldn't maintain a grip, but he slowed his fall down enough to brace himself. He landed on his feet with a jarring blow but threw himself hard into the ground to redistribute the force and rolled through the impact. Jimmy winced as he felt pain well up in his left ankle. He staggered, kneeling on his left knee as he looked around.

Barclay wasn't so lucky. He had fallen face-first with his torso flush against the ground. He leaned forward, putting weight on his head and neck. The Mossberg rifle lay between Jimmy and Barclay. Jimmy crawled over and considered seizing the gun before he heard shouting from down the street, and sure enough, sirens fill the air. He drew a sharp breath inward and stood, barely able to put weight on his left foot.

"You stupid bitch," Barclay gasped out as he looked up at Jimmy. "You've killed us both. You stupid fucking bitch!" Blood poured from Barclay's mouth freely. He spat out a tooth and struggled against the ground, unable to stand.

"Barc, we need to get out of here," Jimmy said as he stood. "Come on. Can you stand?"

"I'm going to kill you," Barclay gasped out through closed, reddened teeth as he writhed on the ground.

Tires squealed on the road about twenty yards from them as the Olds Cutlass came to a stop by the sidewalk.

Big Trace jumped out of the driver's seat.

"Jimmy, Barclay, what the hell?" Trace said as he loped over. "On Thanksgiving? What... what are you doing here?"

"I'll explain," Jimmy said. The sirens drew closer. "We need to get out of here first."

"Fine," Trace said. "Get that rifle. I'll take you to my place."

"That's the first place they're going to look," Jimmy said.

"Wait. Wait a minute. Why..." Trace stared at Jimmy for a moment. "Why would you know that? Wait... is there something I should know?"

Jimmy's face drained of color.

"Let's go." Jimmy picked up the Mossberg rifle and limped towards the yellow Cutlass.

"Here, help me get Barc," Trace said as he walked over to his prone form.

"No! No, leave him. He's not to be trusted," Jimmy said. Trace stared Jimmy down again, then looked down at Barclay, who had risen to one arm and panted in agony.

"If anything, we should put him out of his misery," Jimmy said as he pointed the gun at Barclay's head. Barclay closed his eyes.

"No!" Trace yelled as he stepped in front of the rifle. "Let's go!"

Jimmy turned and limped as quickly as he could muster to the Cutlass. Trace ran around and in front of him. Trace clambered into the front seat so hard, it caused the bottom of the car to lower.

Jimmy tweaked his ankle again as he went around the front of the car to get to the passenger side. Trace yelled to hurry. Jimmy slumped into the front of the car and slammed the door shut, a burning sensation enveloping his foot.

Big Trace put his foot down and accelerated the heavy muscle car just as police cars pulled in behind them. Their flashing red and blue lights dominated the rearview. Trace let out a whooping holler when he realized they weren't being pursued.

Jimmy Glencroft felt differently.

Jimmy turned around to see that the police cars had stopped near where Barclay lay injured.

"Trace, we need to go back," Jimmy pleaded. "If they get Barclay, the whole operation goes down."

"Maybe what we need is for the whole operation to go down!" Trace exclaimed. "I've been trying to get out of this life for years, and now here I am, fleeing twelve during Thanksgiving dinner. This shit don't end, Jimmy! Besides, you said he can't be trusted."

"And that's exactly why we need to stop this car."

"What?!"

"Stop this goddamn car, Trace! I saved your life, man! You owe me one!"

"I ain't owe you shit," Trace said. However, he obliged Jimmy by slamming on the brakes and spinning the car around, taking out a mailbox and a trash can on the curb.

"God damnit! Jim, this my mom's ride! You owe *me* after this," Trace bellowed.

"I'm sure I will..." Jimmy said quietly as he cranked his arm to roll down the window. The car had stopped in a prime position – around the slow, arcing curve of the subdivision road, he had a clear view of the two police cars a block away. Even in the dimming light, he saw the shadows of the officers exiting their vehicles.

Jimmy raised the rifle.

"Bro! Stop!" Trace yelled.

Boom.

The report of Jimmy's shot temporarily deafened them. The shatter of the police car's windshield otherwise could have been heard, even at this distance. Jimmy recalled how Barclay cleared the chamber. He clumsily mimicked the maneuver just as Big Trace punched him in the shoulder to prevent him from taking another shot.

"What's your problem, man?" Trace shouted as he threw the Cutlass back into drive. Across the neighborhood, the police officers piled back into their cars to begin the chase.

"Go, just go, I'll explain," Jimmy urged.

"I can listen and drive at the same time!" Trace yelled as the muscle car roared among parked vehicles on the winding subdivision roads. "Too bad you can't think and breathe at the same time."

"Look, man! If the cops are chasing us instead of looking for Barclay, he'll get a chance to get away, and he can't talk. I could give a shit less if he gets in trouble, but I don't want him to talk."

The air filled with red and blue lights. Jimmy turned forward and tried to relax his foot and his thoughts alike. Big Trace's eyes were wide, his left hand's knuckles taut around the steering wheel. He struggled to operate the 5-speed manual transmission.

"You know how to drive stick, man? In case we need to switch?" Trace asked as the Oldsmobile clambered onto the main road. The police were gaining.

"Why's everyone always ask me that? Don't you have a file on me?"

"This ain't Madden, dude; I don't know if you have a 90 in Manual!" Trace yelled. "We need to get to speed to beat these guys. I'm heading for the outer belt. Got your phone on you? We need help."

"Nah, do you?"

"Fuck, man... just... fuck." Trace sighed. "What were you two doing? Who's the target in my 'hood? I specifically moved out here to get away from this shit when I'm off."

"I think there's a coup going on," Jimmy said. "Barclay tried to recruit me. I don't know why, but he and Landers are trying to off you and Craig."

"I *knew* there was something up with that little freak," Trace said of Landers. "After we shake the cops, we gotta go help Craig – if there's a chance of him getting capped, we need to help."

"Bet."

"And Jimmy?"

"Yeah?"

"If anything happens to me and you make it out, please find a way to help Craig, and make sure my family's alright," Trace pleaded. "Craig has done a lot for me, and I've done this all for my blood. I don't wanna see all this go to waste."

"You've got it, Trace." Jimmy fixated on the rear-view mirror.

"What's the plan?" Jimmy asked. Horns blared all around them as Trace blasted through a red light. One pursuing officer braved the cross-traffic while the other threw itself in a spin to avoid t-boning a semi-truck.

Trace remained silent for a moment as he gunned the Oldsmobile down the road. They made good time to the on-ramp to 270. Traffic was thinner than expected due to the holiday – sales weren't going to start for another few hours.

"I'm going to the Dublin warehouse," Trace said at last.

"Isn't it compromised?" Jimmy asked. "Nobody's been back since the Slavs took it, right?"

"That's why I'm going," Trace said. "I'm going to draw as many cops as possible there. Give 'em a taste of their own medicine. Like we did in Dayton."

"Ah... hoist them with their own petard!"

"Bro, can you just talk normal?!" Trace barked. The Cutlass threatened to tilt over as Trace struggled to shift accordingly and turn onto the highway. He weaved around a couple cars as he got up to speed. The pursuing cop car was about 30 yards behind them now, and a few distant lights indicated that more had joined the chase.

"What about us?" Jimmy asked. He sat up straight and looked around at their surroundings. They accelerated down the open highway, the Cutlass attaining much higher speed as Trace finally managed to put it in its highest gear.

"There's a big garage there with doors on both sides," Trace explained. "It should be empty since we lost all those vehicles in Slade City. I'mma blast through both doors if they're closed, and just hope they're staffed up and ready to take the coppers on. By then, I'm sure Barclay will have let Landers know what's going on, and I think that will leave Craig and Pickens unattended – we can go back and make a play for them."

"And if that doesn't work?"

"We'll need a different kind of prayer." Trace tapped his crucifix.

Silence ensued, but only within the car. Outside, a cacophony of sirens filled the evening as engines roared and tires squealed. A phalanx of police cars paced the Oldsmobile at a short distance. Jimmy craned his neck around to see beyond the convoy. His heart pounded within his chest, and he inhaled deeply to steady himself.

"There's a chopper in the distance, Trace. Our goose is cooked," Jimmy said.

"Huh. Well, it's been nice knowing you, Jim," Trace replied. He smiled softly at his colleague riding shotgun. "We might as well go out with a bang, right?"

"I just can't believe this is what my life came to."

"Me either, still, man... and I been at this a lot longer than you. You religious?"

"Not as much as I used to be," Jimmy said. He let out a deep sigh.

"Me either, man, maybe you and I are a lot more alike than we thought."

"Are we going to bring a whole new meaning to spray and pray, brother?"

Trace laughed. A genuine, throaty laugh, with the broadest smile he mustered since their paths crossed just a few years ago.

"Jim, normally I'd say you say the worst things at the worst times, but I dig it. I dig it, man. Yeah, if this warehouse plan doesn't work, let's make some fuckin' headlines."

Trace reached under his lavender hoodie jacket and produced a pistol, a pack of Black 'n' Mild cigars, and a lighter. He put the gun on the dash, passed the cigars and lighter to Jimmy, and returned his attention to the road ahead.

"Light me up one of those," Trace said. "We're about ten minutes from the warehouse. Say your prayers while you can."

Jimmy obliged, lighting Trace's cigar and passing it over after a hearty puff. Trace bade Jimmy light up as well, and Jimmy proceeded to with his hands trembling. Jimmy rolled the window down a little bit to let the smoke out. Trace laughed again, and this time Jimmy joined in, the two men embracing their fates with a smile on their faces and a wood tip between their lips.

One of the longest minutes of their entire lives passed, and they came upon an exit ramp leading onto 23 South toward Worthington. Before they had a chance to take said exit, two armored police trucks came up the ramp against the grain of the traffic flow. One spun to block a lane of highway while the other sealed off the exit ramp. Big Trace downshifted and jerked the wheel left to guide the Cutlass past the blockade. The nearest police truck moved forward just enough to clip the Olds and send it skidding sideways down the highway. Trace fought the momentum of the spin and jammed the gears as he tried to change course, but there was a THUNK, a pop, and a sudden screech as Jimmy felt himself fall several inches.

The right-front tire was flat.

"See you on the other side," Big Trace Onwudiwe said as he slammed the car into park. The next few moments played out to Jimmy in slow motion. Trace's eyes stood out against the night as he lurched out of the vehicle and hoisted his gun over the roof.

Jimmy lunged across the front seat just as bullets ripped above him in both directions. He clenched his eyes shut, cheek against the black leather, and hunched over the central armrest. Jimmy whispered a prayer for salvation. Trace and a cop both yelled out for him, and he willfully ignored them, just as he willfully ignored the dropped Black 'n' Mild that burned into the flesh of his arm.

More and more gunfire churned overhead. The wind of a lowering helicopter buffeted the car.

Another faster gun. Yelling.

Another pop and drop. Another flat tire.

More bullets. Jimmy felt one go through the seat beneath him.

Gunfire.

Big Trace fell to the ground.

Gunfire continued.

An eternity passed within thirty seconds.

Then, save for the thumping of helicopter rotors, silence.

"*Jimmy.*"

Jimmy gagged on his elation and adrenaline when he heard Trace's voice rasp from the outside the shattered window above. Jimmy sat up, numb to the glass fragments that fell around him.

Big Trace was alive. He pulled himself up on the outside of the car. Jimmy opened the passenger side with difficulty and fell out to the pavement. Jimmy looked up to see three dead cops on the pavement outside their bullet-ridden vehicles.

As soon as he questioned how this happened, Jimmy was answered by the helicopter that landed behind the police. Two masked men stepped out from between the blockade. Both men hoisted high-capacity rifles. Despite the subterfuge, Jimmy could recognize them by one's slim build and Hawaiian shirt and the other's rat-tail mullet draped across his shoulder.

"*Deus ex machina*, bitches!" Landers yelled from behind his red, white, and blue clown mask.

"Little too on the nose, boss," Wainwright said as he pulled down his camo mask to reveal his mustache and yellowed grin.

Jimmy slowly spun in a circle as he became vaguely aware of the pain in his foot and skinned legs once more. The bodies, the blood, the glass – and yet again, that damned blaring of sirens in another fractured night sky. The very helicopter he had once booted someone out of. Big Trace Onwudiwe incredulously walked up beside him with his mouth agape.

"Barclay gave us a call," Landers said. "Guess you two failed your mission."

"Pushed 'im off a roof, did you?" Wainwright asked. "Shame."

"I... look, it was..." Jimmy glanced at Big Trace before he faced Landers. "*Why?* Why Trace? He's one of the best ya'll have. Landers, I trust you'll make this right!"

"I guess I have to tie up the loose end myself," Landers said. Right there in the middle of Interstate 270 on Thanksgiving Day, Rik Landers emptied the rest of his modified AR-15's magazine into Trace Onwudiwe's torso. The syndicate's #2 man was instantly hewn lifeless.

Jimmy screamed, a scream from the core of his being itself. He slumped beside his fallen friend and tried to shake him awake as if Trace had just had a bad dream, but this was all too real.

"Get to the choppah," Rik Landers said with a gesture of his rifle. He stared at the sobbing and shell-shocked Jimmy for a long moment, and when he realized Jimmy wasn't going to budge, he nodded to Wainwright, and the two men retreated back to the helicopter.

"Slade City's still on the table!" Rik Landers called back as they left the scene. "Stonewall Overlook, Jimmy! A new life awaits!"

Jimmy snapped back into awareness as the helicopter rotors fired up again. He reached under Trace's large, lifeless form and yanked free his chain, his prized golden cross. Jimmy stuffed the blood-soaked jewelry into his jeans pocket and took off running.

Despite his wounded foot, Jimmy pushed on as hard and as fast as he possibly could. He vaulted the median, sprinted headlong among freeway traffic, hopped a divider, and tumbled end-over-end down an embankment and into a wooded copse.

Just as Jimmy slumped against the trunk of an oak tree and closed his eyes, the helicopter flew overhead, low and fast, on a straight course due south. Commotion weighed down the air as ambulances and officers converged on the scene of the shootout.

As flashlights lit up behind him, Jimmy struggled to his feet, took a deep breath, and took off running again.

CHAPTER TWENTY-SIX

"You ready for this?" Drago Zupan asked as he hopped in the passenger seat of the purple van.

"Born ready," James Glencroft said as he turned the ignition to power on the minivan with a rumble. He wore red shutter shades tilted upon his forehead between a black Albuquerque Isotopes hat and a black shirt that read in white text, *FLYNT FLO$$Y IS MY FAVORITE RAPPER*. The golden crucifix of Big Trace Onwudiwe, whose dying face was all Jimmy could see any time he tried to sleep, hung around his neck in tribute.

"I'm ready to rave!" Trevor MacKenzie screamed as he threw himself into the van in a heap, a ridiculous sight in his bright yellow crayon costume.

"Not so sure if I am," said Sean Doan, white tank top tight around his skinny body, scratching his arm under his bright blue sock cuffs. He sat behind Jimmy and blinked furiously.

"Come on, Sean, it'll be a blast," Trevor said. "You got to admit, it's nice of Lyndsey to set us with this tip... kind of makes you want to forgive that whole Manny thing, eh?"

"Manny thing?" Jimmy questioned.

"Nothing," Sean cut in. "It's nothing. You're still on my shit list, though, Glencroft, so this score better be worth it."

"We are going to pull up outside the club ackin' a foo', as you call it," Drago stated, his words met with a sharp glare from Sean as the van pulled into the night. "Then while you and Trevor cause a scene, Jimmy and I go in to literally pull the plug on the performance."

Sean shook his head. "I still don't get your guys' beef with Galactico,"

Drago shrugged. "You could get some nice cash if we pull this off." Drago slid on a bright orange trucker cap with blue numbers stitched all over it.

"I need cash, true. But really, man? Why I gotta act a fool? I have a warrant."

Drago grinned a crooked yellow smile. "That means you'll run harder and are less likely to mess it up. I know you can't risk getting time."

Jimmy turned the purple van onto a main thoroughfare. Traffic was dense up and down the road. A light mist cascaded through the air, and the windshield of the van succumbed to the creep of condensation. Jimmy turned up the heat a few notches, looking in the rear-view back at Sean. Jimmy kept one eye on Sean and one eye on the road.

"Hey Trevor, you got your playlist?" Jimmy asked. They were now a short drive away from the club.

"Yessuh," Trevor said, passing his smartphone to Jimmy. "What do you want to play, man? Aren't we almost there?"

Jimmy laughed as he drove with his left hand, utilizing the right hand to connect the van's cassette deck mp3 jack to the phone. "Yeah. We're gonna pull up in style, boys."

Drago grinned at Jimmy. "What do you have in mind?"

Jimmy pulled to a red light and came to a rolling stop as he looked back at the other men. "Gentlemen, we are going to ghost ride the whip."

"Ghost ride?!" All three of the others said simultaneously in various tones. Drago sounded curious, Trevor was excited, and Sean was shocked.

"Yes, ghost ride." Drago's brow furrowed as Jimmy repeated himself once more.

"Brody, I know you don't know," Trevor said. The van rolled on under the green light. "Jimmy will give you a 101 on how to ghost ride."

"Ghost riding is where I put the van in neutral; I get out and start dancing while we blast a hyphy beat," Jimmy explained in a scholarly tone. Trevor cackled in excitement. If Sean blinked any faster, his forehead would take off.

"That sounds incredibly dangerous," Drago said.

Jimmy laughed. "Brody, you'll stay in here and flash the lights on and off while making sure the system is turned to 11. You'll go shift into park if something goes wrong. I'll just dance for a minute or two before I hop back in, so it shouldn't go too bad."

Sean grabbed Jimmy's shoulder. Jimmy shivered when he did so. "What?"

"Man, what do Trevor and I do?" Sean asked. Jimmy winced. He could smell Sean's breath, and it was something atrocious.

"Simple. Swing open the side doors of the van and just bounce up and down. Throw some gang signs, twerk, hell... get out and groove with me. I don't care. Just as long as we get a lot of attention."

"Attention... Man, I ain't about that life..." Sean groaned as they pulled up to the club.

Evolution was situated on Dublin-Granville Road, one of the hottest spots on the North Side of Columbus. The bright blue neon sign atop the building could be seen for a mile down the road. The parking lot was jammed, and even in the chill autumn air, those seen lined up outside the door were quite underdressed. With one hand, Jimmy steered the van into the parking lot, advancing towards the front of the building while lining up "Ghost Ride It" by Mistah F.A.B. on the smartphone. *Tonight Only: AN EVENING WITH CAPTAIN GALACTICO* flashed on the electronic scrolling marquee around the side of the roof. Trevor MacKenzie put his face to the window like an excited dog on a road trip.

"Trim... trim, everywhere!" MacKenzie exclaimed as he ogled the dozens of scantily clad women huddled close in the line along the building.

Drago turned around and smacked MacKenzie lightly. "Focus, man! We're about to ghost ride!"

Almost on cue, Jimmy cranked up the volume and blasted the song, a synth beat searing over thumping subs. He put the van into neutral and swung open the door, awkwardly popping out and stumbling over himself, almost falling to the damp pavement. Jimmy's skin had not quite fully scabbed over, and his ankle was still weak. He recovered and started dancing alongside the van, busting out various moves he learned from years of mascot performance.

"The streets know just what this is, ghost ridin' up and down the strip!"

Drago flashed the headlights as well as the lights inside the van. He kept one eye on the van as it rolled and another eye on those around him. The left door swung open. Sean propped himself up inside, looking around nervously, his brow furrowed, and mouth shut taut. Jimmy motioned for him to start grooving, and Sean shook his head, declining to do so.

"When you get a new car, and you feelin' like a star..."

On the other side of the van, the crayon-clad Trevor MacKenzie embraced the opportunity to act like a fool. He jumped out of the van and started doing a "Crip Walk," kicking his feet rhythmically in a zig-zag motion as people gathered around to look on at the ghost-riding van. People laughed, pointed, or otherwise looked on in fear and disgust at the runaway vehicle. As anticipated, security guards made their way through the throngs of people waiting for the club to open.

"Whatcha gonna do?" Mistah F.A.B. asked over the speakers.

Sean looked over his shoulder and saw the first security guard break through the crowd. He shouted over to Jimmy, who was doing a "Charleston" dance in front and to the left of the slowing van.

"Fuzz!" Sean yelled.

Sean's eyes widened with fear. The ever-oblivious Trevor MacKenzie performed "The Worm" beside the van, propelling his horizontal body up and down in a wave. The sight was every bit as ridiculous as the group had wanted it to be, with many smartphones up among the throng of people as they caught video of the breakdancing yellow crayon.

"GHOST RIDE IT! Ghost ride ya whip!"

Sean smacked the back of the front seat.

"Brody, drive, man! The fuzz!" Sean yelled.

Drago shook his head as he kept flicking lights. "Not until Jimmy is ready."

Sean popped his head out from the side of the van and yelled at Jimmy, who was doing the "Running Man" before a throng of cheering club-goers.

"Jimmy!! You ready, man?! The fuzz!!" Sean yelled as sweat poured down his face. Jimmy looked at him and let out an exasperated sigh. They neared parked cars about twenty yards ahead. *Maybe it was time to stop after all.* Jimmy ran back to the front seat and hopped in, turning the van before becoming a threat and kicking it back into drive. Sean slammed the door, Drago followed suit. MacKenzie danced on, oblivious to the fact that two large security guards were drawing ever nearer. Some people in the crowd intentionally got in the way of the guards to slow their advance. The guards grew aggravated and continued to jostle their way to the front.

Sean clambered across the middle seat of the van and yelled, "Trevor! Get in!"

Jimmy turned around. "The hell, dude? Why are you using our names?"

Sean looked at Jimmy, wide-eyed and panting. He yelled again.

"Yellow! Get the fuck in here!"

Jimmy put his foot to the accelerator while he shut off the smartphone. "He's fine. Trust me. Shut the door. We'll park and come around."

Sean slammed the other door shut as the van accelerated through the parking lot towards a shopping center on the other side. Drago turned to the others and grinned. "That was awesome, mate. Are you sure Trevor is fine by himself up there?"

Jimmy nodded. "Part of the plan, right? I'll drop you off around back by the smoker's patio. Scale the fence and get in there."

"Won't that be weird? Everyone's still outside waiting, I'll be one of the only ones back there," replied Drago.

Jimmy grinned. "I have my ace in the hole. There's early admittance for V.I.P.s. When you climb the fence, just yell out, "Summer of '92!" Trust me on this, bro."

The van swooped around to the back of *Evolution* with zero fanfare. Most folks were still gathered up front. Drago pounded knuckles with Jimmy and hopped out. Drago dashed around the side of the van, keeping the brim of his orange and blue hat low as he ran.

There was a loud cheer from the other side of the building. Jimmy glanced at Sean. Sean didn't say anything, staring wildly back at him.

Jimmy grinned. "Sean, I'll leave you here with the van. Come up front, keep it running. We'll try to call your phone when we're about to bounce. You cool man?"

Sean kept staring, unblinking. He nodded. "Always cool."

Jimmy put the van in park. He removed his hat and took off his shutter shades and Flynt Flo$$y shirt, revealing a standard red t-shirt without any print. Jimmy threw on a hoodie, tossed the rave clothing in the back, opened his door, hopped out, and went jogging around the side of the building, Trace's giant crucifix tucked against his chest. The rain opened up as if the heavens were a merciless dunk tank of karmic retribution.

Trevor MacKenzie was right where he needed to be. He didn't even care that the others had left him. It was time to do his job.

The crayon costume had grown hot. Sweat smeared his yellow face paint, his clothes beneath the costume were soggy. He blinked away sweat, careful not to wipe at it, lest he irritate his eyes. He looked around to see laughing, beautiful people dressed in all manner of color, gathered around in a semicircle in the parking lot. Trevor saw the lights of smartphones and overheard conversations, homing in on words like "YouTube" and "Tik Tok" and "viral."

Trevor made an exaggerated bow, standing on one leg. "Thank you, thank you!" he shouted. He looked around and noticed the commotion to the left as the security guards jostled through the small crowd. Trevor tried to ignore it, focusing his attention on a shorter blonde girl. He dance-walked up to the girl, who smiled and turned red in embarrassment.

"Looks like you need a little color!" Trevor exclaimed as he bent forward, rubbing the tip of his crayon hat on her stomach. She laughed, playing along. He stood up, pointed, and winked at her.

"What's your favorite color, baby?!" Trevor pointed at his costume. "Is it yellow? I'm your fellow!"

The crowd laughed, several phones up and still recording. The two security guards finally arrived.

"I'm gonna ask you to leave," one burly bald guard said, crossing his arms.

"Why?" Trevor asked, tilting his head. "I'm a paying customer like everyone else."

The other security guard, shorter but more muscular, came walking up.

"That don't mean we want you in the club," he said. "Get on out of here."

Trevor laughed. "Come on, toots," he said, wrapping an arm around the random blonde girl. "Let's go rave." He started to walk to the front of the club with her.

The taller security guard shoved Trevor back as the other started cracking his knuckles. The blonde girl staggered towards the shocked crowd, some of whom had gasped. The additional security guard pulled out a walkie-talkie.

"Get on out!" the tall guard yelled again. Trevor stood still and stared up at the guard fearlessly.

"Or what?!" Trevor said, sounding like a child goading on his angry parent.

The security guard nodded to his colleague. "He's on the horn with the 5-0 right now."

"5-0? Man, fuck the 5-0!" Trevor yelled. The crowd let out a cheer.

"Pigs in a blanket! Fry 'em like bacon! Pigs in a blanket, fry 'em like bacon!" Trevor chanted as he clapped his hands. The crowd picked up on the chant and joined in earnest.

The flustered security guard yelled up at the doorman. "Let them in!" The doorman lowered the rope to let the ravers inside, to try to disperse the crowd. Only a few folks entered, the outdoor pre-rave entertainment still capturing the interest and imagination of the many.

Trevor stepped up to the security guard. "What have I done to break the law? I wasn't the one recklessly operating a motor vehicle. I wasn't aware... that there were laws against dancing in parking lots. I wasn't aware there were laws... against being a sexy ass rave crayon."

Trevor got face to face with the security guard, looking up into his eyes. "Go back to your cave, Cro-Mag, and let the rave begin."

The security guard stared right back at Trevor, unflinching. He pulled up his walkie-talkie without breaking his stare. "Let's start the show early, potential situation outside." He lowered his arm.

Still inches from Trevor MacKenzie's face, the guard, "Show's starting!! Everyone inside!!"

Trevor stood still and glared in return. The crowd shuffled inside reluctantly, staring sideways at Trevor to see if anything else would happen. Trevor started to move forward, but the security guard raised his arm to block him. "You, stay here."

"YELLOW!"

Someone was yelling for him, but he couldn't see whom. He looked around the crowd. Many were looking at him, but nobody was shouting.

"YELLOW!! Don't let them in!!"

He finally saw the source of the voice. James Glencroft ran around the side of the building, waving his arms. Rain fell as Trevor felt the wet drops dissolve the paint on his face.

It took him a moment of careful climbing, but Drago finally tumbled over the side of the smokers' patio fence. He gathered himself, got to his feet, and tentatively shouted towards the door, which was ever so slightly open.

"Summer of '92!"

The door swung open, and a man walked out. He was taller than Drago, but most men would still consider him short. The dark brown wingtip shoes matched his leather jacket, his long dark hair framing a stubbled face. He removed his sunglasses and winked.

Kip Kazdorf.

"Kazdorf?! Mate, I had no clue you'd be Jimmy's ace in the hole. What do you know?"

Kazdorf put his sunglasses in a shirt pocket, the top part of his jacket unbuttoned and unzipped. "I know what you know," Kazdorf said with a smirk.

Kazdorf glanced back behind him, then looked forward to Drago. "I know you're working with the feds."

Drago felt the blood rush to his face.

"What else do you know?" Drago asked.

"That's all, really. Don't blame Jimmy. I have a way of keeping him honest. He owes me his dick," Kazdorf said.

"Ugh. Okay, well, I have no choice to trust you. I'm sure you know exactly what I'm here for," Drago said as he cracked his knuckles. "Is this spaceship staying grounded tonight?"

Kazdorf nodded once, then stepped to the side and extended his arm towards a hallway extending off to the side. "Be my guest. It's all on a pallet in a wing behind the stage. Heavily guarded, but I'm sure once you get your guys over here, easy peasy lemon squeezy."

Drago started to walk into the hallway but stopped and glared at Kazdorf before he continued.

"Do you really have to speak like that? Right now?" Drago asked.

Kazdorf shrugged. "Been around Jimmy too much."

Drago walked down the hall. Kazdorf ambled behind him. Together, at the end of the hallway, they looked up at a dimmed red-lit sign that said *STAGE*. There was another sign on the double-door itself that said *Authorized Personnel Only*.

Drago tapped the sign. "How strictly is this enforced?" he asked.

Kazdorf laughed. "Just as strictly as the dress code. Let's head in." He pushed the left side door open, holding it for Drago as they walked into the dimly-lit backstage area.

A small road crew, maybe a half-dozen men, roved around performing various tasks. Two men unsnapped and assembled a platform. Another climbed a ladder and checked lighting cables. Two others knelt on the stage and marked off brightly colored tape in small concentric squares, only visible beneath a curtain. The other individual checked a rack of gear and wrote on a small notepad as he peered through different turntables, keyboards, microphones, and gadgets stacked off to the side.

Kazdorf walked unhindered among the crew. He gestured to Drago to come ahead with him. They turned the corner around a break between a wall and a curtain, and the lights were significantly brighter here. Together they gazed out over the club, which was mostly empty save for bartenders and security milling around, preparing for the night of sin and revelry. The two crew guys nearby worked at a hypnotic pace, bopping to and fro, whipping back and forth between different tape rolls in their belts and pockets, barely having to measure as they marked the spots.

"This is the wing, yeah?" Drago asked Kazdorf as he looked around. This part of the stage was cleaner than the back end, with no clutter between themselves and the crew guys taping the stage.

Kazdorf frowned. "Yeah, you're right. This is odd, Galactico's rig isn't here."

"Well, find it!" Drago whispered harshly at Kazdorf. "You told me it would be here."

Kazdorf held up a finger to silence Drago. "I'll go check the other wing. Stay here."

Kazdorf silently speed-walked across the stage, crouching low and shuffling sideways. He was spider-like in his movement, his limbs making many subtle movements yet entirely in tandem with one another.

As Kazdorf reached the other side, he slid up to the shadow beside the curtain. Glancing around, he slid over behind the wall, head on a constant swivel.

Nothing.

The murmur of voices and some distant shouts fell over the club and performance area. Drago looked up. Kazdorf peered around the corner to behold throngs of partiers and concert-goers pouring into the building from the main foyer.

"Shit, Kip, they're coming in awful early," Drago said. "We need to move, security's going to see me any minute now."

Kazdorf nodded. "Follow me. There's a couple final places to check for this rig."

Together, Kazdorf and Drago rushed to the other side of the stage and down the west hallway. They passed the bar back area, where several workers washed dishes and prepped alcohol for the night's festivities. They peeked in quickly but did not see anything incriminating. They also tried opening the doors to the locker rooms designated for talent, but all were locked. The final entry was marked with a taped-on sign saying *Captain Galactico and Crew Only.* Kazdorf banged on the door repeatedly, yelling, "Galactico! Pasquale! Open the door!"

Immediately after Kazdorf yelled, the door swung open. A stocky, short, tan man with curly, frosted-tip blonde hair stepped out, wearing an open-chested white dress shirt and khakis.

"What do you want, Kip? I got you V.I.P. again; you don't need anything else, do you?" Pasquale asked.

"Pasquale, man, I think you have a problem. Galactico's rig is missing." Kazdorf said.

"Are you serious... what?" Pasquale shut the door behind him. "How do you... why... how... *what?!*"

Kazdorf gestured towards the stage. Together with Pasquale and Brody, they walked hurriedly in that direction. Pasquale was first on the stage. He pulled at his hair hard, and his already-ruddy face reddened even more.

"God damnit, you're right! How could this happen? No one else really knows the importance of that..." Pasquale paced back among the wings, looking around and rubbing his temple.

"We looked everywhere. The kitchen, both hallways, any open door we saw... Nothing," Drago said.

"Who the hell are you anyway?" Pasquale asked. Before Drago had a chance to answer, his face changed sharply from worry to excitement. "The kitchen! Did you go all the way in?!"

"Nope," Kazdorf said. "But we gave it a good look."

"Follow me," Pasquale said. The three men dashed back into the hallway and then the bar back kitchen. Pasquale grabbed a young brunette woman by the shoulder who happened to be nearest to them.

"Doll, mind telling me if you've seen anyone take equipment through here?" Pasquale asked her.

She threw his hand off her, rolling her eyes. "Don't touch me again, P. Some guy in a wife-beater came through saying he was with maintenance. He was hauling a lot of stuff."

"What?! How long ago was this?"

The woman sighed. "He's still out there. You just missed him coming through."

Pasquale slipped, brown oxfords slick on the wet floor. He regained balance and walked quickly through the kitchen. Drago and Kazdorf followed in close suit. Pasquale gained momentum and pushed through double doors that swung open hard, nearly smacking Kazdorf and Drago in their recoil.

As they stepped into the rain, they squinted against the downpour to see the tail lights of a van some distance in front of them, in the parking lot, the back hatch open – and there, apparent in the light of the van, was Captain Galactico's candle rig. It was composed of rotating plinths, the candles affixed on the circumference. A skinny man in a tank top dashed around and shut the van's back hatch, revealing the purple of the van, and when he turned to face the building – the slack-mouthed, distant-eyed look of Sean Doan.

"Sean! What are you doing? Get back here with that!" Drago yelled at him.

At that time, Trevor MacKenzie came dashing around the side of the building in full gallop. Just as soon as Sean ran around the left side of the van and jumped into the driver's seat, Trevor made it to the other side, swung open the door, and dove in. Brody, Kazdorf, and Pasquale took chase as the van's engine gunned, and it took off into the parking lot. Jimmy Glencroft and two security guards rounded the building and joined the chase.

Jimmy gave chase long after everyone else had stopped and gasped for air, or in the case of Kip Kazdorf, refused to get his dress shoes muddy. Jimmy sprinted hard, slogging through puddles and pushing through mud, trying in vain to catch up to the accelerating van. Sean and Trevor got away, driving into an alley between two retail buildings, and taking off into the suburban streets among the homes beyond. Jimmy's van was gone, and with it, two members of his crew and tens of thousands of dollars' worth of industrial-grade hallucinogenic candles. Jimmy fell to a knee, gasped raggedly for breath, and cussed into the night. He gingerly sat down, his ankle throbbing and his flayed skin screaming in irritation, and set to find some comfort in the crags of the concrete.

CHAPTER TWENTY-SEVEN

James Glencroft sat on the sidewalk alongside a brick building in downtown Worthington, just north of Columbus. The soaked man caught a brief respite beneath an awning. Still, all around him, a torrential downpour cloaked the night sky, obscuring the lights of the looming brick mid-rises, the rainfall splattering into the ever-growing puddles, pooling too fast for the drains to take on.

Jimmy lit up a cigarette and closed his eyes, holding the smoke in for a long moment before exhaling. He opened his eyes and looked around. The bars were long closed, and the streets were mostly empty. Only every now and then would a car splash by. It was around 3 AM, and here he was, nowhere to go and nobody to talk to, his chance at a big payday having ridden off with his junkie associates. Jimmy had been moping here a long time, having walked here after his van was stolen, not having the slightest urge to do anything about it.

A car driving in from the south deliberately plowed through the puddle in front of Jimmy, splashing him with a large wave before skidding to a stop a few feet later. Soaked and his cigarette extinguished, Jimmy stood up, yelling profanity at the vehicle. The passenger side door opened, and he saw an arm through the rain gesturing at him to get inside. Jimmy walked up to peer through and see who was within.

Detective Sophie Browning.

Jimmy sighed and plopped into the passenger seat.

"Detective Browning, sorry to soak your seat here – probably would be drier if you didn't splash me," Jimmy said.

"I'm not fussed," Browning replied. "Your smell bugs me more than the rain does. God, I hate the smell of cigarettes."

Browning drove in silence for a few minutes. The windshield wipers beat against the glass as the rain pattered relentlessly.

"Alright, I'll talk first," Browning said as the car rolled through Clintonville, passing small strip malls and residential areas, barely visible through the rain-streaked windows. Jimmy nodded as he pressed his head against the cold glass.

"You haven't been wearing your wire," Browning said. Jimmy continued to stare out the window.

"What happened to the wire, Jimmy? It's been two weeks... no transmissions from you. This is a disappointing development. I could have made this all go away."

Jimmy took a shuddering breath.

"I lost it. During a little scrap," he explained.

"At the warehouse outside of Slade City? Perkins Township, is it?" Browning asked.

"You got me," Jimmy said quietly.

Browning drove for a few more minutes as Jimmy fidgeted with his wet hoodie sleeves and twisted his own fingers over and over again.

"I want witness protection," Jimmy said at last. "There are a lot of scary moving parts here; I never wanted any part of it."

"But you're in it, you're actively participating in it, and that's the reality," Browning said. "That whole thing on the outer belt? The truck theft in Dayton? Hell, that whole debacle at the rave tonight..."

"Wait, you knew about the rave? What, how?"

"Are you really so thick to think the federal government wouldn't tap more than one source?" Browning scorned.

"Well, I know you have Lyndsey working on Sean and Trevor..."

Browning laughed.

"What? Is something funny?"

"Sean and Trevor. That's rich," Browning said.

The color drained from Jimmy's face, and his soaked hoodie became even colder, oh so very cold.

Browning continued to laugh.

Jimmy leaned forward and clunked his head purposefully against the dash above the glove box.

"Secret secrets are no fun," Browning said. "Secret secrets hurt someone."

"You had *Lyndsey* wired... for *me*? Even before I... what? Am I being detained?"

"If you have to ask, you already know," Browning said. "Don't worry, I'll keep this civil as long as you do."

Jimmy curled his arms around his head and sobbed.

"You might want to buckle up, kid. If we're in a wreck and something happens to you before I get a chance to process you, well... it's your funeral," Browning said. "You and Trace seemed to be getting close. Maybe you'll see him sooner than you think."

"You used Lyndsey against me? One of my own best friends, someone I love?" Jimmy asked.

"Yes, of course! You made it far too easy. Love and friendship blind you. I'm going to be cutting her loose. She, Trevor, and Sean are all about to run away together. Friends forever," Browning said with a laugh. "Just your precious 'Lytz' and her two crackhead buddies, doing God knows what together."

"Shut *up!*" Jimmy snapped.

"Oh, I don't think you're in a position to be telling me what to do," Browning said. "No, no... not at all."

"Maybe I am," Jimmy said. "Don't you know about the stockpile of drugs they have?"

Browning smirked and shook her head. "The Dirty D Posse and Slavia United took it. It's probably all split up between every hood in Dayton by now."

"No, Browning! Think! If you knew about the rave, didn't Lyndsey tell you we were going to go steal drugs from Captain Galactico to fund their move out of town?"

"No, it wasn't Lynds..." Browning cut herself off mid-sentence, but it was too late. Jimmy immediately read between the lines.

"Drago, eh? How long has he been in your pocket? Since the poker game? Before that?" Jimmy questioned.

Browning didn't answer.

"Look, I know he's working with you. We've talked."

"Drago Zupan's value to this investigation has greatly exceeded yours," Browning said. "That's why he's getting let out, and you're going downtown."

"But he didn't tell you about the drugs he was chasing down! Are you sure he's not selling you out straight back to Dirty D and Slavia United?"

"Not any more than you've tipped off the syndicate about them being on our radar," Browning said.

"I haven't left a single thing out," Jimmy said. "Where's my lawyer? I feel like he should be here for this."

"You're welcome to his services if you can find out which cognac-soaked brothel he's sleeping on the floor of tonight," Browning said with a hyperactive laugh.

Jimmy remained quiet for a long moment as the gears turned in his head. Browning hooked a hard right off Lane Avenue as she changed course for the western suburbs. As they came to a red light, she fired off a text on a Blackberry.

"The law is for me and not for thee," Jimmy said.

"Nobody cares," Browning replied flatly.

"I do," Jimmy said. "I'm sitting on something that will rock your whole investigation. If you don't give me protection, or at least let my friends and me go, I promise to God above that I'll lean into this."

"Are you threatening a Federal agent?" Browning asked.

"Yes. Yes, I am. Unless you have better advice," Jimmy said.

"All the advice in the world won't help you now. You're desperate."

"Not as desperate as you're going to be when your agency finds out you heard information about an insurrection and didn't act on it," Jimmy said.

"Insurrection? You mean like that shit show at the Capitol?" Browning asked.

"Worse. So much worse. That was amateur hour compared to this," Jimmy said. He didn't even believe the scope of his own words, but he had heard and seen enough from Rik Landers to think it was possible.

"Whatever," Browning responded.

"You need to give me something, Browning! I'm not a bad guy, I promise. I can't get put away. I'm not a criminal, I won't last in prison. I just want my freedom," Jimmy pleaded.

"You should have thought before you blew up Corso and Townshend, and picked up that gun on the roof," Browning chided.

"I'm sitting on something big," Jimmy said. "Please. I need you to help me. Again, I'm not a criminal, I..."

"Fine! Shoot, what is it?" Browning said.

"The syndicate is a front operation for the most organized group of Boogaloo Boys in the nation!" Jimmy exclaimed. "They're right here in Ohio gearing up for an insurrection. A real one."

"Hardly. I have a colleague on that task force, and the alt-right was stamped out *hard* over the last year. The wind was out of their sails once big tech turned on them," Browning said.

"Not the alt-right. The Boogaloo. There's a difference, Browning! You have to look at their motivations, their makeup. We're talking hackers, dark web guys, ex-military, ex-law enforcement guys. I can take you to them. Together we can stop the storm that's coming," Jimmy said, taking a half step ahead of his own mind.

Browning sighed and looked over at Jimmy. "If what you said is true, then you will have earned my trust. I'm on my way to rendezvous with Drago now. Does he know this?"

"If he does, he hasn't let me in on that knowledge, much like he let you down on that drug tip with Sean and Trevor. Oh, by the way, I can lead you to them too. Probably fifty grand of hallucinogenic candles. You can put Sean and Trevor away, and have something for the larger case against the syndicate. But we have to act quickly and make sure we roll with Lyndsey, or they won't trust me when I arrive."

"Christ, Jimmy. Why didn't you tell me about the Boogaloo connection earlier?" Browning asked.

"Same reason you wired Lyndsey against me," Jimmy said. After a moment of silence, he turned to Browning and smiled. "You've done your homework on me. You know I'm a poker player and a damn good one too. Never show your cards before you're all in."

Jimmy's gaze turned to the headlights and windshield wipers and driving rain ahead of him.

"And now... I'm *all in.*"

CHAPTER TWENTY-EIGHT

Jimmy Glencroft burst into his rented house first, closely followed by Detective Sophie Browning and Drago Zupan.

"LYTZ!!!! Lyndsey, are you here?! *Hello?!*" he yelled as he dashed from room to room, checking every nook and cranny, looking around corners, and checking inside closets. Browning inspected the floor, windows, and tables; Drago followed Jimmy around at a safe distance, holding his pistol low at his side.

After Jimmy finished looking in the back bedroom, bathroom, and walk-in closet, he dashed down the hallway. He looked up at the tassel hanging down from the ceiling to pull down the stairs to the attic, but Drago gently reached over and pushed Jimmy's arm down.

"She's not up there," Drago said. "We need to move, friend."

Browning yelled back from the kitchen. "He's right, Jimbo. Nobody's here. But check this out!"

Drago walked over but was beat to the kitchen by Jimmy. Browning snapped picture after picture with her smartphone.

"What is it?" Jimmy asked.

Browning turned and wrinkled her forehead, nodding back towards the stovetop.

"Teatime," Browning said.

The kettle, still atop the warmer, whistled as it steamed to completion.

"Damnit," Jimmy said.

"Right. We must have just missed them. Now Lyndsey can't be our way in. I'll get out an APB for Doan and MacKenzie... Listen, Jimmy. Stay here. I know it's easier said than done. But we can't have you interfering in this. We can't drag other parties further into this than they already are."

"Detective, with all due respect, I want to be involved with this. I can be helpful. I've made it through everything so far," Jimmy pleaded.

"Give me one thing. *One thing* that can help. Choose wisely."

"Lyndsey used to be a squatter when she was hard into drugs," Jimmy said. "Her aunt owns a trailer on the east side of Nawakwa, in the Leeds Creek Mobile Home Park. That's where she always hid when she was in a bad way."

Browning leveled her gaze at Jimmy. "You better be right. If you're wrong, it's over for you. I promise you that."

"I liked you better when I first met you," Jimmy told Browning. "What changed?"

"The two officers that died in that explosion? One of them was my best friend. Officer Townshend and I went all the way back to middle school. He was a good man, Jimbo. He wasn't a 'pig' at all. Now, we haven't pinned that explosion on anyone, but we all know you were there. We heard the shots. That's indisputable. And trust me on this, it would be much easier to put a scrub like you in the pen for Townshend and Corso's murders since we wouldn't have to deal with any heat from the street for your arrest. So, if I were you, I'd keep my mouth shut and stay right here while a professional deals with your meth addict friends and rescues your princess for you."

Browning backed up towards the front door, nodding towards Drago.

"Same goes for you, Euro. Now stay here or face the consequences."

"I thought we had a deal!" Jimmy yelled at Browning. "I've told you everything I know!"

"Nothing said was legally binding," Browning responded. "Maybe you should have waited until we were downtown with your criminal lawyer. Now keep your head low, will you? I wouldn't want to be you once the syndicate finds out you've sold them out as a front operation.

"Stay here. I'll be back for you tonight; maybe then we can work something out."

Browning turned back around as she walked back to her unmarked sedan. She lowered her hand to the gun at her waist, nodded to Jimmy with a furrow of her forehead, then turned, opened the door, and hopped in.

As Detective Browning sped off, Jimmy turned and faced Drago. Drago shrugged softly, mouth agape.

"Drago, man. We *have* to do something. I don't trust Browning."

"Neither do I. She would sell Lytz out to cover herself for anything she messes up." Drago sighed. "I could never trust a cop, Jimmy."

"They've meddled in too much in my life. We need to keep matters in our own hands. They ever actually say anything about a witness protection deal on the table for you?"

Drago shook his head. "Nada. You?"

"I mean, I feel like it's still good," Jimmy said. "Do you think Browning would yank it somehow?"

"No, her commander, he's the one with the final call. She's just trying to make a name. I don't think she has the authority."

"Let's go, then," Jimmy said as he gestured outside towards Drago's Prius. "I sent Browning to the wrong place, but close enough to where they probably are. They'll see the cops and know to split. Are your boys still tailing us at all?"

"Nope," Drago said. "The Dayton shit actually put them on notice. This is just between us, the feds, Lytz, Sean, and Trevor."

"Way too many moving parts in this crap if you ask me," Jimmy said. "Alright, we're wasting time. Browning will probably beat us to Nawakwa by twenty minutes. I'm almost 100% sure where Lytz is."

"Bet. I'll drive, friend."

Drago slapped Jimmy on the back, nodded to him, and ran with him out the front door into the brisk autumn breeze that whipped through Columbus.

"Trev, we have to move, man. This work is hotter than hell," Sean Doan barked out to his partner in crime. Sean wrapped the pallet of candles with tape to hold them in place. He stood in the middle of a cleared-out dining room in a tiny musky home on Nawakwa's east side. He knelt on a dusty wooden floor, the house messy save for this room, all manner of personal effects slung about the place, disorganized and unclean. None of the lights were on, there were no clocks on the stove or the microwave, and a keen eye could see the cockroaches skittle through the shadows from time to time.

Trevor slunk in the corner beside a staircase as he played with a smartphone, a taut grin on his pale face.

"Sean, Sean, I said I'd be on it. I just want to make sure everything's good with your dude in Youngstown," Trevor said.

Sean flung his roll of packing tape against the wall with a smack. "How many times do I have to tell you that Youngstown's good? Nothing is wrong in Youngstown. We gotta roll. Put that shit away before I break it."

Trevor grinned at Sean. "You're edgy as hell, man. How long has it been since you took a bump?"

"How long has it been since you've helped, ass wipe?"

"What's there to help with? You just need to finish taping our load. We have the donut truck; we have the pallet jack. Once we get loaded and get out, it's smooth sailing from here. Well, if Youngstown is still on..."

"Can we *please* stop worrying about Youngstown? It's good!"

Sean slunk over to the roll of tape to pick it back up. From there, he hurried as he finished a half-effort tape job on the pallet. Trevor put his phone to the side and sparked up a menthol, eyeing Sean as he worked. Silence fell upon the house save for Trevor inhaling and exhaling over Sean's tape strapping and ripping.

The relative silence was broken as the back door, which led to the kitchen, swung open. Lyndsey de Rueda staggered in, turned, and slammed the door shut again. She slunk to the floor, sobbing, sinking into her hoodie, and pulling the hood tight over her face.

Sean and Trevor peeked around the corner, saw Lyndsey, and relaxed. They had both reactively drawn their pistols. Trevor sat his gun on the kitchen counter, and Sean put his back in his waistband. Trevor went to comfort Lyndsey, but Sean shoved him against a wall. Trevor staggered back up, threw up his hands in an angry shrug, and turned to look out the window. Like a field goal kicker, Sean took a short running start and delivered a crushing kick to Lyndsey's side. She crumpled and curled into a ball. Trevor turned around, yelling swears at Sean, who had just delivered another sharp kick. Sean stopped, gestured to Trevor to step back, and then returned his attention to Lyndsey.

"What the hell? Why aren't you at the trailer?!" Sean yelled.

"The police! Nawakwa P.D. They came... they were at the trailer..." Lyndsey choked out between sobs.

"And you didn't think to call us? Why didn't you call us?"

"I dropped my phone somewhere in the field... I had to get out right away, or this whole thing would go up in smoke."

"Did they see you?"

"I don't think so. Their sirens were on, so once I heard them, I had time to bail out the back door. I made sure to shut it. I hid behind a tree and watched. There were like three cars. SWAT truck too. They're coming for us hard. I ran here across the field. I'm so scared."

Sean sighed and looked down at the floor a long moment. Out of nowhere, he kicked Lyndsey violently once more. Trevor reached over and jabbed Sean hard in the eye. With that, he stopped his assault and turned to Trevor, anger wrinkling one side of his face while his hand covered the other.

"What the hell, man?!" Sean yelled at him.

"Stop it. That's enough. If you need to do that, do it to someone who can fight back." Trevor shrugged off his unbuttoned outer shirt, standing there in just his tank top and jeans. "Come on, let's throw!"

"STOP!!" Lyndsey shrieked. "For the love of God, both of you, just stop!"

Sean turned as if to kick her again, then sighed and stepped back. Trevor stood still, glaring at Sean, and occasionally glancing at Lyndsey. All three of them breathed heavily.

Lyndsey sat up and pulled down her hood. Tears streaked her pale face. The skin under her eyes hung low, purple and thin, the rest of her face sallow.

"We are all in trouble. We are all in this together. Sean, you need to stop hurting me if we are going to do this. You and Trevor need to stop fighting too. I'm just so tired. I can't be any good to you if this keeps happening."

"I'm so sorry, baby..." Sean said, taking his hand off his eye and reaching down to help Lyndsey up. "You know how I get when I'm nervous... Come here, baby, you know it's okay..."

Lyndsey stood and allowed herself to lean into Sean. Trevor sighed and looked away for a moment, turning around and then watching out the window. He turned back around to see Lyndsey watching him intently. Sean looked away, rubbing her hair and back, clutching hard. Trevor raised an eyebrow. Lyndsey smiled. Trevor mouthed, "What?" Lyndsey winked. Trevor threw up his hands in frustration.

"Sean, baby, do you think you can go check on the pallet? Make sure everything's good?" Lyndsey asked.

"Yes, baby, I've got it. Everything will be okay," Sean said as he rushed to the other room.

As soon as Sean was distracted, Lyndsey pulled down the top of her hoodie just enough to show off a wire transmitter taped to her chest. Trevor's mouth drooped open.

"Trevor, we've come too far. Play along with me and I'll make sure you're okay," she whispered. "Our way out is coming."

"I... I don't know what to say," Trevor muttered in return. "I... thank you for letting me know."

There was a thud at the front door, knocking dust loose and into the air, wafting on the sunbeams. Trevor slid back behind the entryway of the kitchen. Sean, panicking, turned and drew his pistol, a Glock 43. He retreated to the back of the room, planted his feet and stood in the kitchen entryway.

The door finally shook loose, falling open to the side. A short man stepped in, his face and features obscured by the bright light framing him. He pointed a pistol of his own at Sean, who stood brandishing his in the open.

"Sean! Sean Doan! Drop the gun, or I am going to light you up like a Chri...."

The man didn't have a chance to finish his threat. With several echoing cracks, Sean pulled the trigger repeatedly, emptying multiple shots into the man, who shuddered in his tracks and then slumped to the ground. Sean let his arm fall to his side. He glared at the fresh body of the man, cackling evilly, a sharp and wild grin crawling across his face.

Sean's grin fell into a blank expression, and blood burst through the front of his forehead, splattering across the floor below, another crack reverberating through the house as he fell to his knees, and then face-down just inches from the other body. Behind him, with both hands clasped around a smoking gun, Lyndsey de Rueda stood with a Cheshire grin, crying and laughing, her chest rising and falling rapidly, with Trevor slumped in the corner near her, a look of shock and fear on his face. She dropped the gun. Trevor winced and slunk further out of view. She sat down, cross-legged on the floor, looked to the ceiling, and laugh-cried uninterrupted for a long moment as the two men bled out in front of her.

Trevor finally stood up and walked over to the bodies. He stepped over Sean and knelt to see who the other person was. He rolled the body over to expose the face of Drago Zupan, his eyes still open yet lifeless, blood and spittle having frothed out of the corner of his mouth.

"Damnit... Lytz, it was Brody," Trevor called back to her. He stood up, wincing as he looked at the bodies, coughing back a gag as he took a step away. "That must mean..."

Before Trevor could finish his sentence, Jimmy Glencroft strode into the house, a look of sheer pale terror on his face. He looked a long moment at the bodies of Sean Doan and Drago Zupan on the floor, then he finally met Trevor's gaze. Jimmy stepped around him for a second to see Lytz sitting on the floor. He looked back to Trevor.

"Trev, dude... What the hell happened?!" Jimmy asked.

"Sean shot Drago. He didn't even have a chance. Then Lytz popped Sean's melon. One-shot, and boom," Trevor said.

"Holy shit... Lytz, are you okay?"

Lytz continued to stare at the ceiling. Jimmy turned back to Trevor and motioned to the bodies with a wave of his arm.

"Whatever happened here is a serious mistake!" Jimmy said. "You don't have time to hide these bodies. What were you doing? What the hell is going on? We had a *plan*! You, me, Lyndsey – these *dead fucking men* – we were in this together, dude. Why did you turn on me? WHY?"

Trevor, dumbfounded, could only muster a dead-eyed shrug.

"Trevor... you need to get out of this life. I wasn't going to tell anyone this, but I'm going to Slade City to meet a fixer. He's going to help forge a new identity for me, and the syndicate is footing the bill. Maybe I can have him help you and Lytz. You should come with me, and we should leave soon. Someone has called 9-1-1 by now, I'd hope..."

"Jimmy, we can't – well, I can't – I'm not in the system like you. I can still be me. I can still be Trevor MacKenzie. Look... If you do what you're going to do, you can never be Jimmy Glencroft again. Maybe you should come to Youngstown with me and Lytz. You can still be you. Besides," he took a quick glance at Lyndsey, "she's with *the police*. I think we can trust her."

"I'm with them too!" Jimmy yelled. "I've been with them! I just – I think I fucked up by lying to them, and now Drago and Sean are gone, and... we *really* messed up this time, man..."

Jimmy and Trevor stood there, looking at one another, then the dead bodies, and then Lyndsey – who watched everything in silence.

"It's funny," Lyndsey said, "the house we all met in for the first time... here we are. Here *this* is..."

"I wonder what your parents are going to say about this," Jimmy said. "They still own the place, right?"

"Who knows," Lyndsey said. "They haven't spoken to me in years, and I doubt this whole thing will change that."

Jimmy paced in circles. Lyndsey remained sitting and played with her hoodie sleeves as she thought about what just happened, and Trevor stood stock still.

Over the quiet, the three of them heard the distant wail of sirens. A few seconds passed, and there was an obvious crescendo. The sirens were approaching.

"I'm going to Slade City," Jimmy said. "Go to Youngstown. You need to move fast."

Trevor nodded, then dashed to where the pallet of candles stood, not completely wrapped. He set to preparing it for transport, sliding over the pallet jack and getting to work.

"Van's down the street," Trevor reminded Jimmy. He paused his task, reached into his sweats, fished out the keys, and tossed them to his old friend.

Jimmy walked deliberately to Lyndsey and took a knee, extending a hand to her shoulder, looking straight into her eyes. She returned his look, several long strands of her dark hair clinging to the sweat on her face, across her eyes, nose, and mouth. Jimmy reached out to push the strands back around her face and behind her ears.

"Lytz... I'm so sorry for everything that's happened. We can start again. Come with me to Slade City. I don't want to go alone," Jimmy said. He was breathing heavily, his eyes wide. After he spoke, he smacked his tongue against the roof of his mouth, fighting the dryness within.

"Jimmy... I'm going to Youngstown. There's nothing for me here. There's nothing for me *there*." Lyndsey said with a vague southward gesture.

"No, Lytz... I love you. You know I have a hard time with my own emotions. *I love you.* I mean that. I really do. I've loved you for years. Through high school and that year at college, through everything we've fought through... I love you. I mean that. Come with me to Slade City, and we can run away forever to somewhere new."

"How romantic," Trevor said as he shuffled by, pulling the pallet behind him and out the back door, not bothering to steady it as it fell onto the back patio with a thud, a couple candles falling out from under the wrap and either breaking or rolling away.

Lyndsey stared at Jimmy quietly.

"I love you," Jimmy said one more time, his face reddening. He leaned in to kiss Lyndsey's forehead, but she ducked smoothly away from him and stood with a pivot. Jimmy had to thrust a hand down to the floor to keep himself from falling over. He looked up at Lyndsey, tears starting to well in his eyes.

"Goodbye, Jimmy," Lyndsey said.

"Lytz, wait... what you did, you killed Sean... Browning is *not* going to work with you now! She will look for you until she catches you," Jimmy pleaded.

Lyndsey stood up and turned around with a shrug, heading out the back window after Trevor, careful to pick up candles on the ground along the way. Trevor loaded the pallet into the back of the Cream Dream donut truck along with the possessions he could take with him. The engine was rumbling, and Trevor boarded stiffly. When Lyndsey came out, he waved out of the driver's side window, and she darted over to the passenger side. Jimmy watched from the back door as she hopped into the delivery truck without turning around, without waving or saying anything else. Just like that, she was in the truck with a slammed door, and then Trevor gunned the engine, guiding it into the alley and hooking a left towards the main road.

The sirens closed in from down the street. Jimmy stepped back inside for a moment. He looked at the discarded pistols on the ground, still loaded and freshly fired. Drago and Sean, motionless and with blood pooled around them, formed a sinister picture in the light of the living room. The sirens came to a peak and then stopped abruptly, and Jimmy could see the blue and red reflection of them play off the metal of old tins displayed on elevated shelves in the living room. Jimmy scooped up the pistols, rubbed his hands all over the barrels and handles, marking them up with his prints before he put them back on the ground.

Jimmy turned and ran. He ran out of the back door, through the ratty backyard, and turned hard left into the alley, tweaking his knee and falling, cracking his jaw against the pavement. He scrambled up, pushing against loose gravel, cutting into his hands as he took off into another headlong sprint. The whole world dimmed and tunneled around him. He took another sharp left at another street, this a one-way, cars on either side of the road facing him as he ran down the middle. A car pulled out, driving slowly, having just left its driveway. Without stopping, Jimmy vaulted onto the car, running up the hood and front windshield, jumping off the roof and landing behind the moving car, rolling through his landing and continuing. An older man walking his dog on the right-hand sidewalk watched the whole thing, his jaw slacked and ignoring his yapping pooch as he watched Jimmy go.

Jimmy finally arrived at the purple van where Sean had parked it on the left-hand side of the street. He struggled to pull his keychain from his pocket. Once it was fished out, he opened the driver's side door, clambered in, and hurried to start the engine. Once on and rumbling, Jimmy gassed it hard, cutting off a traveling car behind him. As the horn echoed behind him, he sped away towards the highway as fast as the old van could muster.

CHAPTER TWENTY-NINE

How long have I been driving?

Am I being followed? Dirty D, Slavia United, the fucking government – they will all want me.

Who am I? What have I become? What lies ahead?

What will become of my friends? Will I ever see them again?

Will I die? Will I finally meet my family?

James Glencroft rolled down the driver's side window by hand, letting the chill air come in and cool him down. His face flushed red, and he briefly closed his eyes even as he drove, letting the brisk whip of chill soften his color. He opened his eyes again, guiding the van over the gently rolling hill and dale as he accelerated yet again, pushing the gas pedal down until he heard the automatic gear rattle and then jump into the next shift.

Time and time again, Jimmy would check the mirrors. A quick glance to the left. Drive a moment. A glance at the top rear-view. Nothing yet. Glance to the right mirror, glance back to the left one. His attention wandered. He would drift in and out of the lanes. He would drift off and back onto the road. Jimmy's eyes wide open and his extremities and limbs constantly fidgeting and tapping, he was awake, but he drove like a zombie. Only the jolts of the rumble strips or the flash of a nearby vehicle or the pangs of pain and agony would bring him to attention. His speed belied his morose state, increasing as he went – 65, 70, 80...

The sun edged low over the hills of southern Ohio. The sky streaked with wispy white cirrostratus. As the light in the sky faded, the clouds darkened to gray. The sky above Jimmy was a light purple, and the horizon to the west was enhanced with bright orange, the sinking sun kissing the rest of the world goodnight with its flourish of color and charm.

Jimmy drove the van over a long inclining rise. No other cars were near him in the eastbound lane. Every now and then, a semi or a vehicle would go in the other direction, headlights on, dim in the receding sunlight. He lightly drummed his fingers on the wheel, forgetting to breathe, occasionally shuddering through a ragged sigh as his mouth remained open, lips at a light purse. The autumn leaves upon the forested treetops on either side of the highway had long receded, only occasional trees still enjoying full plume. Others yet were almost entirely bare, their naked snarl spotted by an occasional limb and bough with a brush of faded color.

Jimmy drove past a Prius, and he checked the driver's window for Drago Zupan. Jimmy drove past a Buick, and he checked for Manny Rezendes. He came up on a white delivery van, like the one from Dayton, and he thought of Big Trace Onwudiwe. Jimmy realized he still wore Big Trace's crucifix chain, still specked with Trace's blood, heavy on his chest, his heart even heavier within...

Jimmy let out a huge breath as he crested the rise, and the highway took its sharpest turn yet, down and to the right. As he took another right at a tight angle, the forested trees across the road to the left took a break, and the opposite-side lanes faded as that direction of highway took its approach on a lower elevation. From this break in the trees, Jimmy beheld for the first time in such a long, long time; the skyline of Slade City, Ohio.

Tucked in close to the mountainside he drove along, Slade City was darker than the world on the other side. Already hemmed in by the shades of shadow, the city was in transition from light to night. A ragged cluster of some half-dozen 1920s era skyscrapers thrust forth, the tallest of which was a 320-foot art deco concrete building, a spire atop the roof giving the building an impression of being even taller, the lights along the spire glowing purple in the twilight. The other facilities were of a similar era and construct, with nothing astutely modern in shape clear from Jimmy's vantage. The buildings were predominantly brick or concrete, many of which were squat, with only a few (including the tallest) comprising a tiered construct.

Jimmy was so distracted by viewing the sights that he nearly missed his exit. When he glanced up and saw "Downtown / Drake's Landing / Winterview – Exit 71," he immediately slammed on his brakes, decelerating sharply from around 80 MPH to 40. He steered to the right, cutting across another two lanes without looking, blasting across the shoulder and onto the off-ramp, tires squealing as the van tilted slightly, the left tires nearly leaving the pavement as Jimmy took the steep grade and sharp turn downward and to his left, going under the highway and then on a long sloping bridge.

The decline led Jimmy into the fringe of Slade City. Along the left side of the two-lane road stood the mountain's edge. Occasionally a home or a standalone business stood among the flatter grounds. A tow truck company here, a disheveled farmhouse there. Lining up on the right side were lower-class neighborhoods. Jimmy observed the sides of yellow and pale green and faded white houses, mostly one-story and in various states of disrepair. Windows boarded up, roofs caved in yet uncovered, dead vines and plants having overgrown the tops and sides of fences. Here and there, the monotony of the neighborhoods was broken up with a business, some closed and others opened, bars and grills and laundromats, and similar conditions for the homes around them.

More checking of mirrors. More panic upon seeing headlights that could even barely be construed as law enforcement vehicles. More visions in his head of dead friends, of Trace, of Manny, of Drago, the wide-open eyes of the man Jimmy kicked off the helicopter... always falling, never fading...

Jimmy sped up on this narrow road. Only the sporadic set of headlights would pass him from the left. Nobody else was in front of him. It was too dark for him to notice the police cruiser sitting in the parking lot of a dollar store on the right side of the road, disguised by the store's street-level sign. Jimmy was driving 65 MPH; the posted speed limit was 45.

The lights of the cruiser didn't turn on right away. The cop turned onto the road behind Jimmy and accelerated to keep following him at a safe distance. Jimmy was too focused on the road ahead at this point to pay mind to his rear-view mirror. He missed the lights coming on at first. The curves of the road and Jimmy's attention span were enough to cloak them. When the flash finally refracted from his rear-view and into his attention, he gulped deeply, his skin flushed with adrenaline, and he accelerated even faster, coming to a three-way intersection with a traffic light.

One road pointed towards the woods. The other option went towards downtown Slade City, heading down a decline towards the skyscraper cluster shining over the horizon.

Jimmy veered left and uphill as he ran a red light and hopped a sidewalk corner with his back-right tire. He almost overcorrected, but managed to steady the bucking van and regain some speed as he accelerated towards the crest of the rise, a quarter-mile in the distance. The snarled branches of deciduous trees ravaged by the advance of the seasons hung over both sides of the road. Jimmy glanced into his rear-view to see the cop's lights ascending the rise behind him. Now he could hear the siren, a crescendo of alarm. Jimmy gunned the accelerator but could not gain any traction. Between the rev of the engine and the blare of the siren, he could make out a familiar sound, the rumbling rub of the tire against the ground.

His right-rear tire was going flat.

Jimmy looked around frantically. He couldn't see much other than the road ahead and the trees shrouding his view. Jimmy thought he could make out the top of a nearby cell tower. His foot was almost entirely down on the accelerator as he felt the bumping of the right rear steadily increasing in intensity and effect.

Jimmy crested the rise and went on a slight downhill curve to the left. He was so frantic that he didn't see the semi-truck, void of a trailer and with its headlights off, parked on a side drive at the crest. Right as Jimmy's van bolted past, the semi-truck pulled out into the middle of the road, completely blocking both lanes from either direction.

The police cruiser squealed to a halt, spinning itself out and into the drainage ditch on the right-hand side of the road to avoid colliding with the semi-truck. With a black cap pulled tight over his head and wearing all black head to toe, the driver swung open the door and hopped to the road below. The policeman leaped from the ditch with his side-arm drawn. The driver darted around the side of the truck.

"FREEZE!" the policeman yelled as he ran to the semi, hands on his pistol, sweeping his aim across the road and the semi-truck. "SHOW YOURSELF!"

There was a scurry as the officer turned to see the driver vault over the ditch from the back of the truck on the other side; stumbling slightly, he took off into the woods, sprinting between trees headlong downhill. The officer ripped off a few shots, mostly embedding his bullets into trees or losing them to the night sky. He looked around, back at his car, and then down the road, on his radio as he yelled for backup. He knelt on the street, shaking his head before taking off his hat and wiping sweat from his brow.

Down the road, Jimmy sought refuge. He came upon a side road going to the right and slightly uphill. A sign to the right of this road said Welcome to Winterview State Park. The right-rear tire was almost to the rim, grinding against the pavement as he churned onward, the smell of destroyed rubber intoxicating and robust. The engine shuddered a few times as well, an extra whirring sound now coming in over the chunky clunk of the block itself.

Jimmy turned off his headlights and turned right one more time onto a gravel road. The right-rear tire got wedged in the roadside, Jimmy unable to see the boulder until it was too late. He tried to throw the van into reverse to get out of the stoppage but to no avail. Jimmy swung open the door, hopping out and dashing around to the side. He grabbed his backpack, pistol, and coat. Jimmy hurriedly donned the dark padded jacket, pulling his hat tighter over his brow and putting the gun in a roomy pocket.

"After all is said and done, this van deserves nothing less than a Viking funeral," Jimmy said aloud. He tapped the side of his purple minivan one last time and ran into the darkness.

After some distance, the dark trees had closed fully around Jimmy, blocking most moonlight and starlight. The panic in his heart had given way to a dark, whole, complete and somber heaviness. He could now feel the throbbing of his jaw, the tightness in his left knee, and the ever-present road rash and foot pain. Jimmy could not run any longer and drew to a slow walk, breathing deeply as he fished into his pack to find a flashlight.

Before he turned on the flashlight, he listened closely to his surroundings. With it being late in the year, most insects weren't quite as active, most birds had migrated, and evenings in the wood weren't quite as noisy as they were in the summer. An eerie quiet had set into Winterview State Park. There were no sirens, no engines, no gunfire, nothing that Jimmy had anticipated cracking the silence. He turned on the flashlight and limped onward, shoulders slumped, dragging his feet through the dried leaves of the forest floor along the access road.

A half-hour passed, and Jimmy found a break in the trees around a bend ahead. He suddenly recognized where he was, and his pace quickened. Fighting through the throbbing pain, he came to the curve, trees on either side opening to a turnoff, benches sitting along a manmade stone wall. Looking down and across the mountain, Jimmy was treated to a panoramic view of Slade City from a different angle than the highway approach.

Jimmy plopped down on the stone wall, swinging his legs over the edge and letting them hang heavy. He pulled out a cigarette and sparked it, taking a drag deep and holding the smoke before blowing it through his nose. Jimmy leaned over, propping himself on the side of the wall, gazing out over the city as he smoked. He flicked ash, reflecting over his times sitting in this very spot before with Lyndsey de Rueda – during high school, during college – wishing that she could be here even after. He thought about her and Trevor MacKenzie a long moment – wondering if they made it to Youngstown safely, if the evidence at the shooting scene could somehow pin them, or if he had successfully taken the heat. Jimmy was deep in thought, but never so deep he couldn't take another ragged, exhausted pull of sweet nicotine.

Jimmy could see the literal red lights of Slade City's red-light district, along a diagonal strip a half-mile from the skyscrapers downtown. He observed bright stadium lights in a part of town off to the southwest – ah, yes, it was Friday Night – so many dreams were being made, so many dreams were being dashed – all within that 100-yard gauntlet. Finally, on the horizon and barely visible through the city lights, his weary eyes lingered on the bright green light atop a spire, marking the main hall at Slade City College. Jimmy took one final pull of his cigarette, letting the smoke linger in his mouth before finally exhaling. He closed his eyes and laid down against the cold stone of the wall, slumping his bag down beside him.

A black van pulled up alongside him as Jimmy drifted into sleep. Two large men dressed entirely in black, with balaclavas covering their faces and beanies covering their hair, jumped out of the sliding door nearest the edge of the road. Together, they grabbed him and hauled him over to the van without his feet even touching the ground. He was thrown into the van like airline luggage, and one man retrieved Jimmy's pack and threw it in after him. The men didn't say a single word amongst themselves during the whole exchange. They climbed back into the van, and before they shut the sliding door, one slapped the side of the vehicle. The driver gunned the engine, and they drove into the night, alone in the wilderness above Slade City.

About the Author

Tyler Woodbridge was born and raised in Chillicothe, Ohio, but now lives with his wife Laura and daughter Julia in Murfreesboro, Tennessee. Tyler is completing a degree in Marketing so he can more efficiently match messages with people who need them most. In addition to literary pursuits and family time, Tyler also enjoys music, travel, gaming, cinema, television, hiking, sports, and the occasional pale ale.

Books by Tyler Woodbridge

Down From Carlisle (2020)

All In (2021)

Connect with the Author

Tyler Woodbridge on social media:

Facebook – WoodbridgeWrites

Instagram – tylerwoodbridge

Tumblr – woodbridgewrites

Twitter – @woodbridgetyler

Website – www.tylerwoodbridge.com

Want to be credited and even immortalized in future works by Tyler Woodbridge?

Patreon – WoodbridgeWrites

DOUBLE DOWN
THE GAMBLE CONTINUES...

Made in the USA
Middletown, DE
14 September 2021